DEAR MISS KARANA

DEAR MISS KARANA

ERIC ELLIOTT

Heyday, Berkeley, California

Library of Congress Cataloging-in-Publication Data
Elliott, Eric, 1961-
  Dear Miss Karana / Eric Elliott.
    pages cm
  Summary: "While reading Island of the Blue Dolphins at school and learning about the real woman stranded on San Nicolás Island, ten-year-old Tíshmal begins writing emails to 'Miss Karana' in hopes of talking to her spirit"-- Provided by publisher.
  ISBN 978-1-59714-323-3 (pbk. : alk. paper) -- ISBN 978-1-59714-331-8 (e-pub) -- ISBN 978-1-59714-330-1 (amazon kindle)
  1. Luiseño Indians--California--Juvenile fiction. [1. Luiseño Indians--Fiction. 2. Indians of North American--California--Fiction. 3. Luiseño language-- Fiction. 4. Email--Fiction.] I. Title.
  PZ7.1.E445De 2016
  [Fic]--dc23
                        2015010016

Cover art and hummingbird © 2016 by L. Frank Manríquez
Book design by Rebecca LeGates

Orders, inquiries, and correspondence should be addressed to:
        Heyday
        P.O. Box 9145, Berkeley, CA 94709
        (510) 549-3564, Fax (510) 549-1889
        www.heydaybooks.com

Printed in North Kansas City, MO, by KC Books Manufacturing

10 9 8 7 6 5 4 3 2 1

Alexandria Perches pokwáan

For Alexandria Perches

CONTENTS

DEAR MISS KARANA,

Hello, Miss Karana. My name is Tíshmal. My whole bedroom is decorated with hummingbirds. I have a hummingbird bedspread, hummingbird sheets, and hummingbird towels. I also have hummingbird earrings and barrettes, and my favorite dress has hummingbirds all over it. I even have a hummingbird-shaped scrapbook that I put all my favorite things in, like movie and concert ticket stubs, notes, and pictures. I bet you can't guess why I love hummingbirds so much. It's because in my language my name, Tíshmal, means hummingbird. We call our language Chamtéela.

In case you haven't guessed, I am a girl, and I am ten years old. My mom and dad named me Tíshmal after they first held me in their arms. They said that the second I was born, my eyes started darting around like two little humming-birds searching for a flower to stick their beaks into. They were going to name me Epiphany, after my mom's great-aunt, but the minute they saw me, they knew I was much more of a Tísh-mal than an Epiphany. Plus, my eyes are green like a hummingbird's feathers, and I have a red birthmark on my neck, just like a male hum-mingbird's red throat. I'm glad they named me Tíshmal because Epiphany sounds like an old lady's name.

Oh, and I go to a school called Hewéesh. That's a Chamtéela word too. It means hope and joy. I am in fourth grade, and right now we are reading your book. It's called *Island of the Blue*

Dolphins, but you already knew that. I am writing to you because I want to be your friend, and because your island is not too far from my home up here in the hills. My teacher says you were a real person stuck out on your island all alone for a long time. Real people need real friends. I want to be your real friend, Miss Karana.

First of all, Miss Karana, I want to let you know how sorry I am that strangers came and killed so many of your people back when you were all living together out on your island. I am sorry, too, that you had to live alone on your island for so many years, back when there were no phones or bathrooms or anything. I think that it was very brave of you to jump off the rescue boat to stay behind with your little brother. That took real guts, Miss Karana! And, I am very sorry that your little brother died. What was his name again? I have a little brother named 'íswut, and I would be sad, too, if he died. 'íswut means wolf in our language.

3

'íswut annoys me sometimes. He is always trying to, you know, pass gas on me when I'm lying in bed. Yuck! Once he even cooked my doll in the microwave. That smelled really bad too. That's why I say his name should be Şísqila, not 'íswut. In my language, *şísqila* means stinkbug. Actually, his name should be Şísqila Junior, because he learned how to use his stinkbug powers to annoy me from our mom. She's always sneaking up on my dad and doing you-know-what right next to him too. My dad and I aren't like that. I'm a nice young lady, and Dad is a gentleman.

Here's what I don't like: bugs, but especially spiders, olives, sweating, plain acorn mush without gravy and without at least some kind of meat, grapefruit, and movies with lots of blood in them. But what I really hate the most is having to clean up the bathroom, when 'íswut is always the one who leaves a mess and never puts his things away. He never puts the lid back on the toothpaste, and he always squeezes it from the middle, not from the end like you're supposed to.

In the book, it says that dogs killed your brother. When I read that I thought, *They can't be Indian dogs, because our rez dogs fight with each other but they listen to us, especially when we talk to them in Indian!* I wonder how the dogs on your island got so un-Indian. But anyway, if my little brother wasn't around, I'd be sad. That's why, since you are probably an orphaned little mockingbird, I would like to be your e-friend. By the way, in my language, we call lonely people "orphaned little mockingbirds."

My mother "found" your email address on the web. I know SHE was the one who created this address. Now, let's see if she remembers to log in and write me back, pretending to be you. She probably won't because she never even checks her own email. Anyway, even though it isn't a real email address, if you haven't gone West yet maybe you will be able to read what I'm writing to you in my emails.

You see, I figure you're a spirit. My dad always talks to spirits, to people who haven't gone West yet. He's always over at the *táaxanash* with his voice recorder. *Táaxanash* is our word for cemetery. He says spirits talk nicer to him than Mom does and are usually more polite. My dad never lets me or my little brother listen to what he records over there. So if my dad thinks he can record the voices of spirits, why can't I send you emails, since you're a spirit too?

I will write more tomorrow, Miss Karana. I have to go to bed now because my little brother finally went to sleep. I always try to go to sleep after he does: I'm sure you can guess why! I don't want to be attacked by a giant stinkbug.

Your new friend,
Tíshmal

MY FRIEND KARANA,

I forgot to tell you that I am writing to you in Chamtéela and English because I know that you are Indian too, but from farther north. I know that you can't understand most of what I'm writing in my language, but I think you might be able to understand at least SOME of it, if you study it carefully. The people to the east of us are called the Kawíiyayam, or Cahuilla. When I hear Cahuilla people talking their language, I can understand some of what they're saying because their language is sort of close to mine.

Anyway, I'd be happy to teach you a few words in my language. That way, you'll be able to speak to me in Chamtéela. My dad says he always talks Chamtéela over at the *táaxanash* because he knows that everyone who hasn't gone West yet over there is Indian. Indian spirits want to hear our own language, he always says.

I think that I might be able to understand your language too, at least a little bit, if I listen carefully. So, if you want to, if you can find a way, I mean, please go ahead and teach me some of your language. That way, we will both be able to understand each other better.

Our teacher at school, Mr. Qáalaq, says that when the Americans and Chumash Indians came to your island to take you back with them, they couldn't understand your language, and you couldn't understand theirs either. I think it must have been hard on you to see people after eighteen years alone on your island and not be able to understand a word they said.

What is your island like, anyway? Do you guys have lots of oak trees? We do. In town, most of the oak trees are gone, because they dug them up or cut them down to clear the land for new houses. But here on the rez, we respect oak trees like they're part of the family, because they are! Túutu, my grandma, and Kwá"a, my grandpa, say that back in the beginning of time, all the plants and animals could talk Indian. They say that even though plants and animals can't talk anymore, they still understand Indian. I believe them, because I always tell the oak tree by our house how beautiful she is, and every year she gives us a ton of acorns so Túutu can make acorn mush. But I always remind her to add some gravy when she serves it! Did you spend a lot of time talking to the plants and animals on your island? I bet you did, because you had so much time to yourself.

Okay, my friend Karana, I have to stop writing now. We are getting ready for school, and

I don't want to be late. If we're never late to school all year long, then at the end of the year our principal is going to give us an ice-cream party. So, I'm not going to be late, not even once, this entire year.

Your new little sister,

Tíshmal

KARANA, MY NEW AUNTIE,

I'm calling you my auntie, Karana, because you're starting to feel like one of the family. I know you will be a polite member of the family, like me and Dad, not a rude one like Mom and Şísqila 'íswut!

Thank you, Karana, for finding a way to teach me some of your language. Today, Mr. Qáalaq played us one of your songs. He said that you sang this song when the strangers found you. They say that the strangers snuck up on you at home and surrounded you while you were cooking. Then, they jumped out of hiding and showed themselves to you. They say that you were surprised because you didn't realize they had come so near to you. I don't believe that. You knew every inch of your island. Nobody could have snuck up on you like that in your own home.

Mr. Qáalaq also said something that really made me sad. He said you weren't a young lady when they found you. You were a grown woman, a lot older than the young lady who played you in the movie. When I started to think about how you were probably as old as my mom, or maybe even older, I wondered if you ever wanted to have children but couldn't because you were all alone for so many years. That made me want to cry, because I dream about growing up and someday having my own kids, maybe a girl and a boy—but NOT a boy like Şísqila.

Anyway, when the strangers came to your place, you sang the song we heard in class. And guess what? Us kids could understand some of your language! You see? I knew I would be able to understand you, at least a little bit. First we heard the word *Yáamay,* except you said it more like *Yáamuy.* Túutu says that the first two people that ever lived are called 'óomay and Yáamay. They are like Adam and Eve, but Indian style. We know that 'óomay was the first man, and that Yáamay was the first woman. Another name for them is Túukumit, Father Night Sky, and Tamáayawut, Mother Day Earth. What I don't understand is why you sang about Yáamay, the first woman, when the Americans and Chumash Indians came to your home.

They say that you gave them food when they came into your house. Túutu and Kwá"a always give me and my brother food when we visit them. There's always food on the table, and good-tasting food too, whenever the two of us come over. I'm always surprised, because Túutu is like a million years old. And Kwá"a is even older. And if we go over to Túutu and Kwá"a's house with friends, nobody goes away hungry, no matter how many of us go over there. If you go to anybody's house here on the rez, they'll give you plenty of food. Day or night, you'll get stuffed. I've been to other kids' homes in town, off the rez, and sometimes their parents don't even offer me a stick of gum when I visit.

Anyway, it must have been hard for you to cook all that food for all those hungry strangers when they showed up at your door. I bet you saw their ship coming from far away, and you decided right then and there to make something tasty for them. You probably spent the whole day cooking food for them so that everything would be nice and ready when they came to your house. While you were cooking, you probably made up that song, the one we heard in class.

And your house was little, they say. How did all those big men fit into your little house?

Anyway, I have to go to sleep now. Oh, Karana, I almost forgot to tell you about the other word that we could understand in your song. You also sang the word *nişúun*. Here, we say *noşúun,* not *nişúun,* and in my language it means "my heart, my soul," and it can also mean sweetheart or beloved. When I asked Túutu why you said *nişúun* and not *noşúun,* she told me that up north they talk like that, like the 'axáchmay-yam at San Juan Capistrano, and all of those people who live out on the islands.

Wow, I sure wrote a lot, maybe too much. Until tomorrow, Karana.

Your little sister,
Tíshmal

P.S. My mom did forget to check the email account she created when she was pretending to be you. She is really not a computer person. She'd rather rebuild her truck's engine than go online.

KARANA, MY NEW FAVORITE AUNTIE,

Today is Saturday. This morning, I went to an old man's house. His name is Wéh Powéeya. That means Two Tongues.

I don't know what his real name is. We try not call him anything, but when we have to mention his name, we whisper the words *Wéh Powéeya*. He's a grouchy old man. He's mean to people, but we all know that he knows a lot. Most people stay far away from him because they don't want to get yelled at. And like I said, us kids never talk about him, because people say that if you say his name out loud, he'll find out and come and get you. Not even grown-ups talk about him, because they don't want him to come and mess with them either. It's just like everybody says around here: "If you talk about a rattlesnake, you're gonna call one up, and sooner or later one's gonna cross your path." Even though I was scared, I went to his house because I had to ask him about the words you sang in your song, Karana.

Wéh Powéeya's house is way up in the hills. I rode there on my bike. There's only a dirt road up by where his house is. The higher I rode, the darker and bigger the plants got. Down by my house there is space between the trees, but up in the hills the scrub brush is so thick that you can't really see where you are, or even how high up you are. It's just one curve this way, then another curve that way, over and over again, and only every now and then do you get

a glimpse of the valley below. The first time
I got a good look down was when I came to a
burned-up scrub oak tree with no leaves on it.
The drop was so steep that I felt like I might
fall off the road if I stuck to the right side, like
you're supposed to. So, I started peddling down
the center of the road. But then I began to wonder if I would have time to move over if a car
suddenly came around the curve.

The higher up I got, the more the wind
seemed to whistle through the trees. It was kind
of eerie. One time it sounded like the wind
whispered to me *yáaaaawaaaq,* all dragged
out like that, kind of like a coyote howling. I
don't think you have coyotes on your island,
Karana, but over here when a coyote howls
like that, saying *yáawaq,* it means something
like "the end is near" in Indian. And you know
what THAT means! I started wondering whether
the trees up here could still talk, like at the
beginning of time. Were they telling me to turn

around and give up? If my dad was up here with his recorder, would he be capturing spirit voices? It's one thing to hear spirits' voices over at the *táaxanash*. You're supposed to hear them there. But up here in the hills? Just thinking about spirits lurking around the scrub brush gave me goose bumps. But I had to keep going because I just knew that Wéh Powéeya would have some answers for me. I knew he would be able to help me make sense of your words, Karana. I knew you wanted my help, and I knew that you were trying to tell me something, but I couldn't figure out what you wanted me to do on my own.

I was out of breath and sweating like crazy by the time I got up there. I leaned my bike against a big oak tree and walked the rest of the way to Wéh Powéeya's house. I couldn't ride my bike the whole way to his door because there were so many willows growing around his place. They were like a fence. When I walked through them, I just knew that there were probably a thousand spiders hiding in the willow leaves, waiting for me to get within biting distance. When I got through without a scratch or a bite, I turned around and said thank you to the willows for protecting me from all those creepy-crawly things. Wéh Powéeya's little old broken-down house was right behind the willows. The door was open. When I knocked, nobody answered.

I wonder where he is? I said to myself. *Maybe he's still asleep.*

I don't know why, but I decided to follow a little path towards the back of the house. I found a little *wámkish* back there, taller than the top of my head. A *wámkish* is a ceremonial house with no roof where we say prayers and send people West. Because its wall was so high, I couldn't see what was inside it until I got to the opening. I was afraid of what I might see, so I kept my eyes glued to the ground. That's when I saw three rocks buried about halfway

21

into the ground. Then, I saw a pair of gnarly old boots standing on one of the rocks, like what Frankenstein might wear on his feet. I followed those boots up and saw a tall, skinny, old man, too skinny to be Frankenstein, in a long-sleeved shirt that looked too big for him. He looked kind of like an Indian scarecrow, but he had a bandana on his head, not a straw hat. Because of that bandana, his head looked too small for that big shirt. The rock he was standing on was in between the other two rocks, a bit farther behind them. The ground around the rocks looked blue-gray with patches of yellow and other colors. It almost looked like water for a second, but then I figured out that it was just the way the sunlight was hitting the ground that made everything look blue.

The old man was standing there quietly. He was holding a turtle shell rattle in his hand. He was shaking it, but I couldn't hear it because the wind was still howling through the trees. His eyes were closed too.

He must be singing, I thought to myself, *because when people shake rattles they are usually singing too, or trying to remember words to a song.*

I moved a little closer on my tiptoes, like the Cowardly Lion did when he got scared. I know it was a dangerous thing to get so close to this old man that everybody was afraid of, but I just had to see if I recognized the song. I've heard just about every kind of Indian song you can think of. Finally, I was almost standing right next to him, but I still couldn't understand him. It wasn't my language, but it wasn't English either. Every now and then, though, I could understand a word or two. *Whose language IS it?* I wondered.

And then, when I was trying harder than ever to figure out what he was saying, a hummingbird came out of nowhere and hovered right by my ear. Its wings were buzzing so loud that I couldn't even tell whether Wéh Powéeya was still singing or not. If I hadn't been so scared of the old man I might have giggled, because I could feel the hummingbird's beak gently poking at my ear. It kind of tickled. It reminded me of the way my dad had taught me how to ride a bike. One day, he took the training wheels off my stingray and held the bike steady, with one hand on the banana seat and the other hand on the handlebars as he ran along beside me. Then, right before he let go, he whispered in my ear, "Be brave now, Tíshmal." His nose kind of tickled my ear that time, too, and I didn't fall after he let go. That's what the hummingbird felt like in my ear. But then, just as quickly as the hummingbird had buzzed in, it buzzed back out of sight.

Right then Wéh Powéeya opened his eyes. He looked straight at me and growled, "What are YOU doing here, you little spy?" And even though he was growling, his eyes kind of sparkled, Karana.

Then I got really scared, because he was talking to me really mean, just like they say he does to everybody else. I chickened out, because he was even scarier than the spiders or the howling wind. All I could do was say to him as quiet as a mouse, "I wanted to ask you something. But, if you're really busy, never mind. I can come back another day."

"I might not be around anymore, another day. Any day now I might just be heading West. There's no time like the present, little spy, so ask me what you want to know, and then get lost!"

"All right," I said a bit louder. "In school, we are reading a book called *Island of the Blue Dolphins*. Have you ever read it, Noká'?" (*Noká'* means "my grandfather on my dad's side." We use it when we want to show respect to an old man, even if he isn't our real grandfather.)

"I don't read books, just human hearts," he said, still standing on the third rock, the one in the middle behind the other two rocks. "So, what's so important about this dolphin book?"

I couldn't believe it, Karana! He had never heard of your book. Even my mom, who's pretty old, has read your book, but not Wéh Powéeya.

"There is a woman in the story, an Indian woman. Yesterday, Mr. Qáalaq, our teacher, played one of her songs for us. Her language was a little like ours," I said. I was crossing my fingers that he wouldn't bite my head off, the way he was glaring at me. But you know, Karana, even though he looked and sounded scary, I could tell that he wanted something from me too. It wasn't just me who wanted something from him. But I couldn't tell what he wanted yet.

"Sing the song for me," said Wéh Powéeya.

"I can't," I said. "I could just understand a

few words here and there in the song."

"Then say the words that you DID understand."

"I think she said *Yáamay* and *nişúun*," I said.

"Yáamay? Nişúun? She didn't say *NOşúun?"*

"No."

"Are you sure she said *Yáamay,* and not *Yáamuy?"* Wéh Powéeya asked.

"Oh, yeah," I said, "she did say *Yáamuy,* not *Yáamay."*

"Go. Come back tomorrow once you've learned the song," the old man said.

"I don't have the song at home," I said. "It's at school, and tomorrow is Sunday."

"Very well, little miss *I-can't.* You and your pigtails can just hightail it out of here, and don't come back until you CAN sing me that song."

And that was that, Karana. I got out of his way. The whole time I was walking away from him, I could feel him staring at the back of my head like I was going to be his next meal. I wasn't even afraid to pass through the willows—remember them? The ones that just had to be full of spiders? I got on my bike and went home. At least it was all downhill. But I closed my eyes, just for a second, when I coasted past that burned-out old scrub oak. That place really gave me the creeps.

Anyway, I don't know why that old man was so mean to me, Karana. I just wanted to know what you were saying in the song. I'm back home now, it's Saturday evening. Dad's cooking beans and fry bread. That means that in a few hours, Şísqila is going to be fully loaded with ammo. I'm going to have to be extra careful not to fall asleep before he does. But I probably won't sleep much anyway because I'm counting the minutes until I can go back to school Monday morning and learn your song.

Good night, sweet Karana.
Tíshmal

MY DEAR AUNTIE KARANA FROM THE HEART OF THE OCEAN,

This morning, I rode my bike as fast as I could to school. I got there early and ran to my classroom. When I knocked on the door, I heard Mr. Qáalaq's voice saying, "It's already open. Please, come right on in."

I was still out of breath when I went inside. I told Mr. Qáalaq that I wanted a copy of your song, Karana.

Mr. Qáalaq said, "All right, Tíshmal. But why are you so out of breath? And you look all sweaty. Are you running a fever?"

"I went to Wéh Powéeya's house Saturday morning," I said, nice and loud. I completely forgot to whisper his name. "I went there to tell him about the song we listened to, about how there were some words in it that sounded like our words, like *Yáamay* and *noşúun*. He told me not to come back until I learned the song. So I rode my bike here as fast as I could to get it from you. I really, really need to memorize it."

Mr. Qáalaq laughed and said, "Tíshmal, you could have gotten the song from me right then on Saturday morning. Why didn't you send me a *tóomawutal~náawish?* (That's email in Indian, but it really means thunder-writing.) "I have the song on my phone," he said. "I could have sent it to you by *tóomawutal~náawish!*"

Duh, I said to myself for being so silly. Out loud I said, "Can you send it to me now?"

"Yes, Noşwáamay," said Mr. Qáalaq. (*Noşwáamay* means "my daughter." He called

30

me that because that's how a grown man talks nice to a girl like me.)

All day long, I've been listening to your song, during every single recess. And now I can sing it by heart, Karana! By the end of school, I still had five percent left on my phone, just in case I needed to hear it a couple more times.

When the bell finally rang, I jumped on my bike and headed straight home like an arrow. Usually, I have to wait around for 'íswut to put everything in his backpack, which takes forever, before we can ride home together. But luckily, Dad had already picked him up from school early to go to the dentist. Thank God I didn't have to wait for 'íswut to get his act together today.

Once I got home, I told my mom that I wanted to go up into the hills.

"Why do you want to go up there?" she asked from under the sink. She was fixing a leaky pipe. All I could see were her legs sticking out, her welding gear, and a big old metal pipe lying on the floor next to her. But her legs were twitching. That meant she wasn't in a good mood. Usually, she can fix just about anything, but sometimes even she has a hard time, like with plumbing.

"I want to sing a song for Wéh Powéeya," I answered, whispering his name.

"WHAT did you say?" my mom asked kind of slowly, like she was trying not to lose it. She said it the way she says things when she's not happy.

"I want to sing a song for that old man, the one called Wéh Powéeya," I whispered again.

"WAY up there in the hills?" my mom asked.

"Yes. See you later," I said, inching my way towards the door. Sometimes, my mom gets upset real quick, but then she calms down right away. She's like that a lot. She gets mad, and then before she does anything about it, she cools off. So, I figured if I kept heading towards the door, she might just let me go. Plus, she was real busy with the sink.

"Hold on a minute, I want to go with you," my mom said, sliding out from under the sink.

I could tell she meant business.

"No, please. You'll ruin everything, Mom!" I said. I didn't want to be mean, Karana, but let's face it: moms can sometimes get in the way.

"I'll stay in the truck if you like. But, I don't want you going up to that mean old man's house alone. He's a hothead. You know your *kwá"a* is the nicest guy around. He never loses his temper. Well, one time, that old Wéh Powéeya…" my mom whispered. Then she said, "Oh, what's the use? I already said his name. I might as well say it loud from now on.…Once, that Wéh Powéeya was racing up the hill in that beat-up, hunk of junk truck of his. Your *kwá"a* was driving up the hill too, a little ahead of Wéh Powéeya. In nothing flat, Wéh Powéeya caught up to your *kwá"a*. He thought your *kwá"a* was driving too slow. So, Wéh Powéeya honked and yelled at him to pull over. Your *kwá"a* was looking for a safe spot to get out of the way, but before he could, that old Wéh Powéeya just hit the gas, shot past your *kwá"a,* and nearly ran him off the road. You know how narrow it gets up there, and how steep the hill is, right by that scrub oak tree that got hit by lightning." When she said that, I remembered how that place had creeped me out, Karana. That was right where it really felt like the plants were whispering to me. "Your *kwá"a* almost choked to death on the dust cloud Wéh Powéeya kicked up. I've seen him driving in town, you know, stopping at all the stop signs, and driving the speed limit. In town, I guess Wéh Powéeya minds his p's and q's when he's behind the wheel, but the farther he drives up into the hills on the rez, the crazier his driving gets."

After I heard what my mom had to say about Wéh Powéeya, I figured it was better for me not to tell her that I had already gone up to his house on my own, without letting anyone know before I went.

My mom headed towards the door. "Come on," she said.

I followed her. When she opened the front door, I saw she was carrying the big piece of pipe she was going to weld under the sink. I figured she was in such a hurry to get me up there, and get back to finish her welding, that she had forgotten she was carrying it.

So I said, "Mom, you're not going to be doing any welding up there, are you?"

"No, but I need to bring along some kind of protection," she said. "If that crazy old man comes at me, don't think I won't put a dent in his forehead with this piece of pipe."

Oh, I thought to myself, *she really IS worried.*

"He probably won't come after you, at least I don't think so, because he used to be a pushover for kids, especially little girls. He and I used to be pretty close, back when I was a kid, right after his own daughter passed away."

"Wéh Powéeya had a daughter?" I asked. I forgot to whisper again!

"Yes," my mom said. "I was very young at the time. I barely remember going to her funeral, but I do remember seeing her coffin. It was handmade, by Wéh Powéeya, I think, with flowers and hummingbirds painted all over it. I remember thinking how beautiful it was. Your *túutu* picked me up so that I could see the little girl in her coffin. She looked so pretty…like she was going to come out in a classy quinceañera. They even put a little doll in there with her. She was holding the doll in her arms."

"What did she die of?" I asked.

"I don't know," my mom said. "All I know is that she died on the road up in the hills, by that burned-out scrub oak tree, when Wéh Powéeya was bringing her home from the hospital. She had some illness nobody could cure."

"What was his daughter's name?" I asked.

"Noşúun, at least that's what Wéh Powéeya used to call her, back when I was a kid and he and I used to hang together. Except Wéh Powéeya always used to say *Nişúun,* not *Noşúun.*"

Just like in your song, Karana.

My mom started the truck and we made our way up the hill. As we passed that scrub oak with no leaves on it, my mom said, *"Híi, híi, wuníyk!"* (That means something like "Shoo, shoo, stay away from me!")

When we pulled up in front of Wéh Powéeya's house, I got out alone. My mom stayed in the truck. She kept her word, at least.

I passed the willows, and all those hiding spiders I had been so scared of. But before I could even knock, the door flew open and Wéh Powéeya came out with a rifle in his hand. He must have heard my mom's truck pull up because he rushed right past me, through the willows and out towards the truck, with the gun still under his arm. I followed him, forgetting all about the spiders.

"Who are you and what are you doing on my property?" the old man shouted.

"It's me, Nokéek," my mom said from the truck. (*Nokéek* means great-uncle.)

"Wéh Powéeya is your great-uncle?" I said.

"That he is," my mom said.

The old man put down his rifle when he caught sight of me.

"Did you learn it?" He asked me, not even saying hello to my mom.

"Yes," I said.

"Learn what?" my mom asked from the truck. "Tíshmal, have you been up here before?" She raised one eyebrow.

The old man winked at me and said to me with his eyes, *So you didn't tell your mother. Okay, I'll keep my mouth shut, if you keep yours shut too!*

So I didn't say anything. And since my mom had her mind on other things, like that gun, she didn't think to ask again. I took one last look at her in the truck. I could see she didn't have the pipe in her hand. So I took a deep breath and decided to believe with all my heart that Wéh Powéeya was going to help me so I could help YOU, Karana. After all, he did tell me to come back after I learned the words to the song.

"All right," said the old man. "You, Nokéeki-may, stay here." (*Nokéekimay* means great-niece.) "Your daughter and I have some work to do, ALONE."

I felt special when he said "alone" like that. It made all his nasty words from before go away.

"You're the boss," I heard my mom shouting back from the truck, but she didn't say it in a mean way.

When we got behind the house, I said to Wéh Powéeya, "I didn't know that you were my mom's great-uncle."

"There's a lot you don't know," said Wéh Powéeya, standing by the entrance to the *wám-kish*. "Who do you think taught your mom everything she knows? Not your *kwá"a,* that's for sure. Why, that old bump on a log doesn't even know how to get out of first gear. But anyway, go ahead, sing that song, my little don't-know-much girl!"

So, I sang your song, Karana. In the background behind Wéh Powéeya I could see the three rocks.

When I finished, the old man said to me, "You were singing in our other language."

"Our other language?" I asked, feeling like someone had just turned on a lightbulb in a dark room. Suddenly everything started to make sense.

"Not many people know it," he said, "but long ago, two of our ancestors came here from the belly button of the ocean, as they say, from those islands. They brought over their language and their songs. Long ago, we used to speak and sing in two languages, the language from here, and the ocean language. Nowadays, I'm the only one who speaks the ocean language. All the others who used to speak it have headed West. That's why they call me Wéh Powéeya, Two Tongues," he continued. "When I was a kid, everybody called me Páa'ila Róok-kawut, Snapping Turtle. Long ago, when I was young, lots of people used to speak both languages. Now, there's just me, Wéh Powéeya, Old Man Two Tongues. So, out with Snapping Turtle, and in with Wéh Powéeya."

You still ARE a snapping turtle, I thought to myself. Come to think of it, when I saw him for the first time he had looked a little like a turtle in a shell, wearing that shirt that was way too big for him and that bandana that made his head look so small.

"When did those ancestors come over from the belly button of the ocean?" I asked out loud.

41

"A long time ago, before white folks got here," the old man said.

"Can you understand the words to the song?"

"Of course. The woman is telling a man to come back to Yáamay, to Mother Day Earth. Yáamay is Mother Day Earth, and it's also her island out in the ocean. In English, they call it San Nicolás Island or Saint Nic Island, after Santa Claus, I guess. But I don't know what kind of man she was singing about. She says, 'Our home is Yáamay, and a man has to appear here. My soul has been waiting here.'"

"She was alone. She was alone out on that island. She needed a man to show up on Mother Day Earth, her island home," I said, repeating my great-uncle's words back to him to make sure I got it right.

"That's right," said Wéh Powéeya.

After saying thank you to Wéh Powéeya, I went back to the other side of the house, where my mother was waiting for me. I didn't even remember to be afraid of the spiders lurking in the willows.

When I got in the truck, my mom said, "So, he didn't shoot either of us. That's a good thing. Now, tell me what kind of a song you sang to my great-uncle."

"Something from school," I said, which really wasn't a lie at all.

My mom started the truck.

"Aren't you even going to say good-bye to him?" I asked.

"What for?" said my mom. "We're not like that with each other, all lovey-dovey. Besides, he knows we're leaving. And I know he's glad I came."

"How do you know for sure?" I asked.

"He didn't blow a hole in my windshield, did he?" she said with a smile.

She didn't say another word the whole ride back, until I asked her, "So, why didn't you ever take me to meet him, if he's your great-uncle?"

Mom sighed and said, "I've never taken you skydiving, either, have I? Wéh Powéeya never wanted to let me be me. The older I got, the more he tried to change me into somebody I wasn't. Sure, he liked teaching me about engines, but he also tried to get me to wear dresses to school. I was strictly a jeans and T-shirt kind of girl. Still am. By the time I hit high school, I'd just had enough of him trying to make me into his own little Pocahontas doll. I never wanted to let anybody try and change who YOU are. It's my job to protect you, as your mother. Plus, your *túutu* always told me not to take you over to see him, as long as you were a baby."

"Why?" I asked.

"Wéh Powéeya has a lot of power. If he were to die, and if you were close to him, he might try to take you West with him."

"It's been a long time since I was a baby, Mom! Besides, Wéh Powéeya wouldn't do

44

that," I said. "I believe in him," *and in his power,* I felt like saying, but didn't.

"That's just it, Tíshmal," Mom said. "If you believe in powerful people like him, then their power gets stronger."

I didn't say anything, but my heart told me that Wéh Powéeya would never try to hurt me.

When we passed that scrub oak again, this time I said, *"Híi, híi, wuníyk!"*

I'm writing to you in bed now, Karana. Now I really know that you and I are related. I felt it all along in my heart, but now I know for sure. I have Island blood in me. After hearing the meaning of your song, I think you must have been glad that those men came to your home out in the belly button of the ocean, at least at first. Good Night, Karana. I hear Şísqila snoring, so it's time for me to go to bed too.

Until later, my dreamtime friend.

Tíshmal

KARANA, MY DEAREST ORPHANED LITTLE MOCKINGBIRD,

I'm not calling you names. Remember, in my language, when someone is lonely, we say that they are an orphaned little mockingbird. You see, mockingbirds like to talk a lot, but an orphaned little mockingbird has no one to talk to.

Today, Mr. Qáalaq told us what happened to you when you left your little piece of Mother Day Earth, your island. I was very sorry to hear that you passed away just a few weeks after coming to Santa Barbara. He said that you went outside to pray all alone while you were there, and that you always faced the ocean. You were facing your island, off in the west, weren't you? We pray outside too, Karana. Our *wámkish* houses don't have roofs! When we pray for our loved ones who have died, we try to send them West. Who were you trying to send West, Karana? Or were you just homesick? I really love finding out new stuff about you, but the more I learn, the sadder I get.

Mr. Qáalaq told us that you stayed at somebody's house in Santa Barbara, and that a lot of Americans came to see you. What was that like? Did you enjoy having all those strangers around looking at you? Or did you feel like you were in a cage at the zoo?

Mr. Qáalaq also told us that you kept speaking your language to the strangers. I know why you did that: after eighteen years alone, you had plenty to say. Some people say I talk too much already, but if I had to wait eighteen years to talk to somebody, you'd never be able to shut me up either. But the strangers only wrote down four of your words before you passed away.

If I had been there, I would have tried to learn your language all day, every day. I would have shown you lots of things, like fishing gear and plants, so I could learn their names in your language. I figure you did a lot of fishing on your island, and that you gathered a lot of plants, like my ancestors used to do here long ago. We still do gather some stuff, like acorns to make acorn mush (but don't forget the gravy!). When you said the names of things in your language, I would have written them down right away so I wouldn't forget them. I would have pointed to every part of my body to learn your words for everything from head to toe. And I would have walked along the beach with you, to learn the names in your language for all the things from the sea. We could have skipped rocks along the water, if the ocean wasn't too rough.

Mr. Qáalaq put on the white board the four words that the strangers wrote down of your language. He also wrote down what the strangers thought your four words meant in English:

nache	man
puoochay	body
toca	hide
toygwah	sky

It's lunch recess now. Other kids think I'm crazy because I'm writing on the computer instead of playing tetherball or something, but I really needed to talk to you right away to say thank you for the new words you've taught me in your language. I just knew you'd be able to get in touch with me again.

Today after school, when I finish my math homework, I want to go to Wéh Powéeya's

house to ask him if the people of Santa Barbara
wrote down these four words of yours correctly.
My mom says that I can go up to her great-uncle's
house, as long as I finish my homework first,
especially math. I'm not much of a math person,
but I'll do anything, even my math homework
with a smile on my face, if it means I can learn
what your four new words mean, Karana.

Your little sister who always thinks of you,
Tíshmal

KARANA WHO SINGS TO ME,

Right after school, I did go up to Wéh Powéeya's house. On the way up, when I rode by that scrub oak I said a little prayer for his daughter who passed away.

When I knocked on his door, no one answered. So I walked around to the back, just like the first time. And I didn't let the spiders slow me down.

And there he was, singing again, standing on the same rock. His eyes were closed, like last time, so I waited until he finished. Then, I said hello.

Without opening his eyes, he said, "I was expecting you. That's why I'm standing on this rock."

I said to him, "Nokéek, some Americans wrote down four words that the woman said when she was still living in Santa Barbara."

"That woman only said four words when she was up there in Santa Barbara?" he asked.

"No," I said. "They say that she never stopped talking our other language until she passed away, a few weeks after coming to Santa Barbara. But they only wrote down four words."

"Poor thing," said Wéh Powéeya, still standing on the rock. "Well, let's hear 'em."

"The first word is *nache.*"

"There's no such word."

"My teacher says it's supposed to mean 'man,'" I said.

"Oh! You mean *náache*. Yes, it means 'man' AND 'cane,' like a walking stick, in the language of the Island people," said Wéh Powéeya, swaying back and forth a little as he stood on the middle rock.

"Man AND cane? How can it have two meanings?" I asked.

"A cane supports other people. So does a man...a good man, at least." Wéh Powéeya stood up a little straighter, kind of like a soldier.

"Oh, I get it," I said.

"So, what's the second word?" he asked.

"Puoochay."

"Say it again."

"I think it's *puoochay,*" I said more slowly.

"Man, oh, man! That's *pú'u'chey*....It means 'right on her belly button'! Those two words go together." He pointed down at the rock under his feet. "A man...right on her belly button. For so long, there had been no man out on that belly button," said Wéh Powéeya.

"I don't get what you mean," I said. "How can the words 'man' and 'right on her belly button' go together?"

"Look at me. I'm a man. Well, an old man. And here I am, standing on the belly button of Mother Day Earth."

"You're standing on a rock, on the ground," I said.

"Don't you get it? You're looking at me with your own two eyes, and yet you're as blind as a bat. You young people don't believe in anything unless you see it on a screen somewhere. Where is your faith? This ground is a sand painting. The sand painting is Mother Day Earth. The ocean is here," he said, pointing to the ground. "Mother Day Earth is lying in the ocean looking up, while Father Night Sky looks down on her from above. The rocks are islands. These two rocks are the brow and the nose of Mother Day Earth." He pointed to the two rocks a little in front of the one he was standing on. "And I'm standing on Mother Day Earth's belly button, in the middle of the ocean, just like that woman did on her island. When those white men and

Chumash Indians made it out to her island, a man had come to stand with her on Mother Earth's belly button at long last. Anyway, tell me the next word."

"The third word is *toca*," I said.

"That one's easy!" he shouted. He smiled and looked up as we both heard the buzz of a hummingbird's wings zooming past us. "That's *túk'a'* and it means her skin. The skin of Mother Day Earth. Her skin is lying there face up, searching for Father Night Sky."

"Okay, I get it," I said. "Mother Day Earth was looking for Father Night Sky. The woman on the island was looking for a man. Her island didn't feel right without a man on it. The woman on the island was like Mother Day Earth. She needed the other half, a man, who could be like Father Night Sky."

"That's right," said Wéh Powéeya.

Your words that the people wrote down reminded me of the message in your song,

Karana. I was more sure than ever now that you were trying to tell me something. But what?

"And what's the last word?" said Wéh Powéeya.

"*Toygwah,*" I said.

"*Wít, 'iyákko, wít!*" shouted Wéh Powéeya. (*Wít, 'iyákko, wít* means something like OMG.) "That's *Tóykwa* and it means 'to Heaven.' She wants to go up to Heaven and become a star. Poor thing!"

"Poor thing," I said, just like he did. "She wanted to go to Heaven."

"No, not want-ED to go, I think she still wants to go to Heaven, to her final home up in the sky," said Wéh Powéeya.

I knew it, I said to myself.

See, Karana, I knew all along that you were asking for help. I'm so glad you opened up your heart to me.

"Why does their word for Heaven sound like our word *tóoyit?*" I asked. (*Tóoyit* means ice.)

"Spirits are cold," said Wéh Powéeya. "If they're stuck here in the east and haven't crossed over to Tóykwa yet, to the Land of Cold Spirits, then whenever they come around, you can feel them because suddenly it gets cold right by you. That's a sure sign that a spirit is near."

No wonder I've been thinking about getting out my winter clothes! I've been getting the chills ever since I first heard your song, Karana.

Wéh Powéeya didn't say anything else for a long time after that. That made me a little nervous. I just stood there waiting. Finally, he said, "Go home. I don't feel like talking anymore."

Here I am, Karana, at home. I feel sorry for you. I wonder if you ever made it to where you wanted to go, to Tóykwa. I don't think so, because you are still talking to me through Mr. Qáalaq and through your song. But even though I know you're probably getting impatient with me, I do want to say thanks again for teaching me new words in your language. Look, I made a little chart so I won't forget:

náache	a man (and a cane), Father Night Sky
pú'u'chey	right on her belly button, on the belly button of Mother Day Earth, your island
túk'a'	her skin, your island looking up into the sky hoping to find Father Night Sky
Tóykwa	to Heaven, where you want to go

Until tomorrow, my dear Karana.

Your little sister,
another orphaned little mockingbird,
Tíshmal

KARANA NĪŞÚUN,

See, Karana? I now know how to tell you in your own language, I mean in OUR language, that you are special to me. That's why I added the word *nişúun,* which is like *noşúun* in my language. We use our word *noşúun* when we want to tell someone we care about them. It's like "beloved" or "my dear" in English. That was one of the words I learned from your song. I'll never forget what your song says: you say a man has to come to Yáamay, to Mother Day Earth. That's another word for your island. You say our home is Mother Day Earth, and a man has to come to your island, where your soul has been waiting. I hope you don't have to wait much longer, Karana.

Today, Mr. Qáalaq told us that we will get to go on our field trip up north, to Santa Barbara. We've been pen pals with fourth-grade Chumash Indian kids all year long, and they invited us to come visit their reservation and see them dance. They do something called the Swordfish Dance. We don't have anything like that down here in the south. Maybe you and your people, out on Mother Day Earth's belly button, used to do dances like that long ago. We had a bake sale to raise money for the trip, and we printed up a whole lot of flyers and stapled them up everywhere to let people know. And boy did we ever make a whole bunch of money selling goodies—enough to pay for the trip! We are going to spend the night up there, and we will see the Santa Barbara mission too.

You probably don't know it, Karana, but priests built missions all along California. They said they built the missions to teach Indians about God and Heaven. But we knew all about God and Heaven before the priests ever got here. Mom always says that if the priests had just bothered to learn our language and our songs, then they would have understood that we all pretty much believe the same thing. Like our word for God, Karana—it's Chamyúungawish, and that means "the-one-above-our-heads." We believe that there is one God above us in Heaven. And Dad says that WE could have taught those priests a thing or two about what it really means to love your neighbors and to live by the golden rule.

But anyway, Karana, I am looking forward to walking down the same streets that you walked down in Santa Barbara, and maybe seeing the house that you once slept in, even if the Santa

61

Barbara mission is a place that hurt so many of us, a place that maybe hurt you too.

I'm at home now, Karana, and I'm packing things for the field trip.

My dad just came into my room and said, "I'm excited that you're going away on your big field trip, Tíshmanim. I'm really happy for you." Tíshmanim is a nice way of saying my name. It means "little hummingbird girl," all rolled up in one word. It's kind of like if your real name is Cassandra, but some people really close to you call you Cassie.

"Anyway, I wanted you to have this," Dad said, holding out a present all wrapped up nice with pink wrapping paper and a white bow. "It's a little something for your big day up in Santa Barbara."

"Thanks, Dad!" I said as I opened it up.

Guess what? They were new shoes. They have high heels! And they even have little hummingbirds beaded onto them.

"I found them at the powwow last summer," my dad said. "I was just waiting for the right time to give them to you. Since you're going to a fancy place, I thought you could use a pair of heels. I hope they fit."

I tried them on and they fit just right! I thanked my dad and gave him a big hug. Then I practiced walking around in them, and I could. I thought the heels might trip me up because I'd never worn high-heel shoes before, but they didn't.

"Take care of yourself," my dad said. "I won't be there to watch over you like I usually do."

You see, my dad's worried because I've never gone on an overnight field trip before. I've never been anywhere far away alone, not like this. Four girls will be sharing one room with one adult chaperone lady. I hope there won't be any stinkbugs in the room, like Mom and 'íswut. I think it will be fun, but still, I'll probably be thinking about my mom and dad the whole time, and even about my little brother. Maybe I won't be such an orphaned little mockingbird if I think about how you might be there up north too.

Good night, Karana. Sleep tight. Sweet dreams! Listen for the click of my new heels up in Santa Barbara.

Tíshmal

THE BLOG OF MISS TÍSHMAL WÁAŞAQ

Posted by Tíshmal Wáaşaq on Thursday

Hi, everybody. Welcome to my blog! I'm posting this story online because everybody in fourth grade needs to know what I just found out. The lady called Karana, the one in the book called *Island of the Blue Dolphins*, died just a couple of weeks after she got taken to Santa Barbara. I think she died of a broken heart. But she's okay now. I know because I just got back from Santa Barbara on a field trip with my class. I was there helping to put the broken pieces of her heart back together again.

Right after we checked into the hotel, I got all dressed up. I had on hummingbirds from head to toe: my barrettes, my earrings, my hummingbird skirt, of course, and my brand-new hummingbird shoes with one-inch heels that my dad gave me. My dad is cool, Fourth Graders. He knows how to dress. Even if we just go to the supermarket, my dad makes sure his hair is combed and that he's wearing a nice, clean shirt. He says that he has to look good when he goes off the reservation because he's representing our whole tribe. So, because I was going out too, I just had to be the best dressed of all us girls on the field trip. And I WAS, if I do say so myself.

Oh yeah, Fourth Graders, I should have told you earlier: my name is Tíshmal, and my name means hummingbird in my language. I speak an Indian language that we call Chamtéela.

First, our class went to see the Chumash Indians dance and sing. Up in Santa Barbara, people
don't speak Chamtéela. They speak another
Indian language called Chumash. Their dancing
and singing was cool, but I couldn't understand
what they were saying because their language
is way different from mine. It was kind of like
watching Mexican TV. Sometimes when I go
over to other people's houses, their parents, and
especially their grandparents, are watching TV in
Spanish, and I can't tell what the show is about
because I don't know any Spanish. That's the way
the Chumash singing and dancing was for me.

When we sing ceremonial songs in
Chamtéela, we try to send a person West so
they can go up to Heaven to become a star. Of
course, we have lullabies and other kinds of
songs too. But I'm not talking about everyday
songs. I'm taking about the songs you sing in
Chamtéela when someone dies. If you understand our language, then the meaning of our

ceremonial songs is clear. If spirits follow the words, they can find the path up to Heaven. So, you see, Fourth Graders, our ceremonial songs are prayers AND maps, all at the same time. First, the spirits go north, then east, then south, then west, then out to the belly button of the ocean, then up to Heaven to become a star. The belly button of the ocean is Karana's island—that's what she calls her island in her own language.

After the Chumash finished dancing and singing, I tried to find out more about Karana. But none of the Chumash Indians could tell me anything about her. They just said that she was gone, that she had disappeared a long time ago, and that no one could understand her language.

"Not even a few words?" I asked one of the Chumash.

"Nope," he said. "And they say they even brought in Indians from L.A., and they couldn't understand her either."

"Okay, thanks," I said. *They should have gone down south to where we live,* I thought to myself. *We could have at least understood some of what she was saying.* You see, Fourth Graders, my tribe comes from Southern California, from the area south of San Juan Capistrano to the east near Riverside, and all the way down around Oceanside. I'm part Islander too, just like Karana. All of us are part Islanders on my reservation. We even used to speak Karana's language along with Chamtéela.

Anyway, after we talked to the Chumash, we went to Mission Santa Barbara. I could tell that it was a church, even when we were like a mile away, because it was just like every other church I'd ever seen. I was kind of hoping that this church up at Santa Barbara might be different, that at least some part of it might not have a roof so you could look straight up to Heaven when you were praying. I thought that maybe up here the Indians might have been able to talk the priests into making the mission a little bit more like an Indian church, or *wámkish*. A *wámkish* is where we pray the Indian way. It never has a roof. That way, our prayers and the souls of our loved ones who have passed away can shoot straight up to Heaven and become stars.

When our bus pulled into the mission parking lot, I saw a white truck that looked a lot like my mom's. I'm sure you know, Fourth Graders, that parents can be a real pain sometimes. Sure, I love my mom, but she can be a little embarrassing, especially in public.

Mom had promised to let me go on this field trip alone. When I saw a truck that looked like hers, I thought maybe she was spying on me to make sure that I was all right. I didn't need anybody checking up on me. I was really hoping that I was just seeing things.

Back when my mom bought her truck, I had tried to talk her into getting it painted pink, but she just wouldn't listen. And last Christmas, my dad and I got her some really cool stuff to decorate her truck with. The best thing was these pink neon lights that could make it glow from underneath. We also got a pink-and-black zebra-striped dashboard cover and steering-wheel cover, pink hubcaps, big pink heart decals for the doors, and even a license plate frame that glows pink. But Mom never put any of our gifts on her truck. If her truck had pink heart decals on the doors, then I could recognize it anywhere.

Anyway, once we got off the bus, Mr. Qáalaq, my teacher, led our class to the mission entrance. You guys would really like Mr. Qáalaq. He's Indian, just like me. When we watched that old movie about the *Island of the Blue Dolphins,* he stopped it every couple of minutes to tell us everything they got wrong about California Indians in the movie. And believe me, there was a lot wrong with that movie.

So, there we were at the mission entrance. We each got to hold our own ticket as we waited to go in. After the gate person tore mine in two, I carefully put the half she gave back to me in my pocket so I could paste it in my scrapbook back home.

First, we went inside the church building. It was very pretty, a little like the mission church at Pala, the one by our house. But this church was a lot bigger than the one by my house. Over at Pala, you can feel how uneven the floor is under your feet because of the earthquakes over the years. Our *wámkishes* are like that too, because they just have dirt floors. At the church at Pala, you can see the designs on the walls that Indian people made a long time ago with their own two hands. Everything at Pala is just like it was two hundred years ago. The heart of the mission at Pala still feels like home, it still feels Indian. That church still feels a little like a *wámkish,* even though it has a roof on it. But the mission at Santa Barbara felt different, like something from far away, a little like a fancy shopping center.

When we came out of the church, we went to the cemetery. I looked all over for Karana's gravestone, but I couldn't find it anywhere. I just wanted to say a few words to Karana, to make her feel better about dying so far away from her island. But then I looked up and saw my mom standing there, wearing overalls. Ugh, and DOUBLE UGH! So, it WAS her boring white truck in the parking lot! I guess I didn't need her to paint it pink after all.

I was mad. So I told her, "Mom! You promised that you would let me go to Santa Barbara alone. 'You're a young lady now,' you said. 'You can spend one night away from home.' You promised! I thought you believed in me. And just look at how you're dressed. Overalls in church?"

See what I mean about my mom and how embarrassing she can be?

My mom smiled and said, "I don't know how you can keep from falling in those heels. But anyway, you don't understand, Tíshmal. I didn't follow YOU here. I'm here because of him." My mom pointed to an old man wearing a bandana.

"Wéh Powéeya is here too?" I shouted, because I couldn't believe my eyes. But then I thought, *This is how it has to be. This is how we can help her. Karana made this happen!*

There's so much more of the story to tell, Fourth Graders, but my fingers are tired from all this typing! More tomorrow.

DEAR FOURTH GRADERS EVERYWHERE

Posted by Tíshmal Wáaşaq on Friday

Okay, I'm back!

I sure wish you could meet the old man called Wéh Powéeya, Fourth Graders. He's the one who helped me understand the words to Karana's song. Wéh Powéeya means Two Tongues, because he can talk Indian my way, and also Karana's way—he can speak Chamtéela AND our Island language. He's also my great-great-uncle, but I didn't know that till a week ago.

I used to be afraid of Wéh Powéeya. Most people still are, but not me. Now I know that he has a big heart and really just wants things done right, like me.

"Yeah," my mom said. "After you guys left on the school bus, Nokéek showed up at our house. I couldn't believe it, because he never visits anybody. But there he was, knocking on our front door, all nice and proper, wearing a clean shirt and everything. I invited him in, but he said he didn't have time for small talk. He said that he knew you would be coming up here. He said you'd be needing his help. He said he wanted to go on the field trip with you. I told him that you had already left for Santa Barbara. He got all bent out of shape and told me I had to drive him up here right away. So, I dropped everything, and here we are. You don't say no to Wéh Powéeya when he gets like that."

"I wonder what kind of help he thinks I need," I said to my mom, so she wouldn't catch on. But I already knew perfectly well what he meant. See, Fourth Graders, my mom didn't really understand how important it was for me to come and visit this place. But Wéh Powéeya sure got it.

"Who knows?" my mom said. "All I know is that before we made it here, Nokéek started practicing some song, or at least it sounded like a song that he was whispering to himself. I think I'd heard it somewhere before, but I didn't know the words. Other than that song, I didn't hear a peep out of him for the whole trip. I figured, let sleeping rattlesnakes lie. I didn't want to hear a lecture on how it wasn't proper for a young lady to go on a field trip alone without her parents."

"That crazy old man," I said to my mom, just because I felt like I had to say something. See, Fourth Graders, my mom and Wéh Powéeya sort of hate each other's guts, even though they love each other. And because they don't get along, they don't even try to listen to each other. But you know, I don't want to be too hard on my mom because there's no way she could have understood the song he was singing. I'll bet he was singing in Karana's language. I couldn't understand our Island language either until I learned a little of it.

Anyway, there she was, in her messy overalls, standing in front of me right there in the cemetery. I asked her to stay put, but I was nice about it. I wanted to talk to Wéh Powéeya alone. My mom understood and let me go over to him without coming along.

As I was walking away, my mom said with a smile, "I don't think he's packing a pistol here in the cemetery." Then she went over to talk to Mr. Qáalaq, my teacher, to let him know I'd be busy with Wéh Powéeya for a while. Oh yeah, Fourth Graders, you need to know that the old man Wéh Powéeya pulled a gun on my mom not that long ago. It was a big rifle. This is just the kind of crazy stuff he does that scares people. But to me, he wasn't crazy. I think he was just upset all the time because he had a broken heart, like Karana.

When the other kids from my school caught sight of Wéh Powéeya, their eyes got all bugged out and not one of them looked like they wanted to have anything to do with him. That felt great! So I shouted over to the rest of my class, "And, guess what? Wéh Powéeya's my great-great-uncle!" That made them scurry like mice who had just seen a big, mean, and very hungry cat. See, Fourth Graders? Everybody back home was afraid of Wéh Powéeya, everybody but me.

When Wéh Powéeya heard me, he looked at me and said, "Hello, Noşwáamay! Don't you look as cute as a bug's ear? Fancy meeting you here."

I wonder what a bug's ear looks like? I thought to myself. *Noşwáamay* means "my daughter." A man says that to a girl in our language when he wants to talk politely to her, even if she isn't his own daughter. It felt good for him to call me Noşwáamay.

"We're on a field trip," I said. "What are YOU doing here?"

"I just wanted to pay her a little visit," said Wéh Powéeya, pointing to a sign on the wall.

I looked up and read the sign. It said "Juana Maria, Indian woman abandoned on San Nicolás Island eighteen years, found and brought to Santa Barbara by Capt. George Nidever in 1853."

"Who is Juana Maria?" I asked Wéh Powéeya.

"Take a guess, Noşwáamay," he said.

"Don't tell me that Karana's real name was Juana Maria!" I shouted.

"I don't know who that Karana is you're talking about," Wéh Powéeya said. "Where did you get that name from?"

"From the book we read."

"That must be some name the author made up," Wéh Powéeya said. "Who ever heard of an Indian lady named Karana? We'll never know her real name, I guess, but you can bet your bottom dollar that her parents didn't name her Juana Maria. How could they have given her a Spanish name out on that island if they just spoke our Island language? My guess is that people at the mission started calling her Juana Maria after they took her off our island. Anyway, the old-timers used to say that it's impolite to say the real name of a person once they become a spirit. That's why you never hear ceremonial singers saying the name of somebody who's passed away. We never say their name out loud, because we don't want to call their spirit back to this side once they've started to head West. Instead, we use words like *noṣúun* when we sing about a dead person.

Sure, *noṣúun* is a woman's name, but it's also how we talk about people who aren't here anymore."

You probably don't speak Chamtéela, Fourth Graders, so let me explain. The word *noṣúun* means "my heart, my soul," or "my loved one." It's a girl's name too. I know a girl named Noṣúun who goes to my school.

When Wéh Powéeya told me this, I remembered that Mr. Qáalaq, our teacher, had never, ever, ever called the woman Karana either. And I thought to myself, *I will always call Karana "Niṣúun" from now on, because niṣúun (not noṣúun) is the Island word for a loved one who's gone away.*

See how much alike our languages are?

Then I said it out loud. "Her name should be Niṣúun, Nokéek."

But then I remembered that Niṣúun was Wéh Powéeya's daughter's name. You see, Fourth Graders, he had a daughter a long time ago, but

84

she died. I felt really bad inside because the last thing I wanted to do was hurt the old man's feelings.

But Wéh Powéeya said, "Darned if I wasn't just thinking the same thing, Nokéekimay."

So I guess Nişúun wasn't his daughter's real name. It's just what he started calling her after she went West.

We didn't say anything for a while, as we stood by the cemetery wall. Then, Wéh Powéeya pulled out a cigarette, struck a wooden match on somebody's gravestone, and lit the cigarette.

"Nokéek!" I said, "I don't think you're supposed to smoke here! There are people all around us."

"Don't you think I already know that? Don't worry, 'cause I look pretty scary to most people. Nobody's gonna want to get near an old Indian man with a do-rag on his head right here in the middle of this fancy mission, especially when

I'm puffing on a cigarette. I'll scowl at anybody who gets too close." Wéh Powéeya grinned at me from ear to ear. "My scowls can scare just about anybody off, except you…."

"But, Noká', don't you know that tobacco is bad for your health?" I asked, wagging my finger at him.

"I only smoke sacred tobacco to purify my soul and the world around me," he said. "I've had this same pack of cigarettes for months now, 'cause I only smoke before I send people you-know-where."

That's when I finally figured out exactly what we were going to do. I wish I could finish the story, Fourth Graders, but I have to go to bed now. I'll tell you the rest tomorrow!

DEAR FRIENDS

Posted by Tíshmal Wáaşaq on Saturday

Okay, Fourth Graders, so this is what happened.

Wéh Powéeya took out a candle and handed it to me. "Light this," he said.

Does he always carry a candle around in his pocket? I wondered. "I don't have a match," I said out loud, just like a grown-up would.

"Oh, yeah, I forgot you're still just a little pipsqueak," Wéh Powéeya said. He gave me a wooden match. "They probably don't let people light candles in here either, even though this is a cemetery."

Wow, I thought, *Nokéek lets me light candles all on my own.*

"Get a move on. What are you waiting for? I'm already getting goose bumps here," Wéh Powéeya said with a shiver. "Light that candle already, would you?"

You probably don't know this, Fourth Graders, but when Indian spirits are nearby, it sometimes gets cold. That's how I knew that we were really on to something.

Just like in the movies, and just like Wéh Powéeya, I struck the match on somebody's gravestone and lit the candle.

"You see?" Wéh Powéeya said with a smile. "You didn't even burn yourself. I knew you'd be able to do it on your own like a pro. Turn a little bit this way so the mall cop over there can't see you." He pointed to a security guard.

"Why do you want the candle lit, Nokéek?"

"I have to do this old school. She died a long time ago, and so she probably expects a real traditional ceremony. We are going to burn her *tówchanish,* just like in the olden days."

"What's a *tówchanish?*" I asked.

"Way back when, a year after a person's death, people would make and then burn wooden images that looked like the person. Those images are called *tówchanish,*" Wéh Powéeya said, pulling a small handmade doll shaped like a woman out of his pocket. The doll was wearing a *píşkut* and *şixéevish,* just like in the olden days. A *píşkut* is the front skirt that women used to wear, and a *şixéevish* is the back skirt. She even had a *chílkut* on her head. That's a basket cap that women used to wear.

"Why do you want to send her West from right here, Nokéek?" I asked.

"'Cause she's buried right here under our feet," he answered.

"She doesn't have a gravestone here."

"Do you think they would have bothered to make a gravestone for some Indian lady way back then? Take a good look at that sign. What does it say on the bottom?" Wéh Powéeya pointed at the sign again.

"Santa Barbara Chapter, Daughters of the American Revolution, 1928," I read out loud. "What does that mean, Santa Barbara Chapter? And who are the Daughters of the American Revolution?"

"No clue," said Wéh Powéeya. "That part doesn't matter. Look at the date: 1928. That means that they put up that sign who-knows-how-many years after she died. Look at the other date: they found her in 1853. That must be around when she passed away, too, 'cause you said she didn't last long once she left the island. See? They really took their sweet time about marking her grave, didn't they?"

"Maybe she's buried somewhere else around here."

"No way," Wéh Powéeya said. "I already looked everywhere. I also asked our friend, the cop. He said Nişúun didn't have a gravestone here."

I was very glad to hear him call her Nişúun again. But I was also very sad to think that she didn't have a gravestone. "That's not fair. If everybody else has a gravestone, she should too. We should buy a nice one for her. We can write her name, Nişúun, in gi-hugic letters on it."

"Don't worry, Nokéekimay. It doesn't matter. Her spirit is here now, but it won't be for much longer, not if I have anything to say about it. When I was still in the truck with your mom on the way here, I started to call up my *tóotow* from the islands. My *tóotow* is a *tíshmal,* you see. See, there's a *tíshmal* hovering right here, right by the sign."

I looked up and waved at the *tíshmal.* Its little chest looked like it was on fire because the sun was shining right on its red throat feathers. I felt like my chest was on fire too, because my heart was pounding just as fast as the *tíshmal's* wings were beating.

"What does *tóotow* mean again, Noká'?" I asked.

"It's a spirit guide," Wéh Powéeya said.

"How can I get one?"

"It comes to you in a dream when you become a teenager. Plus, you've got to be a boy to get one. So, tough luck, kiddo. I've had mine for a long, long time. Your spirit guide can help you find things."

Sort of like GPS for old-timer Indians, I thought to myself. *Still, it would be nice to get one someday, even if I am a girl.*

It was cool that his spirit guide had the same name as me. But then I started thinking about it: How could he tell which hummingbird was his spirit guide? I had already seen a bunch of hummingbirds at the mission. Were they all his spirit guides?

"How do you know that it isn't just any old *tíshmal?*" I asked, pointing at the hummingbird who was now perched on a branch above us.

"You have to believe, otherwise your power isn't worth a hill of beans," he said. "Plus, my guide met me out in the parking lot and led me inside here, right to this spot. Your mom even tried to shoo him away, but my *tóotow* wouldn't give up. He just kept on hovering in front of me. Any hummingbird that'll put up with your mother trying to swat him has to be my guide. I believe in my guide, and so *tíshmal* believes in me. Look: he's still perched right here on this tree, listening to us talk Indian. He talks our Island language too."

I looked up and saw the *tíshmal* still sitting there, listening to us, and so I believed. "Well. Let's send her West!" I said.

"Oh, shoot," Wéh Powéeya said, "I almost forgot!" He took a few small shells out of his pocket and carefully stuck all but one of them into a fold of his bandana. The last shell he gave to me, saying, "Put this one on the little ledge on top of her sign. She's going West, isn't she?"

Then Wéh Powéeya took four puffs of his cigarette, blowing them out one by one, once to the north, once to the east, once to the south, and once to the west. He took his rattle out of his pocket and started singing. Wéh Powéeya sang his heart out.

He must be singing in the Island language, I said to myself, because I could understand a few of the words here and there. I looked up and was really happy we didn't have a roof over our heads.

Then he handed me the *tówchanish* and said, "Hug the *tówchanish*. Tell Nişúun how glad you are that she came into your life, but that now it's time for her to go up to Tóykwa. You can even dance with the *tówchanish*, if you feel up to it."

The word Tóykwa means "to Heaven." It is a place that's cold for people like you and me who are still alive, but it's nice and warm for spirits. To people like Nişúun, people who have died but haven't gone West yet, even a nice sunny place like Santa Barbara must feel like the North Pole, because our world feels cold to spirits.

So anyway, I did just like Wéh Powéeya said. I told Nişúun how grateful I was that she had taught me some of her language. I told her to listen to the words in the song, because I was sure that the words were telling her how to get up to Tóykwa, where her family was waiting for her, where it was all nice and warm. I told her that I was sorry that she had been stuck here shivering for so long in Santa Barbara. Then, I hugged the *tówchanish* real tight and spun around with her a couple of times. While I was spinning, I imagined seeing Nişúun sitting by a warm fire, all toasty and happy, together with her whole family. Even though I did three complete spins, I didn't fall, not even with my new high heels on.

Then Wéh Powéeya said, "Set the *tówchanish* down right next to the candle on the gravel so it catches fire. Be careful. That thing's full of dried twigs so it will burn real easy."

So I carefully put the *tówchanish* right by the candle, as Wéh Powéeya continued singing. I held her by her head and pushed her feet towards the flame. She caught fire and turned into a pile of ashes within a few minutes.

When he finished singing, he whispered, *"Hóo, hóo, hóo, 'óo,"* as he blew his breath upwards. I knew what that meant: he was sending her soul West, out to the belly button of the ocean, and then up.

Wéh Powéeya took off his bandana, carefully put the shells and his rattle back in his pocket, and said, "Okay. Now, blow out the candle."

I blew it out and watched the smoke twirl up this way and that, then move towards the ocean.

"Look! The smoke is going towards the belly button of the ocean!" I shouted to Wéh Powéeya.

"Of course it's heading towards the belly button of the ocean," said Wéh Powéeya. "Where else would Indian smoke go?"

Even though I was excited, I felt like crying, because I knew in my heart she was gone. I choked back my tears. Right then, my heart felt broken, but I knew it would heal because we had done the right thing. It would have been very selfish for me to try and keep Nişúun here with me.

"Was it Nişúun's soul? Are you sure? Is she finally going to go Tóykwa?" I asked.

"I already told you: I don't read books, just human hearts," Wéh Powéeya said. "Let's go. It's time for us to head for home too, just like Nişúun."

"What about the last shell, the one on the ledge above the sign?" I asked.

"Leave it," he said, "as a reminder that she's gone West now."

Wéh Powéeya just stood there for a minute, looking towards the ocean, like he was day-dreaming. The sun was going down. It was shining right on him, making him look for a second like he was on fire too. He stood there frozen in the light. Then I saw him crack a little tiny smile, and I think I saw him blow a little kiss, but not with his hand like some famous person on a float at the Rose Parade. He just puckered his lips for a second. If I hadn't been paying attention, I wouldn't have even noticed. Then he woke back up, and we headed towards the exit.

And now, Fourth Graders, I just finished putting the ticket stub from the mission into my scrapbook. I wanted to start this blog so that you will all know that Nişúun's story has a happy ending, thanks to one very special *náache* we all know and love. I am happy for

Nişúun, but still I wish we could have spent just one day together before she went away, walking along the beach and skipping stones over the water.

Nişúun's best friend in the east,

Miss Tíshmal Wáaşaq,
who will always believe in Nişúun

P.S. After we got back from up north, Wéh Powéeya's truck broke down right in front of our house. It was in the afternoon, so I was home, and when I saw him out on the road I went out to say hello. Even my brother came out with me, since nobody's scared of Wéh Powéeya anymore.

Wéh Powéeya had his tool chest lying there open on the ground while he was working on his truck. Once I saw all those tools, I got an idea. I said to myself, *I wonder if he can help me out with something else that still needs fixing?*

And he did!

When we were all finished, we stood back to look at all the cool changes.

"Now, at least it looks a little gussied up, like it's ready for a night on the town!" said Wéh Powéeya.

"Do you think everything will stay on?" I asked, because some of the stuff looked a little flimsy. "Do you think Mom will leave it on?"

"You have to believe, Noşwáamay," Wéh Powéeya said. "If you don't, then your power will be like soda that's lost its fizz."

So, I did believe. And you know what? My mom still hasn't taken any of the pink stuff off her truck.

AUTHOR'S NOTE

In the year 1853, a Native American woman
was removed from her home, the island sometimes called Xaráaşa in Chamtéela and San
Nicolás in English, located some sixty miles off
the coast of Southern California. The woman,
often referred to as "the lone woman," had been
living alone on her island for eighteen years,
ever since outsiders sent by Mission Santa Barbara took the rest of her people to the California
coast.

Today, the people of San Nicolás Island are
sometimes referred to as the Nicoleño. Sources

say that most of the Islanders were massacred
by fur trappers in 1815, which led church
authorities to believe the survivors needed to
be rescued. The lone woman was somehow
left behind on the island, apparently because
she didn't get to the beach in time to board
the rescue boat. She was finally brought to the
mainland eighteen years later by a group of
men made up of several European Americans
and at least one Native American, a Chumash
man by the name of Malquiares. After living in
Santa Barbara for six weeks, the woman died.
Her cause of death is unknown. Many people
believe she died of a broken heart.

Scott O'Dell wrote *Island of the Blue Dolphins,* a fictional story based on the woman's
experiences, in 1960. This little book before
you is also inspired by the lone woman's
story, but offers a glimpse into the vibrant
Native American world of today's Southern

California, a world that very much intersects with the world of the lone woman. Told through the eyes of Tíshmal, a ten-year-old Native American girl living on a reservation and attending a reservation school here in Southern California, this story links the life of the lone woman with the Native world of today. Tíshmal learns that her people's contemporary beliefs have much in common with the beliefs of the lone woman, and that their languages share similarities too.

No one in Santa Barbara could understand the lone woman's language. Native Americans from various tribes, speaking different languages, were brought to her, but none could communicate with her. During her brief lifespan of six weeks on the mainland, only four words of her language were ever written down. Those four words are *nache, puoochay, toca,* and *toygwah.* They were written down by well-meaning people who did their best to capture the correct pronunciation.

Decades later, an elderly Chumash man named Fernando Librado from the Santa Barbara area recorded a song he had learned from another man, Malquiares—the very same Chumash man who had been on the voyage to bring the lone woman back from San Nicolás Island. You see, when they found her, the lone woman sang a song. Malquiares remembered that song, and sang it to Fernando Librado, who then, as an elderly man, recorded the song for posterity. That song, plus one other song and the four words recorded of the lone woman's language, are just about all we know of her native tongue.

When I heard the song myself, I realized that the language of the lone woman had more than a little in common with Chamtéela, a Native American language of San Diego, Riverside, and Orange Counties in Southern California that I have spoken and cherished for the last thirty years. Once I heard the song, I felt moved to write this book.

Chamtéela is not my native language. I am a white man who first learned to speak English from my mother. But many years ago, an old lady named Mrs. Hyde planted her language, Chamtéela, in my heart, and I promised her I would do everything I could to help keep her language alive. That's why I work at a school where kids learn in Chamtéela. They even say their times tables in Chamtéela.

While I was still wondering how to reach a young audience with a new book about the lone woman, a student at our school, Alexandria Perches, asked me to help her write a fan letter. Alexandria had become captivated by the story of another famous Native American woman, Ramona, the hero of the novel of the same name by Helen Hunt Jackson. Alexandria wanted to send Ramona a fan letter.

Knowing that Ramona was just as Indian as herself, Alexandria asked me to help put her own English words into Chamtéela so that she could send Ramona a letter in Indian.

This was just the inspiration I needed to begin writing this book, *Dear Miss Karana*. In keeping with Alexandria's logic, I decided to first write this book in Chamtéela. Later, I translated it into English so that you can read it too.

HOW TO SAY CHAMTÉELA WORDS

Below is a guide to all of the Chamtéela words found in this book, listed in alphabetical order. Also included are the few Island words we know. The Island words that were recorded in the nineteenth century are written here using the same spelling system as Chamtéela. The capitalized syllables are the ones to say the loudest.

'axáchmay-yam (ah-HOTCH-mah-yam), Juaneño Indians

Chamtéela (cham-TAY-lah), Our Language, a language of California

Chamyúungawish (cham-YOO-ngaw-weesh), God, the-one-above-our-heads

chílkut (CHEEL-koot), basketry cap worn by women

hewéesh (hey-WAYSH), hope, joy

híi, híi, wuníyk (HEE, HEE woo-NEEK), "shoo, shoo, stay away"

'íswut (ISS-woot), wolf, a man's name

Kawíiyayam (kaw-WEE-yah-yom), Cahuilla, a tribe living to the east of Tíshmal

kwá"a (QUA-ah), grandfather, mother's father

náache (GNAW-chay) man, cane

nişúun (knee-SHOON) my heart, my soul, a woman's name

Noká' (know-CAW), my grandfather, father's father

Nokéek (know-CAKE) my great-uncle, a relative's name

Nokéekimay (know-CAY-key-my), my great-niece, a relative's name

noşúun (know-SHOON), my heart, my soul a woman's name

Noşwáamay (know-SCHWA-my), my daughter, a relative's name

'óomay (OWE-my), the first man, Father Night Sky

páa'ila róok-kawut (PAW-ee-lah ROW-caw-woot), snapping turtle

píşkut (PEESH-koot), front skirt, worn my women

pú'u'chey (POO-oo-chay), "right on her belly button"

Qáalaq (CAW-lock), "riverbank caves in," a Native family name

şísqila (SHIS-kee-lah), stinkbug

şixéevish (she-HAY-veesh), back skirt, worn by women

táaxanash (TAW-hah-nosh), cemetery

Tamáayawut (taw-MAH-yah-woot), Mother Day Earth

tíshmal (TISH-mall), hummingbird, a woman's name

Tíshmanim (TISH-mah-neem), Little Hummingbird Girl, a girl's name

tóomawutal~náawish (TOE-mah-woo-tall GNAW-weesh), thunder-writing, a term used for email

tóotow (TOE-toe), spirit guide

tóoyit (TOE-yeet), ice

tówchanish (TOE-chah-neesh), wooden image burned at a ceremony

Tóykwa (TOY-quah), to Heaven

túk'a' (TOOK-ah), her skin

Túukumit (TWO-coo-mit), Father Night Sky

túutu (TWO-two), grandmother, mother's mother

Wáaşaq (WAH-shock), stretches, a Native family name

wámkish (WAHM-keesh), sacred enclosure like a church or mosque

Wéh Powéeya (WEH poe-WAY-yah), Two Tongues, a man's nickname

wít, 'iyákko, wít (WIT ee-YOCK-co WIT), "oh my God," an expression of amazement

Xaráaşa (hah-RAW-shaw), a Chamtéela name for the island known as San Nicolás in English

Yáamay (YAW-my), the first woman, Mother Day Earth

Yáamuy (YAW-muy), the first woman, Mother Day Earth

yáawaq (YAW-wock), "the end is near"

ACKNOWLEDGMENTS

I would like to thank first and foremost my wife, Sandra, my children, Max, Mariano, and Victoria, my sister Julie and brother Scott for putting up with me, and my cousin Carol for sharing her faith with me; Mrs. Villiana Hyde and Mr. Raymond Basquez Qapárrapish Sr. for teaching me their language, faith, and culture; L. Frank Manríquez for her inspired artwork; Bridgett Barcello, Lindsie Bear, Alexis Dyer, Linda Hodges, Tom Holm, L. Frank Manríquez, John Munoa, R.J. Munoa, Aimee Perches, Emili Siva, Kevin Siva, Catalina Villarruel, Doug

Westfall, Todd Winter, and Molly Woodward for reading, and in many cases rereading, the manuscript, and for their many helpful suggestions; and Alexandria Perches for being such a wonderful role model of how a polite young lady talks and thinks.

ABOUT THE AUTHOR

Villiana Hyde began teaching the Chamtéela language to Eric Elliott in 1987. In 2001, Raymond Basquez Sr. began sharing his faith with Elliott. It was these two elders who planted the seeds that have since blossomed into Elliott's present venture into children's literature. Elliott is a teacher. He lives near the coast, in the San Diego area.

HEYDAY

into California

About Heyday

Heyday is an independent, nonprofit publisher and unique cultural institution. We promote widespread awareness and celebration of California's many cultures, landscapes, and boundary-breaking ideas. Through our well-crafted books, public events, and innovative outreach programs we are building a vibrant community of readers, writers, and thinkers.

Thank You

It takes the collective effort of many to create a thriving literary culture. We are thankful to all the thoughtful people we have the privilege to engage with. Cheers to our writers, artists, editors, storytellers, designers, printers, bookstores, critics, cultural organizations, readers, and book lovers everywhere!

We are especially grateful for the generous funding we've received for our publications and programs during the past year from foundations and hundreds of individual donors. Major supporters include:

Advocates for Indigenous California Language Survival; Anonymous (3); Arkay Foundation; Judith and Phillip Auth; Judy Avery; Carol Baird and Alan Harper; Paul Bancroft III; The Bancroft Library; Richard and Rickie Ann Baum; BayTree Fund; S. D. Bechtel, Jr. Foundation; Jean and Fred Berensmeier; Joan Berman; Barbara Boucke; Beatrice Bowles, in memory of Susan S. Lake; John Briscoe; David Brower

Center; Helen Cagampang; California Historical Society; California Rice Commission; California State Parks Foundation; California Wildlife Foundation/California Oak Foundation; Joanne Campbell; The Campbell Foundation; Candelaria Fund; James and Margaret Chapin; Graham Chisholm; The Christensen Fund; Jon Christensen; Cynthia Clarke; Community Futures Collective; Lawrence Crooks; Lauren and Alan Dachs; Nik Dehejia; Topher Delaney; Chris Desser and Kirk Marckwald; Lokelani Devone; Frances Dinkelspiel and Gary Wayne; Doune Trust; The Durfee Foundation; Megan Fletcher and J.K. Dineen; Michael Eaton and Charity Kenyon; Richard and Gretchen Evans; Friends of the Roseville Library; Furthur Foundation; The Wallace Alexander Gerbode Foundation; Patrick Golden; Erica and Barry Goode; Wanda Lee Graves and Stephen Duscha; The Walter and Elise Haas Fund; Coke and James Hallowell; Theresa Harlan and Ken Tiger; Cindy Heitzman; Carla Hills; Leanne Hinton and Gary Scott; Sandra and Charles Hobson; Nettie Hoge; Claudia Jurmain; Kalliopeia Foundation; Judith Lowry and Brad Croul; Marty and Pamela Krasney; Robert and Karen Kustel; Guy Lampard and Suzanne Badenhoop; Thomas Lockard and Alix Marduel; Thomas J. Long Foundation; Bryce Lundberg; Sam and Alfreda Maloof Foundation for Arts & Crafts; Michael McCone; Nion McEvoy and Leslie Berriman; Moore Family Foundation; Michael J. Moratto, in memory of Major J. Moratto; Stewart R. Mott Foundation; Karen and Thomas Mulvaney; Richard Nagler; National Wildlife Federation; Native Arts and Cultures Foundation; The Nature Conservancy; Nightingale Family Foundation; Steven Nightingale and Lucy Blake; Northern California Water Association; Panta Rhea Foundation; Pease Family Fund; Jean Pokorny; Jeannene Przyblyski; Steven Rasmussen and Felicia Woytak; Susan Raynes; Restore Hetch Hetchy; Robin Ridder; Spreck and

Isabella Rosekrans; Alan Rosenus; The San Francisco Foundation; Toby and Sheila Schwartzburg; Stephen M. Silberstein Foundation; Ernest and June Siva, in honor of the Dorothy Ramon Learning Center; William Somerville; Carla Soracco; John and Beverly Stauffer Foundation; Radha Stern, in honor of Malcolm Margolin and Diane Lee; Liz Sutherland; Roselyne Chroman Swig; TomKat Charitable Trust; Jerry Tome and Martha Wyckoff; Thendara Foundation; Sonia Torres; Michael and Shirley Traynor; The Roger J. and Madeleine Traynor Foundation; Lisa Van Cleef and Mark Gunson; Stevens Van Strum; Patricia Wakida; Marion Weber; Sylvia Wen; John Wiley & Sons, Inc.; Peter Booth Wiley and Valerie Barth; Bobby Winston; Dean Witter Foundation; Yocha Dehe Wintun Nation; and Yosemite Conservancy.

Board of Directors

Getting Involved

To learn more about our publications, events and other ways you can participate, please visit www.heydaybooks.com.

THE WORLD'S CLASSICS
CARMEN AND OTHER STORIES

PROSPER MÉRIMÉE was born in Paris in 1803, the son of an academic painter. After completing his law studies he published *Théâtre de Clara Gazul* (1825), a group of plays that at once made him a prominent figure in the French Romantic Movement, from which, however, he distanced himself shortly after. In 1829 appeared *Chronique du règne de Charles IX*, his only novel, and over the following year he wrote six of the dozen or so stories for which he is chiefly remembered. In 1830 he joined the Civil Service, and in 1834 was appointed Inspector-General of Historic Monuments, a post he held until 1860 and which involved him in extensive travels throughout France. He also travelled widely in England and Spain. During this period he wrote increasingly on architectural and historical matters, but continued to publish occasional stories. In 1843 he was admitted to the Académie des Inscriptions et Belles-Lettres, and the following year was elected to the Académie française. After the publication of *Carmen* in 1846, he wrote no more fiction for twenty years. In 1854 he was appointed a Senator, and thereafter became a prominent figure at the court of Napoleon III. In the last three years of his life he turned again to fiction, with three short stories, none of which was intended for publication. Mérimée died at Cannes in 1870.

NICHOLAS JOTCHAM attended Oxford and Bath Universities, and has worked as a teacher and translator in Spain, France, and the USA. He has also edited a volume of Maupassant's short stories.

THE WORLD'S CLASSICS

PROSPER MÉRIMÉE

Carmen and Other Stories

Translated and with an
Introduction and Notes by
NICHOLAS JOTCHAM

Oxford   New York
OXFORD UNIVERSITY PRESS

Oxford University Press, Walton Street, Oxford OX2 6DP

Oxford New York Toronto
Delhi Bombay Calcutta Madras Karachi
Petaling Jaya Singapore Hong Kong Tokyo
Nairobi Dar es Salaam Cape Town
Melbourne Auckland

and associated companies in
Berlin Ibadan

Oxford is a trade mark of Oxford University Press

First published 1989 as a World's Classics paperback
Reprinted 1990, 1992

British Library Cataloguing in Publication Data

Prosper, Mérimée, 1803-1870
Carmen and other stories.—(World's classics).
I. Title   II. Jotcham, N. (Nicholas)
843'.7

ISBN 0-19-282242-X

Library of Congress Cataloging in Publication Data

Mérimée, Prosper, 1803-1870.
[Selections. English. 1989]
Carmen and other stories / Prosper Mérimée : ed. & translator,
Nicholas Jotcham.
p. cm.—(World's classics)
Bibliography: p.
1. Mérimée, Prosper, 1803-1870—Translations, English.
I. Jotcham, N. II. Title. III. Series.
843'.7—dc 19   PQ2362.A25 1989   88-22568

ISBN 0-19-282242-X (pbk.)

Printed in Great Britain by
BPCC Hazells Ltd
Aylesbury, Bucks

CONTENTS

INTRODUCTION

'I am one of those who have a strong liking for bandits—not that I have any desire to meet them on my travels; but, in spite of myself, the energy of these men, at war with the whole of society, wrings from me an admiration of which I am ashamed.'

(Mérimée's 1851 article on Gogol)

PROSPER MÉRIMÉE is now best remembered as an early exponent of the short-story as a modern genre; as the author of a handful of memorable tales—not all of them short—whose themes are violence, passion, and death; and above all as the author of *Carmen*, which provided the basis for one of the world's most enduringly popular operas and has consequently tended to eclipse the other stories. In addition to his activities as a writer, however, Mérimée left his mark in a number of other fields, as administrator, scholar, archaeologist, authority on medieval architecture, historian, and translator. He rose to be an academician and senator, and was thus a prominent and—in his public life, at least—respectable figure in the bourgeois establishment. Yet this elegant, scholarly man-about-Paris never ceased to hanker after the exotic milieux and primitive societies of which he had written in his Romantic youth.

A contrast between primitive and civilized values informs his work. He inherited, but did not subscribe to, the myth of the noble savage, and he had no need to be reminded of the benefits of civilization. But he disliked the tameness and hypocrisy of mid-nineteenth-century French society, and yearned for distant cultures and remote periods of history—ancient Rome, medieval Spain, sixteenth-century France, the Napoleonic era—which he saw as times when it had been possible for men and women to be true to their natures, when their natural inclinations had not yet been stifled by society's conventions. He numbered Julius Caesar and Pedro the Cruel among his historical heroes, and was an admirer of strong personalities, of men and women of action who lived adventurous lives, and of those who had won glory on the field of battle.

A passionate but reticent man, he admired primitive peoples for their uninhibited spontaneity, for their courage, and, above all, for their energy—a quality he uncritically extolled, regardless of the ends to which it was applied.

Mérimée's fiction presents civilization as a façade behind which lurk brutal passions and dark, mysterious forces, manifested in violence, unreason, occasional irruptions of the supernatural, and erotic love, which, with some exceptions (the idyll of *Colomba*), he presents as a sinister, fatal power, often equated with death, the supreme consummation of desire.

Mérimée juxtaposed the primitive and the civilized, but could not bring himself wholeheartedly to accept or reject either set of values. Despite his nostalgia for primitive societies and his reluctance to repudiate violence, this fastidious, donnish man was hardly cut out to be a brigand or a military hero. Instead, besides portraying aspects of his more urbane self in the male characters of his Parisian stories, and awarding himself a prominent role as the narrator of more exotic tales such as *The Venus of Ille* and *Carmen* (in which, however, he took care always to present himself in an ironic light), he projected the barbarous side of his nature into fictional characters leading lives far removed from his own: representatives of more primitive societies such as Colomba and Mateo Falcone; outcasts such as Carmen; and the outlaws that people his most famous tales—Don José, Brandolaccio, and Castriconi, the scholar-bandit.

Born in Paris on 28 September 1803, the son of an academic painter whose administrative talents later earned him the post of Permanent Secretary of the École des Beaux-Arts, Mérimée grew up in an artistic, cultured, and agnostic middle-class environment. He was apparently never baptised. After attending the Lycée Napoléon he studied law at the University of Paris. He learned English from his anglophile parents and soon developed a taste for Byron, Shakespeare, Scott, and Bulwer Lytton, and began to affect English dress and manners (he admired the English for their reserve and love of action, travelled widely in England, and had many English friends).

In 1822 he met Stendhal, who, though twenty years his senior, was to be a close friend for a number of years. On completing his law studies, he wrote his first story, *La Bataille* (1824, unpublished until 1887), and published four articles on the Spanish theatre in a literary review. At the same time he was working on a group of six dramas embodying the new Romantic theories on the theatre expounded by Stendhal in the pamphlet *Racine et Shakespeare* (1823). The plays were published in 1825 as *Le Théâtre de Clara Gazul, comédienne espagnole* (*Plays by the Spanish Actress Clara Gazul*). The attribution to a fictitious Spanish actress fooled no one, and the identity of the author was an open secret from the outset. Noteworthy for their disregard of the Classical unities of time and place, their radically liberal sentiments, and their anticlericalism, the plays (only one of which was staged in Mérimée's lifetime) are now of interest only to the specialist. At the time, however, they earned him immediate critical acclaim, drawing praise from such eminent literary figures as Goethe and Chateaubriand; and at 22 Mérimée found himself lionized in Romantic circles.

His next work, *The Guzla: Selection of Illyrian poems collected in Dalmatia, Bosnia, Croatia and Herzegovina* (1827) (the title refers to a Serbian stringed instrument, but is also an anagram of *Gazul*), again took the form of a hoax, purporting to be prose translations of original Illyrian ballads. These alleged translations initially deceived a number of experts, and Mérimée later tried to dismiss the work as a hoax pure and simple. But *La Guzla* is more than this: in its fascination with exotic local colour and its identification with the values of an unspoiled primitive society, the work is already fully characteristic of its author.

In January 1828 Mérimée was wounded in a pistol duel with the husband of Émilie Lacoste, with whom he had been having an affair for the past year. This incident is reflected in the story *The Etruscan Vase*. In June of the same year he published *La Jaquerie (Scènes féodales)* (*The Jacquerie: Feudal Scenes*), a long sequence of loosely connected, unstageable dramatic tableaux evoking the fourteenth-century French peasant uprising, and a play, *La Famille de Carvajal* (*The Carvajal*

Family); and in the spring of 1829 the historical novel *Chronique du règne de Charles IX* (*Chronicle of the Reign of Charles IX*), an imaginative recreation of events leading up to the massacre of the French Protestants in 1572.

In terms of literary output, 1829 was Mérimée's most productive year. The novel was soon followed by *Mateo Falcone*, the first of his published short tales, in which he at last discovered the genre that best suited his literary temperament. Between May 1829 and June 1830, besides three more plays, he also produced six stories: *Vision de Charles XI*, a brief, quasi-historical tale of hallucination with supernatural overtones, set in Sweden; *L'Enlèvement de la redoute* (*The Storming of the Redoubt*); *Tamango*; *Federigo* (a retelling of a Neapolitan folk legend, reprinted in the collection *Mosaïque* in 1833, but never subsequently reissued in the author's lifetime); *Le Vase étrusque* (*The Etruscan Vase*); and *La Partie de trictrac* (*The Game of Backgammon*).

In the summer of 1830 Mérimée embarked on a six-month tour of Spain. His impressions are recounted in four *Letters from Spain* (1831–3), which, besides containing some of his most colourful and attractive writing, include material used again in *Carmen* fifteen years later. The visit to Spain was also notable for a chance encounter with don Cipriano Guzman Palafox y Portocarrero, the future Count Montijo, which resulted in Mérimée being introduced to the Countess and her two daughters on his arrival in Madrid. So began a lifelong friendship with the Montijo family, which was to stand him in good stead when, twenty-two years later, the younger of the two daughters, Eugenia, married the Emperor Napoleon III.

Meanwhile, in France, the reactionary Charles X had been deposed in the events of July 1830, and Louis-Philippe installed on the throne as constitutional monarch. Mérimée, who in 1829 had declined an opportunity to serve the previous administration as an attaché in the London embassy, was not too late to partake of the spoils on his return to Paris, as the new regime distributed official posts to able or well connected young men of appropriately liberal views. He was soon appointed *chef de bureau* to Count Apollinaire d'Argout, Minister for the Navy, whereupon he willingly traded in the

rôle of impecunious man of letters for that of affluent senior
civil servant.

His decision to look beyond the horizons of literature seems
to have been motivated primarily by a desire for financial independence and for social advancement. His rapid rise within
the civil service inevitably had an impact on his activities as
a writer. He now had less time to devote to imaginative
writing, and literature had to take second place. By the age of
26 he had produced almost half his purely literary output. He
wrote nothing of major significance between his departure for
Spain and the publication in 1833 of *La Double Méprise* (*The
Double Mistake*), a long story recounting how a virtuous
woman succumbs to the attentions of an unscrupulous libertine. *Mosaïque* (1833) merely gathered together the various
stories and other pieces published elsewhere in reviews over
the previous three years; and between 1834 and 1846—the
year in which he abandoned fiction altogether for twenty
years—he was to publish only six tales.

The year 1834 saw the publication of what is generally
regarded as one of his least successful works, *Les Âmes du
purgatoire* (*The Souls in Purgatory*), which mingles elements of
the Don Juan legend derived from Tirso de Molina's *El
Burlador de Sevilla* with an imaginative reconstruction of the
life of the seventeenth-century libertine Don Miguel Mañara,
whose tomb Mérimée had seen in Seville in 1830. In the same
year he was appointed Inspector-General of Historic
Monuments, a post he was to hold until 1860. Its responsibilities entailed listing all the outstanding buildings in
France and ensuring their preservation. The decision to
appoint him may seem a curious choice, since the previous
year he had begun his fourth *Letter from Spain* with the
words: 'Antiquities leave me cold, especially Roman antiquities; [. . .] I'm no antiquary.' While it is true that initially
he lacked the requisite expertise, he made up for this in his
keen sense for historical research, knowledge of the arts, and
proven talent as an administrator. Besides its administrative
responsibilities, the post was to involve him in often arduous
tours of duty which, over the next eighteen summers, took
him to every corner of France. Although his rôle (and that of

Viollet-le-Duc, his protégé) has not gone uncriticized, his achievement in saving and restoring a substantial portion of France's architectural heritage would alone be sufficient to guarantee him a prominent place in French cultural history.

By the mid-1830s Mérimée was beginning to think of himself primarily as a scholar. During this period he began to write extensively on archaeology and architecture. Around 1837 his taste for history led him to embark upon a *Life of Caesar* (never completed, although the first two parts, *Essay on the Social War* and *The Conspiracy of Catiline*, appeared in 1841 and 1844). On one occasion in 1836 he professed to have given up writing fiction. The next year, however, he published *La Vénus d'Ille* (*The Venus of Ille*), followed in 1840 by *Colomba*, a by-product of a visit to Corsica in 1839, ostensibly to inspect its monuments.

With professional success came a desire for recognition by the Establishment. In 1843 he campaigned successfully for admission to the Académie des Inscriptions et Belles-Lettres, and the following year he was elected to the Académie française. Paradoxically, he arranged for his election to coincide with the publication of *Arsène Guillot*, an attack on the values of Parisian society, which contrasts the virtue of a humble *grisette* who takes a lover in order to support herself and an ailing mother, with the hypocrisy of a pious lady of fashion who sets out to reform Arsène, but ends up by appropriating the girl's lover.

Between 1844 and 1847 he wrote his *History of Don Pedro I, King of Castile*. His most famous story, *Carmen*, written as a relaxation from these historical labours, appeared in 1845. In 1846 he added a fourth chapter to *Carmen*; published *L'Abbé Aubain*, an insubstantial tale recounting through letters how a priest obtains a rich parish in the gift of a pious lady, by pretending to have fallen in love with her; and wrote *Il Vicolo di Madama Lucrezia*, a tale of mistaken identity set in Rome, which he deemed unworthy of publication—a judgement with which posterity has tended to concur. On this note (if we disregard *Les Deux Héritages*, an abortive attempt at a theatrical comeback dating from 1850), Mérimée wrote no more fiction for the next twenty years. At about this time he began to take a scholarly interest in Russian, and in July 1849 he published a translation of Pushkin's *The Queen of Spades*, which was followed by further translations of Pushkin and Gogol, a study of Gogol, and works on various periods of Russian history.

With the marriage of the Emperor Napoleon III to Eugenia de Montijo in 1853, Mérimée, who had known the Empress well since she was a child of 4, soon found himself drawn into court life. He reluctantly acquiesced in his appointment as a senator, but subsequently declined a number of other important official posts. Embittered by the painfully protracted termination of his liaison with Valentine Delessert (which had provided a stable emotional base since 1836), and in increasingly poor health, he divided his time between Paris and the newly fashionable resort of Cannes, when not obliged to accompany the imperial retinue on their frequent travels to one or another of the royal residences.

In the last four years of his life he returned to fiction, with the three tales *La Chambre bleue* (*The Blue Room*, 1866), *Lokis* (1868–9), and *Djoûmane* (1870). Each was written as an entertainment for the Empress and her circle, and none was intended for publication, though he relented in the case of *Lokis*. Opinions differ as to their merit. *Lokis* repeats the formulas applied successfully in the earlier tales. *La Chambre bleue* had originally been conceived as a serious investigation of a moral dilemma facing two lovers, but in its final form it creates a mood of mystery and tension which is then dispelled in a deliberately bathetic conclusion. *Djoûmane* breaks new ground. With its Algerian setting, emphasis on the workings of the subconscious, and themes that lend themselves to a psychoanalytic interpretation, it has sometimes been hailed as a precursor of Surrealism.

From 1868 Mérimée was virtually an invalid, and his death in 1870 (at Cannes, where he is buried in the English Protestant cemetery) was undoubtedly hastened by his distress at the news of the defeat of France at the hands of the Prussians, the collapse of the Empire, and the exile of the Empress Eugénie.

A word needs to be said about Mérimée's attitude towards his own fiction. The question how seriously he takes his own writing is posed as early as *Le Théâtre de Clara Gazul* and *La Guzla*. The former work masquerades as a translation of plays by a Spanish actress, and it has thus been traditional to regard it as a hoax—a view of the work borne out by the fact that it is prefaced by a spurious biography of the fictitious actress, and that the first edition contained a portrait, allegedly of the actress but in fact depicting Mérimée *en travesti*. *La Guzla*, too, purports to be a translation, this time of ballads composed by an Illyrian bandit. Mérimée went to some pains to conceal his authorship of these prose poems, and in a preface to a later edition published in 1842 he even asserted that the sole purpose of the work had been to deceive the public.

Thus, at first sight it would seem that these early works are merely *jeux d'esprit*, devoid of serious content. However, it should be noted that everything Mérimée wrote up to and including the *Chronique* was initially published either anonymously or under a *nom de plume*. It would thus seem more appropriate to regard the *Clara Gazul* plays and *La Guzla*, not as hoaxes, but as serious works published pseudonymously. Mérimée's claim in the 1842 Preface to *La Guzla* that the work was a hoax pure and simple is contradicted not only by the internal evidence, but also by the considerable trouble he is known to have taken over it: it seems inconceivable that he should have lavished so much care and effort on a project whose sole purpose was to deceive the reader.

The fact remains, Mérimée wished us to believe that these works had been intended as hoaxes, a tendency deliberately to belittle his own work that also manifests itself in other forms. In his correspondence he was frequently at pains to disparage his literary writing or to minimize the importance he ascribed to it, asserting that he had been driven to write some stories purely by financial necessity, professing to dislike others, or making light of the creative effort involved in composing them (he claimed, implausibly, to have written *Carmen* in a week, *La Chambre bleue* in one night, and to have dashed off the *Guzla* ballads in pairs before breakfast).

In other ways, too, Mérimée seems intent on casting doubt on the artistic validity of his creations. In imitation of a quaint convention of the seventeenth-century Spanish theatre, each of the plays closes with the actors resuming their everyday identities, announcing that the play is over, and apologizing for its shortcomings—a procedure which Mérimée sometimes takes a stage further, introducing banal references to the actors' supper so as brutally to shatter the tragic mood. Other examples may be found of attempts to disrupt the aesthetic impact of his works: the *Chronique* concludes with an invitation to the reader to invent his own ending to the novel; elsewhere, in Chapter VIII, the narrative is interrupted by a remarkable 'Dialogue between the Reader and the Author', a dramatized discussion of the techniques available to the historical novelist, in the tradition of Molière's *Critique de l'École des Femmes*. While, generally speaking, the stories are recounted by a narrator who is distinct from Mérimée himself, when he does intervene as author, either directly (in the *Chronique*), implicitly (in the way in which he chooses to present *The Game of Backgammon*), or through a semi-fictional persona (the archaeologist's comments at the start of *Carmen*, the professor's at the close of *Lokis*), it is usually to mock, express indifference, or diminish the impact of the story—the extreme example of this being Chapter IV of *Carmen*, discussed at greater length below.

Clearly, Mérimée does care about his fictions. Why, then, should he systematically belittle them, feign indifference to them, and assert that they are not to be taken seriously?

On the one hand, these ploys indicate a wish to protect himself. The desire for anonymity, the use of a *nom de plume*, reveal a lack of confidence in his own literary abilities; assertions that the work is a hoax and other attempts to belittle his own writings are a device to forestall adverse criticism. The same is true of the affectation of indifference, which is also a manifestation of his emotional reticence and reluctance to wear his heart on his sleeve. More than this, however, it is a protective device: like his hero Bernard de Mergy, in Chapter III of the *Chronique*, Mérimée tries to 'arm himself with indifference'; like the dandies at the close of *The Etruscan Vase*, or like Orso as Lydia imagines him when comparing him to Fieschi in the third chapter of *Colomba*, he betrays nothing of his inner emotions. He needs to express his innermost feelings through fiction; but by laying bare his soul he leaves himself vulnerable to attack. He thus protects himself in his personal life by adopting the cold, aloof pose of the dandy, insolent, disdainful, seemingly caring for nothing but external appearances, regarding it as unstylish to show any sign of emotional or intellectual involvement; and in his literary life by writing fiction that is deeply committed, only to disavow and feign indifference to it thereafter. The device of telling his stories through a second narrator distinct from himself further distances him from the fiction (since he is simply relating hearsay); and by casting himself as audience, rather than narrator, of a tale of passion (as in *Carmen*) he is able to give uninhibited expression to his feelings.

Hand in hand with the wish to protect himself goes the wish to protect the reader, by warning him not to take literature too seriously. Mérimée undoubtedly inherited the eighteenth-century view that fiction, involving as it does an element of deception, is somehow disreputable, and that writers of fiction are little better than liars. The endings of many of the stories may be seen as a reminder to the reader that fiction is only make-believe, and that its value as experience is thereby diminished.

The fact is, Mérimée fundamentally—and increasingly—respected history more than fiction, an attitude he states explicitly as early as 1829, when, in Chapter VIII of the *Chronique*, the Author tells the Reader: 'I wish I had the talent to write a History of France: if I had, I wouldn't bother with stories.'

Carmen has its origins in an anecdote recounted to Mérimée by the Countess Montijo in 1830, but over the next fifteen years the tale grew in anticipation of the telling, with the addition of impressions of his travels in Spain, reflections of his own emotional experiences, and information gleaned from his wide reading in Spanish literature, on Roman history, and on the Gypsies.

This sometimes lurid portrayal of a destructive passion still retains its vitality, thanks mainly to the character of its heroine. In Carmen Mérimée created one of the supreme literary incarnations of the *femme fatale*, who surrounds herself with an aura of mystery, magic, and malevolence, with which she exerts a fatal charm on the weak and the unwary, exploiting her sexuality and the mystique she has created, in order to further her own ends.

It is sometimes hard to take don José seriously. On close acquaintance, this doomed hero of romance often seems little better than a churlish adolescent. He is in thrall to Carmen, sees her as the devil, and allows her to unman him. Dependent, passive, weak-willed, and submissive, José is simply a slave to his passions. He blames Carmen, the Temptress, for causing his undoing; and, at the last, he blames the *Calé*; but the truth is, he has only himself to blame.

Carmen is another matter. Dishonest, unruly, promiscuous, shallow, vicious, callous, she is also vivacious, energetic, enterprising, resourceful, indomitable. A lover of her freedom before all else, she cannot allow any one man to call himself her master for long. Above all, the power of the story not merely to entertain, but to move us, resides in the courage and dignity with which she faces death, and in the resignation with which she submits to what she sees as her Fate, which bring to the tale a tragic dimension.

The decision to let don José narrate his own story gives it urgency, conviction, and dramatic force. By contrast, the narrator of Chapters I and II is too much the gentleman, the dandy, and the pedant to admit to any emotional involvement in the events he is recounting. For him, the really interesting issue is the site of the battle of Munda. The result of this narrative technique is a mingling of intense emotion and ironic detachment unique to Mérimée.

Furthermore, in its final form, after the addition of a fourth chapter in 1847, *Carmen* actually has not two but three first-person narrators; Chapters I and II are narrated by a semi-fictional archaeologist on a tour of southern Spain, whose interests and experiences to some extent coincide with Mérimée's own. José Navarro narrates Chapter III. The narrator of Chapter IV, however, is Mérimée himself, the author of a recently published *nouvelle* entitled *Carmen*. Unlike the archaeologist-narrator of the first two chapters, the author-narrator of Chapter IV plays no part in the events of the story.

The 1847 version of *Carmen* reads like a tale to which a covering letter from the author to his publisher has inadvertently been appended.

Chapter IV has been variously seen as evidence that *Carmen* is first and foremost a treatise on the Gypsies; as an attempt to make the narrator more substantial, and Carmen more real by generalizing her traits; as an ironic disclaimer of what has gone before; as an attempt to 'pad out' an over-slim volume; as a catastrophic error of artistic judgement; and as a repudiation of imaginative fiction involving the deliberate destruction of a work of art. It has sometimes been greeted with admiration, more often with bafflement or dismay.

Clearly, it resembles some of the other works in the way it diminishes the tale's impact. In this respect, comparison with the coda to *Lokis* can give us an idea of the effect Mérimée may have been trying to achieve by adding a fourth chapter. And, although the first version of the tale ends impressively with the death of Carmen, it could certainly be said to lack symmetry. However, as it stands, Chapter IV seems merely inept. Mérimée's decision to narrate it in his own persona appears to be more an oversight than a deliberately calculated effect, and irreparably disrupts the unity of tone. The information it gives on Gypsy women's attitudes to superstition and to marriage contradicts, rather than confirms, Carmen's traits. There are discrepancies, too, in the quality of the artistry: with its pedantic yet superficial erudition and its uninspired anecdotes, Chapter IV makes dull reading.

Nevertheless, on balance, it seems more plausible to regard the decision to add Chapter IV as an error of judgement than as an attempt by its author deliberately to ruin the story. The true explanation for the addition is perhaps to be sought in the conflicting claims that literature and scholarship exerted on Mérimée's mind. We have already noted that he had more respect for history than for fiction, and that he did not really regard literature as a reputable pursuit. He saw fiction as a game, whereas history was a serious matter. His abandonment of literature as a career in 1831 suggests that he had already ceased to feel fully committed to it. Early works like *La Jaquerie* and the *Chronique* had contained a strong historical element, in subject and treatment. As time passed his taste for history gradually gained the upper hand. By the time he came to write *Carmen*, as a sort of protracted parenthesis to his *History of Pedro I*, he had grown confused about his priorities and was no longer clear in his own mind whether he was writing a work of imaginative fiction or an academic treatise on the Gypsies.[1] Even after the story had finally appeared in print this problem continued to vex him. In 1846 he added the enigmatic fourth chapter, then gave up writing fiction altogether, to concentrate exclusively on history.

In view of the above considerations, the decision has been taken to print Chapter IV as an appendix to the present edition, enabling present-day readers to experience *Carmen* as did those of Mérimée's contemporaries who first read the tale in its three-chapter version in 1845, before turning to the longer version in 1847.

Of the other stories included in this selection, *Mateo Falcone* (1829), described by Walter Pater as 'perhaps the cruellest story in the world', established a model for the genre which is still valid today. It tells how a Corsican's uncompromising conception of honour and justice compels him to commit an act which leaves him bereft of his most cherished asset.

The story is based on a popular tradition that had already been retold a number of times. Little in the tale is Mérimée's own invention—even the descriptions of Corsica are borrowed from written sources (he did not visit the island until 1839). However, the author's originality lies not in what he invents, but in the manner in which he reassembles concrete details meticulously selected from among his various sources. Every element tells, nothing is superfluous. Effects are achieved

---

[1] This conflict between the claims of erudition and fiction is nowhere more clearly illustrated than in Mérimée's obsession with learned footnotes. This is already apparent in *Mateo Falcone*, which, in its final version, contains eight such footnotes in the space of thirteen pages. It is the result of an unsuccessful and sometimes obtrusive attempt to reconcile two incompatible worlds. Footnotes may have their place in those chapters of *Carmen* recounted by a framework narrator; but whatever the intended purpose of the thirty-eight footnotes that punctuate don José's narrative in Chapter III, their actual effect is undoubtedly to distract and irritate the reader.

with the utmost economy of means (the dangling watch, cupidity made palpable; or the way in which the last sentence serves to place the incident in the wider continuum of human affairs). Tightly organized and overwhelmingly powerful, *Mateo Falcone* is a landmark in the history of the short story.

The Storming of the Redoubt, a description of the taking of the Shvardinó redoubt by the French during Napoleon's Russian campaign of 1812, has been much admired for its concision and technical mastery. It exemplifies Mérimée's admiration for the martial virtues, and impressively conveys one man's view of a battle, in a six-page narrative unique in his *œuvre* for its absence of irony. Whether one regards it as a brilliant exercise in classical control or finds it merely arid is ultimately a matter of personal taste. The fact is, *The Storming of the Redoubt* is not so much a story as an artistic simulation of a brilliant piece of on-the-spot war reporting, and therein lie both its strength and its weakness. Yet, if the abiding impression is one of a technical study expertly carried off, a familiarity with this tale is nonetheless indispensable to a proper understanding of Mérimée's world.

In *Tamango* Mérimée addressed the highly topical issue of the slave trade, which had been abolished in 1815 but continued to flourish clandestinely. The descriptions of the trade and of conditions on board the slave ships are accurate and carefully researched, drawing on a variety of sources, including pamphlets by the English abolitionist Thomas Clarkson. The details of West African customs are taken from works such as Mungo Park's *Travels in the Interior Districts of Africa*. The story, too, he may have found in the literature on the trade, which abounds in descriptions of slave revolts. A similar incident is recounted in Defoe's *Life, Adventures and Piracies of the famous Captain Singleton* (1720); and he may also have had in mind the notorious wreck of the *Méduse* off Senegal in 1816, the fate of whose survivors was the subject of Géricault's painting *The Raft of the Medusa* (1819).

If *Tamango* is, among other things, a piece of abolitionist propaganda, it is nonetheless first and foremost a work of art. Mérimée documents, but refuses to sentimentalize, the Negroes' plight. As for the protagonists, Ledoux and Tamango, there is little to choose between them. In its satirical and didactic elements the tale harks back to Voltaire, but in its violence, its poetry, the elemental force of its climax, and the devastating irony of its conclusion, it is one of Mérimée's most characteristic statements.

The Etruscan Vase is an example of the group of Parisian tales that also includes *La Double Méprise* and *Arsène Guillot*. It is based in part on Mérimée's affair with Émilie Lacoste, which, like Saint-Clair's with Mathilde de Coursy, had culminated in a duel. The resemblances between Mérimée and his hero Saint-Clair are striking. Saint-Clair, however, is at most a partial portrait of his creator, and, like the other dandies in the story, is a composite, whose traits cannot be matched against those of any one member of Mérimée's circle. *The Etruscan Vase* paints a picture of a society which, beneath its veneer of civilization, is permeated with violence, hypocrisy, and irrationality. The sophisticated Saint-Clair allows himself to be tormented by groundless jealousy, and his fate (and that of Mathilde) is precipitated by his inability to control a momentary irrational impulse. Despite its brevity, this subtle, haunting, and elegant work has an almost novelistic density, and reveals a facet of Mérimée's talents very different from those demonstrated in the earlier stories.

The Game of Backgammon recounts how a man's remorse at having cheated at the gaming table drives him to court his own death. Like *Carmen*, the story has two narrators, the captain of the ship and the framework narrator of the tale's opening and close, to whom the captain tells the story of his friend Roger.

In addition to this complex *cadre*, there is also the sub-plot involving Gabrielle. In her temperament, pride, prodigality, promiscuity, and love of independence, even in her theft of a watch, Gabrielle clearly prefigures Carmen. However, her presence in the story, justified by the insight it gives us into Roger's personality and motives, is otherwise superfluous, for Roger explicitly rejects his friend's suggestion that his motive in cheating had been to provide for her.

Roger's self-destructive remorse results primarily, not from his bringing about another man's downfall, but from his attaching more importance to a paltry sum of money than to his honour. For Roger, honour is everything. He is no gambler, and it is to uphold the honour of France that he agrees to play against the Dutchman. The scene of the duels highlights the importance he attaches to a code of honour, thus emphasizing the paradoxical nature of his subsequent dishonourable behaviour. Likewise, the insistence on his natural generosity emphasizes the paradox of his true motive for cheating, which—if we are to believe him—is sheer greed. Nor can Gabrielle's love redeem him: only death can wash away the stain of dishonour.

The ending is often cited as a deliberate anticlimax, illustrating Mérimée's contemptuous attitude towards his own fiction; and certainly, as in many of the other stories, one of its effects is to bring the reader abruptly back to earth. Yet it also in a sense cleverly avoids the anticlimax that would result from going over the same ground twice (we have already been told in the story's opening pages that Roger died in the war, and the precise manner of his death is hardly crucial). The ending does indeed diminish the story which is being told by the captain to his captive audience, but not the story the latter then tells to the reader. The captain's story does not have an ending; the framework narrator's ends with something of a flourish. In a sense, The Game of Backgammon gives us two stories for the price of one.

The Venus of Ille, Mérimée's own favourite among his stories, combines reminiscences of his tours of duty as Inspector of Historic Monuments, a satirical self-portrait in the character of the narrator, and a retelling of an age-old legend which he may have found in one or more of a number of sources, ranging from the twelfth-century chronicler William of Malmesbury to the libretto of Hérold's Zampa. Through the unimpeachable testimony of his pedantic narrator, Mérimée creates an entirely credible setting into which inexplicable events gradually intrude. And, although we are encouraged to infer that the events recounted are supernatural in origin, the climax, when it comes, is all the more satisfying in that the possibility of a natural explanation is not entirely ruled out.

The Venus of Ille may be read as a ghost story, as an early

example of the whodunit, or as a satire on provincial mores and provincial scholarship; but above all, this tale of a goddess of love who demands the lover's death as her tribute uses the devices of myth to hint, obscurely yet disturbingly, at the dual nature of erotic passion, at once seductive and lethal.

Colomba is based on the true story, told to Mérimée in Corsica, of a vendetta between the Bartoli and Durazzo families. Many of the more implausible incidents (such as Orso's one-armed left-and-right shot) are based on real occurrences related to him by their protagonists; other details are drawn from various travellers' accounts of Corsica. Colomba's ballads are modelled on genuine Corsican *ballate*, examples of which he had appended to his *Notes d'un voyage en Corse*, the official report on his tour of the island in 1839.

Colomba is the story which most explicitly illustrates the conflict between primitive and civilized values. Enlightenment, in the shape of Orso della Rebbia, fights a losing battle against the forces of entrenched prejudice and unreason, epitomized by the baleful Colomba. Torn between the conflicting demands of civilization and near-barbarism, embodied by Lydia and Colomba respectively, Orso is no match for his sister's machinations, and ultimately it is Colomba's principles that triumph, with Orso a hapless victim of *force majeure*.

As so often with Mérimée, critics have failed to agree about the work's merits. It has been criticized for an excessive preoccupation with local colour (a hallmark of the Romanticism of the 1820s which, despite the disclaimer at the start of the story, continued to exert its fascination on him until the very end of his literary career). The happy outcome, in which Orso is able to retain both women's affections, has been called weak and contrived. But the idyll of Lydia's and Orso's romance is really no more than a conventional backdrop against which the real, darker business of the story is enacted. If the amiable Orso sometimes comes across as insipid, Colomba is as powerful a creation as Carmen; and it is not Orso or Lydia, but Colomba, who has the last word, in an ending which remains almost without parallel in all literature for sheer venom.

The particular virtues of *Colomba* are not those we have

become accustomed to associate with Mérimée: in its expansiveness (it has the proportions of a medium-length novel), its often pastoral mood, its surprisingly mellow irony, its prevailing comic tone, and its air of good humour—all of which, however, also serve to throw its heroine's malevolence into still starker relief—it is perhaps his richest and most successful work.

The last of these stories, *Lokis*, gives us a variant on the old tale of the man who is the monstrous progeny of a coupling of bear and woman; a tale that may also be found in sources as varied as the thirteenth-century Danish historian Saxo Grammaticus and the Italian Bandello. The immediate stimulus to compose it came from some fantastic tales by Turgenev which he had been translating (it was Turgenev who provided the title) and from his browsing in a Lithuanian grammar. Mickiewicz and Charles Edmond Choiecki provided most of the local colour.

Lokis is the last, and perhaps the least satisfactory, of Mérimée's meditations on the mysterious connection between love and death, and on the dangers of untrammelled erotic passion. The tale spells out the message that in each of us there is a latent animal nature, normally held in check by reason and morality; that bestiality lurks beneath the civilized veneer.

In a number of the details of its plot, and in the figure of the pedantic narrator, the story uncomfortably resembles *The Venus of Ille*. However, whereas in the latter story we are invited to believe in supernatural intervention, in *Lokis* we are required to believe in a genetic impossibility. The Lithuanian local colour seems to be a purely technical exercise in the picturesque, with little organic justification in terms of the story. The recreation of Lithuanian life is superficial and often inaccurate. All too often, Mérimée seems mechanically to fall back on the techniques and formulas that had been such outstanding and innovative features of the tales written nearly forty years previously. The work cannot be accounted a total failure: it has moments of considerable force, and its sinister mood is not readily dispelled. Yet, if *Lokis* is a much more impressive achievement than the other two late tales, it is still nothing like as accomplished as the best early ones.

*

Critics have been notoriously unable to agree as to Mérimée's merits, or as to the relative merits of his various stories. His plots are seldom original, his subject matter is limited in range; his vision of the world is a narrow one, and (except in *Colomba*) he is at his happiest when working on a small scale.

On the other hand, his stories are colourful, readable, and retain their power to affect us. Mérimée ranks, not just as one of the inventors, but as one of the greatest practitioners of the short story, because he brought to it qualities we now take for granted—a style simple and terse, a highly compact structure and economical narrative technique calculated to heighten his stories' effect. His works are free of the ephemeral clutter that now makes much of the literature of the period unreadable. He shows us human nature in the raw, and dramatizes it memorably. His uniqueness resides in the way in which he combines a love of dramatic action with a sceptical cast of mind, enabling him to write of uncontrollable passions and horrific events with elegance, restraint, and ironic detachment. His conception of what constitutes the exotic may have dated; but the stories themselves retain their readability. In short, they have lasted.

NOTE ON THE TEXT

THE text on which this translation is based is that of the last reprinting of each story to which Mérimée himself is known to have made corrections at the proof stage. This is the text that appears in *Mérimée: Théâtre de Clara Gazul, romans et nouvelles*, edited by Jean Mallion and Pierre Salomon, Bibliothèque de la Pléiade, Paris, Gallimard, 1978.

The only departure from this principle is in the case of *Carmen*. Here, the final version of the text is the one reproduced, but Chapter IV has been printed separately as an appendix at the end of the volume (see Introduction, page xix).

Mérimée's stories first appeared in literary reviews, and were later published in collections compiled by himself. Subsequent editions sometimes omitted stories previously included in a collection, or grouped together different selections of stories into a single volume. Below are details of the first publication of each story here translated, and of its first publication in volume form:

Carmen: the first three chapters were published in the *Revue des Deux Mondes* on 1 October 1845. Early in 1847 an edition bearing the date 1846 was published by Michel Lévy, in a volume entitled *Carmen* which also contained the stories *Arsène Guillot* (1844) and *L'Abbé Aubain* (1846). The story's fourth and final chapter, added by Mérimée as an afterthought, first appeared in this edition and was included in all subsequent editions.

Mateo Falcone first appeared in the *Revue de Paris* on 3 May 1829 under the title *Mateo Falcone, mœurs de la Corse*. It was later published by H. Fournier jeune, in 1833, in a volume entitled *Mosaïque*. This collection was something of a miscellany, and brought together *The Storming of the Redoubt*, *Tamango*, *The Etruscan Vase*, and *The Game of Backgammon*, the stories *Vision de Charles XI* and *Federigo*, a group of short *Ballades*, a playlet entitled *Les Mécontents*, and three *Lettres sur l'Espagne*, in addition to *Mateo Falcone*.

The Storming of the Redoubt (*L'Enlèvement de la redoute*) was first published in *La Revue française* in September 1829. It subsequently appeared in *Mosaïque* in 1833.

Tamango appeared first in the *Revue de Paris* on 4 October 1829, and then in *Mosaïque* in 1833.

The Etruscan Vase (*Le Vase étrusque*) was first published in the *Revue de Paris* for 14 February 1830, and later included in *Mosaïque* in 1833.

The Game of Backgammon (*La Partie de trictrac*) appeared in the *Revue de Paris* on 13 June 1830, and was later included in *Mosaïque* in 1833.

The Venus of Ille (*La Vénus d'Ille*) appeared in the *Revue des Deux Mondes* on 15 May 1837. The first edition was published by Magen et Comon in 1841, in a volume that also contained *Colomba* and the story *Les Âmes du purgatoire*.

Colomba was first published in the issue of *Revue des Deux Mondes* for 1 July 1840. The following year it was published by Magen et Comon in the volume also including *The Venus of Ille* and *Les Âmes du purgatoire*.

Lokis was published in the *Revue des Deux Mondes* on 15 September 1869 under the title *Le Manuscrit du professeur Wittembach*, a title adopted for typographical reasons and against the author's wishes. Mérimée had intended making changes to this text before having it published in a volume; however, he died in 1870 without having had an opportunity to revise the story, which was printed in the posthumous *Dernières Nouvelles* in 1873.

The numbered footnotes at the foot of the pages are Mérimée's own.

SELECT BIBLIOGRAPHY

The edition of Mérimée's plays and fiction used in preparing this translation is *Théâtre de Clara Gazul, romans et nouvelles*, ed. Mallion & Salomon (Gallimard: Pléiade, 1978). The following may also be useful:

Romans et nouvelles, ed. M. Parturier, 2 vols. (Paris, Garnier, 1967).
La Guzla, ed. Eugène Marsan (Paris, Le Divan, 1928).
La Jaquerie, suivie de *La Famille de Carvajal*, ed. Pierre Jourda (Paris, Champion, 1931).
Théâtre de Clara Gazul, suivi de *La Famille de Carvajal*, ed. Salomon (Paris, Garnier-Flammarion, 1968).
Nouvelles, ed. M. Crouzet, 2 vols. (Paris, Imprimerie Nationale, collection 'Lettres françaises', vol. i, 1987; vol. ii, 1988).
Correspondance générale, 17 vols. Vols. i–vi, ed. Parturier, with Josserand and Mallion, Paris, Le Divan, 1941–7. Vols. vii–xvii, ed. Parturier, Toulouse, Privat, 1953–64.

The vast bulk of critical work on Mérimée is, of course, in French. More comprehensive bibliographies are contained in Raitt's biography (1970) and in the Pléiade edition; reference may be made to these, and to recent issues of *The Year's Work in Modern Language Studies*.

The following select bibliography lists only critical matter on Mérimée published in English:

Bowman, F. P., *Prosper Mérimée. Heroism, Pessimism and Irony* (Berkeley and Los Angeles, University of California Press, 1962).
—— 'Narrator and myth in Mérimée's *Vénus d'Ille*', *French Review*, 1960.
Dale, R. C., *The Poetics of Prosper Mérimée* (The Hague and Paris, Mouton, 1966).
George, A. J., *Short Fiction in France 1800–50* (New York, Syracuse University Press, 1964).
—— 'Prosper Mérimée and the short prose narrative', *Symposium*, Spring 1956, pp. 25–33.
Gobert, D. L., 'Mérimée revisited', *Symposium*, Summer 1972.
Grover, P. R., 'Mérimée's influence on Henry James', *Modern Language Review*, 63 (October 1968).
Hainsworth, G., 'West African local colour in *Tamango*', *French Studies*, January 1967, pp. 6–23.
Hamilton, J. F., 'Pagan ritual and human sacrifice in Mérimée's *Mateo Falcone*', *French Review*, 55 (1981), 52–9.

Healy, D. McN., 'Mary Shelley and Prosper Mérimée', *Modern Language Review* (July 1941).

Johnstone, G. H., *Prosper Mérimée. A Mask and a Face* (New York, Dutton, 1927).

Lethbridge, R., and Tilby, M. J., 'Reading Mérimée's *La Double Méprise*', *Modern Language Review*, 73 (October 1978).

Lyon, Sylvia, *The Life and Times of Prosper Mérimée* (New York, The Dial Press, 1948).

O'Faolain, S., *The Short Story* (Cork, Eire, Mercier Press, 1973).

Pater, W., 'Prosper Mérimée', in *Studies in European Literature* (Oxford, Clarendon Press, 1900).

Pilkington, A. E., 'Narrator and supernatural in Mérimée's *La Vénus d'Ille*', *Nineteenth-Century French Studies*, Fall–Winter 1975–6.

Porter, L. M., 'The Subversion of the narrator in Mérimée's *La Vénus d'Ille*', *Nineteenth-Century French Studies*, 10 (1982), 268–77.

Raitt, A. W., *Prosper Mérimée* (London, Eyre & Spottiswoode, 1970).

—— 'History and fiction in the works of Mérimée', *History Today*, April 1969.

Reid, I., *The Short Story* (London and New York, Methuen and Barnes & Noble, 1977).

Rosenthal, A. S., 'Mérimée and the supernatural: diversion or obsession?', *Nineteenth-Century French Studies*, May 1973.

Siebers, T., 'Fantastic lies: *Lokis* and the victim of coincidence', *Kentucky Romance Quarterly*, 28 (1981), 87–93.

Smith, M. A., *Prosper Mérimée* (Twayne, 1972).

Spoerri, T., 'Mérimée and the short story', *Yale French Studies*, No. 4, pp. 3–11.

Tilby, M. J., 'Language and sexuality in Mérimée's *Carmen*', *Forum for Modern Language Studies*, July 1979.

—— 'Henry James and Mérimée: a note of caution', *Romance Notes*, 21 (1980), 165–8.

Ullmann, S., *Style in the French Novel* (Cambridge, Cambridge University Press, 1957), 53–8.

CHRONOLOGY OF PROSPER MÉRIMÉE

1803   Born, 7 Carré Sainte-Geneviève, Paris, on 28 September.

1812–19   Attends Lycée Napoléon (the modern Lycée Henri-IV).

1819   Begins law studies at University of Paris.

1822   Meets Stendhal.
Composes a prose tragedy, *Cromwell* (lost).

1823   Graduates in law.
Begins *Le Théâtre de Clara Gazul* (plays).

1824   April, *La Bataille* (first story, published posthumously in 1887).

Four articles on the Spanish theatre published anonymously in *Le Globe*, November.

1825   *Théâtre de Clara Gazul* published, May.

First visit to England.

1827   *La Guzla* published anonymously in Strasbourg, July.

1828   Injured in duel by Félix Lacoste, January.
La Jaquerie and *La Famille de Carvajal* (plays).

1829   *Chronique du règne de Charles IX* (novel), March.

Mateo Falcone, May.

Le Carrosse du Saint-Sacrement (play), June.

Vision de Charles XI (story), July.

L'Enlèvement de la redoute (story), September.

Tamango, October.

Federigo (story), November.

L'Occasion (play), November.

1830   *Le Vase étrusque*, February.

Les Mécontents (play), March.

La Partie de trictrac, June.

Travels to Spain, June. Introduced to the Countess Montijo and her two daughters, the younger of whom, Eugenia, will in 1853 become Empress of France.

July Revolution, abdication of the reactionary Charles X, accession of Louis-Philippe.

Early December, returns to France; drafted into National Guard.

1831 First two *Lettres d'Espagne*, January, March.

Appointed *chef de bureau* in the Naval Secretariat, February.

Appointed *chef de cabinet* to the Minister of Trade, March.

Appointed *chevalier* of the Legion of Honour, May.

1832 Special commissioner for sanitary measures during the cholera epidemic.

Third *Lettre d'Espagne*.

Chef de cabinet to the Minister of the Interior, December.

1833 *Mosaïque* (collection bringing together the stories, ballads, and travel pieces previously published in literary reviews, together with the play *Les Mécontents*), June.

La Double Méprise (story), September.

Fourth *Lettre d'Espagne: Les Sorcières espagnoles (Spanish Witches)*.

1834 Appointed Inspector-General of Historic Monuments, May.

Les Âmes du purgatoire (story), August.

1835 *Notes d'un voyage dans le midi de la France* (official report).

1836 *Notes d'un voyage dans l'ouest de la France* (official report).

Beginning of liaison with Valentine Delessert.

1837 *La Vénus d'Ille*.
Essay on Religious Architecture in the Middle Ages, especially in France.

1838 *Notes d'un voyage en Auvergne* (official report).

1839 Annual tour of duty takes him to Corsica.

1840 *Notes d'un voyage en Corse* (official report).
Colomba.

1841 *Essay on the Social War* (history), May.

Visits Greece, Smyrna, Constantinople.

1843 Elected to Académie des Inscriptions et Belles-Lettres.

1844 Elected to Académie française.

Arsène Guillot (story).

Études sur l'histoire romaine (*Essay on the Social War* and *The Conspiracy of Catiline*).

Begins work on his history of Pedro I.

1845   *Carmen.*

1846   *L'Abbé Aubain* (story) published anonymously.

Il Vicolo di Madama Lucrezia (story) written (published posthumously in 1873).

Chapter IV of *Carmen* written.

1847   First commercial edition of *Carmen* published, with fourth chapter added.

Histoire de Don Pèdre serialized.

1848   February Revolution, abdication of Louis-Philippe.

Serves in National Guard during ensuing uprising.

Louis-Napoléon Bonaparte elected President of the Second Republic.

1849   His first translation from Russian published (Pushkin's *Queen of Spades*).

1850   *Les Deux Héritages* (play).

1852   Appointed *officier* of the Legion of Honour.

Death of his mother.

Episode de l'histoire de Russie. Les Faux Démétrius (history).

Proclamation of the Second Empire, and of Louis-Napoléon Bonaparte as Emperor Napoleon III.

1853   Marriage of Napoleon III to Eugenia de Montijo. Appointed senator, June.

Abandons annual tours of duty as Inspector of Historic Monuments.

Translation of Gogol's *Government Inspector*.

1854   End of liaison with Valentine Delessert.

1856   Beginnings of ill-health.

1860   Resigns post as Inspector-General of Historic Monuments.

Appointed *commandeur* of the Legion of Honour.

1865   *Les Cosaques d'autrefois* (history).

1866   Appointed *grand officier* of the Legion of Honour.

Writes *La Chambre bleue* (story) for Empress Eugénie (published posthumously in 1871).

1868   First version of *Lokis*.

1869   *Lokis* published.

1870   Writes *Djoûmane* (story, published posthumously in 1873).

Outbreak of Franco-Prussian War.

Empress Eugénie proclaimed Regent, July.

Capitulation of France, 1 September.

Mérimée dies in Cannes on 23 September. Buried in English Protestant cemetery.

1871   During the Commune the house at 52, rue de Lille, in which he had lived since the death of his mother, is burned down. All his papers are destroyed.

1875   First performance of *Carmen*, music by Bizet, libretto by Meilhac and Halévy.

Carmen

(1845)

Πᾶσα γυνὴ χόλος ἐστίν· ἔχει δ᾽ ἀγαθάς δύο ὥρας
Τήν μίαν ἐν θαλάμῳ, τήν μίαν ἐν θανάτῳ.

PALLADAS.*

I

I HAD always suspected that the geographers were talking
nonsense when they located the site of the Battle of Munda
in the territory of the Bastuli-Poeni, near present-day Monda,
about two leagues north of Marbella. My own theories about
the text by the anonymous author of the *Bellum Hispaniense*,
and some information I had gleaned in the Duke of Osuna's
excellent library, led me to believe that the memorable spot
where, for the last time, Caesar played double or quits against
the champions of the Republic was to be found in the vicinity
of Montilla*. Finding myself in Andalusia early in the autumn
of 1830, I undertook a fairly lengthy excursion in order to
clear up what remaining doubts I had. A paper I shall be
publishing shortly, will, I hope, dispel any last vestiges of
doubt from the minds of all serious archaeologists. While
waiting for my dissertation to resolve once and for all the
geographical problem which is holding all learned Europe in
suspense, I want to tell you a little story. It in no way pre-
judges the fascinating question of the site of the battle of
Munda.

At Córdoba I had hired a guide and two horses, and I had
set off with nothing but Caesar's *Commentaries** and a few
shirts for luggage. One day, as I was roaming the plain of the
upper reaches of the Carchena, half-dead with exhaustion,
parched with thirst, and burned by the scorching sun, I was
heartily cursing Caesar and the sons of Pompey when I noticed,
some distance from the path I was following, a small area of
green grass dotted with reeds and rushes. It indicated that
there was a spring close by. Sure enough, on approaching, I

saw that what I had first taken for grass was a marsh into
which flowed a stream that appeared to emerge from a narrow
gorge between two high spurs of the Sierra de Cabra. I decided
that upstream I would find fresher water, fewer leeches and
frogs, and perhaps some shade amongst the rocks. At the
entrance to the gorge my horse whinnied, and another horse,
that I could not yet see, immediately answered it. I had gone
no more than a hundred paces when the gorge suddenly opened out to reveal a sort of natural arena, afforded perfect shade
by the height of the escarpments surrounding it. A traveller
could have found no more inviting spot in which to halt. At
the foot of sheer rocks the spring gushed and bubbled, falling
into a small pool whose bed was carpeted with snow-white
sand. Five or six fine green oak-trees, sheltered at all times
from the wind and watered by the spring, ringed the edge of
the pool, over which they cast a deep shadow. To complete
the picture, around the pool fine, lush grass offered a bed
better than one could have hoped to find in any inn for ten
leagues around.

The honour of discovering this beautiful spot had not been
mine. There was already another man resting there, who had
no doubt been asleep when I entered the place. Awakened by
the neighing of the horses, he got up and went over to his
steed, which had been taking advantage of his master's sleep
to have a good browse in the grass round about. He was a
young fellow, of medium height, but sturdy in appearance and
with a sombre, proud expression. His complexion, which
might once have been fair, had been tanned by exposure to the
sun until it was darker than his hair. In one hand he gripped
his horse's halter, and in the other a brass blunderbuss. I must
admit that at first I was rather taken aback by the blunderbuss
and the fierce expression of the man holding it; but I had
ceased to believe in the existence of robbers, for I had heard
many tales of them but had never yet met any. Besides, I had
seen so many respectable farmers arm themselves to the teeth
before setting off for market that the sight of a fire-arm did not
justify my questioning the stranger's good character. And in
any case, I said to myself, what would he want with my shirts
and my Elzevir* *Commentaries*? I therefore greeted the man

with the blunderbuss with a friendly nod, and asked with a smile if I had disturbed his sleep. Without replying he looked me up and down; then, as if satisfied with his examination, he turned his attention to my guide, who was now approaching. I saw the latter turn pale and stop, showing evident signs of terror. My first thought was that we had encountered a brigand. But immediately prudence counselled me to show no sign of uneasiness. I dismounted, told the guide to unbridle the horses, and, kneeling down by the side of the spring, plunged my head and hands into it; then I took a good long gulp, lying flat on my stomach like the bad soldiers of Gideon*.

Meanwhile, I observed my guide and the stranger. The former was approaching with considerable reluctance. The other seemed to have no evil intentions towards us, for he had set his horse loose again, and his blunderbuss, which at first he had held at the ready, was now pointed towards the ground.

Feeling it best not to take offence at the scant regard he had seemed to show for me, I stretched myself out on the grass and casually asked the man with the blunderbuss whether he had a lighter with him. At the same time I took out my cigar-case. The stranger still made no reply, but rummaged in his pocket, took out his lighter, and lost no time in striking a light for me. He was clearly thawing, for he sat down opposite me, though without relinquishing his weapon. Having lit my cigar, I chose the best of those that were left and asked him whether he smoked.

'*Sí, señor*,' he replied. These were the first words he had uttered, and I noticed that he did not pronounce the *s* in the Andalusian manner,[1] from which I deduced that he was a traveller like myself, though one less interested in archaeology.

'You'll find this quite a good one,' I said to him, presenting him with a genuine Havana regalia.

He nodded slightly, lit his cigar from mine, thanked me with another nod, then began to smoke it with the keenest pleasure.

---

[1] The Andalusians lisp the *s*, confusing it in pronunciation with the soft *c* and the *z*, which Castilians pronounce like an English *th*. One can recognize an Andalusian merely by the way he pronounces the word *señor*.

'Ah!' he exclaimed, releasing the first puff through his mouth and nostrils, 'it's a long time since I smoked!'

In Spain, a cigar offered and accepted establishes relations of hospitality, as does the sharing of bread and salt in the East. The man proved to be more talkative than I had expected. Moreover, although he claimed to be from the *partido* of Montilla, he seemed to have rather a poor knowledge of the area. He did not know the name of the delightful valley in which we found ourselves; he could not name a single village in the vicinity; and, furthermore, when I asked him whether he had seen any ruined walls, large broad-rimmed tiles, or carved stones in the area, he confessed that he had never paid any attention to such things. On the other hand, he showed himself to be an authority on the subject of horses. He criticized mine (admittedly, this was not difficult); then he gave me the pedigree of his own, which was a product of the famous Córdoba stud farm, and which was indeed a noble animal—so tireless, its master claimed, that it had once covered thirty leagues in one day, at a gallop or a brisk trot. In the middle of his long speech the stranger broke off abruptly, as if taken aback and vexed at his own indiscretion.

'I was in a great hurry to get to Córdoba,' he said in some confusion. 'I had to fetch the judges for a trial.'

As he spoke he was looking at my guide, Antonio, whose eyes were lowered.

The shade and the spring so delighted me that I remembered that my friends in Montilla had put some slices of excellent ham in my guide's pannier. I got him to fetch them, and I invited the stranger to share in this improvised picnic. If it was some time since he had smoked, I reckoned that he probably hadn't eaten for at least forty-eight hours. He devoured the food like a starving wolf. It crossed my mind that his meeting me had been providential for the poor fellow. Meanwhile my guide ate little, drank still less, and spoke not at all, although he had been talking nineteen to the dozen ever since the start of our journey together. The presence of our guest seemed to make him uneasy and some sort of mistrust kept them from one another, although I was unable to guess its precise cause.

After the last scraps of the bread and ham had disappeared and we had each smoked a second cigar, I ordered the guide to bridle our horses and was about to take my leave of my new friend when he asked me where I was intending to spend the night.

Too late to heed a sign from my guide, I replied that I was going to the Venta del Cuervo*.

'No place for a person like yourself to stay, señor. I am going there myself, and if you will allow me to accompany you, we will travel together.'

'With great pleasure,' I said, mounting my horse. My guide, who was holding the stirrup for me, again tried to catch my eye. I responded by shrugging my shoulders, as if to assure him that I was perfectly easy in my mind, and we set off on our way.

Antonio's mysterious signs, his general air of uneasiness, and some remarks that the stranger had let slip, especially his tale of the thirty-league gallop and the implausible explanation he had offered for it, had already enabled me to form an opinion about my travelling companion. I had no doubt that the man I was dealing with was a smuggler, or perhaps a robber. But what odds was it to me? I knew the Spanish character well enough to be quite certain that I had nothing to fear from a man who had shared food and tobacco with me. His very presence was a guarantee of protection, should we run into any trouble. Besides, I was delighted at this chance to learn what a brigand is like. It isn't every day that you encounter one, and there is a certain pleasure in finding yourself in the presence of a dangerous individual, especially when you sense that he is feeling mild and amenable.

I was hoping gradually to induce the stranger to confide in me, and, ignoring the glances my guide kept darting at me, I led the conversation round to the topic of highwaymen. Naturally I spoke of them with respect. There was at that time in Andalusia a famous bandit by the name of José-María, whose exploits were on everyone's lips. 'Perhaps this is José-María,' I said to myself. I recounted the tales I knew of this hero, all of which showed him in a favourable light, and I was vocal in my admiration for his valour and magnanimity.

'José-María is nothing but a scoundrel,' said the stranger coldly.

'Is he passing judgement on himself or simply being over-modest?' I wondered; for, by dint of studying my companion, I had managed to fit him to the description of José-María I had seen displayed on the gates of so many towns in Andalusia. 'Yes, it's him all right: fair hair, blue eyes, large mouth, good teeth, small hands; a fine shirt, velvet jacket with silver buttons, white hide gaiters, a bay horse. . . . No doubt about it! But I shall respect his incognito.'

We arrived at the *venta*. It was as he had described it, that is to say, one of the most wretched I had yet encountered. One large room did duty as kitchen, dining-room, and bedroom. A fire burned on a flat stone hearth in the middle of the room and the smoke escaped through a hole in the roof, or rather hovered beneath it in a pall a few feet above the ground. Half a dozen old mule blankets lay on the ground along one wall: these were the travellers' beds. Twenty yards from the house, or rather from the single room I have just described, stood a sort of shed which served as a stable. The only human beings to be found in this charming abode, at any rate at that moment, were an old woman and a small girl of 10 or 12, both the colour of soot and dressed in squalid rags. 'So this', I said to myself, 'is all that is left of the population of ancient Munda Baetica! O Caesar, o Sextus Pompey, how astonished you would be if you were to return to the world!'

'Ah! Señor don José!' the old woman exclaimed in surprise, on seeing my companion.

Don José scowled and raised his hand in a gesture of authority which at once silenced the old woman. I turned towards my guide and, by a scarcely perceptible sign, intimated to him that he could tell me nothing I did not already know about the man in whose company I was going to spend the night.

Supper was better than I had expected. On a small, low table, we were served an aged fowl in a white sauce, with rice and large quantities of peppers, followed by peppers fried in oil, and to finish with, *gazpacho*, a sort of salad consisting of peppers*. Three such highly seasoned dishes caused us to

have frequent recourse to a skin of Montilla wine, which proved
to be delicious. After we had eaten, noticing a mandolin hanging on the wall (there are mandolins everywhere in Spain) I
asked the little girl who was serving us whether she could play
it.

'No,' she replied, 'but don José plays, and very well, too.'

'Be so good as to sing me something,' I said to him. 'I am
passionately fond of your national music.'

'I can refuse nothing to such a good señor, who gives me
such excellent cigars,' exclaimed don José good-humouredly.
He took the mandolin that was handed to him, and sang to his
own accompaniment. His voice was rough but agreeable, the
melody plaintive and exotic. Of the words I understood
nothing.

'Unless I am mistaken,' I said, 'the song you have just sung
is not Spanish. It resembles the *zortziko* I have heard in the
Basque Provinces,[1] and the words must be in Basque.'

'Yes,' replied don José, his face growing sombre. He placed
the mandolin on the ground and, folding his arms, gazed at
the dying fire with an expression of profound melancholy. By
the light of a lamp placed on the little table, his face, its
expression at once noble and fierce, reminded me of Milton's
Satan*. Perhaps, like him, my companion was thinking of the
abode he had left behind and of the exile he had earned by
some transgression. I tried to rekindle the conversation but he
did not respond, remaining immersed in his sad thoughts. The
old woman had already gone to bed in a corner of the room
screened off by a tattered blanket that hung from a rope. The
little girl had followed her into this retreat reserved for the fair
sex. At this point my guide rose and asked me to follow him
to the stable; but at his words don José suddenly came to, and
asked him abruptly where he was going.

'To the stable,' answered the guide.

'What for? The horses have enough fodder. Sleep here, the
señor will let you.'

'I'm afraid the señor's horse may be sick. I should like the

[1] The privileged provinces, enjoying particular *fueros* (rights): Álava,
Vizcaya, Guipúzcoa, and part of Navarre. Basque is the language of the
region.

señor to see for himself. Perhaps he will know what must be done.'

It was obvious that Antonio wanted to speak to me in private; but I was anxious not to arouse don José's suspicions and, at this stage in the proceedings, it seemed to me that the best course was to show complete trust. So I said to Antonio that I knew nothing about horses and that I wanted to sleep. Don José followed him to the stable, whence he soon returned alone. He told me that there was nothing wrong with the horse, but that my guide considered it such a priceless animal that he was rubbing it down with his jacket to make it sweat, and proposed to devote the rest of the night to this recreation. Meanwhile I had stretched myself out on the mule blankets, carefully wrapped in my coat so as to avoid contact with them. Don José asked my pardon for taking the liberty of joining me, then lay down by the door, after first priming his blunderbuss, which he was careful to place beneath the pannier he was using as a pillow. We wished one another goodnight, and five minutes later we were both sound asleep.

I had thought I was tired enough to be able to sleep in such surroundings; but, after an hour, I was roused from my first slumbers by a highly disagreeable itching sensation. As soon as I had ascertained its cause I got up, convinced that it was better to spend the rest of the night out of doors than beneath that inhospitable roof. I tiptoed to the door, stepped over the spot where don José lay enjoying the sleep of the just, and managed to leave the house without waking him. Beside the door was a wide wooden bench; I stretched myself out on it and tried to make myself comfortable for the night. I was about to fall asleep for the second time when I saw in front of me what looked like the silhouettes of a man and a horse, both moving in total silence. I sat up, and recognized Antonio. Surprised to see him out of the stable at such an hour, I rose and went to meet him. He had halted, having already seen me.

'Where is he?' asked Antonio softly.

'In the *venta*. He's asleep, the bugs don't bother him. But why are you taking the horse away?'

Then I noticed that, in order to avoid making any noise as

they left the outhouse, Antonio had carefully wrapped the animal's hooves in the remnants of an old blanket.

'Talk more quietly, for God's sake,' said Antonio. 'You don't know who that man is. It's José Navarro, the most notorious bandit in Andalusia. I've been trying to warn you all day, but you chose to ignore my signs.'

'What does it matter to me if he's a bandit?' I replied. 'He hasn't robbed us, and I'll lay odds he doesn't intend to.'

'That's all very well. But there's a reward of two hundred ducats for anyone who turns him in. I know of a lancers' post a league and a half from here, and before the night's out I shall be back, with a few strong lads. I would have taken his horse but it's so vicious that no one but Navarro can go near it.'

'Devil take you,' I said to him. 'What harm has the wretched man done you, that you should denounce him? Besides, are you certain he's the brigand you say he is?'

'Absolutely. Just now he followed me into the stable and said to me: "You're acting as if you recognize me. If you tell the good señor who I am I'll blow your brains out." Stay by him, señor, you have nothing to fear. So long as he knows you are here he will suspect nothing.'

As we spoke, we had already come far enough away from the *venta* for the horseshoes to be inaudible. In no time at all Antonio had removed the rags he had wrapped around the horse's hooves and was preparing to mount. I tried pleading with him and threatening him in an attempt to make him stay.

'I am a poor devil, señor,' he said. 'I can't afford to turn down two hundred ducats, especially when it means ridding the countryside of the likes of that vermin. But be on your guard: if Navarro wakes up he'll go for his blunderbuss, and then you'd best watch out! As for me, it's too late for me to turn back now. You must do whatever you think best.'

The wretch was in the saddle. He spurred his horse, and I had soon lost sight of him in the darkness.

I was extremely vexed with my guide, and somewhat uneasy. After a moment's reflection I made up my mind and returned to the *venta*. Don José was still sleeping, no doubt taking the opportunity to recover from the fatigue of several eventful days and nights. I had to shake him roughly to wake him. Never shall I forget his fierce look and the way he reached for his blunderbuss, which, as a precaution, I had placed some distance from his bed.

'Señor,' I said to him, 'I must ask you to forgive me for waking you, but I have a silly question I must put to you: would you be glad to see half a dozen lancers arrive here?'

'Who told you of this?' he asked menacingly, leaping to his feet.

'What does it matter where I heard the information, so long as it is true?'

'Your guide has betrayed me! But he'll pay for it. Where is he?'

'I don't know . . . in the stable, I think. But I was told . . .'

'Who told you? It can't have been the old woman.'

'No one I know. . . . Look, without more ado, have you got reason to leave before the soldiers arrive, or haven't you? If you have, waste no time, if not, goodnight and please forgive me for interrupting your sleep.'

'Ah, that guide of yours! I distrusted him from the start. But I'll settle with him! Farewell, señor. May God repay you the service I owe you. I am not so thoroughly evil as you suppose. . . . Yes, there is still something within me that deserves the pity of a man of honour. Farewell, señor; my one regret is that I cannot repay you.'

'In return for what I have done for you, don José, promise me that you will suspect no one, and renounce all thoughts of vengeance. Here, take some cigars for your journey; *bon voyage!*' And I offered him my hand.

He shook it without replying, picked up his blunderbuss and his pannier, and, after saying a few words to the old woman in some argot I could not understand, he ran to the outhouse. A few moments later I heard him gallop off into the countryside.

I returned to my bench and lay down, but I did not fall asleep again. I asked myself whether I had been right to save a robber, and perhaps a murderer, from the gallows, merely because I had shared some ham and some Valencian-style rice with him. Had I not betrayed my guide, who was upholding the cause of law and order? Had I not exposed him to the risk of incurring a blackguard's vengeance? Yes, but what about the obligations of hospitality? Primitive notions, I said to myself; I shall be answerable for all the crimes this bandit goes on to commit. Yet can one dismiss as primitive that instinctive call of conscience which is resistant to all reasoning? Perhaps, in the delicate situation in which I found myself, it would not have been possible for me to escape without some self-reproach. I was still in a state of complete uncertainty as to the rights and wrongs of my action when I saw half-a-dozen horsemen appear, with Antonio prudently bringing up the rearguard. I went to meet them and informed them that the bandit had fled over two hours earlier. Questioned by the corporal, the old woman replied that she knew Navarro but that, since she lived alone, she would never have dared risk her life by denouncing him. She added that when he came to her inn it was his habit always to leave in the middle of the night.

I had to go some leagues out of my way in order to present my passport and sign a statement before an alcalde, after which I was permitted to resume my archaeological investigations. Antonio bore me a grudge, suspecting that it was I who had prevented him from collecting the two hundred ducats' reward. However, we parted amicably in Córdoba, where I gave him the largest tip the state of my finances would allow.

II

I spent some days in Córdoba. I had been referred to a manuscript in the library of the Dominican friary, in which I was to find some interesting information on ancient Munda. The friars made me very welcome, and I spent my days in their friary and my evenings walking about the town.

Towards sunset in Córdoba, many people with nothing better to do congregate on the street above the right bank of the Guadalquivir. At this spot, the air is heavy with the stench from a tannery that still produces the fine leather for which the region has long been famous; but this is a small price to pay for the sight with which the spectator is rewarded. A few minutes before the angelus a large number of women gather at the river's edge below the street, which is on a fairly high embankment. No man would venture to mingle with that company. As soon as the angelus has been rung, night is deemed to have fallen. At the last stroke of the bell all these women remove their clothes and leap into the water. A pandemonium of shouts and laughter ensues. From the street above, the men gaze at the bathers, peering in a vain attempt to see what is going on. Yet those white and indistinct forms visible against the dark azure of the river set poetic minds at work, and with a little effort it is not difficult to imagine one is watching Diana and her nymphs bathing, without the risk of incurring the fate of Actaeon*.

There is a story that some wags once got up a subscription in order to bribe the cathedral bell-ringer to ring the angelus twenty minutes before the appointed time. Although it was still broad daylight the nymphs of the Guadalquivir did not hesitate and, taking their cue from the angelus rather than from the sun, they performed their ablutions—which are always of the simplest—with a clear conscience. I was not present on that occasion. During my visit the bell-ringer was incorruptible, the twilight impenetrable, and only a cat could have distinguished between the most wizened old crone that sold oranges and the prettiest girl in Córdoba.

One evening at dusk I was leaning on the parapet of the embankment, smoking, when a woman came up the flight of steps that led down to the river, and sat down near me. In her hair was a large spray of jasmine, whose flowers give out an intoxicating scent in the evening. She was simply, even poorly, dressed, all in black, like most working-class girls in the evenings. (Respectable women wear black only in the morning; in the evening they dress *a la francesa*.) As she drew level with me, the girl, who had been bathing, allowed the mantilla covering her head to fall back over her shoulders and, *by the dark light that shines down from the stars**, I saw that she was slight, young, good-looking, and had very large eyes. I at once threw away my cigar. She understood this very Gallic gesture of politeness, and hastened to tell me that she enjoyed the smell of tobacco, and that she even smoked herself when she could get hold of the mild cigarettes she liked. By good fortune I had a few of these in my case, and I lost no time in offering her some. She condescended to take one, and lit it from a piece of burning rope brought to us by a child for a small payment. As our tobacco-smoke mingled, the beautiful bather and I conversed together for so long that we found ourselves almost alone on the embankment. I thought it would not be indiscreet to propose going to have an ice at the *nevería*.[1] After a modest hesitation, she accepted the invitation; but before deciding, she asked what time it was. I made my watch strike the hour, and this seemed to astonish her a great deal.

'What ideas you foreigners dream up! Where are you from, señor? I suppose you are English?'[2]

'French, and your humble servant. And I take it you are from Córdoba, señorita, or señora?'

'No.'

'But you do come from Andalusia. I think I can tell that from your soft speech.'

'If you're so clever at recognizing people's accents, you must be able to guess what I am.'

'I think you come from the land of Jesus, two steps from paradise.' (I had learned this metaphorical description of Andalusia from my friend Francisco Sevilla*, the well-known picador.)

'Paradise! Round here they say that's not for the likes of us.'

'Then you must be Moorish, or . . . ' I stopped, hardly daring to say 'Jewish'.

'Come, come; you can see perfectly well that I'm a Gypsy. Do you want me to tell you *la baji*[3]? Have you heard people talk of Carmencita? That is my name.'

At that time, fifteen years ago, I was such an unbeliever that I did not recoil in horror at finding myself in the presence of

[1] Café with an ice-house, or rather a snow-store. Few villages in Spain cannot boast a *nevería*.

[2] In Spain, any traveller not carrying samples of calico or silk is taken for an Englishman (*Inglesito*). The same is true in the Levant. At Chalcis I had the honour to be introduced as a Μιλόρδος Φραντζέσος (French Milord).

[3] To tell your fortune.

a witch. Very well, I said to myself; last week I dined with a highwayman, so today why not eat ice-cream with a servant of the devil? A traveller should try to see everything.

I had another motive for cultivating her acquaintance. After leaving school I had, I confess to my shame, spent some time studying the occult sciences, and had even tried several times to call up the spirit of darkness. Long since cured of my interest in such pursuits, I was nevertheless still curious about all forms of superstition, and was looking forward to learning what heights the magic art had attained among the Gypsies.

As we talked, we had entered the *nevería*, and we sat at a small table lit by a candle enclosed in a glass globe. I now had a chance to examine my *gitana* at leisure, whilst a few respectable folk stared at me over their ices, amazed to see me in such company.

I very much doubt that Señorita Carmen was of pure Gypsy stock; at any rate, she was infinitely prettier than any other woman of her race I had ever encountered. According to the Spaniards, for a woman to be beautiful she must have thirty positive qualities; or, to put it another way, it must be possible to apply to her ten adjectives each of which describes three parts of her person. For instance, she must have three things that are dark: dark eyes, dark eyelashes, and dark eyebrows; three that are delicate: her hands, her lips, and her hair; and so forth—for the rest, see Brantôme*. My Gypsy-girl could not lay claim to such perfection. Her skin, though perfectly smooth, was nearly the colour of copper. Her eyes were slanting, but remarkably wide; her lips rather full, but finely chiselled, affording a glimpse of teeth whiter than blanched almonds. Her hair, perhaps rather coarse, and black with a blue sheen like a raven's wing, was long and shining. Not to weary you with too lengthy a description, I will sum her up by saying that for every fault she had a quality which was perhaps all the more striking from the contrast. She had a strange, wild beauty, a face that was disconcerting at first, but unforgettable. Her eyes in particular had an expression, at once voluptuous and fierce, that I have never seen on any human face. 'Gypsy's eye, wolf's eye' is a phrase Spaniards apply to people with keen powers of observation. If you don't have time to visit the zoo in the Jardin des Plantes to study the look in a wolf's eye, watch your cat when it is stalking a sparrow.

Naturally it would have been ridiculous to have one's fortune told in a café, so I asked the pretty witch to allow me to accompany her to her home. She raised no objection, but again wanted to know how the time was passing, and again asked me to make my watch strike the hour.

'Is it really gold?' she asked, scrutinizing it with excessive attention.

Night had fallen when we left; most of the shops were shut, and the streets almost deserted. We crossed the bridge over the Guadalquivir, and in an outlying district we stopped in front of a house of anything but palatial appearance. A child opened the door to us. The Gypsy spoke a few words to it in a language I did not recognize, but which I subsequently realized was Romany, or *chipe calli*, the language of the Gypsies. The child at once took itself off, leaving us in a fairly large room whose sole furnishings consisted of a small table, two stools, and a chest—unless you include the jug of water, a heap of oranges, and a bundle of onions.

As soon as we were alone the Gypsy took from the chest a pack of cards that seemed to have come in for a lot of use, a magnet, a dried chameleon, and various other paraphernalia of her art. Then she told me to cross my left palm with a silver coin, and the magic ceremonies commenced. I need not tell you of her predictions; as for her way of going about things, she was obviously no mean sorceress.

Unfortunately it was not long before we were disturbed. The door was suddenly flung violently open and a man swathed from head to foot in a brown cloak entered the room, upbraiding the Gypsy in the most uncivil fashion. I did not understand what he said, but the tone of his voice made it clear that he was in an extremely bad temper. On seeing him the Gypsy showed neither surprise nor anger, but ran up to meet him and, with extraordinary volubility, spoke several sentences to him in the mysterious language she had already used in my presence. The word *payllo*, which recurred often, was the only one I understood. I knew this to be the word

Gypsies use to refer to any man not of their own race. Supposing myself to be the man under discussion, I was ready for an awkward scene; I already had my hand on the leg of one of the stools and was calculating the precise moment at which it would be appropriate to throw it at the intruder's head. The man pushed the Gypsy away roughly, advanced towards me, then, taking a step back, said:

'Ah, señor! It's you!'

Looking at him, I recognized my friend don José. At that moment I rather regretted not having left him to hang.

'Why, it's you, my dear fellow!' I exclaimed, with the heartiest laugh I could muster. 'The señorita was on the point of telling me some most interesting things when you interrupted us.'

'The same old story! This has got to stop!' he said between his teeth, fixing her with a ferocious look.

Meanwhile the Gypsy went on speaking to him in her language. She gradually became more excited. Her eyes grew bloodshot, her expression terrifying, her features contorted, and she stamped her foot. She seemed to be exhorting him to take some course of action about which he was showing some hesitation. What it was, I thought I understood only too well from the way she moved her little hand quickly back and forth under her chin. I was tempted to believe that they were talking of cutting someone's throat, and I had my suspicions that the throat in question might be my own.

Don José responded to this torrent of eloquence with only a few brief utterances. At this the Gypsy darted him a look of profound scorn; then, seating herself cross-legged in a corner of the room, she selected an orange, peeled it, and began to eat it.

Don José took me by the arm, opened the door, and led me out into the street. We walked about two hundred paces in total silence. Then, extending his hand, he said:

'Straight ahead, and you'll come to the bridge.'

At once he turned his back on me and walked rapidly away. I returned to my inn feeling a trifle sheepish, and more than somewhat annoyed. To make matters worse, when the time came to undress I discovered that my watch was missing.

Various considerations prevented me from going next day to claim it back, or from requesting the *corregidor** to be so good as to have it traced. I finished my work on the Dominicans' manuscript and left for Seville. After several months' wanderings through Andalusia, the time came to return to Madrid, and I had once again to pass through Córdoba. I did not intend to stay there long, for I had taken a dislike to that beautiful town and to the lady bathers of the Guadalquivir. However, I had to see a few friends again and deliver some messages, and this entailed my spending three or four days in the ancient capital of the Moslem princes.

As soon as I reappeared at the Dominican friary, one of the friars who had always shown great interest in my research on the site of Munda welcomed me with open arms, exclaiming:

'God be praised! Welcome, my dear friend. We all took you for dead, and I myself have recited any number of *Paters* and *Aves* for the salvation of your soul—not that I regret them. So they didn't murder you—for we know that you were robbed.'

'How come?' I asked him in some surprise.

'Yes, indeed: you know that fine repeater watch you used to make strike the hour, in the library, when we told you it was time to go to service? Well, it's been found, and it will be returned to you.'

'It's true that I'd mislaid it,' I broke in, somewhat abashed.

'The scoundrel is behind bars, and since he was known to be a man who would shoot a Christian to rob him of a peseta, we were scared to death he'd done away with you. I'll go with you to the *corregidor* and we'll get them to return your beautiful watch to you. Then, when you're back in France you won't be able to say there's no justice here in Spain.'

'Quite frankly,' I said to him, 'I'd sooner lose my watch than give evidence against some poor wretch that will lead to his being hanged, especially because, well . . .'

'Oh, set your mind at rest. He's been tried on a number of other counts, and you can't hang a man twice. Besides, it's not a question of hanging: the man who robbed you is an *hidalgo*, so in two days' time he will be garrotted, with no reprieve.[1]

[1] In 1830 this was still the privilege of the nobility. Today, under the constitutional regime, commoners have won the right to be garrotted.

So you see, one robbery more or less will make no difference
to his case. Would to God he had only stolen! But he has committed a number of murders, each more hideous than the one
before.'

'What is his name?'

'In these parts he goes by the name of José Navarro, but he
has another name, a Basque one, that you and I could never
hope to pronounce. Look, he's not the sort of man one
encounters every day, and since you like getting to know the
idiosyncrasies of our country, you mustn't miss this opportunity of learning how felons take their leave of the world here
in Spain. He's in the prison chapel.* Brother Martínez will
take you to see him.'

My friend the Dominican friar was so insistent that I should
see the preparations for this '*verry preety leetle hanging*'*
that I could not refuse the offer. I went to see the prisoner,
taking with me a packet of cigars which, I hoped, would help
him to overlook my indiscretion.

I was ushered in to don José's presence as he was eating
his meal. He nodded to me rather coldly and thanked me
politely for the gift I had brought him. After counting the
cigars in the packet I had put at his disposal, he selected a few
and returned the rest to me, remarking that he would not
be needing more.

I asked him whether, with money or the influence of my
friends, there was anything I could do to mitigate his fate.
At first he shrugged his shoulders, smiling sadly; then,
on second thoughts, he asked me to have a mass said for the
salvation of his soul.

'And would you have another one said, for someone who
has offended you?' he added timidly.

'Certainly, my friend,' I said. 'Though to the best of
my knowledge no one in this country has offended me.'

He took my hand and shook it gravely. After a moment's
silence he went on:

'May I be so bold as to ask you to do something else for
me? When you return to your country, perhaps you will be
passing through Navarre. At any rate you'll be going through
Vitoria, which is not very far from there.'

'Yes,' I said, 'I shall indeed be passing through Vitoria. But it's not inconceivable that I may make a detour in order to visit Pamplona, and I'm sure I would be glad to go out of my way on your behalf.'

'If you go to Pamplona you'll see plenty of things to interest you—it's a beautiful town. I will give you this medallion.' (He showed me a small silver medallion which hung from a chain round his neck.) 'You can wrap it up . . .'—he paused for a moment to control his emotion—'and deliver it, or see it is delivered, to an old woman whose address I shall give you. You should say I am dead, but not how I died.'

I promised to carry out his commission. I saw him again the next day, part of which I spent with him. It was then that he told me the sad tale you are about to read.

III

'I was born,' he said, 'in Elizondo, in the valley of Baztán. My name is don José Lizarrabengoa, and you are familiar enough with Spain, señor, to be able to tell at once from my name that I am a Basque and an Old Christian*. If I call myself *don*, it is because I am entitled to do so, and if we were in Elizondo I would show you my genealogy on parchment. They wanted me to go into the Church, and I was given some schooling, but little good did it do me. I was too fond of playing pelota—that was my undoing. When we Navarrese play pelota we don't spare a thought for anything else. Once when I'd won a game, a lad from Álava province picked a quarrel with me. We took up our *maquilas*,[1] and once again I was the victor; but I had to leave the province as a result.

'I met up with some dragoons and enlisted in the Almansa Cavalry Regiment. We mountain folk are quick to learn military ways. I soon became a corporal, and had already been promised promotion to sergeant when it was my misfortune to be put on guard at the cigar factory in Seville. If you've been to Seville you must have seen that big building* outside the town walls, near the Guadalquivir. I can still picture the

---

[1] Iron-tipped sticks used by the Basques.

gate with the guard on duty outside. The Spaniards play cards or sleep when they're on guard; but as a true man of Navarre I tried always to have something to keep me occupied. I was making a chain with some brass wire, so I could attach the priming needle for my rifle to it.

'Suddenly my comrades said: "There goes the bell—the girls will be coming back to work."

'You probably know, señor, that around four or five hundred women work in the factory. They roll the cigars in a large room in which men aren't allowed without a pass from the *Veinticuatro*,[1] because when it's hot the girls don't believe in over-dressing, especially the younger ones. When these factory-girls return to work after lunch, lots of young men go and watch them pass, and make all sorts of propositions to them. Few of the girls would refuse the offer of a mantilla made out of taffeta, and anyone with a taste for such sport has only to reach out for the fish to swim into his hand.

'While the others watched, I stayed on my bench near the gate. I was young then; I was still homesick, and I didn't believe any girl could be pretty unless she wore blue skirts and hair plaited over her shoulders.[2] Besides, Andalusian women frightened me; I wasn't yet used to them and their ways, forever mocking, never a serious word. So there I was engrossed in my chain when I heard some townsfolk saying, "Here comes the *gitanilla*." I raised my head, and saw her. It was a Friday; I'll never forget it. I saw Carmen, whom you know, and at whose place we met a few months ago.

'She was wearing a very short red skirt, beneath which you could see her white silk stockings with holes in them and dainty red morocco-leather shoes fastened with flame-coloured ribbons. Her mantilla was parted so as to reveal her shoulders and a big bunch of acacia flowers which she had in the front of her blouse. She had another acacia bloom in one corner of her mouth, and she moved forward swaying her hips like some filly out of the Córdoba stud. In my part of the world everyone

---

[1] The magistrate responsible for law and order, and for municipal administration.

[2] The usual costume of country women in Navarre and the Basque Provinces.

would have crossed themselves at the sight of a woman dressed like that; but there in Seville everyone paid her some risqué compliment on her appearance. She replied to them all, eyeing them archly, with her fist on her hip, brazen like the true Gypsy she was. At first I didn't find her attractive, and I returned to my task; but, acting as women and cats usually do, refusing to come when they are called, but coming when they are not called, she stopped in front of me and said, addressing me in the Andalusian manner:

' "*Compadre*, will you give me your chain, to keep the keys to my strongbox on?"

' "It's for my priming needle," I replied.

' "Your priming needle!" she laughed. "The señor must go in for lace-making, since he needs needles!" Everyone around us began to laugh. I could feel myself blushing and could think of nothing to say to her in reply.

' "Very well, my love," she went on. "Make me seven ells of black lace for a mantilla, needle-seller of my heart!"

'And taking the acacia flower from her mouth, she flicked it at me with her thumb, right between the eyes. Señor, it was like a bullet hitting me. I didn't know where to hide myself, I stood there like a block of wood. When she had gone into the factory, I saw the acacia flower that had fallen to the ground at my feet. I don't know what came over me, but I picked it up without my companions noticing and tucked it away in my tunic for safe keeping. That was my first piece of folly!

'I was still thinking about it two or three hours later when a porter arrived in the guardroom, breathless and with alarm written all over his face. He told us that a woman had been murdered in the big room where they roll the cigars, and that the guard would have to be sent in. The sergeant told me to take two men and go in and see. I picked two men and went on up. Just imagine, señor: the first thing I found when I went into the room was three hundred women in their under-garments and precious little else, all shouting, screaming, gesticulating, kicking up the most unholy row. On one side lay one of the women, sprawled flat on her back, with blood all over her and two knife-slashes across her face in the

shape of a letter X. Facing the injured woman, who was being
helped by some of the better-natured girls, I saw Carmen,
held by five or six of her cronies. The injured woman was
shouting, "A priest, a priest! I'm dying!" Carmen said
nothing. She was clenching her teeth and rolling her eyes like
a chameleon.

' "Now what's all this?" I asked.

'I had great difficulty in discovering what had happened, for
the factory-girls were all talking at once. The injured woman
had apparently been boasting that she had enough money in
her pockets to buy a donkey at the Triana* market. Carmen,
who had a sharp tongue in her head, said, "Isn't a broomstick
good enough for you, then?" Stung by the reproof, perhaps
because she knew she wasn't blameless on that score, the other
woman replied that she wasn't herself an authority on
broomsticks, not having the honour to be a Gypsy or an
adopted daughter of Satan, but that señorita Carmencita
would shortly be making the acquaintance of her donkey,
when the *corregidor* took her for a ride, with two lackeys
following behind to keep the flies off her*.

' "I'll make some gashes on those cheeks of yours for the
flies to drink from," said Carmen, "and I'll paint a chequer-
board on them."[1] Thereupon she began slashing away,
carving crosses on the woman's face with the knife she used
for cutting the ends off the cigars.

'It was an open-and-shut case. I took Carmen by the arm.
"Young lady," I said to her politely, "you must come with
me." She darted me a look, as if of recognition; but then she
said resignedly, "Let's go. Where's my mantilla?" She put it
over her head so that only one of her big eyes was visible, and
followed my two men, as meek as a lamb.

'When we arrived at the guardroom the sergeant said it was
a serious matter, and that she must be taken to prison. I was
again given the task of escorting her. I placed a dragoon on
either side of her and marched behind them, as a corporal
should on such occasions. We set off for the town. At first the
Gypsy remained silent, but in the Street of the Serpent—you

[1] *Pintar un jabeque*, to paint a xebec. A xebec, a type of Spanish boat,
generally has red and white checks painted along its sides.

know how it lives up to its name, the way it twists and turns*
—she began by letting her mantilla fall to her shoulders, so as
to show me her face with its cajoling expression, and, turning
towards me as far as she could, she said:

' "Where are you taking me, officer?"

' "To prison, poor child," I replied as kindly as I was able,
as every good soldier should speak to a prisoner, especially a
woman.

' "Alas, what will become of me? Officer, have pity on me!
You are so young, so kind!" Then, more quietly, she said:
"Let me escape and I'll give you a piece of the *bar lachi*, that
will make all women desire you."

'The *bar lachi*, señor, is a piece of lodestone with which the
Gypsies claim you can cast all sorts of spells, if you know how
to use it. Give a woman a piece grated into a glass of white
wine, and she will find you irresistible. As solemnly as I could,
I replied:

' "We aren't here to talk nonsense. You must go to prison;
those are the orders, there's no help for it."

'We Basques have an accent that makes us easily recogniz-
able to Spaniards, although not one of them can learn so much
as a *bai, jaona*.[1] So it wasn't difficult for Carmen to guess
that I was from the Basque Country. As you know, señor, the
Gypsies have no country of their own. Being always on the
move, they speak every language, and most of them are equally at home in Portuguese, French, Basque, or Catalan. They
can even make themselves understood among the Moors and
the English. Carmen had quite a fair knowledge of Basque.

' "*Laguna, ene bihotzarena*—companion of my heart," she
said suddenly. "Are you from the Basque Provinces?"

'Our language is so beautiful, señor, that when we hear it
spoken far from home our hearts leap at the sound of it.—I
should like to have a Basque confessor,' the bandit added,
more softly.

After a silence he went on.

' "I'm from Elizondo," I replied in Basque, deeply moved
at hearing my language spoken.

---

[1] Yes, sir.

' "And I'm from Etxalar!" she said. "Your village is only four hours' journey from ours. I was kidnapped by Gypsies, who brought me to Seville. I've been working at the cigar factory so as to earn enough money to return to Navarre and be with my poor mother, who has no one but me to support her, and a little *baratz*[1] with a couple of dozen cider apple trees. Ah! how I wish I were back at home, among the white mountains! They insulted me because I wasn't from this land of thieves and pedlars of rotten oranges. And those sluts ganged up on me because I told them that all the *jaques*[2] of Seville with their knives wouldn't frighten one of our lads with his blue beret and his *maquila*. My comrade, my friend, will you do nothing to help a fellow-countrywoman?"

'She was lying, señor, as she always lied. I wonder whether that girl ever spoke one word of truth in her life; but whenever she spoke, I believed her—I couldn't help it. She spoke Basque atrociously, yet I believed her when she said she was from Navarre. You only had to look at her eyes, her mouth, and her complexion to tell she was a Gypsy. I was mad, I overlooked the most obvious things. I was thinking that if any Spaniards had taken it into their heads to speak ill of my homeland I would have slashed them across the face, exactly as she had just done to her companion. In short, I was behaving like a drunken man; I was beginning to talk like a fool, and I was on the point of acting like one too.

' "If I were to push you, my fellow-countryman, and if you were to fall," she continued in Basque, "it would take more than those two Castilian conscripts to stop me."

'As God is my truth, I forgot my orders, I forgot everything, and I said to her:

' "Well then, my dear, my sister, try. And may Our Lady of the Mountains be your aid!"

'At that moment we were passing one of those narrow alleys of which there are so many in Seville. Suddenly Carmen turned and punched me in the chest. I allowed myself to fall backwards. She leaped over me and began to run, showing us a fine pair of legs. "Run like a Basque", they say; she could

---

[1] Paddock, garden.   [2] Braggarts.

run with the best of them, and her legs were as swift as they were shapely. I got up at once, but turned my lance[1] so as to block the alleyway, with the result that no sooner had my men started to pursue her than they found their way barred. Then I began to run too, and they followed after me, but there was no chance of our catching her, what with our spurs, our sabres, and our lances! In less time than it takes to tell, the prisoner had got away. Furthermore, all the gossips in the neighbourhood aided and abetted her in her escape, jeering at us and sending us off on the wrong scent. After much marching to and fro, we had to return to the guardroom without a certificate of receipt from the prison governor.

'To avoid punishment, my men said that Carmen had spoken to me in Basque; and, to be honest, it did seem rather unlikely that a strapping lad like me could so easily be floored by a punch from such a small girl. It all seemed a bit of a mystery, or rather, it all seemed only too clear. When we came off guard I was reduced to the ranks and sentenced to a month's detention. It was the first punishment I'd earned during my time in the army. I could kiss goodbye to those sergeant's stripes I'd thought were as good as mine!

'My first days in prison were a very sad time for me. When I joined up I had imagined I would become an officer at the very least. My compatriots Longa and Mina became generals; Chapalangarra*, who, like Mina, is a liberal and an exile in your country, rose to the rank of colonel, and I've played pelota a score of times with his brother, who was just an ordinary lad like myself. Now I kept telling myself: "All the time you've served with a clean record has gone for nothing. You've earned yourself a black mark. In order to get back into your superiors' good books you'll have to work ten times harder than when you enlisted as a recruit!" And what had I got myself punished for? For the sake of a villainous Gypsy girl who had made a fool of me and who was doubtless going about the town stealing at that very moment. Yet I could not prevent myself from thinking of her. Would you believe it, señor, those silk stockings with the holes in, that she'd given me a good glimpse of when she ran away—I couldn't get them

---

[1] All Spanish cavalrymen are equipped with lances.

out of my mind. I used to look out into the street through the prison bars, and among all the women who went past I never saw a single one who could hold a candle to that devil in female form. And then, despite myself, I used to smell the acacia flower she had thrown at me, which was dry now, but still kept its scent. The girl was a witch, if ever there was one . . .

'One day the gaoler came in and gave me a loaf of Alcalá bread.[1] "Here," he said, "look what your cousin has sent you."

'I took the loaf, extremely surprised, since I didn't have a cousin in Seville. "Perhaps there's some mistake," I thought, looking at the bread. But it looked so appetizing and smelt so good that, without troubling to discover where it came from or who it was intended for, I determined to eat it. When I tried to cut it my knife encountered something hard. On investigating I found a small English file that had been slipped into the dough before the bread was baked. There was also a gold two-piastre coin in the loaf. There could be no further doubt: it was a present from Carmen. For the people of her nation freedom is everything, and they would set fire to a town if it meant avoiding a day's imprisonment. Besides, the girl was crafty, and this loaf was a way of pulling a fast one on the gaolers. In an hour, I could saw through the thickest bar with the little file, and with the two-piastre coin I could trade in my uniform greatcoat for civilian clothes at the nearest second-hand clothes shop.

'You can imagine that a man like myself, who had many times taken young eagles from their nests on our rocky crags, was not going to think twice before climbing from a window less than thirty feet above street level. But the truth of the matter was, I didn't want to escape. I still had my soldier's honour, and I considered desertion a great crime. Still, I was touched by this sign that I was not forgotten. When you're in prison, it's good to know you have a friend out there who is thinking of you. I was a bit offended by the gold coin, and

[1] Alcalá de los Panaderos, a small town two leagues from Seville, where delicious rolls are baked. They are said to owe their quality to the water of Alcalá, and are delivered to Seville in large quantities every day.

would have liked to give it back; but where was I to find my benefactor? It was easier said than done.

'After my ceremonial reduction to the ranks I thought I had nothing further to suffer; but I had to swallow one more humiliation. On leaving prison, I was ordered on duty and made to stand sentry as a private. You cannot imagine what a man of spirit feels in such circumstances. I think I would as soon have been shot. At least then you are out there alone in front of your troop; you feel you are of some importance, and that you are the centre of attention.

'I was put on sentry duty at the colonel's front door. He was a rich, good-natured young fellow, who believed in enjoying himself. All the young officers had been invited to his home, together with a number of townspeople, including some women—actresses, or so it was said. To me it seemed as if the whole town had arranged to congregate at his door so as to take a look at me.

'Suddenly the colonel's carriage arrived, with his batman seated on the box. Who should I see getting out but the *gitanilla*. This time she was decked out like an altar in her jewels and finery, all gold and ribbons. She wore a spangled dress, blue shoes that were also spangled, and she was covered from head to foot in flowers and braid. In her hand she held a tambourine. There were two other Gypsy women with her, a girl and an old woman. They always have an old woman to lead them, and an old man with a guitar, also a Gypsy, to play and accompany their dancing. As you know, Gypsies are often invited to social gatherings to entertain guests by performing their dance, the *romalis*, to say nothing of other forms of amusement.

'Carmen recognized me, and our eyes met. I don't know why, but at that moment I wished the ground would swallow me up. "*Agur, laguna*,"[1] she said. "Officer, you are mounting guard like a recruit!" And before I had found a word to say in reply, she was inside the house.

'The guests had all gathered in the patio and, in spite of the

[1] Good day, comrade.

crowd, through the grille[1] I could see more or less everything that was going on. I could hear the castanets and the tambourine, the laughter and cheers; sometimes I caught a glimpse of her head as she leaped up with her tambourine. Then I heard more officers saying a number of things to her that made the colour mount to my cheeks. I could not hear her replies. It was that day, I think, that I fell in love with her in earnest. Several times I felt like entering the patio, going up to those conceited idiots who were flirting with her, and running them all through with my sabre.

'My ordeal lasted a good hour. Then the Gypsies emerged and the carriage took them away. As she passed, Carmen looked at me again with that expression with which you're familiar, and said to me in an undertone: "My fellow Basque, people who enjoy good fried fish go to Triana to get it, at Lillas Pastia's tavern." Agile as a young goat she leaped into the carriage, the coachman whipped up his mules, and the whole happy band set off for heaven knows where.

'You can easily guess that the moment I came off duty I went to Triana. But first I had myself shaved and smartened myself up as though I was going on parade. She was at the tavern of Lillas Pastia, an old man who kept a fish restaurant, a Gypsy with a face as black as a Moor. Many townspeople used to go to his place to sample his wares, particularly, I suspect, since Carmen had taken up residence there.

' "Lillas," she said as soon as she saw me, "that's enough for today. *Mañana será otro día!*[2] Come on, fellow-countryman, let's go for a walk."

'She covered her face with her mantilla, and I found myself in the street with her, with no idea where I was going.

' "Señorita," I said to her, "I believe I have you to thank for a present that was sent to me when I was in prison. The bread I ate; the file I shall use to sharpen my lance, and I'll

---

[1] Most houses in Seville have an inner courtyard surrounded by porticos, where one can sit in summer. The courtyard is covered by an awning which is kept moist during the day and drawn back in the evenings. The door leading on to the street is almost always open, and the passage leading to the courtyard (*el zaguán*) is barred by an elegant wrought-iron grille.

[2] Tomorrow is another day (Spanish proverb).

keep it as something to remember you by; but as for the money, you can have it back."

' "Why, he's still got the money!" she exclaimed with a laugh. "Just as well, too, I'm not exactly flush at present. But what does it matter?—a dog that roams will find a bone.[1] Why don't we squander the lot? You can treat me."

'We had taken the road back to Seville. As we entered the Street of the Serpent she bought a dozen oranges and got me to tie them up in my handkerchief. A little further on she also bought a loaf, some sausage, and a bottle of *manzanilla**; then finally she went into a confectioner's. She threw down on the counter the gold coin I had given back to her, together with another she had in her pocket, and some silver coins; after which she asked me to put down what I had. I only had a peseta and a few cuartos, which I gave her, deeply ashamed not to have more. I thought she was intending to buy the whole shop. She took all the best and most expensive items, *yemas*,[2] *turrón*,[3] and candied fruit, until the money had all been spent. I had somehow to carry it all in paper bags.

'You probably know the Calle del Candilejo, where there is a bust of don Pedro the Justicer.[4] It ought to have given me pause.

---

[1] *Chuquel sos pirela, cocal terela* (Gypsy proverb).

[2] Candied egg yolks.

[3] A kind of nougat.

[4] King Pedro I, known to us as Pedro the Cruel, whom Queen Isabel the Catholic used always to call Pedro the Justicer, liked to roam the streets of Seville in the evenings in search of adventure, like Caliph Haroûn-al-Raschid*. One night, in a back street, he fell foul of a man who was serenading his lady-love. They fought, and the King killed the amorous knight. Hearing the sound of swords an old woman leaned out of her window and lighted the scene with the small lamp (*candilejo*) she held in her hand. Now although he was agile and sturdy, don Pedro suffered from an extraordinary disability: when he walked his knee-joints cracked loudly. Hearing this sound, the old woman had no difficulty in recognizing him. The following day the *Veinticuatro* on duty came to submit his report to the King. 'Sire, a duel took place last night in such and such a street. One of the participants was killed.' 'Have you discovered the murderer?' 'Yes, Sire.' 'Why has he not already been punished?' 'Sire, I await your orders.' 'Enforce the law.' Now the King had just issued a decree ordering that duellists should be beheaded, and their heads exposed on the site of the duel. The *Veinticuatro* got out of this predicament like a man of spirit: he had the head sawn off a statue of the King, and exposed it in a recess halfway along the street where the murder had taken place. The

We stopped in that street, in front of an old house. She went
into the alley and knocked at the entrance. A Gypsy woman,
a true servant of Satan, opened the door for us. Carmen said a
few words to her in Romany. At first the old woman grumbled.
To placate her, Carmen gave her two oranges and a handful
of sweets, and let her have a taste of the wine. Then she put
her cloak on the woman's back and led her to the door, which
she secured with the wooden bolt. As soon as we were alone
she began to dance and laugh like a madwoman, singing,
"You are my *rom*, I am your *romi*".[1] There I was, standing
in the middle of the room, laden with all the things she had
bought, not knowing where to put them. She threw
everything on to the floor and flung her arms around my neck,
saying, "I pay my debts! I pay my debts! That's the law of the
Calé!"[2] What a day that was, señor! When I think of that day
I forget about what awaits me tomorrow.'

For a moment the bandit was silent. Then, after relighting
his cigar, he continued:

'We spent the whole of that day together, eating, drinking,
and what have you. She ate sweets like a child of six, then
crammed handfuls of them into the old woman's water jar.
"That's to make some sherbet for her," she said. She took
some *yemas* and spattered them against the wall. "Now the
flies will leave us in peace," she said. She got up to every
possible kind of trick and nonsense. I told her I would like to
see her dance; but where were we to find any castanets? At
once she took the old woman's only plate, broke it in pieces,
and began to dance the *romalis*, clicking the bits of crockery

King and all the people of Seville found this an excellent jest. The street
took its name from the lamp held by the old woman, the only witness to the
event.

So runs the popular tradition. Zuñiga gives a rather different version of the
story (see *Anales de Sevilla*, vol. II, p. 126). Whatever the truth of the matter,
there is still a Calle del Candilejo in Seville, and a stone bust in the street,
which is said to depict don Pedro. Unfortunately the bust is modern. In the
seventeenth century the original had become badly worn, and the Town
Council had it replaced by the one that can be seen today.

[1] *rom*, husband; *romi*, wife.
[2] *Calo*; feminine *calli*, plural *calé*. Literally 'black', the name by which the
Gypsies refer to themselves in their own language.

just as if they were real castanets made of ivory or ebony. Rest assured, there was never a dull moment when that girl was around.

'Evening came, and I heard the drums sounding the retreat.

' "I must get back to barracks for roll-call," I said to her.

' "To barracks?" she said scornfully. "Are you a slave, that you must run at their beck and call? What a canary you are! You dress like one, and you act like one too![1] Go, then, since you're so chicken-hearted."

'I stayed, already resigned to a spell in the guardroom.

'In the morning, she was the first to talk about leaving. "Listen, Joseito," she said, "have I repaid you? Our law would say that I owed you nothing, since you are a *payllo*; but you're a good-looking boy and I liked you. Now we are quits. Good day to you."

'I asked her when I would see her again.

' "When you are less of a simpleton," she replied with a laugh. Then, more gravely, she went on: "Do you know, my friend, I think I love you a little. But it can't last, dog and wolf don't stay friends for long. Perhaps, if you were to submit to Gypsy law, I should like to become your *romi*. But that's all nonsense, such things can never be. No, believe me, my friend, you've got off lightly! You've had a brush with the devil—yes, the devil. He isn't always black, and he hasn't wrung your neck. I may wear wool but I'm not a sheep.[2] Go and place a candle before your *majari*,[3] she's certainly earned it. Come—once more, farewell. Think no more of Carmencita, or else she may wed you to a widow with wooden legs."[4]

'As she spoke she was unfastening the bolt that secured the door, and once out in the street she wrapped herself in her mantilla, turned on her heel and vanished.

'She was right. I would have been wise to think no more of her; but since that day in the Calle del Candilejo I could think of nothing else. I used to walk around all day in the hope of

---

[1] Spanish dragoons wear yellow.
[2] *Me dicas vriardâ de jorpoy, bus ne sino braco* (Gypsy proverb).
[3] The blessed one, i.e. The Virgin.
[4] The gallows, the widow of the last man hanged.

meeting her. I would ask the old woman and Pastia if they had any news of her. They both told me she had gone to Laloro[1]—that's what they call Portugal. No doubt Carmen had told them to say this, but I soon learned they were lying. A few weeks after my day in the Calle del Candilejo, I was on sentry duty at one of the town gates. A short distance from the gate, a breach had been made in the city wall. During the day men were working to repair it, and at night they posted a sentry to stop smugglers. That day I saw Lillas Pastia hanging about the guard-house and chatting with some of my fellow-soldiers. They all knew him, and his fried fish and fritters better still. He came up to me and asked if I had any news of Carmen.

' "No," I said.

' "Well, you soon will have, *compadre*."

'He was not mistaken. That night I was put on sentry duty at the breach. As soon as the corporal had taken himself off, I saw a woman coming up to me. I knew instinctively that it was Carmen. However, I shouted, "Keep away! No one passes!"

' "Don't come that fierce act with me," she said, identifying herself.

' "Carmen! Is that you?"

' "Yes, my fellow-countryman. Let's get straight to the point: would you like to earn a *duro*? Some men are going to come by with some packages. Don't interfere with them."

' "No," I replied, "I must stop them from passing. Those are my orders."

' "Orders! Orders! You didn't think of that in the Calle del Candilejo!"

' "Ah!" I replied, overcome at the mere memory. "That was worth forgetting my orders for. But I want no money from smugglers."

' "Well then, if you don't want money, would you like us to go and eat again at old Dorotea's place?"

' "No," I said, half-choking with the effort. "I cannot."

' "Very well, if you're going to be difficult, I know who to

---

[1] The Red (Land).

go to. I'll invite your superior officer to come to Dorotea's with me. He seems a nice fellow, and he'll arrange for some lad to be posted sentry who sees only what he ought to see. Farewell, canary, I'll laugh the day the orders are to hang you."

'I was weak enough to call her back, and I promised to let the entire Tribe of Egypt pass, if need be, on condition I received the only reward I wanted. She at once swore to honour her promise the very next day, and ran to inform her friends, who were waiting a stone's throw away. There were five of them, Pastia among them, all laden with English merchandise. Carmen was acting as look-out. She was to give the alarm by clicking her castanets the moment she spotted the watch patrol; but she had no need to do so. The smugglers' business was done in a moment.

'The next day I went to the Calle del Candilejo. Carmen kept me waiting, and arrived in a bad temper. "I don't like having to ask people twice," she said. "You did more for me the first time without knowing whether you were going to get anything out of it. Yesterday you haggled with me. I don't know why I've come, I don't love you any more. Go on, get out of here! And there's a *duro* for your trouble!"

'I very nearly threw the money in her face, and it cost me an enormous effort to restrain myself from striking her. We quarrelled for an hour, then I left in a fury. I wandered around the town for some time, walking aimlessly this way and that, like a madman. In the end I went into a church, sat down in the darkest corner, and wept bitterly.

'Suddenly I heard a voice: "Dragon's tears, dragoon's tears— I shall make a love potion with them."

'I raised my eyes. Carmen stood before me.

' "Well, my fellow-countryman, are you still angry with me?" she asked. "It must be that I love you, whether I like the fact or not, for since you left me I don't know what's been the matter with me. You see, now it's my turn to ask you if you will come to the Calle del Candilejo."

'So we made it up. But Carmen's temperament was as capricious as the weather in our mountains, where the sun never shines more brightly than when a storm is imminent.

She had promised to see me again at Dorotea's, but she didn't turn up. And Dorotea again insisted that she had gone to Laloro on Gypsy business.

'Having learned from experience how much credence to lend this story, I looked for Carmen in all her usual haunts, and I called in at the Calle del Candilejo twenty times daily. One evening I was with Dorotea, whom I had almost won over by standing her the occasional glass of *anís*, when Carmen entered, followed by a young lieutenant from our regiment.

' "Go quickly!" she said to me in Basque. I stood there stunned, with fury in my heart.

' "What are you doing here?" asked the lieutenant. "Go on, make yourself scarce!"

'I could not move an inch, I stood stock-still as if paralysed. Angry that I did not move, and that I hadn't even taken off my forage cap, the officer seized me by the scruff of the neck and shook me roughly. I don't know what I said to him. He drew his sabre and I unsheathed my own sword. The old woman grabbed my arm, and the lieutenant gave me a cut on the forehead from which I still have the scar. I stepped back and elbowed Dorotea out of the way so that she fell back; then, as the lieutenant was pursuing me, I pointed my sword at him and he impaled himself on it. At this Carmen extinguished the lamp and, in her own language, told Dorotea to make her escape. I myself fled into the street and set off blindly at a run. I had the impression that someone was following me. When I became aware of my surroundings once more, I found that Carmen had not left me.

' "What a great fool you are, Canary!" she said. "You do nothing but put your foot in it! There, didn't I tell you I'd bring you bad luck? Still, there's a cure for every ill when you have a *Flamenca de Roma*[1] for a sweetheart. First of all, tie this handkerchief round your head and throw away that sword-belt. Wait for me in this alley. I'll be back in two minutes."

[1] A slang term for a Gypsy woman. *Roma* is not an allusion to the Eternal City, but to the nation of the Roma or 'married folk', a name by which the Gypsies refer to themselves. The first Gypsies seen in Spain probably came from the Low Countries: hence the name *flamenco* (Flemish).

'She vanished, and soon brought me back a striped cloak that she had fetched from somewhere or other. She made me take off my uniform and put the cloak on over my shirt. In that get-up, wearing the handkerchief with which she had bound the wound on my forehead, I looked not unlike one of those Valencian peasants who come to Seville to sell their *horchata*.[1] Then she took me into a house rather like Dorotea's, at the end of a small alley. She and another Gypsy woman washed and bandaged me better than any army surgeon would have done, and gave me something to drink. Finally they placed me on a mattress, and I fell asleep.

'The women had probably mixed into my drink some of those soporific drugs whose secret they possess, for I woke very late the following day. I had a bad headache and was a bit feverish. It took me some time to recall the terrible events in which I had been involved the day before. After dressing my wound, Carmen and her friend squatted on their heels by my mattress, and had what seemed to be a brief medical consultation in *chipe calli*. Then they both assured me that I would soon be well, but that I must leave Seville as soon as possible, since if I was caught there I would be shot without mercy.

' "Young man," said Carmen, "you'll have to find something to do. Now that the King no longer provides your rice and dried cod,[2] you'll have to give some thought to earning a living. You're too stupid to steal *à pastesas*,[3] but you are agile and strong. If you've got the pluck, take yourself off to the coast and become a smuggler. Didn't I promise to get you hanged? Better that than be shot. Besides, if you know how to set about it, you'll live like a prince, as long as the *miñones*[4] and the coastguards don't collar you."

'Such were the engaging terms in which that diabolical female spoke to me of the new career she had in store for me—the only one, to tell the truth, still open to me now that I had committed a capital offence. I must confess, señor, I

---

[1] A pleasant drink made from *chufas* (tiger-nuts), a bulbous root.
[2] The usual fare of the Spanish soldier.
[3] *Ustilar à pastesas*, to steal skilfully, rob without violence.
[4] Type of irregular infantry unit.

didn't need much persuading. I thought that such a rebellious and hazardous existence would bring me closer to her. I thought that from then on I could be sure of her love. I had often heard tell of a group of smugglers who roamed Andalusia on fine horses, blunderbuss in hand, each with his mistress riding pillion behind him. I could already picture myself trotting up and down the mountainsides with the pretty Gypsy girl seated behind me. When I spoke to her of it she laughed fit to burst, and told me that there was nothing to beat a night spent in the open, when each *rom* retires with his *romi* to their small tent, that consists of three hoops with a blanket laid over the top.

' "Once we are up in the mountains," I said, "I shall be sure of you! Then there'll be no lieutenants to share you with."

' "Ah! You're jealous!" she replied. "More fool you. How could you be so stupid? Can't you see that I love you, since I've never asked you for money?"

'When she talked like that I felt like strangling her.

'To cut a long story short, señor, Carmen procured me an outfit of civilian clothes, wearing which I left Seville unrecognized. I went to Jerez with a letter from Pastia to an *anís* merchant at whose place smugglers used to meet. I was introduced to these people, whose leader, who went by the name of El Dancaire, took me into his band. We set off for Gaucín, where I joined Carmen, who had arranged to meet me there. On our expeditions she acted as spy for our group, and there never was a better one. She was just back from Gibraltar, and had already made arrangements with the skipper of a vessel for the shipment of some English merchandise that we were to be on the coast to receive. We went to wait for it near Estepona, then we hid some of it up in the mountains; the rest we loaded up and took with us to Ronda. Carmen had gone on ahead of us. Once again it was she who told us when it was safe to enter the town.

'That first journey and a few of the subsequent ones were happy times. I preferred the life of a smuggler to that of a soldier. I used to give presents to Carmen. I had money and a mistress. I had few regrets, for, as the Gypsies say, a pleasurable itch is no itch at all.[1] Everywhere we were well received. My companions treated me well, and even showed me some marks of esteem. The reason for this was that I had killed a man, and there were some among them who did not have such an exploit on their conscience.

'But what was most important to me in my new life was that I saw Carmen often. She was more affectionate than ever towards me; yet she would not acknowledge in front of our companions that she was my mistress, and she had even made me swear every oath under the sun that I would say nothing to them of our relationship. I was so weak in the presence of this creature that I submitted to her every whim. Besides, it was the first time I had seen her behave with the reserve that befits a respectable woman, and I was simple enough to believe she really had turned over a new leaf.

'Our band, which consisted of eight or ten men, seldom met as a group except at critical moments, and usually we were scattered around the towns and villages in twos and threes. Each of us was supposed to have a trade: one was a coppersmith, another a horse-dealer; as for me, I used to trade in haberdashery, but I seldom showed myself in places of any size, on account of the trouble I'd got into in Seville. One day, or rather one night, we had arranged to rendezvous below Véjer de la Frontera. Dancaire and I arrived there before the rest of them. He seemed in high spirits.

' "We're going to be joined by another companion," he said to me. "Carmen's just pulled off one of her finest strokes. She's sprung her *rom* from the gaol at Tarifa."

'I was already beginning to understand Romany, which almost all my companions spoke, and at the word *rom* my blood suddenly ran cold.

' "What? Her husband? You mean she's married?" I asked our captain.

' "Yes," he replied. "To García the One-eyed, a Gypsy as cunning as she is. The poor lad was sentenced to hard labour. Carmen wormed her way so successfully into the prison surgeon's good graces that she's secured her husband's

[1] *Sarapia sat pesquital ne punzava.*

release. Ah, that girl's worth her weight in gold! She's been trying to get him out for two years now. Nothing worked, until they took it into their heads to change the surgeon. It seems she pretty soon managed to strike a bargain with the new one."

'You can imagine the joy with which I greeted this news. I soon met García the One-Eyed. He was certainly the ugliest monster a Gypsy ever gave birth to. Dark-skinned and darker still of soul, he was the most arrant rascal I've met in all my life. Carmen was with him, and when she called him her *rom* in my presence, you should have seen the looks she gave me, and the faces she pulled when García's back was turned. I was furious, and I didn't speak to her all that night.

'The next morning we had packed our bundles and were already on our way when we realized that a dozen horsemen were at our heels. The Andalusian braggarts, always full of murderous talk, at once grew faint-hearted. It was every man for himself. Dancaire, García, a good-looking lad from Écija whom they called El Remendado, and Carmen were the only ones to keep their presence of mind. The rest had abandoned the mules and run for the ravines where the horses could not follow them. We could not save our animals, and we hurriedly unloaded our choicest contraband and lifted it onto our backs, then tried to get away down the steepest slopes through the rocks. We threw our bundles ahead of us and followed them as best we could, careering downhill on our heels. All this time the enemy were sniping at us. It was the first time I'd been under fire, and it made little impression on me. When you are being watched by a woman, scorning death is nothing to be proud of. We all got away except for poor Remendado, who received a bullet in the back. I threw down my bundle and tried to pick him up.

' "You fool!" shouted García. "What business have we with a corpse? Finish him off, and don't go losing those cotton stockings!"

' "Drop him, drop him!" Carmen shouted at me.

'Exhaustion forced me to set him down for a moment in the shelter of a rock. García came forward and emptied his blunderbuss in Remendado's face.

' "It'd take a clever man to recognize him now," he said, looking at the face which a dozen bullets had reduced to a pulp.

'You see, señor, what an admirable life I led.

' "That evening we found ourselves in a copse, utterly spent, with nothing to eat, and our livelihood gone with the loss of our mules. What did that infernal García do but take a pack of cards from his pocket and, by the light of a fire they had lit, begin a round of cards with Dancaire. Meanwhile I lay looking up at the stars, thinking about Remendado and telling myself that I would as soon be in his place. Carmen was squatting near me, and from time to time she sang softly and rattled her castanets. Then, drawing close as if to whisper something to me, she kissed me two or three times, though something in me resisted her.

' "You are the Devil incarnate," I said to her.

' "Yes," she replied.

'After a few hours' rest she set off for Gaucín, and the next morning a little goatherd came and brought us bread. We spent the whole day there, and that night we headed for Gaucín. We were waiting for news from Carmen. None came. At daybreak we saw a muleteer preceding a well-dressed woman with a parasol and a little girl who seemed to be her servant. García said to us:

' "Here come two mules and two women, a present from Saint Nicholas*. I'd sooner have four mules, but never mind, I'll take charge of them!"

'He took his blunderbuss and went down towards the path, concealing himself amidst the scrub. Dancaire and I followed a little way behind. When we were within range we showed ourselves and shouted to the muleteer to stop. On seeing us, instead of showing alarm, which our unkempt appearance alone would have justified, the woman burst into peals of laughter.

' "Ah! the *lillipendi* take me for an *erani*!"[1] It was Carmen, but so well disguised that I would not have recognized her if she had spoken in another language. She leaped from her

---

[1] The fools take me for a fine lady.

mule, spoke for a few moments in an undertone with Dancaire
and García, then said to me: "Canary, we shall meet again
before they hang you. I'm going to Gibraltar on Gypsy
business. You'll soon hear word of me."

'We parted after she had told us of a place where we could
lie low for a few days. That girl was like a guardian angel for
our band. We soon received some money from her, and, what
was more important to us, the information that on such-and-
such a day two wealthy Englishmen would be setting out to
travel by a particular road from Gibraltar to Granada. A word
to the wise is enough. They were well and truly laden with
gold sovereigns. García wanted to kill them, but Dancaire and
I vetoed this. Apart from their shirts, of which we had urgent
need*, we took only their money and their watches.

'Señor, a man turns into a villain without realizing what is hap-
pening to him. You fall for a pretty girl, get into a fight over her;
misfortune befalls you; you have to take to the mountains; and
from smuggling you've turned to robbery before you know where
you are. We thought things had got too hot for us round Gibraltar
after the business with the Englishmen, and we withdrew into the
mountains around Ronda. I remember you once mentioned José-
María to me; it was there that I met him. He used to bring his
mistress with him on his expeditions. She was a pretty girl, sensible, modest, and well-mannered, who never spoke an uncivil
word and was utterly devoted to him. In return he made her very
unhappy. He was always chasing after other girls, he ill-treated
her, and sometimes he'd take it into his head to get jealous. Once
he stabbed her; she only loved him the more for it. Women are like
that, especially Andalusian women. She was proud of the scar on
her arm, and used to show it to people as if it were the most
beautiful thing in the world. What's more, José-María was the
worst companion imaginable! On one of our expeditions he fixed
things so that he reaped all the profits, while we got all the blows
and the inconvenience. But let me return to my story.

'We had heard no news of Carmen. Dancaire said, "One of
us must go to Gibraltar to find out what's happened to her.
She must have been organizing some deal. I'd go myself, but
I'm too well known there."

' "The same goes for me," said García. "I've played so

many tricks on the Lobsters![1] And as I've only got one eye I'm not easy to disguise."

' "Had I better go then?" I asked, delighted at the very thought of seeing Carmen again. "Tell me what has to be done."

'The others said to me: "Make arrangements to go by boat, or overland by way of San Roque, whichever you prefer, and when you get to Gibraltar, ask at the port for the address of a woman called La Rollona, who sells chocolate. When you've found her she'll tell you what the score is over there."

'It was agreed that we would all three set off for the Sierra de Gaucín, and that at Gaucín I would leave my two companions and travel on to Gibraltar disguised as a fruit seller. At Ronda a man who was in league with us had procured me a passport. At Gaucín I was given a donkey. I loaded it with oranges and melons and started on my way. On arrival at Gibraltar I found that La Rollona was well known there, but that she had died, or else gone to *finibus terrae*.[2] I was satisfied that her disappearance explained how we had come to lose contact with Carmen. I put my donkey in a stable and, taking my oranges, I went about the town as if to sell them, but in reality to see whether I could find a familiar face. You find every kind of riff-raff there, from the four corners of the earth, and it's like the Tower of Babel, for you can't go ten paces along a street without hearing ten different languages spoken. I saw plenty of Gypsies, but I hardly dared trust them. We were weighing one another up—it was obvious that we were all crooked: the question was, whether we belonged to the same gang. After two days running around on a wild-goose chase, I had learned nothing concerning La Rollona or Carmen, and was thinking of making a few purchases before returning to my companions when, walking down a street at dusk, I heard a woman's voice at a window, calling out to me: "Orange seller!"

'I looked up and saw Carmen leaning from a balcony, in the

---

[1] Name given by Spanish common folk to the British on account of the colour of their uniform.

[2] To prison, or 'the devil knows where'.

company of an officer in a red uniform, with gold epaulettes and curled hair, every inch the wealthy aristocrat. Carmen herself was superbly dressed, all in silk, with a shawl over her shoulders and a gold comb in her hair; and, as usual, the creature was laughing fit to burst. In broken Spanish, the Englishman called to me to come up, saying that the lady wanted some oranges; and Carmen added in Basque: "Come up, and don't be surprised at anything you see."

'The fact is, nothing she did could have surprised me. I don't know whether I felt more joy or sorrow at finding her again. There was a tall, powdered English servant at the door, who ushered me into a magnificent drawing room. Carmen at once said to me in Basque:

' "You don't speak a word of Spanish, and you've never met me before." Then, turning to the Englishman, she went on: "I told you so. I could tell he was a Basque right away; you'll be able to hear what an odd language it is. Doesn't he look stupid, like a cat that's been caught in the larder!"

' "And you," I said to her in my own language, "look like an impudent jade, and I could cheerfully slash you across the face in front of your lover."

' "My lover!" she said. "Did you work that out all by yourself? You mean you're jealous of this idiot? You're even more of a simpleton than you used to be before our evenings in the Calle del Candilejo. Fool that you are, can't you see that at the moment I'm engaged in Gypsy business—and a brilliant stroke of business it is too. This house is mine; the Lobster's guineas will be mine. I've got him by the nose, and I'll lead him to a place there's no returning from."

' "And if you engage in any more Gypsy business of this sort," I said, "I'll make sure it's the last time you get the chance."

' "Oh, indeed? Are you my *rom*, to give me orders? García approves: what concern is it of yours? Don't you think you should be quite content to be the only one who can call himself my *minchorrò*?"[1]

' "What's he saying?" asked the Englishman.

---

[1] My lover, or rather, my passing fancy.

' "He says he's thirsty and could do with a drink," replied Carmen. And she fell back on a sofa, overcome with mirth at her translation.

'When that girl laughed, señor, there was no talking sensibly. Everyone laughed with her. The big Englishman began to laugh too, like the fool he was, and ordered the servant to bring me something to drink.

'While I was drinking she said: "You see that ring he has on his finger? If you like I'll give it to you."

' "I'd give a finger to be up in the mountains with your gentleman friend, and each of us with a *maquila* in his fist," I replied.

' "What does *maquila* mean?" asked the Englishman.

' "*Maquila* means an orange," said Carmen, still laughing. "It's a funny word for an orange, isn't it? He says he'd like to get you to eat some *maquila*."

' "Would he?" said the Englishman. "Well, bring some more *maquila* tomorrow."

'While we were talking, the servant entered and announced that dinner was served. At this the Englishman got up, gave me a piastre, and offered his arm to Carmen, as if she were incapable of walking without assistance. Still laughing, Carmen said to me:

' "I can't invite you to dinner, my friend; but tomorrow, as soon as you hear the drum for parade, come back, and bring some oranges with you. You'll find a room better furnished than the one in the Calle del Candilejo, and then you'll see whether I'm still your Carmencita. And afterwards we can discuss Gypsy business."

'I made no reply. From the street, I heard the Englishman calling to me, "Bring your *maquila* tomorrow!", and Carmen's peals of laughter.

'I left with no idea of what I would do, I hardly slept, and the next morning I found I was so angry with the treacherous creature that I resolved to leave Gibraltar without seeing her again; but, at the first roll of the drum, all my determination forsook me. I took my bundle of oranges and I hurried to the house where Carmen was staying. Her blind was half-open, and I could see one of her great dark eyes peeping round it, watching out for me. The powdered servant ushered me in at once. Carmen sent him off on some errand, and as soon as we were alone, she gave vent to one of her hypocritical shrieks of mirth and flung her arms around my neck. I had never seen her so beautiful: decked out like a madonna, and perfumed, amid the silk upholstery and the embroidered curtains. Ah! and there was I, dressed like the robber I was.

' "*Minchorrò!*" said Carmen. "I feel like smashing this room to bits, setting fire to the house, and running off to the sierra." Then she was lavish in her caresses; she laughed, danced, and tore her flounces—a monkey could not have competed with her for capers, grimaces, and mischievousness.

'When she had calmed down, she said: "Listen, now to Gypsy business. I shall ask him to take me to Ronda, where I have a sister who is a nun . . ." (here more peals of laughter ensued). "The road takes us past a spot of which you will be notified. You'll all set upon him and strip him bare. The best thing would be to bump him off. But", she added, with the diabolical smile she wore at certain moments—and when she smiled like that, no one felt like returning her smile—"you know what you must do? Make sure García is the first to show himself. The rest of you hold back a little; the Lobster's brave, he's a good shot, and he's got good pistols. Am I making myself clear?" Her words were interrupted by another gust of laughter which made me shudder.

' "No," I said. "I hate García, but he is my comrade. Perhaps one day I'll rid you of him, but then we'll settle scores the way it's done in my part of the world. It's only chance that's made a Gypsy of me, and in certain respects I shall always remain a *Navarro fino*,[1] as the proverb says."

' "You are a fool, a simpleton, a real *payllo*," she retorted. "You're like the dwarf who thought he was big when he spat a long way.[2] You don't love me, get out of here."

'When she told me to go, I could not do so. I promised I would set off, go back to my companions, and wait for the

---

[1] A true man of Navarre.
[2] Gypsy proverb: *Or esorjié de or narsichislé, sin chismar lachinguel* (The most a dwarf can do is to spit a long way).

Englishman. In return, she promised to feign illness until the time came to leave Gibraltar for Ronda. I stayed another two days in Gibraltar. She had the nerve to come disguised to my inn to visit me. I set off. I had my own plans.

'I returned to our rendezvous, already knowing when and where Carmen and the Englishman would be passing. I found Dancaire and García waiting for me. We spent the night in a wood, beside a fire of pine-cones that made a wonderful blaze. I suggested a game of cards to García. He accepted. In the second game I accused him of cheating. He began to laugh. I threw the cards in his face. He went for his blunderbuss. I placed my foot on it and said to him:

' "They say you can fight with a knife like the best *jaque* in Málaga. Do you want to take me on?"

'Dancaire tried to separate us. I had already punched García two or three times. Anger had given him courage. He drew his knife, and I drew mine. We told Dancaire to keep his distance and let us fight it out fairly. Seeing that there was no way of stopping us, he stood aside. García was already crouched like a cat ready to spring at a mouse. He held his hat in his left hand to parry my thrusts, and his knife in front of him, in the Andalusian mode of defence. I took up the Navarrese stance, facing him head-on, with my left arm raised, my left leg forward, and my knife against my right thigh. I felt stronger than a giant. He flew at me like a dart. I turned on my left foot and he encountered empty air; but my knife found his throat, and went in so deep that my hand met his chin. I turned the blade so hard that it broke. It was over. A gush of blood as thick as my arm forced the blade out of the wound. He fell on his face as stiff as a post.

' "What have you done?" exclaimed Dancaire.

' "Listen," I said. "There wasn't room for both of us. I love Carmen, and I want no rivals. Anyway, García was a scoundrel, and I still remember what he did to poor Remendado. There are only two of us now, but we're men of honour. Come, will you have me as a friend, in life and death?"

'Dancaire offered me his hand. He was a man of 50.

' "To hell with these love affairs!" he exclaimed. "If you'd asked him for Carmen he would have sold her to you for a piastre. We are the only two left. How will we manage tomorrow?"

' "Leave it to me," I replied. "I don't care a damn for anyone or anything any more."

'We buried García and moved our camp two hundred paces further on. The next day Carmen and her Englishman passed with two muleteers and a servant. I said to Dancaire: "I'll see to the Englishman. Frighten the others off, they're not armed."

'The Englishman had courage. If Carmen hadn't jogged his arm I would have been a dead man. The long and the short of it was that I won Carmen back that day, and my first words were to tell her she was a widow.

'When she learned how it had come about, she said to me: "You will always be a *lillipendi*! García ought to have killed you. You and your Navarrese defence—why, he'd put paid to better fighters than you. It's because his time had come. So will yours."

' "And yours too," I replied, "if you are not a true *romi* to me."

' "So be it," she said. "More than once I've seen in the coffee-grounds that we would be together to the end. Bah! Time will tell!" And she clacked her castanets, as she always did when she wanted to banish some disturbing idea.

'It's easy to get carried away talking about oneself. All these details probably bore you, but I've almost finished.

'This life we were leading went on for quite some time. Dancaire and I had collected together a group of companions who were more reliable than the first lot, and we went in for smuggling, and sometimes, I must confess, for highway robbery too, but only as a last resort, when there was nothing else for it. Besides, we didn't ill-treat the travellers, and we contented ourselves with taking their money. For a few months I was happy with Carmen. She continued to be useful to us in our operations, keeping us informed of any good business that might come our way. At times she was in Málaga, at times in Córdoba or Granada; but at a word from me she would leave everything and come and join me in some remote *venta*, or even at our camp. Only once, in Málaga, did she give me any cause for uneasiness. I knew she had singled out a very rich merchant, on whom she was no doubt intending to try her

Gibraltar trick again. In spite of everything Dancaire could say to dissuade me, I set off and entered Málaga in broad daylight. I looked for Carmen, and at once took her away with me. We had it out in a fierce altercation.

' "Do you know," she said to me, "that ever since you've been my *rom* in earnest, I've loved you less than when you were my *minchorrò*? I don't want to be plagued, still less ordered around. What I want is to be free and to do as I please. Take care not to overstep the mark. If you anger me I'll find some fine lad who will do to you what you did to One-Eyed García."

'Dancaire patched it up between us; but we had said things to one another which rankled, and things were never the same afterwards.

'Soon after, misfortune overtook us. We were surprised by soldiers. Dancaire was killed, along with two of my comrades. Two others were captured. I myself was seriously wounded and, but for my good horse, I would have been captured by the soldiers. At the end of my tether, and with a bullet lodged in my body, I went and hid in a wood with my only remaining companion. On dismounting I fainted, and I thought I was going to die in the undergrowth like a shot hare. My comrade carried me to a cave we knew, then he went to fetch Carmen. She was in Granada, and at once hastened to my side. For a fortnight she did not leave me for a moment. She did not sleep; she nursed me with skill and devotion such as no woman ever showed for her beloved.

'As soon as I was able to stand, she took me to Granada in the utmost secrecy. The Gypsy women find safe hiding places everywhere, and I spent more than six weeks in a house two doors away from the *corregidor* who was hunting me. More than once I looked from behind a shutter and saw him passing. At last I recovered. But I had pondered deeply whilst on my sick-bed, and I was planning to change my way of life. I spoke to Carmen of leaving Spain and trying to live honestly in the New World. She laughed at me.

' "We weren't born to plant cabbages," she said. "It is our destiny to live at the expense of the *payllos*. Listen, I've arranged some business with Nathan ben-Joseph in Gibraltar.

He's got some cotton goods ready to come through—it's only you he's waiting for. He knows you are alive, he's counting on you. What would our partners in Gibraltar say if you broke your word?"

'I allowed myself to be prevailed upon, and embarked again on my ugly trade.

'While I was in hiding in Granada there was a bullfight, to which Carmen went. On her return she talked a lot about a very skilful picador called Lucas. She knew the name of his horse, and how much he had paid for his embroidered jacket. I gave no thought to the matter. A few days later Juanito, my surviving comrade, told me he had seen Carmen with Lucas at a merchant's in the Zacatín. I began to be alarmed. I asked Carmen how and why she had got to know the picador.

' "We may be able to make use of him," she replied. "The river that makes a noise has either water or stones in it.[1] He earned twelve hundred *reales* at the bullfight. There are two possibilities: either we must have his money, or else, since he's a good horseman and a brave young fellow, we can enlist him in our band. Some of them have been killed and will have to be replaced. Take him along with you."

' "I want neither his money nor his services, and I forbid you to speak to him," I replied.

' "Take care," she said. "When someone defies me to do a thing, it is soon done."

'Fortunately, the picador went away to Málaga, and I turned to the business of getting the Jew's cotton goods ashore. I had plenty to do on that expedition, as had Carmen, and I forgot about Lucas. Perhaps she forgot about him too, for a while at least. It was about that time, señor, that I met you, first near Montilla, then again in Córdoba. I shall not speak to you of our last encounter—perhaps you know more about it than I do. Carmen stole your watch. She also wanted your money, and especially that ring on your finger, which she claimed was a magic ring and which she was most anxious to acquire. We had a violent quarrel and I struck her. She turned pale and wept. It was the first time I had seen her weep, and it affected

---

[1] *Len sos sonsi abela / Pani o reblendani terela* (Gypsy proverb).

me profoundly. I begged her to forgive me, but she sulked for a whole day, and when I left again for Montilla she refused to kiss me.

'I was still despondent when three days later she came looking for me, cheerful and blithe as a lark. All was forgotten, and we were like lovers who have known one another for two days. When the time came to part she said to me:

' "There's a *fiesta* in Córdoba. I shall go to it, and when I know which people are going home with money in their pockets, I'll let you know."

'I let her go. Alone, I thought about the *fiesta* and about Carmen's change of mood. She must have had her revenge already, I said to myself, since she came back of her own free will.

'A peasant told me that there were some bullfights taking place in Córdoba. My blood suddenly boiled, and I set off like a madman and went to the bullring. They pointed out Lucas to me, and on the front-row seats I recognized Carmen. I only needed to watch her for a moment to be sure of my ground. When the first bull came on, Lucas played the gallant, as I had expected. He plucked the rosette[1] from the bull and offered it to Carmen, who straightaway put it in her hair. The bull took it upon himself to avenge me: Lucas was knocked down, with his horse on his chest and the bull on top of both of them. I looked at Carmen; she had already left her seat. I wasn't able to get out from where I was sitting, and had to wait until the bullfight was over. Then I went to the house that you know, and I lay low there all that evening and part of the night. About two o'clock in the morning Carmen came back, and was somewhat surprised to see me.

' "Come with me," I said.

' "Very well," she said. "Let's go."

'I went and fetched my horse, set her on the crupper,

---

[1] *La divisa*, a bow of ribbons whose colour shows on which ranch the bull was raised. The bow is attached to the bull's hide by a hook, and it is regarded as the height of gallantry to pluck it from the live animal and present it to a woman.

and we rode for the rest of that night without exchanging a single word. At daybreak we stopped at a remote *venta* close by a little hermitage. There I said to Carmen:

' "Listen. I shall forget the past. I shall reproach you with nothing. But swear to me one thing: that you will come with me to America and settle down there."

' "No," she said sullenly. "I don't want to go to America. I'm happy where I am."

' "That's because you are near Lucas. But think about it carefully—even if he recovers, he won't make old bones. Anyway, why should I lay the blame at his door? I'm tired of killing all your lovers; I shall kill you instead."

'She stared at me with her wild look, and said:

' "I've always felt that you would kill me. The first time I saw you I had just met a priest at the door of my house. And last night, when we left Córdoba, didn't you notice anything? A hare ran across the road between your horse's legs. It is fated."

' "Carmencita," I asked her, "don't you love me any more?"

'She made no reply. She was sitting cross-legged on a mat, tracing figures on the ground with her finger.

' "Let's begin a new life, Carmen," I entreated her. "Let's go and live somewhere where we will never be separated. You know that not far from here we have a hundred and twenty gold *onzas* buried under an oak tree. And we have other money with the Jew ben-Joseph."

'She began to smile, and said: "First me, then you. I knew it had to be so."

' "Think carefully," I went on. "My patience is exhausted, I'm at the end of my tether. Make up your mind, or I shall take my own decision."

'I left her and began to walk in the direction of the hermitage. I found the hermit praying. I waited for him to finish. I would have liked to pray myself, but I could not. When he rose to his feet I went up to him.

' "Father," I said to him, "will you pray for someone who is in great peril?"

' "I pray for all those who are afflicted," he said.

' "Can you say a mass for a soul that may be going to meet its Maker?"

' "Yes," he replied, staring at me. And, as there was something strange about my manner, he tried to draw me into conversation.

' "Haven't I seen you somewhere before?" he asked.

'I placed a piastre on his bench. "When will you say the mass?" I asked him.

' "In half an hour. The innkeeper's son from the inn over there is coming to serve. Tell me, young man, is there something on your conscience that is troubling you? Will you listen to the counsel of a Christian?"

'I could feel I was on the verge of tears. I told him I would return, and made my escape. I went and lay on the grass until I heard the bell. Then I approached, but I stayed outside the chapel.

'When mass was over I returned to the *venta*. I was almost hoping that Carmen would have fled; she could have taken my horse and got away. But I found her still there. She didn't want anyone to be able to say of her that I had made her afraid. During my absence she had unpicked the hem of her dress and taken the lead weights out of it. Now she was at a table, looking at a bowl full of water into which she had just poured the molten lead. She was so engrossed in her magic that at first she did not notice my return. First she would take a piece of lead and turn it sadly this way and that, then she would sing one of those magic songs invoking María Padilla, the mistress of don Pedro I, who was said to be the *Bari Crallisa*, the great Queen of the Gypsies.[1]

' "Carmen," I said. "Will you come with me?"

'She got up, threw aside her wooden bowl, and put her mantilla over her head as if in readiness to leave. My horse was brought to me, she mounted behind me, and we set off.

'After journeying a little way I said to her: "So, my Carmen, you will follow me, won't you?"

[1] María Padilla was accused of bewitching don Pedro I. According to popular tradition, she had presented Queen Blanche of Bourbon with a gold belt, that to the bewitched king looked like a live snake. Hence the repugnance he always showed for the unfortunate princess.

' "I will follow you till death, yes, but I will no longer live with you."

'We were in a lonely gorge. I stopped my horse.

' "Is it to be here?" she asked; and with a leap she had dismounted. She took off her mantilla, threw it to her feet, and stood motionless, one fist on her hip, staring at me.

' "You want to kill me, I can see that," she said. "It is fated. But you shall not make me submit."

' "I beg you," I said, "see reason. Listen to me! I will forget the past—though you know it's you who have been my undoing. It was for you that I became a robber and a murderer. Carmen! My Carmen! Let me save you, and save myself with you!"

' "José," she replied, "you are asking the impossible of me. I no longer love you. But you still love me, and that's why you want to kill me. I could easily tell you another lie, but I'd sooner spare myself the trouble. Everything is over between us. As my *rom*, you have the right to kill your *romi*. But Carmen will always be free. *Calli* she was born, *calli* she will die."

' "Then do you love Lucas?" I asked her.

' "Yes, I loved him, as I loved you, for a moment, perhaps less than I loved you. Now I no longer love anything, and I hate myself for having loved you."

'I fell at her feet, I took her hands, I moistened them with my tears. I reminded her of all the moments of happiness we had spent together. I offered to remain a brigand to please her. Anything, señor, anything! I offered to do anything for her, if only she would love me again!

'She said: "To love you again is impossible. I do not want to live with you."

'Fury gripped me. I drew my knife. I would have liked her to show fear and beg for mercy, but that woman was a demon.

' "For the last time," I cried, "will you stay with me?"

' "No! No! No!" she cried, stamping her foot. And she took from her finger a ring I had given her, and threw it into the bushes.

'I struck her twice. The knife was García's—the one I had taken from him after breaking my own. She fell at the second thrust without uttering a sound. I can still see her great dark eyes that stared at me, then grew clouded, and closed.

'For a good hour I stood aghast, contemplating the corpse. Then I remembered how Carmen had often told me she would like to be buried in a wood. I dug a grave for her with my knife, and placed her in it. I spent a long time looking for her ring, and eventually I found it. I put it by her in the grave, together with a little cross. Perhaps I was wrong to do that. Then I mounted my horse, galloped to Córdoba, and gave myself up at the first guard-house. I told them I had killed Carmen, but I would not say where her body was. The hermit was a holy man, he prayed for her! He said a mass for her soul. . . . Poor child! The *Calé* are to blame, for bringing her up as they did.'

Mateo Falcone

(1829)

AS you leave Porto-Vecchio, heading inland in a north-westerly direction, the ground rises fairly steeply and, after a three-hour journey along winding paths obstructed by great masses of rock, and sometimes broken by ravines, you come to the edge of a very extensive maquis. This is the home of the Corsican shepherds, and of those who have fallen foul of the law. I should explain that, in order to save themselves the trouble of manuring their fields, Corsican farmers set fire to an area of woodland. Too bad if the flames spread further than intended; come what may, one can be sure of a good crop if one sows seeds on this land that has been fertilized by the ash from the trees that grew on it. When the ears of grain have been harvested (they leave the straw, which would be troublesome to gather), the tree-roots that have remained in the soil, untouched by the flames, sprout thick clumps of shoots the following spring, which within a few years grow to a height of seven or eight feet. This kind of dense brushwood is known as *maquis*. It is made up of various species of tree and shrub, tangled and intertwined at Nature's whim. A man would need an axe to force a way through, and sometimes the maquis can be so dense and overgrown that even the wild sheep cannot penetrate it.

If you have killed a man, go to the maquis above Porto-Vecchio, and you will be able to live in safety there, with a good rifle, gunpowder, and bullets. Don't forget to take a brown cloak with a hood,[1] which does duty for blanket and mattress. The shepherds will give you milk, cheese, and chestnuts; and you will have nothing to fear from the law or from the dead man's relatives, except when you have to go down to the town to replenish your ammunition.

When I was in Corsica in 18——,* Mateo Falcone had his home half a league from the maquis. He was a man of some

[1] *Pilone.*

means for that district, who lived nobly—that is, without working—from the produce of his flocks that were driven to pasture on the mountains round and about by shepherds who lived like nomads. When I saw him, two years after the event I am about to relate, he looked 50 years old at most. Picture to yourself a small but robust man with tightly curled, jet-black hair, an aquiline nose, thin lips, large bright eyes, and a complexion tanned like the revers of a top-boot. His skill with a rifle was said to be extraordinary, even for Corsica, where there are so many good marksmen. For instance, Mateo would never have shot a wild sheep with buckshot, but would kill it at a hundred and twenty paces with a bullet in the head or in the shoulder, as the mood took him. He used his weapons with as much ease by night as by day, and I have been told of one of his feats of skill which may perhaps seem incredible to anyone who has never travelled in Corsica. At eighty paces, a lighted candle would be placed behind a transparent sheet of paper the size of a plate. He would take aim, then the candle would be extinguished, and one minute later, in total darkness, he would fire, piercing the paper three times out of four.

With such a prodigious talent, Mateo Falcone had earned himself a great reputation. He was said to be both a dangerous enemy and a staunch friend; moreover, he was always ready to oblige, gave alms to the poor, and lived on good terms with everyone in the district of Porto-Vecchio. But rumour had it that in Corte, where he had taken a wife, he had disposed most effectively of a rival, who was said to be as formidable in war as in love: at any rate, Mateo was given credit for a rifle-shot which caught the rival off his guard as he was standing shaving at a small mirror hanging in his window. When the affair had blown over, Mateo married. His wife Giuseppa first bore him three daughters (to his fury), then finally a son, whom he named Fortunato. This boy was the hope of the family, the heir to his father's name. The daughters had married well: their father could count on the daggers and blunderbusses of his sons-in-law if the need arose. The son was only 10 years old, but already showed great promise.

One autumn day Mateo set out early with his wife to go and

inspect one of his flocks in a clearing in the maquis. Little Fortunato wanted to go with him, but the clearing was too far away; and besides, someone had to stay behind to look after the house; so his father refused to allow him to accompany them. As we shall see, he had cause to regret his decision.

He had been away for several hours, and little Fortunato was lying quietly in the sun, gazing at the blue mountains and thinking about the following Sunday, when he would be going to have lunch in town with his uncle the *caporal*,[1] when his meditations were suddenly interrupted by the sound of a gunshot. He got up and looked towards the plain, whence the sound had come. Other gunshots followed at irregular intervals, coming closer all the time. Finally, on the path leading from the plain to Mateo's house, there appeared a man in a pointed cap of the sort worn by the mountain folk, bearded, in rags, and dragging himself along with great difficulty, leaning on his gun. He had just been shot in the thigh.

This man was a bandit[2] who had gone by night to buy gunpowder in the town and had been ambushed on the way by Corsican *voltigeurs*.[3] After putting up a vigorous defence he had managed to get away, hotly pursued and taking shots at them from behind the rocks. But the soldiers were close behind him, and his wound meant that it would be impossible for him to reach the maquis before they caught up with him.

He went up to Fortunato and said to him:

'Are you Mateo Falcone's son?'

'Yes.'

'I am Gianetto Sanpiero. The yellow collars[4] are after me. Hide me, I can't go any further.'

---

[1] The *caporali* were formerly chiefs appointed by the Corsican communes when they revolted against the feudal lords. Today this name is still sometimes given to a man who, by virtue of his land, his alliances, and his dependants, exercises influence and a sort of *de facto* magistrature over a *pievè* or canton. According to an ancient custom the Corsicans are divided into five castes: nobles (*magnifici* and *signori*), *caporali*, citizens, plebeians, and foreigners.

[2] The word is here synonymous with *outlaw*.

[3] A body of troops levied by the Government a few years ago to assist the gendarmerie in maintaining law and order.

[4] At that time a *voltigeur* wore a brown uniform with a yellow collar.

'But what will my father say if I hide you without his permission?'

'He will say you did the right thing.'

'How can I be sure?'

'Hide me quickly, they're coming.'

'Wait till my father comes back.'

'Wait? Damn it, they'll be here in five minutes! Come on, hide me, or I'll kill you.'

With perfect composure, Fortunato replied:

'Your gun isn't loaded, and there are no cartridges left in your *carchera*.'[1]

'I've still got my stiletto.'

'But can you run as fast as me?' With a bound, he was out of reach.

'You are no son of Mateo Falcone! Would you have me arrested on your very doorstep?'

The child seemed perturbed.

'What will you give me if I hide you?' he asked, drawing closer.

The bandit rummaged in a leather pouch that hung from his belt, and took from it a five-franc piece, which he had no doubt set aside for buying gunpowder. Fortunato smiled at the sight of the silver coin. He seized it and said to Gianetto:

'Have no fear.'

At once he made a large hole in a pile of hay that stood beside the house. Gianetto hid in it, and the child covered him over so as to allow him room to breathe, yet so that no one would suspect that there was a man concealed in the hay. He also thought of a most ingenious ruse, worthy of a true savage. He went and fetched a cat and her kittens and placed them on the pile of hay, to make it look as if it had not been disturbed recently. Then, noticing traces of blood on the path near the house, he carefully covered them with dust, after which he went and lay down again quite calmly in the sun.

A few minutes later six men in brown uniforms with yellow collars, led by an adjutant, arrived at Mateo's door. The adjutant was a distant relative of Falcone. (It is a well-known fact

---

[1] A leather belt doubling as a cartridge-pouch and wallet.

that in Corsica degrees of kinship are traced much further back than is the case elsewhere.) His name was Tiodoro Gamba. He was a zealous man, much feared by the bandits, several of whom he had already tracked down.

'Good day, little cousin,' he said to Fortunato, accosting him. 'How tall you've grown! Did you see a man pass this way just now?'

'Oh, I'm not as tall as you yet, cousin,' the child replied with seeming naïvety.

'You soon will be. Tell me now, did you see a man pass by?'

'Did I see a man pass by?'

'Yes, a man wearing a pointed black velvet hat and a jacket with red and yellow embroidery.'

'A man with a pointed hat and a jacket with red and yellow embroidery?'

'Yes. Answer me quickly and stop repeating my questions.'

'This morning the priest came past our house on his horse, Piero. He asked me how Papa was, and I told him that . . .'

'Ah, you're trying to be clever, you little devil! Tell me quickly which way Gianetto went. He's the man we're after, and I'm certain he took this path.'

'Who knows?'

'Who knows? I do! I know you saw him.'

'How can I have seen someone pass by, if I was asleep?'

'You weren't asleep, you little jackanapes. The shots woke you.'

'What makes you think your guns are so noisy, cousin? My father's blunderbuss is much louder.'

'The devil take you, you confounded little scamp! I'm quite certain you saw Gianetto. You may even have hidden him. Come on, lads! Into the house with you, and see whether our man is inside. He was hobbling along on one leg, and the wretch has got too much sense to try to make it to the maquis in that state. Anyway, the bloodstains stop here.'

'And what will Papa say?' asked Fortunato with a derisive laugh. 'What will he say when he hears that someone entered his house while he was out?'

'You little rogue!' said Adjutant Gamba, taking him by the ear. 'I can soon make you change your tune, you know! If I give you twenty strokes with the flat of my sabre, perhaps then you'll talk.'

And Fortunato still laughed mockingly. 'My father is Mateo Falcone!' he said with emphasis.

'Do you realize, you little devil, that I can take you away to Corte or Bastia? I'll make you sleep in a cell, on straw. I'll clap you in leg-irons and have you guillotined if you don't tell me where Gianetto Sanpiero is.'

The child burst out laughing at this ridiculous threat. 'My father is Mateo Falcone!' he repeated.

'Sir,' muttered one of the soldiers, 'don't let's get on the wrong side of Mateo.'

Gamba was plainly in a quandary. He spoke in a low voice to his soldiers, who had already searched the whole house. This was not a very lengthy operation, for a Corsican's cabin comprises one single square room. The furnishings consist of a table, benches, chests, hunting equipment, and a few household utensils. Meanwhile, little Fortunato stroked his cat, and seemed to take a malicious delight in the perplexity of the soldiers and his cousin.

A soldier went up to the pile of hay. Seeing the cat, he gave the hay a half-hearted prod with his bayonet, shrugging his shoulders as if sensing that his precaution was absurd. Nothing stirred; and the child's face betrayed not the slightest emotion.

The adjutant and his men were at their wits' end. Already they were looking gravely in the direction of the plain, as if tempted to head back the way they had come, when their chief, realizing that threats would make no impression on Falcone's son, decided to make one last attempt, and see what effect cajolery and bribes would have.

'Little cousin,' he said. 'You seem a wide-awake lad. You'll go far. But you're trifling with me, and if I weren't afraid of vexing my cousin Mateo, I'm hanged if I wouldn't take you along with me.'

'You don't say!'

'But when my cousin gets back I'll tell him the whole story, and he'll give you a flaying as a reward for having lied.'

'Is that so?'

'You'll see. Look, be a good lad and I'll give you something.'

'And I'll give you a piece of advice, cousin. If you waste any more time, Gianetto will be in the maquis, and then it'll take more than one fine fellow like you to fetch him out again.'

The adjutant took from his pocket a silver watch that was worth at least ten crowns, and, seeing little Fortunato's eyes light up at the sight of it, he held the watch suspended from its steel chain and said:

'You little rogue, wouldn't you like to have a watch like this hanging around your neck? You could stroll around the streets of Porto-Vecchio, proud as a peacock, and people would ask you what time it was, and you'd say, "Look at my watch." '

'When I'm grown up, my uncle the *caporal* will give me a watch.'

'Yes; but your uncle's son has got one already—not as nice as this one, either. And he's younger than you, too.'

The child sighed.

'Well, do you want this watch, little cousin?'

Fortunato eyed the watch furtively, like a cat that has had a whole chicken placed before it. Sensing it is being teased, it dare not lay a paw on it, and from time to time it looks away, so as not to succumb to temptation. But it licks its chops continually, and seems to be saying to its master, 'What a cruel trick to play on me!'

Yet Adjutant Gamba seemed to be sincere in his offer of the watch. Fortunato did not reach out his hand, but, smiling bitterly, said to him:

'Why are you having me on?'[1]

'I swear I'm not. Just tell me where Gianetto is and the watch is yours.'

Fortunato could not suppress a smile of incredulity. And, fixing his dark eyes on those of the adjutant, he tried to read in them how much faith he could place in his words.

'May I lose my commission', exclaimed the adjutant, 'if I don't give you the watch on those terms. My men here are witnesses, and I cannot go back on my word.'

As he spoke he brought the watch closer and closer until it was almost touching Fortunato's pale cheek. The child's face clearly showed the struggle between cupidity and the claims of

[1] *Perché me c. . . ?*

hospitality that was raging within him. His bare chest was heaving, and he seemed to be fighting for breath. And still the watch swung, twisted, and occasionally bumped against the tip of his nose. At last his right hand slowly rose towards the watch; his fingertips touched it; and he felt its full weight in his palm, though the adjutant still held the end of the chain. The dial was pale blue, the case newly furbished; in the sunshine it seemed ablaze. . . . The temptation was too great.

Fortunato raised his left hand too, and, with his thumb, pointed over his shoulder at the pile of hay behind him. The adjutant understood at once. He let go of the end of the chain; Fortunato found himself sole possessor of the watch. He rose with the agility of a fawn and moved ten paces away from the pile of hay, which the soldiers at once began to demolish.

Very soon the hay began to move and a man emerged from it, drenched in blood and with a dagger in his hand. But as he tried to rise to his feet his wound, which had stopped bleeding, prevented him from standing up. He fell. Throwing himself on him, Gamba tore the stiletto from his grip. Instantly he was tightly bound, despite his struggles.

Gianetto, lying on the ground trussed like a bundle of firewood, turned his head towards Fortunato, who had stepped forward again. 'Son of a ——,' he said to him, with more contempt than anger. The child threw back the silver coin he had accepted from him, feeling that he no longer deserved it; but the outlaw seemed not to notice the gesture. With great composure he said to the adjutant, 'My dear Gamba, I can't walk; you're going to have to carry me into town.'

'You were running faster than a roebuck a moment ago,' retorted the victor pitilessly. 'But set your mind at rest; I'm so pleased to have caught you that I could carry you on my back for a league without getting tired. In any case, my friend, we'll make you a litter out of some branches and your overcoat, and we can get horses at Crespoli's farm.'

'That's good,' said the prisoner. 'And just put a bit of straw on the litter, so I'll be more comfortable.'

While the soldiers were busy improvising a stretcher with chestnut branches and dressing Gianetto's wound, Mateo Falcone and his wife suddenly appeared round a bend leading to the maquis. The woman was plodding laboriously forward, bent beneath the weight of an enormous sack of chestnuts, while her husband sauntered along with only a rifle in his hand, and another slung over his shoulder; for it is unbecoming for a man to carry any burden but his weapons.

Mateo's first thought on seeing the soldiers was that they had come to arrest him. But why should such an idea cross his mind? Had Mateo perhaps tangled with the law? No; he enjoyed a good reputation. He was, as they say, *a man of high standing*. But he was a Corsican and a man of the mountains, and there are few Corsicans from the mountains who, if they delve in their memories, cannot find some peccadillo—a gunshot, a knifing, or some such trifling matter. Mateo had a clearer conscience than most, for it was more than ten years since he had pointed his gun at a man. But nevertheless he was circumspect, and he prepared to defend himself vigorously should the need arise.

'Woman,' he said to Giuseppa, 'put down your sack and be ready.' She instantly obeyed. He handed her the gun that was slung over his shoulder, which might get in the way. He loaded the one he was carrying and advanced slowly towards the house, keeping close to the trees at the roadside, and ready, at the slightest sign of hostility, to dash behind the largest trunk, where he could fire from under cover. His wife walked at his heels, carrying his spare gun and his cartridge-pouch. In the event of combat it is the task of a good wife to load her husband's weapons.

The adjutant, for his part, felt extremely ill at ease at the sight of Mateo advancing with measured steps, gun at the ready and finger on the trigger. 'If by any chance', he thought, 'Mateo should turn out to be a relative of Gianetto, or if he were a friend of his and meant to protect him, the very wads* from his two guns would hit two of us, as sure as a letter reaches its destination. And if he were to take aim at me, notwithstanding our kinship . . .'

In this dilemma, he took the courageous course of advancing alone to meet Mateo and tell him of the affair, hailing him like an old acquaintance. But the short distance that separated him from Mateo seemed interminable.

'Hey there, old comrade!' he called. 'How are things, my old friend? It's me, your cousin Gamba.'

Mateo had halted with no word of reply, and as the other spoke he slowly raised the barrel of his gun until, at the moment when the adjutant reached him, it was pointing towards the sky.

'Good day, brother,'[1] said the adjutant, offering him his hand. 'I haven't seen you in ages.'

'Good day, brother.'

'As I was passing, I came to say hello to you and cousin Pepa. We've had a long haul today, but, although we're exhausted, there's no call to feel sorry for us, for we've made a splendid catch. We've just collared Gianetto Sanpiero.'

'God be praised!' exclaimed Giuseppa. 'He stole a milch goat from us only last week.'

These words delighted Gamba.

'Poor devil,' said Mateo. 'He was hungry.'

'The rogue defended himself like a lion,' continued the adjutant, somewhat disconcerted. 'He killed one of my men and, not content with that, he broke Corporal Chardon's arm. Not that that matters—Chardon's only a Frenchman. And then he went and hid so well that the devil himself wouldn't have discovered him. If it hadn't been for my little cousin Fortunato I'd never have been able to find him.'

'Fortunato?' exclaimed Mateo.

'Fortunato?' repeated Giuseppa.

'Yes. Gianetto had hidden under that pile of hay over there. But my little cousin showed me what the game was. I'll tell his uncle the *caporal*, so he can send him a fine present for his pains. And both your names will appear in the report I shall be sending to the Public Prosecutor.'

'Damnation!' muttered Mateo.

They had rejoined the squad of soldiers. Gianetto had already been placed on the litter in readiness for departure. When he saw Mateo in the company of Gamba, he smiled sardonically. Then, turning towards the door of the house, he spat on the threshold and said: 'House of a traitor!'

---

[1] *Buon giorno, fratello* (the usual greeting among Corsicans).

Only a man resigned to death would have dared call Falcone a traitor. One quick dagger-thrust would instantly have repaid him for the insult once and for all. Yet Mateo merely raised his hand to his brow like a man reduced to despair.

Fortunato had gone inside the house on seeing his father arrive. He soon reappeared with a bowl of milk, which he offered to Gianetto with downcast eyes.

'Keep away from me!' roared the outlaw, in a voice of thunder. Then, turning to one of the *voltigeurs*, he said to him:

'Give me a drink, comrade.'

The soldier handed him his water-bottle, and the bandit drank the water offered to him by a man with whom he had just exchanged rifle shots. Then he asked to have his hands tied across his chest instead of behind his back. 'I like to lie comfortably,' he explained.

They hastened to comply with his request. Then the adjutant gave the signal to depart, bade farewell to Mateo, who did not reply, and set off back towards the plain at a brisk march.

Almost ten minutes passed before Mateo spoke a word. The child glanced uneasily first at his mother, then at his father, who was leaning on his gun, contemplating him with an expression of concentrated fury.

'A fine beginning!' said Mateo at last, in a voice that was calm, but terrifying to anyone who knew the man.

'Father!' cried the child, advancing with tears in his eyes as if to throw himself at his feet. But Mateo shouted, 'Out of my sight!' And the child stopped and stood sobbing a few paces from his father.

Giuseppa stepped forward. She had just noticed the watch-chain, one end of which was dangling from Fortunato's shirt.

'Who gave you that watch?' she asked severely.

'My cousin the adjutant.'

Falcone seized the watch and hurled it against a stone, dashing it into a thousand pieces.

'Woman,' he said, 'is this child mine?'

Giuseppa's brown cheeks turned brick-red.

'What are you saying, Mateo? And do you realize who you are talking to?'

'This child is the first of his line to have committed a betrayal.'

Fortunato's sobs and hiccoughs redoubled, and Falcone continued to stare at him like a lynx. Finally he struck the ground with the butt of his gun, then shouldered it and set off again on the path leading to the maquis, calling on Fortunato to follow him. The child obeyed.

Giuseppa ran after Mateo and seized him by the arm.

'He is your son,' she said in a trembling voice, fixing her dark eyes on those of her husband as if trying to read his thoughts.

'Leave me alone,' replied Mateo. 'I am his father.'

Giuseppa kissed her son and retreated, weeping, into the cabin. She fell to her knees before an image of the Virgin and prayed fervently. Meanwhile, Falcone walked a couple of hundred paces along the path and did not stop until he reached a small ravine, into which he descended. He sounded the earth with the butt of his gun and found it soft and easy to dig. The place seemed suitable for his purpose.

'Fortunato, go and stand by that big stone.'

The child did as he was ordered, then he knelt down.

'Say your prayers.'

'Father! Don't kill me, father!'

'Say your prayers!' repeated Mateo in a terrible voice.

Stammering and sobbing, the child recited the *Pater* and the *Credo*. At the end of each prayer his father uttered a loud 'Amen!'

'Are those all the prayers you know?'

'Father, I know the *Ave Maria* too, and the litany my aunt taught me.'

'It's rather long, but no matter.'

The child finished the litany in a whisper.

'Have you finished?'

'Oh, father, mercy! Forgive me! I won't do it again! I'll beg my uncle the *caporal* until Gianetto is reprieved!'

He went on speaking. Mateo had loaded his gun and was taking aim, saying to him, 'May God forgive you!' The child made a desperate effort to get up and clasp his father by the knees, but he was too late. Mateo fired, and Fortunato fell stone dead.

Without a glance at the corpse, Mateo set off for the house to fetch a spade with which to bury his son. He had gone only a few paces when he met Giuseppa, who had run up in alarm on hearing the shot.

'What have you done?' she cried.

'Justice.'

'Where is he?'

'In the ravine. I'm going to bury him. He died like a Christian; I shall have a mass sung for him. Have them tell my son-in-law Tiodoro Bianchi to come and live with us.'

The Storming of the Redoubt

(1829)

A MILITARY friend of mine who died of fever in Greece a few years ago once described to me the first engagement in which he had been involved. I was so struck by his account that I wrote it down from memory at the first opportunity. Here it is:

'I rejoined the regiment on the evening of 4 September. I found the colonel in the encampment. At first he received me fairly brusquely, but after he had read General B****'s letter of recommendation his manner changed, and he spoke a few kind words to me.

'I was introduced by him to my captain, who had just that moment returned from a reconnaissance. The captain, whom I had little time to get to know, was a tall man with a dark complexion and a harsh, unattractive face. He had risen from the ranks, and had won his commission and his cross on the field of battle. His voice, which was hoarse and weak, contrasted oddly with his almost gargantuan stature. I was told that he owed this strange voice to a bullet that had pierced him clean through at the Battle of Jena.

'Learning that I was fresh from the military school at Fontainebleau, he pulled a wry face and said: "My lieutenant was killed yesterday."

'I realized that he meant, "You're going to have to take his place, and you're not up to it." An acid retort came to my lips, but I restrained myself.

'The moon rose behind the Cheverino redoubt*, which was two cannon-shots distant from our encampment. It was large and red, as it often is when it rises. But that evening it seemed to me exceptionally large. For a moment the redoubt stood out, a black silhouette against the bright disc of the moon. It looked like the cone of a volcano during an eruption.

'An old soldier beside whom I was standing commented on the moon's colour.

' "It's very red," he said. "That's a sign that it will cost us dear to capture this precious redoubt we've heard so much about."

'I have always been superstitious, and this portent, especially coming at that particular moment, made a deep impression on me. I lay down but could not sleep. I got up and walked around for some time, looking at the immense line of camp-fires extending along the heights beyond the village of Cheverino.

'When I felt that my pulse had been sufficiently calmed by the fresh, keen night air, I returned to my place by the fire, wrapped myself carefully in my greatcoat, and closed my eyes, hoping not to open them again till daybreak. But sleep would not come to my aid. Imperceptibly my thoughts took a gloomy turn. I told myself I did not have a single friend among the hundred thousand men who covered that plain. If I was wounded I would be sent to a hospital and treated uncaringly by ignorant surgeons. I remembered all I had heard about surgical operations. My heart pounded violently, and mechanically I arranged my handkerchief and wallet against my breast, so as to act as a makeshift cuirass. I was dog-tired, yet every time I dozed off, some sinister thought would return with renewed force and wake me with a start.

'However, fatigue won out, and when reveille was sounded I was fast asleep. We fell in, the roll was called, then we piled arms again, and all the signs seemed to suggest that we were in for a quiet day.

'Around three o'clock an aide-de-camp arrived with a dispatch. We were again ordered to parade under arms. Our skirmishers spread out over the plain. We followed them slowly, and after twenty minutes we saw all the Russian outposts fall back and return into the redoubt.

'An artillery battery moved into position on our right flank, and another on our left, both well in advance of us. They began a heavy bombardment of the enemy, which met with a vigorous response, and the Cheverino redoubt soon disappeared behind thick clouds of smoke.

'Our regiment was almost protected from the Russian fire by an undulation of the ground. Their cannon-balls, few of which were intended for us (for they preferred to fire at our gunners), passed over our heads, or at worst showered us with earth and small stones.

'As soon as we were given the order to advance, my captain gave me a searching look, and I felt obliged to stroke my youthful moustache two or three times as nonchalantly as I was able. In fact, I was not afraid, my only concern being that someone might suppose I was afraid. Those harmless cannon-balls further contributed to my state of heroic calm. My pride told me I was in real danger, since I was under bombardment at last. I was delighted to find myself so unconcerned, and I thought of the pleasure I would derive from recounting the taking of the Cheverino redoubt, back in Madame de B****'s salon in the rue de Provence.

'The colonel passed by our company. He spoke to me. "Well, it looks as if you're in for a stormy début."

'I gave him my most martial smile, brushing from my coat sleeve some dirt thrown up by a cannon-ball that had fallen thirty paces away.

'The Russians must have realized their cannon-balls were having little effect, because they started using shells, which could reach us more easily in the hollow where we were posted. A fairly large splinter knocked off my shako and killed a man standing beside me.

' "My compliments," said the captain as I rose from retrieving my shako. "You're safe now for the rest of the day."

'I had already come across this military superstition, which considers that the axiom *non bis in idem** is as valid on the battlefield as in a court of law. I proudly replaced my shako.

' "Rather a drastic way of getting you to raise your hat!" I said as cheerfully as I could. This poor joke struck me as excellent in the circumstances.

' "I congratulate you," continued the captain. "You'll come to no further harm, and you'll be commanding a company by this evening, for I can feel my number is up. Every time I've been wounded the officer beside me was hit by a spent bullet. And what's more," he added in an undertone, sounding almost ashamed, "their names all began with a P."

'I pretended to be unimpressed. Most people would have done the same; most people, too, would have been affected, as

I was, by these prophetic words. As a raw recruit, I felt I could confide my feelings to no one, and that I must always appear calmly intrepid.

'After half an hour the Russian fire diminished appreciably. Thereupon we left our cover in order to march on the redoubt.

'Our regiment was composed of three battalions. The second was to outflank the redoubt from the entrance side; the other two were to make the assault. I was in the third battalion.

'Emerging from behind the sort of spur that had been protecting us, we were greeted by several volleys of rifle-fire, which inflicted only minor casualties among our ranks. The whistling of the bullets came as a surprise to me. I kept turning my head, eliciting some humorous comments from my comrades, who were more familiar with this sound than I was.

' "When all is said and done," I said to myself, "a battle isn't such a terrible thing."

'We were advancing at the double, preceded by skirmishers. Suddenly the Russians shouted "*Oura!*" three times—three distant cheers—then fell silent again and held their fire.

' "I don't like this silence," said the captain. "It bodes no good for us."

'I thought our own men were making rather too much noise, and I could not prevent myself from mentally comparing their tumultuous clamour with the enemy's imposing silence.

'We quickly reached the foot of the redoubt. The stockades had been shattered and the earth churned up by our cannon-balls. The soldiers threw themselves onto this latest scene of destruction, shouting "*Vive l'Empereur!*" louder than one would have expected of men who had already shouted so much.

'I raised my eyes, and never will I forget the sight I saw. Most of the smoke had risen, and remained hanging like a pall twenty feet above the redoubt. Through a bluish haze you could see the Russian grenadiers behind their half-destroyed parapet, with their rifles raised, motionless like statues. I can still see each soldier, his left eye fixed on us, his right eye concealed by his raised rifle. In an embrasure a few feet from us, a man stood by a field gun, holding a lighted fuse.

'I shuddered, and thought my final hour had come.

' "This is where the fun begins. Here goes!" cried the captain. Those were the last words I heard him speak.

'A roll of drums echoed around the redoubt. I saw all the rifles point down at us. I closed my eyes, and heard a dreadful crash followed by screams and groans. I opened my eyes again, surprised to find myself still alive. The redoubt was once again shrouded in smoke. I was surrounded by dead and wounded. The captain lay at my feet. His head had been shattered by a cannon-ball, and I was covered with his brains and blood. Out of my whole company only six soldiers and myself were left standing.

'A moment of stunned surprise followed this carnage. Placing his hat on the point of his sword, the colonel led the ascent of the parapet, shouting "*Vive l'Empereur!*" He was at once followed by all the survivors. I have virtually no clear recollection of what ensued. Somehow or other we entered the redoubt. We fought hand-to-hand amid smoke so thick that we could not see one another. I believe I struck home, for my sword had blood all over it. Finally I heard a shout of "Victory!" and, as the smoke dispersed, I saw that the floor of the redoubt was totally concealed by blood and corpses. The guns especially were buried beneath heaps of dead. About two hundred men in French uniforms stood around in disorganized groups, some loading their rifles, others wiping their bayonets. Among them were eleven Russian prisoners.

'The colonel lay on his back, covered in blood, on a shattered ammunition wagon near the entrance. Some soldiers were crowding around him. I approached.

' "Where's the senior captain?" he was asking a sergeant.

'The sergeant shrugged his shoulders eloquently.

' "And the senior lieutenant?"

' "This is the gentleman who arrived yesterday," said the sergeant imperturbably.

'The colonel smiled bitterly.

' "Well, sir," he said to me. "You are commander-in-chief. Have the entrance to the redoubt fortified at once with those wagons, the enemy is in force. But General C**** will see to it that you are supported."

' "Colonel," I said, "are you seriously wounded?"

' "A b—— goner, my boy. But the redoubt has been taken." '

Tamango

(1829)

CAPTAIN LEDOUX* was a first-rate seaman. He had started out serving before the mast and risen to under-helmsman. At the battle of Trafalgar his left hand was shattered by a splinter of wood. He had it amputated and was discharged with a good reference. Leisure was not to his liking, and when the opportunity arose to return to sea, he served as lieutenant on board a privateer. With his prize money* he was able to purchase books and study the theory of navigation (he was already fully conversant with its practical aspects). In time he became captain of a pirate lugger with three cannon and a crew of sixty, and the Jersey coasters still remember his exploits.

The Peace Treaty* came as a blow to him. During the war he had amassed a small fortune which he had been hoping to increase at the expense of the British. He was now obliged to offer his services to peaceable merchants, and since he was known to be a man of resolution and experience, no difficulty arose about giving him the command of a ship. When the slave-trade was abolished* and those engaging in it found it necessary not only to escape the vigilance of the French customs officers, which was not so very difficult, but also—and this was the tricky part—to give the British cruisers the slip, Captain Ledoux became invaluable to the traffickers in ebony.[1]

Unlike most sailors who have vegetated for years on end in subordinate positions, he did not have the deep-seated horror of innovation and devotion to established routine that all too often they take with them into the higher ranks. On the contrary, Captain Ledoux had been the first to recommend his outfitter to use metal cisterns for storing water and keeping it fresh. On his vessel, the manacles and chains with which the slave ships are equipped were manufactured according to the latest process and carefully lacquered to protect them from

[1] The name by which the slave-traders refer to themselves.

rust. But the thing that redounded most to his credit among the slave-traders was the brig he had had built to his own specifications for use in the slave-trade, a sharp-built sailing ship, long and narrow like a man-of-war yet capable of carrying a very large number of blacks. He called it the *Espérance*. He had specified that the space between-decks should be cramped and low, measuring only 3 feet 6½ inches from floor to ceiling, claiming that this allowed a slave of average height enough room to sit upright in comfort. And why should they need to stand? 'When they get to the colonies,' Ledoux used to say, 'they'll spend more than enough time on their feet!'

· The blacks were arranged in two parallel lines, their backs to the vessel's sheathing, leaving a space between the rows of feet which on other slave ships serves only as a passageway. Ledoux had the idea of fitting more negroes into this space, lying at right angles to the rest. In this way, his ship could hold ten more negroes than others of the same tonnage. They could have squeezed more in at a pinch, but you have to be humane and allow a black man at least five feet by two in which to flex his limbs during a voyage lasting six weeks or more. 'After all,' Ledoux said to his outfitter, in justification of this liberality, 'these blacks are human beings, just as much as white men.'

The *Espérance* sailed from Nantes on a Friday, as some superstitious folk were later to point out. The customs officers who gave the brig a thorough inspection failed to discover six large chests filled with chains, manacles, and those irons that for some reason are called *barres de justice**. Nor were they at all surprised by the prodigious quantity of water the *Espérance* was to carry, although according to her papers she was going only as far as Senegal, to trade in wood and ivory. Admittedly the passage is not a long one, but then you can't be too careful. What if the ship were becalmed? Where would they be without water?

So the *Espérance* set sail on a Friday, fully rigged and fully fitted out. Ledoux might perhaps have liked her to have rather sturdier masts; however, for the duration of his command he had no cause for complaint on that score. The voyage to the African coast passed swiftly and without mishap. He dropped anchor—in the Joale River, I believe—at a time when the British cruisers were not patrolling that particular part of the coast. At once the local slave-dealers came on board. He could not have chosen a better time: Tamango, a celebrated warrior and dealer in men, had just herded a large number of slaves down to the coast and was selling them off at knock-down prices, as a man will if he knows he has the power and the wherewithal to supply the market promptly, should the commodities in which he deals suddenly become scarce.

Captain Ledoux had himself put ashore and paid his formal visit to Tamango. He found him in a straw hut that had been hastily erected for him, in the company of his two wives and a few lesser traders and slave-drivers. Tamango had dressed up to receive the white captain. He was wearing an old blue military tunic which still had a corporal's stripes on it. From each shoulder hung two gold epaulettes attached to the same button, one bobbing about in front and one to the rear. Since he wore no shirt and the tunic was rather too short for a man of his height, a considerable expanse of black skin, resembling a broad belt, was visible between the white band at the base of his tunic and his Guinea cotton pants. A large cavalry sabre hung from a cord at his side, and in his hand he held a handsome double-barrelled gun of British manufacture. In this rig-out, the African warrior adjudged himself more elegant than the most consummate dandy to be found in Paris or London.

Captain Ledoux contemplated him for some time in silence, while Tamango drew himself up like a grenadier being inspected by a foreign general, and revelled in the impression he supposed himself to be making on the white man. After appraising him with an expert eye, Ledoux turned to his first officer and said:

'I could get at least a thousand crowns for this chap if I could get him to Martinique alive and in one piece.'

They sat down, and a sailor who spoke some Wolof acted as interpreter. When the first polite compliments had been exchanged a cabin-boy brought a hamper full of bottles of brandy; they drank, and to put Tamango in a good mood, the captain presented him with a handsome powder-flask made of copper, bearing an embossed portrait of Napoleon. The present was accepted with appropriate marks of gratitude, they emerged from the hut and sat down in the shade with the bottles of brandy in front of them, and Tamango gave the signal to bring on the slaves he had for sale.

They appeared in a long line, bent with fatigue and fright, each with his neck held in a fork more than six feet long whose two prongs were joined at the nape by a wooden cross-bar. When the order to advance is given, one of the slave-drivers takes the handle of the first slave's fork over his shoulder; the first slave shoulders the fork of the man immediately behind; the second carries the third slave's fork; and so on down the line. If a halt is called the leader thrusts the pointed end of his fork-handle into the ground, and the whole column stops. It goes without saying that there can be no question of running away when you have a thick pole six feet long fastened round your neck.

As each male or female slave passed before him, the captain shrugged his shoulders, declaring the men puny, the women too old or too young, and he deplored the degeneration of the negro race. 'Everything is deteriorating,' he said. 'In the old days things were different. The women were five feet ten tall, and just four of the men could have turned a frigate's capstan and raised the best bower-anchor.'

However, even as he criticized them, he was making a preliminary selection of the sturdiest and handsomest blacks. For these he was prepared to pay the asking price, but for the rest he was counting on a substantial reduction. Tamango, for his part, defended his own interests, praised his merchandise, and spoke of the scarcity of men and the perils of the trade. He concluded by naming a price, I'm not sure how much, for the slaves the white captain wanted to take on board his ship.

On hearing the interpreter translate Tamango's proposal into French, Ledoux, almost bowled over with surprise and indignation, muttered a few dreadful oaths and stood up, as if to have no further truck with anyone so unreasonable. At this Tamango tried to stop him leaving, and managed with some difficulty to get him to sit down again. Another bottle was opened and discussion resumed. This time it was the black man's turn to find the white man's proposals wild and

preposterous. They shouted and haggled for a long time, prodigious quantities of brandy were consumed. But the brandy
had very different effects on the two contracting parties: the
more the Frenchman drank, the more he reduced his bids; the
more the African drank, the more he lowered the asking price.
Thus, by the time the hamper was empty they had struck a
bargain. A few shoddy cotton goods, some gunpowder, some
flints, three casks of brandy, and fifty dilapidated rifles were
traded for a hundred and sixty slaves. To ratify the treaty, the
captain shook the hand of the black man, who was well on his
way to being drunk, and the slaves were at once handed over
to the French sailors, who promptly removed their wooden
forks and replaced them with iron collars and manacles—
proof, if any were needed, of the manifest superiority of our
European civilization.

There still remained about thirty slaves: children, old men,
and crippled women. The ship was full.

Tamango, who did not know what to do with these rejects,
offered to sell them to the captain for a bottle of brandy apiece.
The offer was tempting. Ledoux remembered how, at a performance of *The Sicilian Vespers** in Nantes, he had seen a
number of corpulent individuals enter an already crowded
auditorium and still manage to find seats, thanks to the com-
pressibility of the human body. He took the twenty thinnest
of the thirty slaves.

Tamango now asked only a glass of brandy for each of the ten
that remained. It occurred to Ledoux that children pay half-fare
on public transport, and occupy only half a seat. So he took three
children. But he flatly refused to take so much as one more black.

Seeing that he still had seven slaves on his hands, Tamango
seized his gun and pointed it at the first of the women. She
was the mother of the three children.

'Buy her,' he said to the white man, 'or else I'll kill her. A
little glass of brandy, or I'll fire.'

'And what the devil am I supposed to do with her?' replied
Ledoux.

Tamango fired, and the slave fell dead to the ground.

'Right, now for the next!' he exclaimed, taking aim at a
feeble old man. 'A glass of brandy, or else . . .'

One of his wives jolted his arm and the gun went off in the air. She had recognized the old man her husband was going to kill as the *guiriot* or medicine-man who had once predicted to her that she would become queen.

Seeing his will opposed, Tamango, whom the brandy had driven into a frenzy, lost all self-control. He struck his wife brutally with the butt of his rifle, then turned to Ledoux and said:

'Here, I give you this woman.'

She was pretty. Ledoux looked at her, smiling, then took her by the hand.

'I'll manage to find room for her,' he said.

The interpreter was a humane man. He gave Tamango a papier-mâché snuff-box and asked him for the six remaining slaves. He released them from their forks and allowed them to take themselves off wherever they saw fit. At once they ran off, scattering in all directions, at their wits' end how to find their way back to their homes two hundred leagues from the coast.

Meanwhile the captain took his leave of Tamango and set about getting his cargo aboard as quickly as possible. It was not advisable to linger up-river, since the cruisers were liable to reappear, and he intended to set sail the next day. As for Tamango, he lay down on the grass in the shade, and began to sleep off the effects of the brandy.

When he awoke the vessel was already under sail and heading downstream. Tamango, whose head was still fuddled from the previous day's intemperance, called for his wife Ayché. He was informed that she had had the misfortune to incur his displeasure, and that he had made a present of her to the white captain, who had taken her on board his ship. At this news Tamango struck himself on the head in astonishment, then took his gun, and, as the river followed a winding course on its journey to the sea, ran by the shortest route to a small loop half a league from the river's mouth. There he was hoping to find a boat in which he would be able to join the brig, whose progress would be delayed by the river's meandering course. He was not mistaken: sure enough, he had time to leap into a boat and join the slave-ship.

Ledoux was surprised to see him, and still more so to hear him ask for his wife back.

'A gift's a gift,' he replied, and turned his back on him. The black man insisted, offering to return some of the items he had received in exchange for the slaves. The captain began to laugh, and told him that Ayché was an extremely fine woman and that he was intending to keep her. At this poor Tamango burst into floods of tears and uttered piercing cries of pain, like some poor devil undergoing a surgical operation. He rolled about the deck calling for his beloved Ayché, then struck his head against the planking as if attempting to dash his brains out. The captain remained unmoved, pointing to the shore as a sign that it was time for him to leave. But Tamango persisted. He even offered him his gold epaulettes, his gun, and his sword, but to no avail.

During this dispute the officer of the *Espérance* said to the captain:

'Three of the slaves died on us last night, we've got room. Why not take this great brute of a fellow along with us? He's worth more than the three dead ones put together.'

Ledoux reflected that he could easily get a thousand crowns for Tamango; that this voyage, which showed every sign of being highly lucrative for him, would probably be his last; and that, furthermore, now that he had made his fortune and was retiring from the slave trade, it mattered little what sort of a reputation he left behind him on the Guinea coast. In any case, the shore was deserted and the African warrior entirely at his mercy. All that remained was to relieve him of his weapons, since it would have been dangerous to lay hands on him while he was still in possession of them. So Ledoux asked him for his gun, as if he wanted to examine it and see whether it really was worth as much as the beautiful Ayché. While testing the action he was careful to empty it of its priming charge. Meanwhile the officer was wielding the sword; and as Tamango now found himself unarmed, two sturdy sailors pounced on him, threw him to the ground flat on his back, and proceeded to bind him hand and foot.

The black man made a heroic resistance. Recovering from his initial surprise, and despite being at a disadvantage on account of his position, he put up a protracted struggle against the two sailors. Helped by his prodigious strength, he managed to rise

to his feet. With a blow of his fist he floored the man who was
holding him by the scruff of the neck, left the other sailor
clutching a piece of his tunic, and flew at the officer like a
madman in order to snatch his sword from him. The officer
struck him on the head with it, inflicting a long but shallow
wound. Tamango fell a second time. At once they bound him
securely hand and foot. While defending himself he had
uttered cries of fury, thrashing around like a wild boar caught
in the meshes of a net, but when he realized that resistance
was useless he closed his eyes and did not make another movement. Only his rapid and heavy breathing showed that he was
still alive.

'I'll be damned!' exclaimed Captain Ledoux. 'Those blacks
he sold us will laugh themselves silly when they see that now
he's in the same boat as they are! Perhaps now they'll finally
realize there really is such a thing as Providence.'

Meanwhile, the unfortunate Tamango was bleeding to death.
The kindly interpreter, who the day before had saved the lives of
six slaves, went up to him, bound his wound, and spoke a few
words of consolation to him. What he said I don't know. The black
man lay motionless like a corpse. Two sailors had to pick him up
like a sack and carry him off to the place allocated to him between-
decks. For two days he refused all food and drink, and seldom
opened his eyes. His companions in captivity and erstwhile
prisoners greeted his appearance in their midst with stunned
amazement. Such was the fear he still inspired in them that not
one among them dared jeer at the misfortune of this man, who had
brought about their own misfortunes.

Helped by a strong land-wind, the vessel was rapidly putting the African coast behind her. The captain was no longer
concerned about the British cruiser, and now thought only of
the enormous profits awaiting him once he reached his
destination in the colonies. His cargo of ebony was unscathed.
There had been no infectious diseases. Only twelve of the
weakest negroes had died of the heat—so few it hardly
mattered.

To ensure that his human cargo suffered as little as possible
from the hardships of the crossing, he considerately allowed
his slaves up on deck once a day. Taking turns, a third of them

at a time, these wretched creatures had an hour in which to
lay in a full day's supply of air. Some of the crew watched over
them, armed to the teeth for fear of mutiny. In addition, they
were careful never completely to remove their irons. Sometimes one of the sailors who could play the violin treated them
to a recital. On these occasions it was remarkable to see them
all turn their black faces towards the musician, gradually lose
their expression of abject despair, laugh loudly, and even
applaud, when not prevented from doing so by their chains.

Exercise is essential to good health. Consequently, one of
the captain's salutary practices was to get his slaves to dance
frequently, as horses are made to prance on deck during a long
sea crossing.

'Come on now, boys and girls, enjoy yourselves!' the captain
bellowed, cracking an enormous coaching whip. And at once
the poor blacks would leap and dance.

For a while Tamango's wound kept him below the hatch-
ways. At last he appeared on deck. First, standing proudly,
head held high, surrounded by the timid throng of slaves, he
gazed sadly but serenely at the immense expanse of water surrounding the ship. Then he lay down on the planking of the
upper deck, or rather collapsed onto it, without even taking
the trouble to arrange his irons so that they would be less
uncomfortable. Ledoux was seated on the poop-deck, placidly
smoking his pipe. Beside him stood Ayché, wearing, not irons,
but an elegant blue cotton dress, her feet clad in pretty
morocco leather slippers, holding a tray laden with liquor, and
ready to serve him a drink. It was evident that she performed
important services for the captain. One of the blacks, who
detested Tamango, pointed to get him to look in that direction. Tamango turned his head, saw her, gave a cry; and,
rising impetuously, ran towards the poop-deck before the
sailors guarding him were able to prevent this gross infringe-
ment of naval discipline.

'Ayché!' he thundered; and Ayché uttered a cry of terror.
'Do you suppose there is no Mumbo Jumbo* in the land of
the white men?'

Sailors were already running up with their sticks raised. But
Tamango was returning calmly to his place with folded arms,

as if unaware of their presence, whilst Ayché burst into tears, seemingly paralysed with fright by these mysterious words.

The interpreter explained the significance of this terrible Mumbo Jumbo, the mere mention of which caused so much horror.

'It's the bugbear of the black peoples,' he said. 'When a husband is afraid his wife is doing what so many wives do, in France as well as in Africa, he threatens her with Mumbo Jumbo. Believe it or not, I once saw Mumbo Jumbo myself, and I wasn't taken in. But these blacks are a simple lot, they understand nothing.

'Picture it, then: one evening while the women were enjoying themselves dancing, holding a *folgar*, as they call it in their lingo, we suddenly heard strange music coming from out of a small, very dense and dark wood. But we couldn't see who it was that was making the music—the musicians were all hidden in the wood. There were reed flutes, wooden drums, *balafos**, and guitars made out of calabash halves, all playing a melody fit to drive the devil to his grave. The moment the women heard the tune they all began to tremble. They tried to run away, but their husbands prevented them. The women knew only too well what they were in for.

'Suddenly a great white figure appeared out of the wood, as tall as our topgallant mast, with a head as big as a bushel measure, eyes the size of hawse holes, and a fiery mouth like the devil's itself. It was moving very, very slowly, and it ventured no more than half a cable's length out of the wood. "It's Mumbo Jumbo!" the women screamed. They were shrieking like fishwives. Then their husbands said to them: "Now then, you jades, tell us whether you've been behaving. If you lie, Mumbo Jumbo will come, and eat you up raw." Some of them were gullible enough to confess, whereupon their husbands thrashed them within an inch of their lives.'

'So what was the white figure, this Mumbo Jumbo, then?' asked the Captain.

'Why, it was some fellow dressed up in a big white sheet, holding a hollowed-out gourd with a lighted candle in it for the head, on top of a long pole. There was no more mystery to it than that—it doesn't take much ingenuity to hoodwink these blacks. All the same, Mumbo Jumbo is a clever invention of theirs. I wish my wife believed in him.'

'Speaking for mine,' said Ledoux, 'she may not be afraid of Mumbo Jumbo, but she's certainly afraid of Martin-Bâton*, and she knows only too well what would happen if she tried any funny business. A Ledoux doesn't take things lying down, and even though I've only got one hand, it can still wield a cat-o'-nine-tails pretty effectively. As for that fellow over there, with his talk of Mumbo Jumbo, tell him he'd better behave and not frighten the little lady, or else I'll flog him till that black skin of his is as red as a raw steak.'

With these words the captain went below to his cabin, summoned Ayché, and tried to console her. But neither caresses nor even blows—for there is a limit to anyone's patience—could make the beautiful negress see reason. Floods of tears streamed from her eyes. The captain went back up on deck in a bad temper and picked a quarrel with the officer of the watch about his handling of the ship.

During the night, when the crew were almost all fast asleep, the men on watch heard a deep chant, solemn and mournful, coming from between-decks, followed by the hideously shrill scream of a woman. Immediately afterwards the harsh voice of Ledoux cursing and threatening and the sound of his terrible whip echoed round the ship. A moment later all was quiet again. When Tamango appeared on deck the next day, his face was bruised, but he was as proud and resolute as before.

The moment Ayché noticed him she left the poop-deck, where she had been sitting beside the captain, ran swiftly to Tamango, knelt before him, and, her voice heavy with despair, said to him:

'Forgive me, Tamango, forgive me!'

Tamango stared at her for a moment, then, observing that the interpreter was some distance away, said to her:

'A file!'

And, turning his back on Ayché, he lay down on the deck.

The captain reprimanded her severely, even slapping her a few times, and forbade her to speak to her former husband. But he had no inkling of the significance of the brief words they had exchanged, and he did not question her on the matter.

Meanwhile, Tamango was shut up with the other slaves, exhorting them day and night to make a valiant effort to regain their freedom. He spoke of how they outnumbered the white men, and drew their attention to the increasing negligence of their warders. Then, without going into any precise details, he told them he would be able to bring them back to their country, boasted of his knowledge of the occult sciences, of which the black peoples are great devotees, and threatened to call down the devil's wrath on anyone who refused to assist him in his venture. During his harangues he spoke only the language of the Fulani, with which most of the slaves were familiar, but which the interpreter did not understand. The speaker's reputation, and the fact that the slaves were accustomed to fear and obey him, rendered his eloquence all the more cogent, and long before he himself felt ready to put his plans into effect, the blacks were urging him to fix a day for their deliverance. He answered the conspirators in veiled terms, telling them that the time was not yet ripe, and that the devil, who appeared to him in dreams, had not yet given him the signal, but that they were to be constantly at the ready. Meanwhile he overlooked no opportunity to put his warders' vigilance to the test. Once, a sailor had left his rifle propped up against the ship's gunwales, and was passing the time watching a shoal of flying fish that was following the vessel. Tamango took the gun and began to handle it, producing a grotesque imitation of the movements he had seen sailors going through at drill. They were quick to relieve him of the gun; but he had established that he could handle a weapon without immediately arousing suspicion; and when the time came to use one, it would be a rash man who tried to take it from his hands.

One day Ayché tossed him a biscuit, making a sign incomprehensible to anyone but himself. The biscuit contained a small file: on this the success of the plot depended. At first Tamango was careful not to show the file to his companions. But, when night had fallen, he began to mutter unintelligible words, accompanying them with bizarre gestures. By degrees he became more excited until his voice rose to a shout. To hear

the changing intonations of his voice you would have supposed he was engaged in animated conversation with some
invisible person. All the slaves trembled, convinced that the
devil was at that very moment there in their midst. Tamango
put an end to this scene by uttering a cry of joy.

'My companions,' he exclaimed, 'the spirit I have invoked
has finally granted me what he promised, and I have in my
hands the instrument of our deliverance. All you will now
need to gain your freedom is a little courage.'

He allowed those closest to him to handle the file, and,
primitive as it was, his stratagem succeeded in deceiving men
more primitive still.

At last the great and long-awaited day of vengeance and
liberty dawned. Bound by a solemn oath, the conspirators had
drawn up their plan after careful deliberation. The most determined among them, led by Tamango, were to seize their
warders' weapons when their turn came to go up on deck.
Others were to go to the captain's cabin and take the guns that
were kept there. Those who had managed to file through their
irons would lead the attack; but, despite several nights'
dogged work, the majority of the slaves were still in no position to take an active part in the operation. Consequently,
three sturdy blacks were given the task of killing the man who
kept the keys to their irons in his pocket, and of then immediately releasing their companions.

That day Captain Ledoux was in excellent spirits. Breaking
his rule, he reprieved a cabin-boy who had earned a flogging.
He complimented the officer of the watch on his handling of
the ship, declared his satisfaction to the crew, and announced
that in Martinique, where they were to arrive shortly, every
man would receive a bonus. Presented with this agreeable prospect, the sailors were already thinking of the uses to which the
money could be put. They were thinking of brandy and the
coloured women of Martinique when Tamango and the other
conspirators were brought up on deck.

They had taken care to file their shackles so that it could not
be seen that they had been cut, yet so that they would break
if the least force were exerted. In any case, they clashed them
so vigorously that it sounded as if they were wearing two sets

each. After breathing in a few lungfuls of air they joined hands and began to dance, while Tamango intoned his family's war-chant,[1] which in days gone by he had sung before going into battle.

The dance went on for some time. Then, as if worn out, Tamango lay down full length at the feet of a sailor who was leaning nonchalantly against the ship's gunwales. All the conspirators did the same. Each sailor was thus surrounded by several blacks.

Suddenly Tamango, who had just unobtrusively broken his shackles, gave a great roar, which was to serve as the signal. He pulled violently at the legs of the sailor standing near him, brought him to the ground, planted his foot on the man's stomach, and snatched his gun, with which he then dispatched the officer of the watch. At the same time the sailors guarding them were all attacked, disarmed, and instantly slaughtered. On all sides the war-cry went up. The petty officer, who had the key to the irons, was among the first to die. Thereupon a horde of blacks swarmed onto the deck. Those who could not find weapons seized the bars from the capstan or the oars from the longboat.

From that moment the European crew was doomed. A few sailors nevertheless made a last stand on the poop, but they lacked the necessary weapons and resolution. Ledoux was still alive, his courage undiminished. Realizing that Tamango was the life and soul of the conspiracy, he was reckoning that, if once he succeeded in killing him, he would then be able to make short work of his accomplices. So he rushed at him, sword in hand, calling out to him at the top of his voice.

At once Tamango dashed at him. He held a gun by the barrel and was using it as a club. The two chiefs came together on one of the fore-and-aft catwalks, the narrow gangways connecting the forecastle and the poop. Tamango was the first to strike. The white man moved aside slightly and dodged the blow. The butt struck the planking with such force that it shattered and the gun flew from Tamango's hands. He was now defenceless, and, smiling with demonic glee, Ledoux

[1] Every Negro chief has his own war-chant.

raised his arm and was on the point of running him through.
But Tamango was as agile as the panthers of his homeland.
He rushed into the arms of his adversary and seized the hand
in which he held his sword. One man was doing his utmost
to keep possession of his weapon, the other, to wrench it from
him. In the course of this violent struggle, both fell, though
the African came off worst. Thereupon, nothing daunted,
Tamango gripped his adversary with all his might and, like a
lion attacking its prey, bit him in the throat so savagely that
the blood gushed from it. The sword slipped from the captain's failing grip. Tamango seized it; then rising to his feet
with the blood dripping from his mouth, he uttered a shout
of triumph and drove the sword again and again into the body
of his enemy, who was already at the point of death.

Victory was no longer in the balance. The few remaining
sailors tried to beg the rebels' mercy, but they were pitilessly
slaughtered to the last man; not even the interpreter, who had
never done them any harm, was spared. The first officer died
a hero's death. He had retreated to the stern, next to a small
cannon of the kind that is mounted on a swivel and loaded
with grape-shot. With his left hand he aimed the gun, while
with his right he defended himself with a sword, thereby
drawing a crowd of blacks around him. Then, pressing the
firing mechanism, he cut a swathe through the middle of
this serried mass, littered with dead and dying. A moment
later he was hacked to pieces.

When the corpse of the last white man had been
dismembered, chopped up, and thrown into the sea, the
blacks, their thirst for vengeance sated, raised their eyes
towards the ship's sails, which were still filled by a fresh gale,
and which, despite their victory, seemed still to be under
orders from their oppressors, and to be bearing the victors
away into a land of bondage.

'We have achieved nothing,' they thought sadly. 'And will
this great fetish of the white men still take us back to our
country, now that we have shed the blood of its masters?'

Some said that Tamango would know how to make it obey.
At once they called loudly for Tamango.

He was in no hurry to make his appearance. They found

him in the aft cabin, standing with one hand resting on the
captain's bloodstained sword; the other he was holding out
abstractedly to his wife Ayché, who was kneeling before him
and kissing it. The joy of victory did not diminish the feeling
of dark uneasiness betrayed by his whole bearing. Less
primitive than the others, he was more aware than them of his
predicament.

At long last he appeared on deck, affecting a calmness he did
not feel. Urged by a hundred tumultuous voices to direct the
vessel's course, he stepped slowly towards the helm, as if
slightly to postpone the moment which, for himself and for
the others, would determine the extent of his power.

Not a negro on the whole ship, even the stupidest of them,
had failed to notice the influence that a certain wheel, and the
box located in front of it, had on the ship's movements; but
the mechanism had always remained a mystery to them.
Tamango examined the compass for a long time, moving his
lips as if reading the letters he could see inscribed on it. Then
he raised his hand to his forehead, adopting the pensive
attitude of a man engaged in some mental calculation. All the
blacks were gathered around him open-mouthed, their eyes
starting from their heads, anxiously following his every movement. Finally, with the mingled fear and confidence that
ignorance confers, he gave a violent turn to the ship's wheel.

At this unprecedented piece of steersmanship, the good ship
Espérance leaped on the billows like a noble steed that rears when
spurred by an impetuous rider. It was as if, to show her indignation, she were determined to sink, taking her ignorant helmsman
to the bottom with her. With the relationship between the setting
of sails and helm suddenly disrupted, the vessel heeled over so
violently that it seemed she was indeed going to sink. Her long
yards plunged into the sea. Several men were knocked down; some
fell overboard. But soon the vessel rose proudly against the waves,
as if to battle once more with destruction. The wind redoubled its
efforts, and suddenly the two masts fell with a terrible crash, snapped off a few feet short of the deck, and covered it with debris
and a heavy web of rigging.

The panic-stricken negroes ran for cover beneath the hatch-
ways, crying out in terror. But now that the wind no longer

encountered any resistance, the vessel righted herself and allowed herself to be tossed lightly by the waves. The bravest of the blacks now returned to the deck and cleared it of the wreckage with which it was cluttered. Tamango stood motionless, with his elbow resting on the binnacle and his face hidden in the fold of his arm. Ayché was at his side but dared not speak to him. Little by little the blacks drew near them; a murmur arose, which soon turned into a storm of censure and abuse.

'Deceiver! Impostor!' they exclaimed. 'You are the cause of all our troubles! It was you who sold us to the white men, it was you who forced us to revolt against them. You boasted to us of your knowledge, you promised to bring us back to our country. Fools that we were, we believed you! And now we are staring death in the face because you have offended the white men's fetish!'

Tamango raised his head proudly, and the blacks who surrounded him stepped back in awe. He picked up two guns, motioned his wife to follow him, passed through the crowd, which drew back to make way for him, and headed for the vessel's bows. There he erected a kind of barricade out of empty barrels and planks; then he sat down in the middle of this sort of blockhouse, from which the bayonets of his two guns projected menacingly.

They left him in peace. Some of the rebels were weeping; others were raising their hands to the heavens, calling upon their fetishes and those of the white men. They knelt before the compass, whose ceaseless movement was a source of wonder to them, imploring it to take them back to their homeland; while the rest lay on the deck in a state of abject despondency. Among these despairing creatures were women and children howling with fright, and a score of wounded crying out for the help that no one had thought to offer them.

Suddenly a negro appeared on deck, his face radiant, and announced that he had discovered where the white men kept their brandy. From his joy and his bearing, it was evident that he had just been sampling it. This news caused the hapless blacks to leave off shouting for a moment. They ran to the store-room and gorged themselves on liquor. An hour later they were to be seen leaping about the deck, laughing and indulging in every brutish excess of drunkenness. For the rest of the day and all that night they danced and sang, to an accompaniment of groans and sobs from the wounded.

They awoke the next morning to renewed despair. During the night a number of the wounded had died. The vessel was drifting in a sea of corpses. There was a heavy swell and the sky was hazy. They took counsel. One after another, several novice magicians, who had not dared speak of their skill in Tamango's presence, offered their services. A number of potent incantations were tried. As each attempt failed their despair increased. Finally their thoughts turned to Tamango, who still had not emerged from his blockhouse. When all was said and done, he was the most knowledgeable among them, and only he could extricate them from the appalling situation in which he had placed them. An old man approached him, bearing overtures for peace. He asked him to come and advise them. But Tamango was as inflexible as Coriolanus*, and turned a deaf ear to his entreaties. During the night, amid the confusion, he had laid in a store of ship's biscuits and salt meat. He seemed determined to remain aloof in his retreat.

There was still the brandy. At least it allowed them to forget the sea, their captivity, and imminent death. They slept and dreamed of Africa, imagining forests of gum trees, straw-thatched huts, baobabs that shaded a whole village. The previous day's orgy resumed. In this way several days passed. Shouting, weeping, tearing their hair, then drowning their sorrows and sleeping: such was their life. Several died of drink; a few threw themselves into the sea or stabbed themselves.

One morning Tamango emerged from his stronghold and advanced as far as the stump of the mainmast.

'Slaves,' he said. 'The spirit has appeared to me in a dream and has shown me how to deliver you from this fate and bring you back to your country. You deserve to be abandoned for your ingratitude, but I have taken pity on these weeping women and children. I forgive you. Listen to me.'

All the blacks lowered their heads respectfully and clustered around him.

'Only the white men', continued Tamango, 'know the

powerful words that will make these great wooden houses move. But these small boats resemble those of our homeland, and we can control them as we wish.'

He was pointing to the longboat and the other small craft with which the brig was equipped.

'Let us fill them with supplies, board them, and row in the direction of the wind. My master and yours will make it blow towards our country.'

They believed him. Never was there a more insane scheme. Ignorant of the use of the compass and with no knowledge of the stars, he was doomed to rove aimlessly. He believed that if he kept rowing straight ahead he would eventually come upon some land inhabited by black men; for black men possess the land, and white men live on their ships—so his mother had told him.

Everything was soon ready for the embarkation; but only the longboat and one dinghy were seaworthy. These were not sufficient to accommodate the eighty or so negroes who still survived. All the sick and wounded had to be left behind. Most of them asked to be killed before being abandoned.

After being launched with infinite difficulty, and with too many people aboard, the two craft left the ship in a choppy sea that threatened to engulf them at any moment. The dinghy was the first to stand away. Tamango and Ayché had boarded the longboat, which, since it was much the more cumbersome and more heavily laden, soon fell a considerable way behind. The plaintive cries of some of the unfortunates who had been left on the brig were still audible when a fairly large wave struck the longboat on the broadside, filling it with water. In less than a minute it sank. The disaster was witnessed by the occupants of the dinghy, and the rowers pulled with redoubled vigour, for fear of having to pick up the survivors. Almost all those who had boarded the longboat were drowned. Only about a dozen managed to make it back to the ship. Among them were Tamango and Ayché. In the setting sun they saw the dinghy disappearing over the horizon, but what became of it, no one knows.

Why should I inflict on the reader a harrowing description of the torments of hunger? Twenty or so persons in a confined space, tossed by a stormy sea, burned by the scorching sun, squabbled daily over the meagre vestiges of their provisions. Each scrap of biscuit was fought over, and the weaker died, not because the stronger killed him, but because he left him to die. After a few days, no one was left alive on board the *Espérance* except Tamango and Ayché.

One night, the sea was stormy, a violent wind raged, and the darkness was so intense that the ship's prow was invisible from her stern. Ayché lay on a mattress in the captain's cabin, with Tamango seated at her feet. Both had been silent for some time.

'Tamango,' Ayché finally exclaimed, 'I have been the cause of all your sufferings!'

'I am not suffering,' he replied abruptly. And he threw the half-biscuit he still had left onto the mattress, by his wife's side.

'Keep it for yourself,' she said, gently pushing away the biscuit. 'I'm not hungry any more. In any case, what's the point of eating? My time has come, hasn't it?'

Tamango rose without replying, made his way unsteadily up onto the deck, and sat down at the foot of a broken mast. With his head slumped over his chest, he whistled his family's war-chant. Suddenly a great shout rang out above the noise of the wind and the sea; a light appeared. He heard more shouts, and a great black ship glided rapidly past his own, so close that her yards were directly above his head. He glimpsed two faces lit up by a lantern hanging from a mast. The men shouted again, and at once their ship was carried away by the wind and vanished into the darkness. The men on watch had undoubtedly seen the wrecked vessel, but the heavy weather made it impossible to turn about. A moment later Tamango saw the flash of a gun being fired, and heard the report; then he saw the flame from another gun, but heard no sound; then he saw nothing more.

The next day not a sail was to be seen on the horizon. Tamango lay down again on his mattress and closed his eyes. During the night his wife Ayché had died.

*

Some time afterwards a British frigate, the *Bellona*, sighted a ship with her masts down, apparently abandoned by her crew. A longboat came alongside, and on board they found a dead negress and a negro so emaciated and scrawny that he looked as if he had been mummified. He was unconscious, but there was still a flicker of life in him. The surgeon took him into his care and treated him, and by the time the *Bellona* reached Kingston, Tamango was in perfect health. He was asked to tell his story. He told them all he knew. The Jamaican planters wanted to have him hanged as a negro rebel. But the Governor, who was a humane man, took an interest in his case, finding his actions justifiable, since after all he had merely exercised his right of self-defence. Besides, the men he had killed were only Frenchmen.

They dealt with him as they usually deal with the negroes from a confiscated slave-ship: he was freed, by which I mean, made to work for the Government. But he was paid sixpence a day and his keep. He was a man of strikingly fine appearance. He came to the attention of the colonel of the 75th, who sent him to be trained as a cymbal-player in the regimental band. He learned some English, but seldom talked much. On the other hand, he drank excessive quantities of rum and tafia. He died in hospital of a chest infection.

The Etruscan Vase

(1830)

AUGUSTE SAINT-CLAIR was not liked in what people call society. The main reason for this was that he set out to please only those who pleased him. These he cultivated, the rest he avoided. To make matters worse, he was absent-minded and indolent. One evening, as he was leaving the Théâtre-Italien, the Marquise A—— asked him what he had thought of Mademoiselle Sontag's singing*. 'Yes, madame,' replied Saint-Clair, smiling graciously and with his mind on other things. This preposterous reply could not be ascribed to timidity, for he was accustomed to addressing members of the nobility, great men, and even women of fashion with as much aplomb as if he had been conversing with an equal. The Marquise concluded that Saint-Clair was monstrously impertinent and conceited.

One Monday, Madame B—— invited him to dine. She talked with him a good deal, and on leaving her house he declared that he had never met a more agreeable woman. Madame B—— would spend a month amassing witticisms at other people's houses, then squander them all in her own home in the course of an evening. Saint-Clair saw her again on the Thursday of the same week. This time he was a trifle bored. One further visit determined him never to set foot in her salon again. Madame B—— bruited it about that Saint-Clair was an ill-mannered young man and totally lacking in the social graces.

He had been born with a tender and loving heart; but at an age at which one all too readily forms impressions that last a lifetime, his over-emotional nature had earned him the mockery of his comrades. Proud and ambitious, he set great store by the good opinion of others, as children do. From that time on he was at pains to conceal any outward signs of what he regarded as a humiliating weakness. He achieved his aim, but his victory cost him dear. He was able to conceal from others the emotions of an over-affectionate heart, but, by bottling them up, he made them a hundred times more painful. When he was in company he was dismissed as insensitive and frivolous; and when he was alone his restless imagination devised torments for himself that were all the harder to bear since nothing would have induced him to reveal them to another living soul.

Truly, how difficult it is to find a friend!

Difficult? Is it possible? Were there ever two men who had no secrets from one another? Saint-Clair had no faith in friendship, and people knew it. The young men with whom he mixed regarded him as cold and reserved. He never questioned them about their secrets; yet all his thoughts and most of his actions were a closed book to them. The French like talking about themselves; consequently, Saint-Clair was the reluctant repository of a good many confidences. His friends (this word is used of anyone we see more than once a week) complained of his unwillingness to confide in them; and indeed, someone who, without being requested to do so, shares his secret with us, usually takes umbrage if we fail to return the compliment. People take it for granted that their indiscretion should be reciprocated.

'That fellow Saint-Clair's as tight as a clam,' Alphonse de Thémines, a handsome cavalry captain, remarked one day. 'I'll never feel able to trust him with the smallest confidence.'

'I believe he's something of a Jesuit,' Jules Lambert chipped in. 'I heard someone swear blind he'd met him twice coming out of Saint-Sulpice. It's impossible to tell what he's thinking. Personally, I shall never feel at ease with him.'

They separated. On the Boulevard Italien Alphonse ran into Saint-Clair, walking with his head down and with eyes for no one. Alphonse stopped him, took him by the arm, and before they had reached the rue de la Paix he had given him a blow-by-blow account of his affaire with Madame ——, whose husband is so jealous and so brutal.

That same evening Jules Lambert lost all his money at écarté, whereupon he went off dancing. While dancing he brushed against another man who had also lost all his money, and who was in an extremely bad mood as a consequence. This led to a sharp exchange of words and a challenge to a duel. Jules asked Saint-Clair to act as his second and, whilst he was about it, borrowed some money from him, which he never did remember to repay.

When all is said and done, Saint-Clair was a fairly easy chap to get on with. His faults harmed no one but himself. He was obliging, often good company, seldom boring. He had travelled a lot, read a lot, and never spoke of his travels and his reading unless pressed to do so. Added to which, he was tall and handsome, with an expression that was noble and intelligent, though almost always too serious, and a captivating smile.

I was forgetting one important point: Saint-Clair was something of a ladies' man, and preferred their conversation to that of men. Was he in love? That was the question. But one thing was sure: that, if this aloof individual was in love, then the object of his preference must be the pretty Countess Mathilde de Coursy.

She was a young widow at whose home he was always to be seen. The following evidence was cited as proof of their intimacy: first, Saint-Clair's almost ceremonious politeness towards the Countess, and vice versa; secondly, the fact that he went out of his way never to utter her name in public, or, if obliged to refer to her, never commended her in any way; thirdly, the fact that, before being introduced to her, Saint-Clair had been a passionate lover of music, whereas the Countess had been equally fond of painting (since their meeting, their tastes had changed); lastly, that when the Countess had gone to take the waters the previous year, Saint-Clair had followed on six days later.

It is my duty as a historian to report that one July night, shortly before dawn, the garden gate of a house in the country opened, and a man emerged from it stealthily, like a thief who is afraid of being caught in the act. The house belonged to Madame de Coursy, and the man was Saint-Clair. A woman wrapped in a pelisse accompanied him to the gate, and craned her neck forward so as to have the pleasure of seeing him for a little longer, whilst he walked away down the lane that ran along the garden wall. Saint-Clair halted, glanced about him in a circumspect manner, and motioned the woman to go back indoors. The sky that summer night was light enough to enable him to make out her pale face, still watching him, motionless in the same spot. He retraced his steps, went back up to her, and embraced her tenderly. He had been intending to get her to go back indoors, but he still had a hundred and one things to say to her. They had been conversing for ten minutes when they heard the voice of a peasant going off to work in the fields. A kiss was exchanged, the gate closed, and in one stride Saint-Clair found himself at the end of the lane.

He was following a path with which he seemed to be familiar. At times he fairly bounded for joy, taking swipes at the bushes with his cane as he ran; then suddenly he would stop or slow to a saunter, looking up at the sky which was starting to turn crimson in the east. In short, to see him, you would have taken him for a madman, delirious with joy at having broken out of his cell.

After walking for half an hour he found himself at the door of a small, isolated house he had rented for the summer. He had a key. He entered, then threw himself on to a large sofa, where he lay gazing into space, with a gentle smile playing about his lips, sunk in a reverie. At that moment, his only thoughts were happy ones.

'How happy I am!' he kept saying to himself. 'At last I've found a heart that understands mine!—Yes, I've found my ideal. I've found someone who is a friend as well as a mistress. What a strong character! What a passionate soul! To be sure, she never loved anyone before she met me.'

Soon (for vanity always worms its way into the affairs of this world) he thought: 'She is the most beautiful woman in Paris.' And he mentally reviewed her charms. 'She chose me from among so many. She had the élite of society for her admirers. That colonel in the Hussars who is so handsome and so gallant, without being too conceited. That young author who paints such exquisite watercolours and who's such a good comic actor. That Russian Lovelace who served under Diebitsch* in the Balkans. And most of all, Camille T——, who's an intelligent fellow if ever there was one, and has elegant manners and a fine sabre scar on his forehead. She sent them all packing!' Then came the refrain: 'How happy I am! How happy I am!' And he got up, opened the window—for he was stifling—paced the room, then curled up on his sofa.

A happy lover is almost as insufferable as an unhappy lover. A friend of mine, who often found himself in one or other of these states, discovered that the only way he could get me to listen to him was to treat me to a first-class midday meal, during which he was free to talk of his amours, on the strict understanding that, after the coffee, we would talk of other things.

As I cannot take all my readers out to lunch, I shall spare them Saint-Clair's amorous musings. Besides, one cannot remain up in the clouds for ever. Saint-Clair was tired. He yawned, stretched, saw that it was broad daylight. It was high time to get some sleep. When he awoke, he looked at his watch and saw that he barely had time to dress and dash off to Paris, where he was invited to a luncheon party with various other young men of his acquaintance.

They had just uncorked another bottle of champagne. I leave it to the reader to decide how many had preceded it. Suffice it to say that the stage had been reached—it comes all too soon at a bachelor dinner—when everyone wants to speak at once, and when those who can take their drink begin to fear for those who cannot.

'I wish', said Alphonse de Thémines, who never let an opportunity to talk about England slip by, 'that it were the fashion in Paris, as it is in London, for everyone to propose a toast to his mistress. That way we would know just who our friend Saint-Clair is pining for.' And as he spoke he refilled his own and his neighbours' glasses.

Somewhat embarrassed, Saint-Clair was preparing to reply when Jules Lambert forestalled him. 'I thoroughly approve of the custom,' he said, 'and I hereby adopt it.' And, raising his glass, he said: 'To all the milliners in Paris! I of course exclude those over the age of 30, the one-eyed, the crippled, and so forth.'

'Hurray! Hurray!' shouted the young anglophiles.

Saint-Clair rose, glass in hand. 'Gentlemen,' he said, 'my

heart is not as capacious as that of our friend Jules, but it is more constant. My constancy is all the more commendable in that for some time now I have been separated from the lady of my affections. However, I'm sure that you will all approve my choice, always supposing, of course, that you are not already my rivals. Gentlemen, I give you Judith Pasta!* May it not be long before Europe's foremost tragic actress visits us again!'

Thémines wanted to find fault with the toast, but was silenced by the cheers. Having parried this thrust, Saint-Clair thought he could breathe freely for the rest of the day.

The conversation then turned to the theatre. By way of theatrical censorship they got on to politics. From the Duke of Wellington they shifted to English horses, and from horses to women, by an association of ideas that is readily comprehensible; since the two most desirable possessions for a young man are first a fine horse, and secondly a pretty mistress.

Then they talked of the ways in which one might acquire these eminently desirable objects. A horse one can buy. One can buy women too, but of that sort the less said the better. After modestly pleading his lack of experience on this delicate matter, Saint-Clair concluded that the prerequisite for attracting a woman is to stand out from the crowd, to be in some way exceptional. But was there a standard method for making oneself exceptional? He thought not.

'So you mean', said Jules, 'that a cripple or a hunchback is more likely to attract a woman than a healthy man with a normal physique?'

'You're taking the argument to its logical conclusion,' Saint-Clair replied. 'But if I must, I am prepared to accept the full consequences of my proposition. You can rest assured that, if I were a hunchback, for instance, rather than blowing my brains out, I'd set out to make a few conquests. To start with I would concentrate on two kinds of women: those who are genuinely sensitive, and those—there are many of them—who like to think of themselves as original—"eccentric", the English call it. To the first I would depict the horror of my situation, nature's cruelty to me. I would try to make them pity my lot in life, I'd let them begin to suspect I was capable of passionate love. I would kill one of my rivals in a duel, then take a mild overdose of laudanum. In a few months they would have ceased to notice my deformity, whereupon I would be watching out for the first onset of affection. As for those women who regard themselves as eccentric, their hearts are easily won. Just insist that it is a hard and fast rule that a hunchback cannot be happy in love. They will immediately want to prove you wrong.'

'Quite the Don Juan!' exclaimed Jules.

'Gentlemen,' said Colonel Beaujeu, 'since we had the misfortune not to be born hunchbacks, let's cripple ourselves instead!'

'I wholeheartedly concur with Saint-Clair's opinion,' said Hector Roquantin, who was barely 3 feet 6 inches tall. 'Never a day goes by without the most beautiful and fashionable women giving themselves to men it would never occur to you handsome chaps to think of as your rivals.'

'Hector, get up, please, and ring for some more wine,' said Thémines with the utmost composure.

The dwarf rose to his feet, and everyone thought with amusement of the fable of the fox that had had its tail cut off.*

'Personally,' said Thémines, resuming the conversation, 'the longer I live the more I'm convinced that tolerably good looks'—and as he said this he glanced complacently at himself in the mirror opposite—'. . . tolerably good looks and good taste in clothes are the exceptional qualities guaranteed to win over the most hard-hearted.' And, with a flick of his finger, he dislodged a breadcrumb that had fallen on the lapel of his jacket.

'Bah!' exclaimed the dwarf, 'good looks and a suit of clothes from Staub* will get you the sort of women you keep for a week and tire of the second time you see them. If you want to be loved—really loved—you need more than that. You need . . .'

'All right,' Thémines interrupted. 'Do you want a perfect illustration? You all knew Massigny; you all know what sort of a fellow he was—manners like an English stable-boy, about as much conversation as his horse. But he was as handsome as Adonis and wore his cravat like Beau Brummell. All in all, he was the most boring individual I've ever met.'

'He almost bored me to death,' said Colonel Beaujeu. 'Can you imagine, I once had to travel two hundred leagues with him.'

'Did you hear', Saint-Clair asked, 'that he was responsible for the death of poor old Richard Thornton, whom you all knew?'

'But surely you know', Jules replied, 'that he was killed by brigands near Fondi?'

'Quite so. But as you'll see, Massigny was at least an accessory to the crime. A number of travellers, including Thornton, had arranged to travel to Naples in a group as a protection against brigands. Massigny wanted to join their party. As soon as Thornton got wind of this he went on ahead, aghast, I suppose, at the prospect of spending all those days with him. He set off alone, and the rest you know.'

'Thornton was right,' said Thémines. 'Of the two deaths he chose the more merciful. Anyone else would have done the same in his place.' Then, after a pause, he continued: 'Will you grant me, then, that Massigny was the most boring man on earth?'

'Granted!' the company exclaimed unanimously.

'Let's not exclude anyone unfairly,' said Jules. 'Let's make an exception for ****, especially when he's expounding his political theories.'

'You will likewise grant me', Thémines went on, 'that Madame de Coursy is an intelligent woman if ever there was one?'

There was a moment's silence. Saint-Clair lowered his head and felt that everyone was looking at him.

'Who could doubt it?' he said at length, still bowed over his plate and apparently engrossed in studying the flowers painted on the china.

'I maintain,' said Jules, raising his voice, 'I maintain that she's one of the three most attractive women in Paris.'

'I knew her husband,' said the Colonel. 'He often used to show me charming letters from his wife.'

'Auguste,' Hector Roquantin interrupted. 'You must

introduce me to the Countess. They say that you rule the roost in her household.'

'At the end of the autumn, when she's back in Paris . . .' murmured Saint-Clair. 'I . . . don't think she receives visitors in the country.'

'Will you kindly listen?' shouted Thémines. Silence was restored. Saint-Clair shifted on his seat like a prisoner in the dock.

'You didn't see the Countess three years ago, Saint-Clair, you were in Germany at the time,' Alphonse de Thémines continued with exasperating composure. 'You can't imagine what she was like then—beautiful and fresh as a rose, incredibly vivacious, and as bright as a butterfly. Well then, which of her numerous admirers do you suppose was honoured with her favours? Massigny! The stupidest and most dull-witted of men made the most brilliant of women fall in love with him. Do you really think a hunchback could have achieved as much? Come, take my word for it—a handsome face, a good tailor, and take your courage in both hands!'

Saint-Clair was in an appalling position. He was on the point of flatly denying the truth of the allegation; but the fear of compromising the Countess restrained him. He would have liked to say something in her defence, but he was at a loss for words. His lips quivered with rage, and he racked his brains in vain for some roundabout way of starting a quarrel.

'What!' exclaimed Jules, astonished. 'Do you mean to say that Madame de Coursy gave herself to Massigny? *Frailty, thy name is woman*!*'

'Of course, a woman's reputation is of so little consequence', said Saint-Clair in a tone of dry contempt, 'that it's quite permissible to destroy it for the sake of some clever remark, and . . .'

As he spoke, he recalled with horror an Etruscan vase he had seen a hundred times on the Countess's mantelpiece in Paris. He knew that it had been a present from Massigny on his return from Italy; and—what made it worse—when she left Paris for the country she had taken the vase with her. And every evening Mathilde would remove the bouquet from her dress and place it in the Etruscan vase.

The words died on his lips. He now saw and thought of only one thing: the Etruscan vase.

'Conclusive proof!' the critic will scoff. 'Just imagine anyone suspecting his mistress for such a trivial reason!'

My dear Critic, have you ever been in love?

Thémines was in too good a mood to take offence at the tone Saint-Clair had adopted towards him. He replied with easy good humour: 'I'm simply repeating what people said in society. At the time you were in Germany, nobody doubted the truth of it. Besides, I hardly know Madame de Coursy; it's eighteen months since I called on her. It's possible I was misinformed and that Massigny lied to me. To get back to the point we were discussing, even if the particular example I've just given is untrue, the fact remains that I'm right. You all know that the most brilliant woman in France, whose works . . .'

The door opened and Théodore Néville walked in. He had recently returned from Egypt.

'Théodore! Back so soon?' He was besieged with questions.

'Have you brought back a real Turkish costume?' asked Thémines. 'Have you got an Arab horse and an Egyptian groom?'

'What sort of a man is the Pasha?' asked Jules. 'When will he declare independence?* Did you see anyone beheaded with a single sword-stroke?'

'What about the almehs?*' asked Roquantin. 'Are the women in Cairo beautiful?'

'Did you see General L——?' asked Colonel Beaujeu. 'How has he organized the Pasha's army? Did Colonel C—— give you a sword for me?'

'What about the pyramids?'

'And the Nile cataracts?'

'The statue of Memnon?'

'And Ibrahim Pasha?*'

Et cetera, et cetera. Everyone was talking at once. Saint-Clair thought only of the Etruscan vase.

Théodore, who had sat down cross-legged—a habit he had picked up in Egypt and was finding it hard to rid himself of in France—waited for his questioners to tire, whereupon he answered them as follows, speaking rapidly enough to make it difficult for anyone to interrupt him.

'The pyramids? Gad, sir, a *regular humbug*! They're nowhere near as high as people suppose. Why, the spire of Strasbourg Cathedral is only four metres lower. I'm sick to death of antiquities. Don't even mention them to me. The very sight of a hieroglyph would make me pass out. The place is full of travellers curious about such things. Personally, what interested me was the appearance and customs of the bizarre blend of peoples that throng the streets of Alexandria and Cairo—Turks, Bedouin, Copts, fellahin, moghrabbin, and what have you.* I made a few hasty notes while I was in quarantine. What an abominable experience that was! I hope none of you fellows is afraid of catching something! I just sat there calmly, smoking my pipe, surrounded by three hundred plague victims. Ah, Colonel, what a fine body of cavalry they've got there, so well mounted! I'll show you some superb weapons I brought back with me. I have a djerid that belonged to the famous Mourad Bey.* I have a yataghan for you, Colonel, and a khandjar for Auguste. You shall see my mashlah, my burnous, and my haik.* Do you know, I could have brought some women back if I'd wanted to? Ibrahim Pasha has shipped so many over from Greece that you can pick 'em up for a song. But you know what my mother is like. . . . I talked a lot with the Pasha. He's a clever chap, by Jove; no prejudices. You can't imagine how thoroughly he understands our affairs. Gad, sir, he knows every smallest secret of our Government. I picked up some priceless information about the state of the parties in France from talking to him. He's taking a lot of interest in statistics at the moment. He subscribes to all our newspapers. Do you realize, he's a rabid Bonapartist! He's forever going on about Napoleon. "Ah, what a great man, your *Bounabardo*!" he said to me. *Bounabardo* is what they call Bonaparte.'

'*Giourdina, c'est-à-dire Jourdain*',* murmured Thémines under his breath.

'At first,' continued Théodore, 'Muhammad Ali was extremely cold with me. You know how extremely suspicious the Turks always are. He took me for a spy, would you believe, or a Jesuit. He can't abide the Jesuits. But after a few visits he realized I was an open-minded traveller, anxious to get a genuine insight into the customs, morals, and politics of the East. At that he unbent and spoke openly to me. During my last audience—it was the third he had granted me—I took the liberty of saying to him, "I cannot imagine why Your Highness does not declare himself independent of the Porte."—"By Heaven," he said to me, "I would gladly do so, but I'm afraid that the liberal newspapers, which control everything in your country, will not support me if I proclaim Egyptian independence." He's a handsome old man, with a fine white beard, who never laughs. He gave me some excellent sweetmeats. But of all the things I gave him, the one that pleased him most was Charlet's collection of illustrations* depicting the uniforms of the Imperial Guard.'

'Is the Pasha a Romantic?' asked Thémines.

'He takes little interest in literature. But of course you know that the literature of the Arabs is intensely Romantic. They have a poet called Melek Ayatalnefous-Ebn-Esraf who recently published a set of *Meditations* which make Lamartine's seem like classical prose.* On my arrival in Cairo I engaged an Arabic teacher, with whom I began to read the Koran. Although I only took a few lessons, I learned enough to grasp the sublimities of the Prophet's style, and to realize how bad all our translations are. Look, do you want to see some Arabic script? This word in gold letters is *Allah*, which means "God".'

As he spoke he pointed to an extremely grubby letter he had taken from a scented silk purse.

'How long did you spend in Egypt?' asked Thémines.

'Six weeks.'

And the traveller continued to hold forth, describing everything *from the cedar tree even unto the hyssop*.* Almost immediately after his arrival Saint-Clair left and headed back to his house in the country. His horse's impetuous gallop prevented him from thinking coherently. But he felt obscurely that his happiness in this world had been destroyed for ever, and that he had a dead man and an Etruscan vase to thank for it.

When he reached home he threw himself onto the sofa on

which, the night before, he had analysed his happiness at such
exquisite length. The idea he had cherished most fondly was
that, unlike other women, his mistress had never loved, and
never could love, anyone but him. Now this beautiful dream
was fading in the face of the sad and harsh reality. 'I am enjoying the favours of a beautiful woman, and nothing more. She
is intelligent. That only makes her the more to blame. She was
capable of loving Massigny! Granted, she loves me now, with
all her heart, in so far as she is capable of love. She loves me
as she loved Massigny! She yielded to my attentions, to my
blandishments, to my importuning. But I was mistaken.
There was no affinity between our hearts. Massigny or me, it
makes little difference to her. He was handsome, she loved
him for that. Sometimes my lady finds me entertaining. Very
well, she said to herself, I might as well love Saint-Clair, since
the other one is dead. And if Saint-Clair dies, or becomes
tedious, then we shall see!'

I firmly believe that when some unfortunate wretch tortures
himself in this way, the Devil is there, invisible, eavesdrop-
ping. It provides an entertaining spectacle for the enemy of
mankind. And when the victim feels his wounds healing the
Devil is there to open them again.

Saint-Clair seemed to hear a voice murmuring in his ear:

> . . . *the singular honour*
> *To be the successor* . . .

He sat up and stared wildly around him. How happy he
would have been to find someone there in his room! He would
probably have torn him limb from limb.

The clock struck eight. The Countess was expecting him at
half past. Supposing he failed to keep the assignation? Come
to think of it, why should he bother to see Massigny's mistress
again? He lay down again on the sofa and closed his eyes. 'I
shall go to sleep', he thought. He lay still for half a minute,
then leaped to his feet and ran to the clock to see what time
it was.

'How I wish it were half-past eight!' he thought. 'Then it
would be too late to go and see her.' In his heart of hearts he

knew he had not the courage to stay at home. He wanted some pretext. He wished he had been seriously ill. He walked about the room, then sat down and picked up a book, but could not read a line. He sat at his piano and could not summon the strength to open it. He whistled, he gazed at the clouds, he tried to count the poplars outside his windows. At last he went back to look at the clock and found that less than three minutes had elapsed.

'I cannot prevent myself from loving her!' he exclaimed, grinding his teeth and stamping his foot. 'I am hers to command, I am her slave, as Massigny was before me! Well, then, wretch that you are, obey, since you haven't enough courage to break this chain that you detest!' He took his hat and rushed out.

When a passion gets the better of us, our wounded self-esteem finds some consolation in viewing our weakness from a position of pride. 'It's true that I'm being weak,' we tell ourselves. 'But, if I wished to be otherwise . . .'

He was slowly making his way up the path that led to the garden gate, and while still some distance away he could see a woman's white face clearly visible against the dark of the trees. In her hand she held a handkerchief which she waved as if motioning to him. His heart was pounding, his knees trembled. He did not have the strength to speak, and he had become so timid that he was afraid lest the Countess should detect his ill humour from his expression.

He took the hand she held out to him, kissed her on the forehead (for she had pressed herself against his breast), and followed her into her rooms, silent, struggling to suppress the sighs which, it seemed, must rend his breast.

The Countess's boudoir was lit by a single candle. They both sat down. Saint-Clair noticed that his lady was wearing a single rose in her hair. The night before, he had presented her with a fine English engraving of Lely's portrait showing the Duchess of Portland with her hair dressed in this way,* with the words: 'I prefer that simple rose to all your elaborate coiffures.' He was not fond of jewellery, and took the same view as the lord who used coarsely to observe, 'Women in their finery and caparisoned horses, the Devil himself wouldn't recognize them.' The night before, while fidgeting with one of the Countess's pearl necklaces (for he always needed to be holding something when he was talking), he had said:

'Jewels are only good for hiding blemishes. You are too pretty to need them, Mathilde.'

That evening the Countess, who heeded even his most casual remarks, had left off her rings, necklaces, ear-rings, and bracelets.

The first thing he noticed about a woman's toilette was her footwear, and, like so many other men, he had his own very definite ideas on the subject. Before sunset there had been a heavy shower. The grass was still quite wet. Yet the Countess had been walking on the damp sward in her silk stockings and black satin shoes. Supposing she were to catch a chill?

'She loves me,' Saint-Clair told himself, and, thinking of himself and his folly, he sighed and looked at Mathilde, unable to suppress a smile, torn between his ill humour and the pleasure of seeing an attractive woman doing her best to please him in all those little ways that lovers prize so highly.

Meanwhile, the Countess's expression radiated a mixture of love and playful mischievousness which only made her the more adorable. She took something from a Japanese lacquered casket and, holding out her little hand with the object concealed in her clenched fist, she said:

'The other day I broke your watch. Here it is, repaired.'

She returned the watch to him and looked at him with an expression at once tender and mischievous, biting her lower lip as if to prevent herself from laughing. Heavens! how beautiful her teeth were! How brilliantly they contrasted with the deep pink of her lips! (How foolish a man looks when he remains unmoved by a beautiful woman's blandishments.)

Saint-Clair thanked her, took the watch, and was about to place it in his pocket.

'Go on,' she continued. 'Look at it. Open it and see whether it's been repaired properly. You're so knowledgeable, you've studied at the École Polytechnique*, you ought to take a look at it.'

'Oh, I don't know much about such things,' said Saint-Clair. And without much interest he opened the watch-case. What was his surprise to discover a miniature portrait of

Madame de Coursy painted on the inside! How could he continue to sulk now? His expression grew radiant. He thought no more of Massigny. He remembered only that he was in the company of an attractive woman, and one who adored him . . .

The lark, the herald of the morn,* was beginning to sing, and long streaks of pale light tinged the clouds in the east. It was at this hour that Romeo bade farewell to Juliet. It is the moment when lovers traditionally take their leave of one another.

Saint-Clair was standing in front of a mantelpiece with the key to the garden in his hand, gazing intently at the Etruscan vase we have already mentioned. At the bottom of his heart he still bore it a grudge; but he was in a good humour, and he was beginning to consider the simple possibility that Thémines might have been lying. While the Countess, who wanted to escort him to the garden gate, was wrapping a shawl around her head, he tapped the detested vase with the key, at first gently, then progressively harder, so as to lead one to suppose that he was going to shatter it at any moment.

'Oh, do please be careful!' exclaimed Mathilde. 'You'll break my lovely Etruscan vase!' And she snatched the key from his hand.

Saint-Clair was extremely annoyed; but he submitted. He turned his back to the mantelpiece so as not to yield to temptation, and, opening his watch, began to contemplate the portrait he had just been given.

'Who is the artist?' he asked.

'Monsieur R——. Why, it was Massigny who brought him to my attention. Since his visit to Rome, Massigny had discovered he had excellent taste in art, and he set himself up as Maecenas to all the young artists. Really, I think it's a good likeness, though it does flatter me somewhat.'

Saint-Clair felt like hurling the watch against the wall so as to render it well and truly irreparable. However, he controlled himself and replaced it in his pocket; then, noticing that it was already daylight, he walked out of the house, entreated Mathilde not to accompany him, strode across the garden, and a moment later was alone in the open fields.

'Massigny! Massigny!' he cried with concentrated fury.

'Will I find you everywhere? Of course, the artist who painted that portrait painted another one for Massigny too! Fool that I was! For a moment I supposed that I was loved as deeply as I myself love, merely because she wore a rose in her hair and left off her jewellery! She's got a whole desk full of the stuff! Massigny, whose only concern was the way women dressed—how fond he was of jewellery! Yes, she's accommodating, I'll say that for her. She knows how to adapt to her lovers' tastes. Great God, I'd a hundred times rather she was a courtesan who had given herself for money. Then at least I could believe that she loves me, since she is my mistress and I pay her nothing.'

Soon another thought, still more distressing, came into his head. In a few weeks the Countess would be coming out of mourning. Saint-Clair was intending to marry her as soon as her year of widowhood was over. He had given his promise. Promise? Not so; he had never spoken of it. But such had been his intention, and the Countess had been aware of it. He felt he had as good as given his word. The day before, he would have given a kingdom to hasten the moment when he could publicly avow his love; now he shuddered at the very thought of sharing his future with Massigny's erstwhile mistress.

'And yet I must!' he told himself. 'It must be so. I suppose she thought, poor woman, that I was aware of her past intrigue—they say it was common knowledge. In any case, she does not know me, she is incapable of understanding me. She supposes I love her only as Massigny loved her.'

Then, not without pride, he told himself: 'For three months she has made me the happiest of men. The rest of my life is a small price to pay for that happiness.'

He did not go to bed, and rode through the woods all that morning. Down a lane in the Forest of Verrières he saw a man astride a fine English horse, who hailed him from afar and at once accosted him. It was Alphonse de Thémines. Solitude is particularly welcome when one is in the frame of mind in which Saint-Clair found himself: consequently, his meeting with Thémines changed his irritation into a smouldering rage. Thémines was unaware of this, or else took a malicious delight in vexing him. He talked, laughed, and joked without noticing that his companion remained unresponsive. Seeing a narrow ride, Saint-Clair at once led his horse down it, hoping that this intrusive fellow would not follow him. But he was mistaken. A bore does not so easily relinquish his prey. Thémines turned his horse's head and quickened his pace so as to catch up with Saint-Clair and continue the conversation more comfortably.

I have said that the ride was a narrow one. It was scarcely wide enough for two horses to walk abreast. So it was hardly surprising that, although an excellent horseman, Thémines brushed against Saint-Clair's foot as he drew level with him. Saint-Clair, whose rage had reached fever pitch, could no longer control himself; he rose in his stirrups and struck Thémines's horse hard across the nose with his riding crop.

'What the devil are you playing at, Auguste?' exclaimed Thémines. 'Why are you striking my horse?'

'Why are you following me?' stormed Saint-Clair.

'Have you taken leave of your senses, Saint-Clair? Have you forgotten who it is you are talking to?'

'I know only too well that I'm talking to a conceited ass.'

'Saint-Clair! You must be mad. Listen here, you have until tomorrow to apologize to me, or else you will answer for your impertinence.'

'Until tomorrow then, sir.'

Thémines reined in his horse; Saint-Clair urged his forward. Soon he vanished into the forest.

He felt calmer now. A belief in premonitions was a failing of his. He felt that he would be killed the next day, in which case it would be a fitting end for one in his situation. One more day to live through; then tomorrow, no more anxieties, no more torments. He returned home, gave his servant a note to deliver to Colonel Beaujeu, wrote a few letters, then ate a hearty dinner and, punctually at half-past eight, presented himself at the little garden gate.

'What's the matter with you today, Auguste?' asked the Countess. 'You are strangely exhilarated, yet for all your jokes I don't feel like laughing. Yesterday you were a bit glum, and

I was so cheerful! Today we've exchanged roles. The fact is, I've got a fearful headache.'

'Yes, my darling, I admit I was extremely tiresome yesterday. But I went out riding today, and now that I've taken some exercise I'm feeling on excellent form.'

'Whereas I got up late, I overslept this morning, and I had bad dreams.'

'Bad dreams? Do you believe in dreams?'

'Perish the thought!'

'I believe in them. I'll wager you dreamt that something dreadful was going to happen.'

'Heavens, I never remember my dreams. Though, come to think of it, I do remember dreaming of Massigny. So you see, it wasn't a very entertaining dream.'

'Massigny! On the contrary, I should have thought it would have given you great pleasure to see him again.'

'Poor Massigny!'

'Poor Massigny?'

'Auguste, will you please tell me what's the matter with you this evening. There's something diabolical about your smile. You seem to be mocking yourself.'

'Ah, now you're treating me as badly as those old dowagers you're so friendly with.'

'You know, Auguste, today you've got the same expression you wear when you're with people you dislike.'

'Don't be malicious! Come, give me your hand!' He kissed her hand with ironic gallantry, and they stared at one another for a moment. Saint-Clair was the first to avert his gaze. He exclaimed:

'How difficult it is to live in this world without being thought ill-intentioned! We ought never to speak of anything except the weather and hunting, or else spend our time talking to those old ladies of yours about the budgets of their charitable committees.'

He picked up a piece of paper lying on a table. 'Why, here's a bill from your fine-laundress. Let's talk about that, my dearest. Then you won't be able to accuse me of being ill-intentioned.'

'Really, Auguste, you amaze me.'

'This spelling here reminds me of a letter I found this

morning. I should explain, I've been sorting through my papers—I need to put things in order occasionally. Anyway, I came across a love letter written to me by a seamstress I was in love with when I was 16. She has her own inimitable way of spelling, with every word as complicated as possible. Her style is worthy of her spelling. Well, at that time I had rather a high opinion of myself, and I thought that any mistress who didn't write like Madame de Sévigné was unworthy of me, so I broke it off with her. Reading her letter again today, I realized that that seamstress must really have loved me.'

'What? A woman you kept?'

'In the lap of luxury, on fifty francs a month! But my guardian didn't give me much of an allowance. He used to say that a young man with money is the ruin of himself and of others.'

'And what became of this woman?'

'How should I know? I expect she died in the workhouse.'

'Auguste, if that were true you wouldn't talk about it in that offhand way.'

'If you must know, she made a respectable marriage. And when I came of age I made over a small dowry to her.'

'How kind you are! Why do you want to appear ill-natured?'

'Oh, very kind. . . . The more I think about it, the more I'm convinced that girl really did love me. But at the time I couldn't see the sincere feeling that lay beneath the ridiculous exterior.'

'You should have brought your letter along with you. I wouldn't have been jealous. Women are more sensitive to these things than men, and we can tell at once from the style of a letter whether the writer is sincere or feigning a passion he does not feel.'

'And yet, how often you allow yourselves to be ensnared by fools or conceited idiots!'

As he spoke he was looking at the Etruscan vase, and in his eyes and voice there was something sinister that Mathilde did not notice.

'Come now! Every man likes to think of himself as a Don Juan. You suppose you are taking us in, whereas often you only find a Doña Juana even more artful than you.'

'I can imagine that, with your superior intellect, you ladies

can detect a fool a mile off. So I don't doubt that our friend
Massigny, who was both a fool and a conceited idiot, died a
virgin and martyr.'

'Massigny? But he wasn't that foolish. Besides, there are
foolish women too. Let me tell you a story about Massigny—
but I must already have told it to you, surely?'

'Never,' Saint-Clair replied falteringly.

'On his return from Italy Massigny fell in love with me.
My husband knew him. He introduced him to me as a man of
intelligence and taste. The two of them were made for one
another. At first Massigny courted me assiduously. He gave
me watercolours he'd bought at Schroth's*, passing them off
as his own work, and he talked to me about music and painting, in a superior way that was most entertaining. One day
he sent me the most astonishing letter. In it he wrote, amongst
other things, that I was the most respectable woman in Paris,
which was why he wanted to become my lover. I showed the
letter to my cousin Julie. We were both quite reckless then,
and we decided to play a trick on him. One evening we had
a number of visitors, including Massigny. My cousin said to
me: "I'm going to read you a declaration of love I received this
morning." She took the letter and read it out amidst gales of
laughter. Poor Massigny!'

Saint-Clair fell to his knees with a cry of joy. He seized the
Countess's hand and smothered it with kisses and tears.
Mathilde was speechless with astonishment, and thought at
first he must be ill. Saint-Clair could say nothing but "Forgive
me! Forgive me!" At last he got up. He was ecstatic. At that
moment he was happier than he had been when Mathilde first
said to him, 'I love you.'

'I am the most foolish and guilty of men,' he exclaimed. 'For
two days I suspected you, yet I made no attempt to talk it over
with you.'

'You suspected me? And of what, pray?'

'What a wretch I am! I was told you'd been in love with
Massigny, and . . .'

'Massigny!' And she began to laugh. Then, at once regaining her composure, she said:

'Auguste, how could you be so foolish as to entertain such

suspicions, and such a hypocrite as to conceal them from me!'
Tears welled in her eyes.

'I beg you, forgive me!'

'How could I do otherwise, my love? But first let me swear
to you . . .'

'I believe you, I believe you. Say no more.'

'But what in Heaven's name could have induced you to suppose anything so unlikely?'

'Nothing, nothing whatsoever but my confounded imagination and, and . . . You know that Etruscan vase? I knew it had
been given to you by Massigny.'

The Countess clasped her hands in amazement. Then, amid
peals of laughter, she exclaimed:

'My Etruscan vase! My Etruscan vase!'

Saint-Clair could not prevent himself from laughing too,
though the tears were pouring down his cheeks. He seized
Mathilde in his arms and said: 'I shall not let you go until you
have forgiven me.'

'Yes, I forgive you, great fool that you are!' she said, kissing
him tenderly. 'How happy you've made me today; this is the
first time I've ever seen you cry. I thought you never wept.'

Then, freeing herself from his embrace, she seized the
Etruscan vase and hurled it to the floor, shattering it into a
thousand fragments. (It was a rare piece, and had never been
catalogued. On it was depicted, in three colours, a combat
between a Lapith and a Centaur.)

For a few hours Saint-Clair was the most ashamed and the
happiest of men.

'So the news is true, then?' Roquantin asked Colonel Beaujeu,
meeting him that evening at the Café Tortoni.

'Only too true, old boy,' replied the Colonel sadly.

'Tell me how it happened.'

'Oh, everything went off according to form. Saint-Clair
began by telling me he was in the wrong, but that he wanted
to face Thémines's fire before apologizing to him. I could not
but approve. Thémines wanted to draw lots to see who should
fire first. Saint-Clair insisted it should be Thémines. Thémines
fired; I saw Saint-Clair spin round once and fall down stone

dead. I've noticed before how soldiers who have been shot often spin round in that strange way before dying.'

'Most extraordinary,' said Roquantin. 'And what did Thémines do?'

'Oh, the only thing one can do in such circumstances. He threw his pistol to the ground in remorse. He threw it down so hard that the hammer broke. It was a Manton pistol, from England. I don't know whether he'll be able to get it repaired here in Paris.'

The Countess saw no one for three whole years. Winter and summer she remained in her house in the country, seldom leaving her room, waited on by a mulatto woman who knew of her liaison with Saint-Clair, and to whom she did not address two words a day. After three years her cousin Julie returned from a long voyage. She forced her way into the house and found poor Mathilde so thin and pale that she thought she was looking at the corpse of the woman who had been so beautiful and vivacious when they last met. With great difficulty she managed to induce her to leave her retreat, and took her off with her to Hyères. The Countess languished there for three or four months more, then died of a chest infection—brought on by domestic cares, according to Doctor M——, who attended her.

The Game of Backgammon

(1830)

THE motionless sails clung limply to the masts; the sea lay smooth as a sheet of glass; the heat was stifling, the calm oppressive.

On a sea voyage, the passengers' resources for keeping one another amused are soon exhausted. After four months cooped up together in a wooden structure a hundred and twenty feet long, people become, alas, only too well acquainted. When you see the first officer bearing down on you, you know that first you are in for an account of Rio de Janeiro, whence he is returning; and that he will go on to tell you of the famous bridge of boats at Essling*, which he helped to construct while serving with the marine infantry. After a fortnight you come to recognize even his pet expressions, the punctuation of his sentences, and the inflexions of his voice. Has he once failed to pause sadly after uttering for the first time in his story the words *the Emperor*? 'If you'd seen him then!!!' (three exclamation marks), he invariably adds. And then there's the episode of the trumpeter's horse; and the cannon-ball that rebounded, taking with it a cartridge-pouch containing seven thousand five hundred francs' worth of gold and jewels; and so on and so forth.

The lieutenant is quite a politician. Every day he provides a commentary on the latest issue of *Le Constitutionnel**, which he has brought with him from Brest. Or, if he quits the sublimities of politics to descend to literature, he will regale you with an analysis of the latest vaudeville he has attended.

And that was a damned good story, the one the purser used to tell! How he held us spellbound, the first time he told us about his escape from the prison ship at Cádiz!* But after we had heard it for the twentieth time, good grief! it was more than flesh and blood could stand! And the sub-lieutenants, and the midshipmen—the very thought of their conversation makes my hair stand on end!

As for the captain, generally speaking he is the least tedious member of the ship's company. A despotic ruler, he is tacitly at odds with all his officers. He angers them, sometimes oppresses them, but for all that, there is some satisfaction to be gained from cursing him. If he has some bee in his bonnet that is a source of irritation for his subordinates, there is still some pleasure to be had from seeing your superior look ridiculous, and that at least is some consolation.

The officers of the ship on which I was sailing were the salt of the earth, good fellows to a man, who loved one another like brothers but were all unutterably bored with one another. The captain was the mildest of men, and extremely easy-going, which is indeed unusual. He never wielded his dictatorial authority save with reluctance.

Yet how the voyage dragged! Especially when we were becalmed just a few days before we were due to sight land!

One day, after a dinner which, for want of anything better to do, we had spun out for as long as was humanly possible, we had all assembled on deck to witness the unchanging but invariably majestic spectacle of a sunset at sea. Some of us were smoking, others re-reading for the twentieth time one of the thirty or so volumes that made up our wretched library. Everyone was bored to tears. A sub-lieutenant seated beside me was passing the time by dropping the dagger customarily worn by naval officers when not in full dress uniform, point downwards into the planking of the deck, as intently as if engaged in some crucial operation. It is as good a way as any of whiling away the time, and one that calls for some skill if the dagger is to stick into the wood with its handle pointing straight up. Wishing to do as the sub-lieutenant was doing, and having no dagger of my own, I asked the captain to lend me his; but he refused. He was singularly attached to the weapon, and would have been sorry to see it used for such a trivial pursuit. The dagger had once belonged to a valiant officer who, unfortunately, had died during the recent war. I sensed that a story was on the way, and I was not mistaken. The captain began without further prompting. The officers in the vicinity, each of whom already knew the misfortunes of Lieutenant Roger off by heart, at once withdrew discreetly. Here is the captain's story, more or less as he told it:

'Roger was three years older than me, and when I first met him he was a lieutenant, whereas I was a sub-lieutenant. I can assure you that he was one of the best officers in the fleet, added to which he was kind-hearted, intelligent, well educated, and talented—in short, a most agreeable young man. Unfortunately he was somewhat proud and touchy. I suspect this may have had something to do with the fact that he was illegitimate, and that he was afraid his birth would be held against him. But to tell the truth, his greatest failing was his passionate and constant desire to excel in every situation. His father, whom he had never met, made him an allowance that would have been more than sufficient for his needs, were it not for the fact that Roger was the soul of generosity. Everything he had was his friends' for the asking. As soon as he received his quarterly allowance, he would be besieged by people coming up to him with a sad and careworn expression. "What's the matter, my friend?" he would say. "You look as if you haven't got two pennies to rub together. Here's my purse; take what you need, and come and have dinner with me."

'There came to Brest a very pretty young actress called Gabrielle, and it wasn't long before she began to make conquests among the sailors and officers in the garrison. She was not conventionally beautiful, but she had a good figure, pretty eyes, dainty feet, and a decidedly brazen manner—all qualities most attractive to a young man in his early 20s. On top of all this, she was reputed to be the most temperamental creature of her sex; and her behaviour on stage confirmed this reputation. Sometimes she acted exquisitely, giving as accomplished a performance as any first-rate actress. The next day, in the same role, she would be wooden and insensitive, delivering her lines as a child recites its catechism. We young men were particularly struck by the following story that was told of her. It appears that she had been kept in the lap of luxury in Paris by a senator who, so they said, was infatuated with her. One day, whilst at her home, this man had put his hat on. She asked him to take it off again, and went on to complain of his lack of respect for her. The senator began to laugh, shrugged his shoulders, and, settling back comfortably in an armchair, said, "When I'm in the company of a woman I pay for, the least

I can expect is to be able to make myself at home." An unladylike slap delivered by Miss Gabrielle's fair hand immediately paid him back for this reply, and sent his hat spinning to the other end of the room. On this note their relationship ended abruptly. Bankers and generals had made the lady considerable offers, but she had turned them all down, saying that she preferred to become an actress in order to be dependent on no one.

'When Roger saw her and learned her story, he decided that she was the girl for him, and with the somewhat brutal frankness for which we sailors are sometimes reproached, this is how he set about informing her how moved he was by her charms. He bought the most beautiful and rarest flowers he could find in Brest, made them up into a bouquet which he tied with a handsome pink ribbon; and into the bow he neatly tucked a rouleau of twenty-five napoleons*. It was all he had at the time. I remember going backstage with him during the interval. He paid Gabrielle a curt compliment on the grace with which she wore her costume, gave her the bouquet, and asked her leave to visit her at her home. All this was conveyed in half a dozen words.

'Whilst she saw only the flowers and the handsome young man who was offering them to her, Gabrielle smiled at him, accompanying her smile with the most graceful of curtsies. But when she held the bouquet in her hands and felt the weight of the gold, her expression changed more swiftly than the surface of the sea when it is whipped up by a hurricane in the tropics. And to tell the truth she caused almost as much devastation, for with all her might she hurled the bouquet and the money at my poor friend's head—he bore the marks of the assault for more than a week afterwards. The stage manager's bell rang and Gabrielle went back on stage, but she acted extremely badly.

'Picking up his bouquet and his roll of gold coins in some confusion, Roger took himself off to a café, where he presented the bouquet (minus the money) to the barmaid, and drank a good deal of punch in an attempt to forget the cruel beauty. But he could not forget her; and, in spite of the resentment he felt at being unable to show himself in public with his black eye, he fell madly in love with the irascible Gabrielle. He wrote her twenty letters a day—and what letters! Submissive, tender, respectful, letters fit for a princess. At first they were returned to him with their seals unbroken; then they went unanswered. However, Roger still held out some hope, until the day we discovered that the woman who sold oranges at the theatre was wrapping her oranges in Roger's love letters, which Gabrielle had been giving her in a refinement of spitefulness. This was a terrible blow to our friend's pride, yet his passion did not diminish. He talked of asking the actress to marry him, and when he was told that the Naval Minister would never consent to this, he declared that in that case he would blow his brains out.

'It was at this point that the officers of a regiment of the line garrisoned in Brest tried to get Gabrielle to sing a verse from a topical song, a request she refused to comply with out of sheer caprice. Officers and actress were both so obdurate that the officers brought the curtain down with their hissing, while the actress fainted. You know what audiences can be like in a garrison town. It was agreed among the officers that the next day and on the following days the guilty party would be hissed relentlessly, that she would not be allowed to act a single role until she had made honourable and humble amends for her crime. Roger had not attended the performance in question, but he learned that same evening of the scandal that had set the whole theatre in an uproar, and of the plans that were being hatched for revenge the following day. At once he decided on his course of action.

'The next day Gabrielle went on stage to a deafening chorus of boos and catcalls from the seats occupied by the officers. Roger, who had deliberately seated himself close to the troublemakers, stood up and addressed the ringleaders in such insulting terms that the full force of their fury was at once turned against him. At this, with the utmost composure he took his notebook from his pocket, writing down the names that people were shouting out at him from all sides. He would have challenged the whole regiment to a duel if a number of naval officers had not turned up and, out of *esprit de corps*, picked quarrels with most of his adversaries. There was a most terrific brawl.

'The whole garrison was confined to quarters for several days; but when we were given our freedom again there was a devil of a score to settle. About sixty of us assembled on the parade ground. Alone, Roger fought three officers in succession. He killed one and seriously wounded the other two without himself receiving so much as a scratch. I was less fortunate: a confounded lieutenant, who had once been a fencing master, dealt me a severe wound in the chest which nearly proved fatal. I can assure you, it was quite some sight, that duel—though battle would be a better word to describe it. The navy easily came off best, and the regiment had to leave Brest.

'As you can imagine, our superior officers did not forget the originator of the quarrel. For a fortnight he had a guard posted at his door.

'When he was released from house-arrest, I came out of hospital and went to see him. Imagine my surprise, on entering his quarters, at finding him seated at table and dining *tête-à-tête* with Gabrielle. They seemed to have been on extremely good terms for some time. They were already calling one another *tu* and drinking out of the same glass. Roger introduced me to his mistress, saying that I was his best friend, and told her that I had been wounded in the minor skirmish of which she had been the prime cause. This earned me a kiss from the fair lady. She was of a thoroughly martial disposition.

'They spent three blissfully contented months together, never leaving one another for a moment. Gabrielle seemed to love him to distraction, and Roger declared that before meeting Gabrielle he had not known what love was.

'A Dutch frigate entered port. Its officers invited us to dinner. Large quantities of all kinds of wine were consumed, and when the table had been cleared, not knowing what else to do, since these chaps spoke very little French, we began to gamble. The Dutchmen seemed to have plenty of money; and their first officer in particular wanted to play for such high stakes that not one of us cared to play against him. Roger, who didn't usually gamble, felt that on this occasion his country's honour was at stake. So he played, and for any stakes the Dutch lieutenant cared to name. The first game he won; then he lost.

After each winning and losing several games they left it at that, and parted.

'We returned the Dutch officers' invitation to dinner. Again we gambled. Roger and the Dutch officer were again pitted against one another. To cut a long story short, they met every day for several days, either in a café or on board ship, trying their hand at all sorts of games, but mainly backgammon, and constantly raising the stakes until eventually they were playing for twenty-five napoleons a game. It was an enormous sum of money for poor officers like ourselves—more than two months' pay! After a week Roger had lost everything he possessed, not to mention three or four thousand francs he had borrowed anywhere he could lay his hands on them.

'As you can imagine, Roger and Gabrielle had ended up living together and pooling their resources. In practice Roger, who had just received a substantial share of prize money*, had contributed ten or twenty times more to the common purse than the actress. Yet he still considered that the money belonged primarily to his mistress, and he had kept only about fifty napoleons for his own personal expenses. Nevertheless, he had to dip into their reserves so as to be able to carry on playing. Gabrielle did not once reproach him.

'Their common funds went the same way as his pocket money. Soon Roger was reduced to gambling his last twenty-five napoleons. He played with hideous concentration, with the result that the game was long and fiercely contested. At one point Roger, who was holding the dice cup, had only one more chance to win. I think he needed to throw a six and a four. It was late at night. An officer who had been watching them play for a long time had finally fallen asleep in an armchair. The Dutchman was tired and drowsy, and he had also drunk a lot of punch. Only Roger was properly awake, and he was in a state of acute desperation. He cast the dice with a shudder. He hurled them onto the table so hard that a candle was knocked to the floor. The Dutchman looked first at the candle, which had just spilled wax all over his new trousers; then he looked at the dice. They were a six and a four. Deathly pale, Roger took the twenty-five napoleons. They continued to play. Fortune now favoured my unhappy friend, though he made blunder after blunder and blocked his points as if he had been trying to lose*. The Dutch officer grew stubborn, doubled the stakes, then increased them tenfold. He kept losing. I can picture him now. He was a large, fair-haired, phlegmatic man, whose face looked as if it were made of wax. At last, after losing forty thousand francs, he got up and paid over the money, his face betraying not the slightest sign of emotion.

'Roger said to him: "This evening's play doesn't count. You were half asleep. I don't want your money."

' "Don't talk nonsense," replied the phlegmatic Dutchman. "I played very well, but the dice were against me. I'm sure always to be able to win, even giving you a four-point lead. Goodnight!" And he left.

'The next day we learned that, in despair over his loss, he had returned to his room, drunk a bowl of punch, and shot himself through the head.

'The forty thousand francs Roger had won were spread out on a table, and Gabrielle was contemplating them with a smile of satisfaction. "Look how rich we are!" she said. "What are we going to do with all this money?"

'Roger did not reply. He seemed to have been in a daze since the Dutchman's death.

' "We must have a real fling," continued Gabrielle. "Easy come, easy go. Let's buy a barouche and snap our fingers at the admiral and his wife. I want diamonds and cashmere shawls. Why don't you put in for some leave, and we'll go to Paris—we'll never get through all that money here!" She paused to observe Roger, who had not heard her and who was staring at the floor with his head in his hands, apparently turning over the most sinister thoughts in his mind.

' "What on earth's the matter with you, Roger?" she exclaimed, placing a hand on his shoulder. "I think you're sulking with me. I can't get a word out of you."

' "I'm so unhappy!" he said finally, choking back a sigh.

' "Unhappy? Bless my soul, surely you haven't got a guilty conscience about fleecing that fat *mynheer*?"

'He raised his head and cast a haggard glance at her.

' "What does it matter?" she continued. "So he took it to

heart and blew out what few brains he had—so much the worse for him. I have no sympathy for people who gamble and lose. And his money is certainly better placed with us than with him. He'd only have spent it on drink and tobacco, whereas we'll find a thousand and one extravagant ways of spending it, each more stylish than the one before."

'Roger was pacing the room with his head slumped over his chest, his eyes half-closed to hold back the tears. It would have made your heart bleed to see him.

' "Do you know," she said, "anyone who wasn't acquainted with your romantic sensibility might easily think you'd cheated."

' "And supposing I had?" he cried in a hollow voice, coming to a halt in front of her.

' "Why, you're not clever enough to cheat," she replied with a smile.

' "Yes, Gabrielle, I did cheat. I cheated, like the cad I am."

'She realized from his emotion that his words were only too true. She sat down on a sofa and did not speak for some time. Finally, in a voice thick with emotion, she said:

' "I'd sooner you had killed ten men than cheated."

'For a mortal half-hour they were silent. They both sat on the same sofa, and never once looked at one another. Roger was the first to rise. In a fairly calm voice he said goodnight to her.

' "Goodnight!" she replied drily and coldly.

'Roger told me later he would have killed himself that same day if he hadn't been afraid our friends would guess the reason for his suicide. He didn't want to die leaving his name disgraced.

'The next day Gabrielle was her usual chirpy self. It was as if she had already forgotten the confession of the previous night. Roger, however, had become sombre, unpredictable, and surly. He seldom left his room, avoided his friends, and often went whole days without saying a word to his mistress. I attributed his sadness to laudable but excessive sensitivity, and I tried several times to console him; but he sent me packing, affecting utter indifference to the fate of his hapless partner. Once he even burst out in a violent tirade against the

Dutch nation, asserting that there was not a single honest man to be found the length and breadth of Holland. At the same time he was secretly making enquiries about the Dutch officer's family, but no one could give him any information about them.

'Six weeks after the unfortunate game of backgammon, Roger found in Gabrielle's rooms a note from a midshipman, apparently thanking her for certain favours she had accorded him. Gabrielle was disorder personified, and had left the note on her mantelpiece. I don't know whether she had been unfaithful to him, but Roger believed she had, and his anger was dreadful to behold. His love, that and a few vestiges of his pride, were the only things that still gave life any meaning for him, and now the thing that mattered most to him was suddenly about to be destroyed. He showered abuse on the haughty actress and, what with his violent temper, I don't know how he prevented himself from striking her.

' "No doubt this conceited young whelp gave you plenty of money," he said to her. "That's the only thing you care for, and you would let any unwashed sailor enjoy your favours provided he had the wherewithal to pay for them."

' "And why not?" the actress replied coldly. "Yes, I would accept money from a sailor—but *I would not steal*."

'Roger uttered a cry of rage. Trembling, he drew his dagger, and for a moment stared wild-eyed at Gabrielle. Then, summoning up all his strength, he threw the weapon to the ground and fled from the apartment so as not to yield to the temptation that was obsessing him.

'Late that same night I passed by his lodging and, seeing a light in his room, I went in to borrow a book from him. I found him busy writing. He did not leave off what he was doing, and seemed scarcely to be aware of my presence. I sat down near his desk and contemplated his features. They were so careworn that anyone who didn't know him as well as I did would have had difficulty in recognizing him. Suddenly I noticed on the desk a letter addressed to me that had already been sealed. I at once opened it. In his letter Roger announced that he was going to take his own life, and entrusted me with a number of commissions. As I read he carried on writing, paying no attention to me. He was writing a letter of farewell to Gabrielle. You can imagine my astonishment, and what I must have said to him, dismayed as I was by his decision.

' "What? You can't want to kill yourself—you are so happy!"

' "My friend," he said, sealing up his letter. "You know nothing of all this. You don't know me. I am a scoundrel. I am so despicable that a prostitute can insult me, and I am so conscious of my baseness that I dare not strike her."

'He went on to tell me the whole story of the game of backgammon, which you already know. Listening to him, I was at least as moved as he was. I didn't know what to say. I clasped his hands, with tears in my eyes, but could find no words. Finally it occurred to me to put it to him that he had no reason to reproach himself with deliberately causing the Dutchman's downfall, and that after all, the man had lost only twenty-five napoleons as a result of his . . . well, cheating.

' "So," he exclaimed with bitter irony, "I'm a petty thief instead of a big one. I had so much ambition, and I'm nothing but a cheap little pilferer!" And he burst out laughing. The tears welled from my eyes.

'Suddenly the door opened. A woman entered and threw herself into his arms. It was Gabrielle. "Forgive me!" she cried, embracing him fiercely. "Forgive me! I realize now, I love only you. I've loved you more than ever since you did the thing you reproach yourself with. If you like, I'll steal. I've stolen already. Yes, stolen—a gold watch. Can one stoop any lower?"

'Roger shook his head incredulously, but his face seemed to light up. "No, my poor child," he said, pushing her gently away, "death is the only course open to me. I am suffering too much. I can't endure the pain, here in my heart."

' "Very well, Roger, if you wish to die, I shall die with you! Without you, what is life to me? I'm brave, and I've fired guns before. I'm as capable of killing myself as the next person. For a start, I've acted in tragedies, so I've had plenty of practice." She had begun speaking with tears in her eyes, but this last idea caused her to laugh, and Roger too could not suppress a smile. "You are laughing, Lieutenant!" she exclaimed, clapping her hands and kissing him. "You shall not kill yourself!"

And she went on kissing him, weeping, laughing, and swearing like any sailor—for she wasn't one of those women who are shocked by bad language.

'Meanwhile, I had taken custody of Roger's pistols and dagger, and I said to him, "My dear Roger, you have a mistress and a friend who love you—believe me, you can still find happiness in this world." I embraced him and went out, leaving him alone with Gabrielle.

'I think we could only have succeeded in postponing his fatal project, if he had not received orders from the Naval Ministry to take ship, as second-in-command, on a frigate that was going to cruise in the Indian Ocean, having first penetrated the squadron of British ships that was blockading the port. There was a good deal of danger involved. I intimated to him that it was better to die gloriously, under fire from the British cannon, than to take his own life, thereby dying an inglorious death of no service to his country. He promised not to kill himself. Of the forty thousand francs, he gave half to disabled seamen and to the widows and orphans of sailors. The rest he gave to Gabrielle, who at first vowed to devote the money exclusively to good works. The poor girl certainly intended to keep her word, but her zeal was short-lived. I later learned that she had given a few thousand francs to the poor, and spent the rest on frills and furbelows.

'Roger and I took ship on a fine frigate, the _Galatée_. Our crew were stout-hearted, well drilled, and well disciplined. But our captain was an ignoramus, who thought himself a second Jean Bart* because he swore more proficiently than a master gunner, murdered the French language, and had never studied the theory of his profession, of which he was a fairly mediocre practitioner. However, at first, luck was on his side. We got out of the roads without mishap, thanks to a gale which forced the blockading squadron to take to the open sea, and we began our expedition by burning a British corvette and an East Indiaman off the coast of Portugal.

'We were sailing slowly towards the Indian Ocean, our progress hampered by the winds and by the inept navigation of our captain, whose incompetence made our voyage even more dangerous. Sometimes we were pursued by superior forces, sometimes we chased merchant vessels—never a day went by without some new adventure. But neither our hazardous existence nor the strain of his duties as second-in-command of the frigate could take Roger's mind off the melancholy thoughts that haunted him relentlessly. He, who had once been regarded as the most energetic and brilliant officer in our port, now did only the bare minimum expected of him. As soon as he went off duty he would shut himself up in his cabin without books or paper. The poor fellow spent hours on end lying on his bunk, unable to sleep.

'One day, noticing his dejection, I took it upon myself to say to him, "Good heavens, my dear Roger, you're tormenting yourself about nothing at all. All right, so you filched twenty-five napoleons from some fat Dutchman. To judge by your remorse, anyone would think it had been a million. Tell me now, did you feel remorse when you had an affair with the Prefect's wife at ****? Yet far more than twenty-five napoleons was at stake then."

'He turned over on his mattress without answering me.

'I went on: "After all, your crime, since you wish to call it a crime, had an honourable motive, and was inspired by high-minded feelings."

'He turned his head and looked at me in fury.

' "Yes, indeed, for what would have become of Gabrielle if you had lost? Poor girl, she would have sold her last chemise for you. If you had lost, she would have been destitute. It was for her, out of love of her, that you cheated. There are people who kill, or kill themselves, for love. You did more than that, Roger. For men like us, it takes more courage to . . . well, to steal, to put it bluntly, than to kill oneself."

'Perhaps now,' the captain said to me, breaking off from his tale, 'I seem ridiculous to you. But I can assure you, at that moment my friendship for Roger gave me an eloquence that is no longer mine to command. And, hang it all, when I spoke to him like that it was in good faith—I believed every word I said. Ah, I was young then!

'For some time Roger did not reply. He reached out his hand to me. "My friend," he said, seeming to make a great effort to pull himself together, "you think too highly of me. I am a craven scoundrel. When I cheated in that game against the Dutchman, my only thought was of winning twenty-five napoleons. I wasn't thinking of Gabrielle; that's why I despise myself. To care less about my honour than about twenty-five napoleons—what turpitude! Yes, I would be happy if I could tell myself I had stolen to save Gabrielle from poverty. Not so—I wasn't thinking of her. At that moment I wasn't a lover—I was a gambler, I was a thief. I stole money so as to keep it for myself. And that act has so coarsened and degraded me that my courage and my love have deserted me. I live still, but I no longer think of Gabrielle. It's all up with me."

'He seemed so unhappy that if he had asked me for my pistols to kill himself with, I think I would have given them to him.

'One Friday—a day of ill omen—we came upon a sizeable British frigate, the *Alcestis*, which began to pursue us. She carried fifty-eight cannon, whereas we had only thirty-eight. We hoisted all our sail so as to escape her, but she had the better turn of speed, and was gradually gaining on us. It was obvious that before nightfall we would be obliged to face the enemy in unequal combat. Our captain summoned Roger to his cabin, where they spent a good quarter of an hour conferring. Roger came back up on deck, took me by the arm, and drew me aside.

' "Within the next two hours," he said, "we will be joining battle. That brave fellow leaping around the poop deck over there has taken leave of his senses. There are two possible courses of action open to us: the first, and more honourable, would be to allow the enemy ship to catch up with us, then mount a vigorous assault and board them with a hundred stalwart lads. The alternative, not a bad course, but rather a cowardly one, would be to lighten our ship by jettisoning some of our cannon. Then we could hug the shore of Africa which we can see over there to port. The English would have no choice but to let us get away, for fear of running aground. But our so-called captain is neither a coward nor a hero: he's going to let the ship be smashed to smithereens from a distance by cannon fire; then, after a few hours' fighting, he will surrender honourably. Worse luck for you—you've got the hulks at Portsmouth* in store for you. Personally I don't intend to live to see them."

' "Perhaps," I said, "our first shots will inflict enough damage on the enemy to compel them to call off the chase."

' "Listen. I don't want to be taken prisoner. I prefer to get myself killed. It's time for me to put an end to all this. If by some misfortune I'm only wounded, give me your word that you'll throw me overboard. The sea is a fitting deathbed for a true sailor like me."

' "What nonsense!" I exclaimed. "And what a favour to ask of me!"

' "You will do what it is a good friend's duty to do. I know I must die. I only consented not to kill myself in the hope of being killed instead—don't forget that. Come, give me your word. If you refuse, I shall ask that petty officer over there, and he won't refuse me."

'After thinking for some time, I said: "I give you my word that I'll do as you wish, should you be mortally wounded, and past hope of recovery. In that event I agree to spare you unnecessary suff⸱ing."

' "I shall be mortally wounded, or else killed." He gave me his hand, and I shook it hard. After that he was calmer, and he even began to show some semblance of martial cheerfulness.

'Around three in the afternoon the enemy's bow chasers began to strike our rigging. Thereupon we clewed up some of our sails, turned our broadside to the *Alcestis*, and began to batter away at the British ship, which responded vigorously. After about an hour's fighting, our captain, who had a knack of doing everything at the wrong moment, decided to try boarding them. But we already had a number of dead and wounded, and the rest of our crew had lost their enthusiasm for battle. Our rigging had also taken a pounding, and our masts were in poor shape. Just as we spread our sails to draw closer to the enemy ship, our mainmast gave up the unequal struggle and fell with a fearful crash. The *Alcestis* took advantage of the ensuing confusion. She approached to within half a pistol-shot of our stern, then fired a full broadside. Our unfortunate frigate, which had only two small cannon in that quarter with which to retaliate, was pierced from stern to bow. At that moment I was standing next to Roger, who was busy giving orders for the backstays, which still supported the shattered mast, to be cut. I felt him grip my arm tightly. I turned and saw him lying sprawled on the deck in a pool of blood. He had been wounded in the belly by a piece of case-shot.

'The captain ran to him. "What are we to do, Lieutenant?" he cried.

' "Nail our flag to that mast-stump and scupper the ship."

'The captain left him at once, little relishing this advice.

' "Come," Roger said to me. "Remember your promise."

' "It's nothing," I said. "You'll pull through!"

' "Throw me overboard," he cried, swearing horribly and seizing me by the skirt of my coat. "You can see I'm a goner. Throw me into the sea. I don't want to live to see us surrender."

'Two sailors came to carry him below decks. "To your cannon, you scum!" he burst out. "Load them with case-shot and aim at the men on deck.—And as for you, if you break your word I'll curse you for the most cowardly and basest of men!"

'His wound was clearly fatal. I saw the captain call a midshipman and give the order to surrender. "Give me your hand to shake," I said to Roger.

'At the very moment when our flag was lowered in surrender . . .'

'Captain! A whale, to port!' interrupted a sub-lieutenant, running up to us.

'A whale!' exclaimed the captain, breaking off his story, beside himself with joy. 'Quick! Man the longboat! Man the yawl! Man all the longboats! Fetch the harpoons! Fetch ropes!' Etcetera, etcetera.

I never did discover how poor Lieutenant Roger died.

The Venus of Ille

(1837)

*Ἵλεως ἦν δ' ἐγώ, ἔστω, ὁ ἀνδριὰς
καὶ ἤπιος, οὕτως ἀνδρεῖος ὤν.*

ΛΟΥΚΙΑΝΟΥ ΦΙΛΟΨΕΥΔΗΣ *

I WAS descending the final slope of Mount Canigou, and although the sun had already set, on the plain I could make out the houses of the little town of Ille*, which was my destination.

'I don't suppose you know where Monsieur de Peyrehorade lives?' I asked the Catalan who had been acting as my guide since the previous day.

'Why, of course I do!' he exclaimed. 'I know his house as well as I know my own. If it weren't so dark I'd point it out to you. It's the finest house in Ille. He's a rich man, is Monsieur de Peyrehorade, and he's marrying his son to a girl who's wealthier still.'

'And is this marriage to take place soon?' I asked him.

'Soon? I daresay they've already hired the musicians for the wedding feast. Perhaps this evening, or tomorrow or the day after, I couldn't say. The wedding's taking place at Puygarrig, because it's Mademoiselle de Puygarrig that young Monsieur de Peyrehorade is marrying. Oh yes, it will be a grand occasion!'

I had been given an introduction to Monsieur de Peyrehorade by my friend Monsieur de P——. He was, my friend had told me, a most erudite antiquary, and infinitely obliging. He would be delighted to show me all the ruins for ten leagues around. I had been counting on him to give me a conducted tour of the country around Ille, which I knew to be rich in ancient and medieval monuments. This marriage, which I was now hearing of for the first time, looked like upsetting all my plans.

I'm going to be in everybody's way, I said to myself. But I was expected; now that my arrival had been announced by Monsieur de P——, I would have to present myself.

'I'll bet you, sir,' my guide said to me as we came onto the plain, 'I'll bet you a cigar I can guess what you're going to do at Monsieur de Peyrehorade's.'

'Why, that's not very hard to guess,' I said, offering him a cigar. 'At this time of day, after a six-league trek over Mount Canigou, supper is the main item on the agenda.'

'Yes, but what about tomorrow?—Come on, I'll lay odds you've come to Ille to see the idol. I guessed as much when I saw you drawing those pictures of the saints at Serrabona.'*

'Idol? What idol?' The word had aroused my curiosity.

'Why, didn't they tell you in Perpignan how Monsieur de Peyrehorade came to unearth an idol?'

'An earthen idol? Do you mean a terracotta statue, one made out of clay?'

'No, no, a real copper one. It must be worth a packet, weighs as much as a church bell. We found her deep in the ground, at the foot of an olive tree.'

'Were you present at the discovery, then?'

'Yes, sir. A fortnight ago, Monsieur de Peyrehorade told us, me and Jean Coll, to grub out an old olive tree which had caught the frost last year, for it was a hard winter, you know. So there was Jean Coll going at it for all he was worth, takes a swing with his pick, and I heard this "dong", as if he'd struck a bell. What's that? I says. So we dug and dug, and gradually this black hand appears, like a dead man's hand reaching up out of the ground. So then I got frightened, I went off to monsieur, and I said to him: "Dead men, master, under the olive tree. Better call the priest!" "What dead men?" he says to me. He came, took one look at the hand, and exclaimed, "An antiquity, an antiquity!" Anyone would have thought he'd found treasure. And there he was, digging away with the pick and with his hands, working almost as hard as the two of us put together.'

'And what did you eventually find?'

'A great black woman, more than half naked, begging your pardon, sir; solid copper, and Monsieur de Peyrehorade told us it was an idol from pagan times—you know, from the time of Charlemagne!'

'I see. Some bronze Virgin plundered from a convent.'

'A Virgin? Oh, dear me, no! I'd soon have recognized it if it had been a Virgin. It's an idol, I tell you—you can tell from the look of her. She looks at you with those big white eyes of hers . . . it's as if she was staring at you. You can't look her in the eyes.'

'White eyes? No doubt they are embedded in the bronze. It sounds as if it may be a Roman statue.'

'Roman, that's it! Monsieur de Peyrehorade says it's a Roman lady. Ah! I can see you're a scholar like him!'

'Is it intact, in a good state of preservation?'

'Oh, there's nothing missing, sir! It's a lovely bit of work, even better than the painted plaster bust of Louis-Philippe in the town hall. All the same, I don't like the look of her. She looks vicious . . . and what's more, she is, too.'

'Vicious? Has she done you any harm?'

'Not me exactly. But let me tell you. We was trying for all we was worth to get her upright, Monsieur de Peyrehorade too, he was pulling on the rope as well, though he's got no more strength than a chicken, bless him! After a lot of heaving we got her upright. I was picking up a bit of tile to wedge her with when, crash! down she went flat on her back again. "Watch out!" I said. Not quick enough, though, because Jean Coll didn't have time to get his leg out of the way.'

'And was he hurt?'

'Why, his poor leg was snapped clean through like a vine-prop. Poor lad, when I saw what had happened I was furious. I was all set to smash up the idol with my pick, but Monsieur de Peyrehorade held me back. He gave Jean Coll some money, but all the same he's still in bed a fortnight after it happened, and the doctor says he'll never walk as well on that leg as on the other. It's a shame, he was our best runner and, apart from Monsieur de Peyrehorade's son, the best *pelota** player. Young master Alphonse was proper upset about it, because Coll and him, they used to play against one another. What a sight it was to see them returning the balls—thump! thump! they never touched the ground.'

Discoursing in this vein we entered Ille, and I soon found myself in the company of Monsieur de Peyrehorade. He was a little old man, still hale and hearty, powdered, red-nosed, and with a jovial, bantering manner. Before he had even had time to read Monsieur de P——'s letter, he had sat me down at a generously spread table and had introduced me to his wife and son as a distinguished archaeologist who was destined to rescue Roussillon from the oblivion to which scientific indifference had condemned it.

While tucking in with zest, for nothing whets the appetite better than the keen mountain air, I was studying my hosts. I have already said a word about Monsieur de Peyrehorade. I should add that he was vivacity personified. He was constantly talking, eating, getting up, running to his library, bringing me books, showing me etchings, pouring me wine; he was never still for two minutes. His wife, who was rather too plump, like most Catalan women over the age of 40, struck me as an out-and-out provincial, totally absorbed in running her household. Although there was enough supper for at least six people, she ran to the kitchen, ordered pigeons to be killed and maize cakes fried, and opened I don't know how many pots of preserves. In a moment the table was laden with dishes and bottles, and I should certainly have died of indigestion if I had so much as tasted everything I was offered. However, with each dish I refused there were renewed apologies. They were afraid I should not be comfortable in Ille. Resources are so limited in the provinces, and Parisians are so hard to please!

Amid his parents' comings and goings, Monsieur Alphonse de Peyrehorade sat motionless like a Roman *Terminus**. He was a tall young man of 26, whose features were fine and regular but somewhat expressionless. His athletic figure and build certainly bore out the reputation he enjoyed locally of being an indefatigable *pelota* player. That evening he was dressed elegantly, exactly in the style illustrated in the latest number of the *Journal des modes*. But he seemed to me to be inconvenienced by his clothes; he was as stiff as a peg in his velvet collar, and moved his whole body as he turned. His large, sunburned hands and short nails contrasted strangely with his attire: they were the hands of a ploughman emerging from the sleeves of a dandy. Furthermore, although he scrutinized me keenly on account of my Parisian credentials, he spoke to me only once in the course of the evening, and that was to ask me where I had bought my watch chain.

'Well now, my dear guest,' Monsieur de Peyrehorade said to me as supper drew to an end, 'I have you at my mercy. You are in my house, and I'll not let you go until you've seen all the curiosities our mountains have to offer. You must get to know our Roussillon, and you must do it justice. You can't imagine how much there is to show you. Phoenician, Celtic, Roman, Arab, and Byzantine monuments—you will see everything from the cedar tree to the hyssop*. I shall take you everywhere, and I shall not spare you a single brick.'

A fit of coughing obliged him to break off. I took this opportunity to tell him that I should be sorry to inconvenience him at a time of such significance for his family. If he would be so good as to give me the benefit of his excellent advice on what excursions I should make, then, without putting him to the trouble of accompanying me, I should be able . . .

'Ah! You're referring to that boy's wedding,' he exclaimed, interrupting me. 'A mere trifle. It will be all over two days hence. You shall celebrate with us, as one of the family. The bride-to-be is in mourning for an aunt who died leaving her all her money, so there will be no reception, no ball. A pity, you'd have been able to see our Catalan girls dancing. They are pretty, and perhaps you would have felt like taking a leaf out of Alphonse's book. One marriage, they say, leads to another. . . . On Saturday, once the young couple are married, I shall be free, and we'll begin our excursions. I must ask your pardon for inflicting a provincial wedding on you. For a Parisian, bored with parties . . . and a wedding without a ball, at that! However, you will see a bride . . . what shall I say?—you will be delighted with her. But then you are a serious-minded man, you're not interested in women any more. I've got better things to show you. Wait till you see the fine surprise I've got up my sleeve to show you tomorrow.'

'Upon my word,' I said, 'it's not easy to have a treasure in one's house without everyone getting to hear about it. I think I can guess the surprise you have in store for me. But if it's your statue we're talking about, the description my guide gave me of it has only served to arouse my curiosity and to predispose me to admire it.'

'Ah! he told you about the idol—for that's what they call

my beautiful Venus Tur. . .—but I shan't say another word. Tomorrow you shall see her in daylight, and then you can tell me whether I am justified in considering her a masterpiece. To be sure, you couldn't have arrived at a better moment! There are some inscriptions which, ignorant as I am, I have interpreted to the best of my ability. But perhaps you, a scholar from Paris, will laugh at my interpretation, for the fact is, I have written a monograph. I, your humble servant, an elderly provincial antiquary, have put pen to paper. . . . I want to make the presses groan. If you would be so good as to read and amend what I have written, I might hope. . . . For example, I am very curious to know how you will construe this inscription on the pedestal: *CAVE* . . .—but I shall ask you nothing yet! Tomorrow, tomorrow! Not another word about the Venus today!'

'You are right not to keep going on about your idol, Peyrehorade,' said his wife. 'Can't you see you are preventing monsieur from eating? Why, he has seen much more beautiful statues than yours in Paris. At the Tuileries there are dozens of them, bronze ones, too.'

'Such is the ignorance, the blessed ignorance of the provinces!' Monsieur de Peyrehorade interrupted. 'Fancy comparing a marvel of antiquity with Coustou's* lifeless figures!

> With what irreverence
> My wife doth speak of the gods!*

'Do you know, my wife wanted me to melt down my statue to make a bell for our church. She would have been the sponsor, you see. A masterpiece by Myron*, sir!'

'Masterpiece? Masterpiece? A fine masterpiece she is, breaking a man's leg!'

'I tell you, my dear,' said Monsieur de Peyrehorade resolutely, extending towards her a right leg clad in shot silk, 'if my Venus had broken this leg of mine, I would not regret it.'

'Good heavens, Peyrehorade, how can you say such a thing! Fortunately the man is recovering. . . . Even so, I can't bring myself to look at a statue that does such wicked things. Poor Jean Coll!'

'Wounded by Venus, sir,' said Monsieur de Peyrehorade with a hearty laugh. 'Wounded by Venus, and the rascal complains.

Veneris nec praemia noris*.

'Which of us has not been wounded by Venus?'

Monsieur Alphonse, whose French was better than his Latin, gave a knowing wink, and looked at me as if to say: 'And you, Parisian, do you understand?'

Supper finished. It was an hour since I had eaten anything. I was tired, and I could not manage to stifle my frequent yawns. Madame de Peyrehorade was the first to notice the fact, and observed that it was time to go to bed. At this they again began to apologize for the poor accommodation I was going to have. It would not be like Paris. There are so few comforts in the provinces. I must show indulgence towards the people of Roussillon. In vain did I protest that after a journey through the mountains I would be delighted with a heap of straw for a bed; they continued to beg me to forgive poor countryfolk if they did not treat me as well as they would have wished. At last I went up to the room that had been prepared for me, accompanied by Monsieur de Peyrehorade. The staircase, whose upper flight was of wood, ended in a corridor extending to either side, with several bedrooms opening onto it.

'To your right', my host said to me, 'are the rooms I am setting apart for the future Madame Alphonse. Your bedroom is at the end of the other corridor. Of course,' he added, doing his best to sound discreet, 'you realize that newlyweds must have privacy. You are at one end of the house, they are at the other.'

We entered a well-appointed bedroom, in which the first object that caught my eye was a bed seven feet long, six feet wide, and so high that one needed a step-ladder to hoist oneself into it. After showing me where to find the bell, checking for himself that the sugar bowl was full and that the flasks of eau de cologne had been duly placed on the washstand, and asking me several times if I needed anything, my host wished me goodnight and left me alone.

The windows were shut. Before undressing I opened one of

them so as to breathe in the fresh night air which, after that long supper, seemed delicious. Opposite lay Mount Canigou, a magnificent sight in any weather, but which that evening, by the light of a resplendent moon, seemed to me the most beautiful mountain in the world. I stood for a few minutes contemplating its marvellous outline, and was about to close my window when, lowering my eyes, I noticed the statue on a pedestal about a hundred yards from the house. It stood at one corner of a quickset hedge separating a little garden from a large square of perfectly level ground which, I later learned, was the town *pelota* court. This ground, which was the property of Monsieur de Peyrehorade, had been made over by him to the community, in response to insistent demands by his son.

At that distance it was hard for me to make out the appearance of the statue; I could only judge its height, which seemed to me to be around six feet. At that moment two local lads were crossing the *pelota* court, quite near the hedge, whistling the pretty Roussillon tune *Montagnes régalades*. They stopped to look at the statue; one of them even addressed it in a loud voice. He spoke in Catalan, but I had been in Roussillon long enough to be able to get the gist of what he said.

'So there you are, you hussy!' (the Catalan term was stronger). 'There you are!' he said. 'So it's you that broke Jean Coll's leg! If you were mine I'd break your neck.'

'Huh! What with?' said the other. 'She's made of copper, and it's so hard that Étienne broke his file trying to cut into her. It's copper from pagan times, and harder than I don't know what.'

'If I had my cold chisel' (apparently he was a locksmith's apprentice) 'I'd soon gouge those big white eyes out for her, like prising almonds out of their shells. There's more than a hundred sous' worth of silver in them.'

They began to walk away.

'I must just say goodnight to the idol,' said the taller of the two apprentices, stopping suddenly.

He bent down, and doubtless picked up a stone. I could see him straighten an arm, then throw something, and immediately the bronze emitted a resonant note. At the same moment the apprentice put his hand to his head and uttered a cry of pain.

'She threw it back at me!' he exclaimed.

And the two young lads took to their heels. Evidently the stone had rebounded off the metal and punished the rascal for this act of sacrilege against the goddess.

I shut the window, laughing heartily.

'Another vandal punished by Venus. May all destroyers of our ancient monuments get their heads broken in the same way!' On this charitable thought, I fell asleep.

It was broad daylight when I woke. At one side of my bed stood Monsieur de Peyrehorade, in his dressing-gown; at the other, a servant sent by his wife, holding a cup of chocolate in his hand.

'Come on, Parisian, up we get! How lazy they are in the capital!' my host was saying as I dressed hastily. 'Eight o'clock and still in bed. I've been up since six. This is the third time I've come upstairs. I tiptoed to your door: nothing stirring, no sign of life. It's not good for you to sleep so much at your age. And you haven't even seen my Venus yet! Quick, drink this cup of Barcelona chocolate, it's real contraband. . . . You won't get chocolate like that in Paris. Get your strength up, for once you are standing before my Venus we won't be able to tear you away.'

In five minutes I was ready: that is to say, half-shaved, ill-buttoned, and burned by the scalding chocolate I had gulped down. I went down into the garden and found myself looking at a splendid statue.

It was indeed a Venus, and a marvellously beautiful one. The upper part of her body was naked, as was customary among the ancients when depicting great divinities. Her right hand was raised to the level of her breast, with the palm turned inwards, the thumb and first two fingers extended, and the other two slightly bent. The other hand, held near her hip, supported the drapery that covered the lower part of her body. The attitude of the statue recalled that of the *Mora Player*, which for some reason or other is known as *Germanicus*. Perhaps someone had wanted to portray the goddess playing the game of *mora**.

Be that as it may, nothing could be more perfect than the body of that Venus; nothing softer or more voluptuous than her contours; nothing more elegant or more noble than her drapery. I had been expecting some work of the Lower Empire; what I saw was a masterpiece from the finest period of statuary. What especially struck me was the exquisite truth of the forms, so perfect that one could have thought them moulded from nature, had nature ever produced such models.

The hair, brushed up from the brow, seemed at one time to have been gilded. The head, which was small, like that of almost all Greek statues, was tilted slightly forward. As for the face, it had a strange quality which defies description, and which resembled that of no other ancient statue I can recall. It had none of that calm and severe beauty of the Greek sculptors, who systematically imparted a majestic immobility to every feature. Here, on the contrary, I observed with surprise that the artist had clearly intended to render a mischievousness bordering on the vicious. All the features were contracted slightly: the eyes a little slanting, the mouth turned up at the corners, the nostrils somewhat flared. Disdain, irony, cruelty could be read in that face, which, notwithstanding, was incredibly beautiful. The fact is, the more one looked at that admirable statue, the more one became aware of the distressing truth that such wonderful beauty could go hand in hand with a total absence of feeling.

'If ever there was a model for this statue,' I said to Monsieur de Peyrehorade, 'and I doubt that Heaven ever brought forth such a woman, how I pity her lovers! She must have delighted in letting them die of despair. There is something ferocious in her expression, and yet I have never seen anything so beautiful.'

'*C'est Vénus tout entière à sa proie attachée!*'* exclaimed Monsieur de Peyrehorade, satisfied at my enthusiasm.

Her expression of diabolical irony was perhaps heightened by the contrast between the very bright eyes, of inlaid silver, and the blackish-green patina with which time had overlaid the rest of the statue. Those bright eyes produced an illusion of reality, of life. I recalled what my guide had told me, that she made those who looked at her lower their eyes. It was almost true, and I could not help being momentarily angry with myself for feeling ill at ease in the presence of this bronze figure.

'Now that you have admired everything in detail, my dear fellow-student of bric-à-brac,' said my host, 'let us hold a learned colloquium. What is your view of this inscription, which you have not yet noticed?'

He was pointing at the base of the statue, on which I read these words:

CAVE AMANTEM.

'*Quid dicis, doctissime?**' he asked me, rubbing his hands. 'Let's see if we can agree on the meaning of this *cave amantem*.'

'Well,' I replied, 'there are two possible meanings. One could translate it as: "Beware of him who loves you, mistrust lovers". But I don't know whether, if that were the sense, *cave amantem* would be very good Latin. Having seen the lady's diabolical expression, I am more inclined to believe that the artist wanted to put the beholder on his guard against this terrible beauty, and I would therefore translate as follows: "Beware if *she* loves you" .'

'Hmm!' said Monsieur de Peyrehorade. 'that's a splendid meaning. But, if you'll forgive me, I prefer the first translation, on which, however, I shall elaborate. You know who was the lover of Venus?'

'She had several.'

'Yes, but the first was Vulcan. Don't you think what is meant is: "Despite all your beauty, your disdainful air, you shall have an ugly, lame blacksmith for a lover"? An object-lesson, sir, for coquettes.'

I could not suppress a smile, so far-fetched did the explanation seem to me.

'Latin is a shocking language for concision,' I observed, to avoid open disagreement with my antiquarian friend; and I stepped back a few paces so as to get a better view of the statue.

'One moment, my dear colleague,' said Monsieur de Peyrehorade, seizing me by the arm to detain me, 'you have not seen everything yet! There is another inscription. Climb onto the pedestal and look on the right arm.' As he spoke he was helping me up.

I clung rather unceremoniously to the neck of the Venus, with whom I was beginning to get on familiar terms. For a moment I even looked her boldly in the face, and from close up I found her even more vicious and even more beautiful. Then I noticed that engraved on the arm were what looked to me like some characters in ancient cursive script. With much recourse to spectacles*, I spelled out the following inscription, while Monsieur de Peyrehorade repeated each word as I uttered it, with sounds and gestures of approval. What I read was:

> VENERI TVRBVL. . .
> EVTYCHES MYRO
> IMPERIO FECIT.

After the word *TVRBVL* in the first line, it looked to me as if a few letters had been worn away; but *TVRBVL* was perfectly legible.

'Meaning . . .?' my host asked me, beaming, but with a glint of mischief in his smile, for he was quite sure that *TVRBVL* was going to give me a hard time.

'There's one word that I haven't worked out yet,' I said. 'The rest is easy. "Eutychus Myron* made this offering to Venus at her command." '

'Excellent. But *TVRBVL*, what do you make of that? What is *TVRBVL*?'

'*TVRBVL* has me baffled. I'm racking my brains to try to find some well-known epithet for Venus that might come to my aid. Let's see, what would you say to *TVRBVLENTA*? Venus who disturbs, who disrupts. . . . As you can see, I am still preoccupied with her vicious expression. *TVRBVLENTA*, that's not too bad an epithet for Venus,' I added modestly, for I was not myself very satisfied with my explanation.

'Venus the turbulent! Venus the reveller! So you think that my Venus is a Venus of the taverns? Not a bit of it, sir, my Venus keeps good company. But now I shall explain

TVRBVL . . . to you. Promise me one thing: not to reveal my discovery until my paper has been printed. The fact is, you see, I'm rather proud of my find. . . . You must leave us poor devils in the provinces a few ears of corn to glean. You Paris scholars are so well off!'

From the top of the pedestal, on which I was still perched, I promised him solemnly that I would never stoop so low as to plagiarize his discovery.

'For *TVRBVL*. . ., sir,' he said, drawing closer and lowering his voice lest anyone other than myself should hear him, 'read *TVRBVLNERAE*.'

'I am none the wiser.'

'Listen carefully. A league from here, at the foot of the mountain, there is a village called Boulternère. The name is a corruption of the Latin word *TVRBVLNERA*—nothing is commoner than these inversions. Boulternère, sir, was a Roman city. I had always suspected as much, but I never had any proof. This is the proof I was seeking. This Venus was the local deity of the city of Boulternère; and the word Boulternère, whose ancient origin I have just demonstrated, proves something more curious still, namely, that before being a Roman city, Boulternère was a Phoenician city!'

He paused for a moment to get his breath and to enjoy my surprise. I managed to suppress a strong inclination to laugh.

'In fact,' he resumed, '*TVRBVLNERA* is pure Phoenician: *TVR*, pronounced *Tour*. *Tour* and *Sour* are the same word, aren't they?—"Sour" is the Phoenician name for Tyre (there's no need to remind you of the meaning). *BVL* is "Baal"; Bâl, Bel, Bul—minor differences in pronunciation. As for *NERA*, that gave me a bit of trouble. Having failed to find a Phoenician word, I am tempted to believe that it comes from the Greek νηρός, humid, marshy. In that case this would be a hybrid word. In order to justify νηρός, I will show you at Boulternère how the streams from the mountain form stagnant pools there. On the other hand, the termination *NERA* may have been added much later in honour of Nera Pivesuvia, wife of Tetricus, who may have granted some favour to the city of Turbul. But on account of the pools I prefer the derivation from νηρός.'

He took a pinch of snuff with a self-satisfied air.

'But enough of the Phoenicians—let's get back to the inscription. I therefore translate it: "To Venus of Boulternère Myron dedicates at her command this statue, his work." '

I took good care not to criticize his etymology, but I wanted to have a chance to show some proof of my own perceptiveness, and I said: 'Not so fast, sir. Myron dedicated something, but I certainly don't see that it need have been this statue.'

'What!' he exclaimed. 'Wasn't Myron a famous Greek sculptor? The talent must have been handed down in the family; it was one of his descendants who made this statue, nothing could be more certain.'

'But I can see a small hole on the arm,' I replied. 'I think it was for attaching something, a bracelet, for example, that this Myron offered to Venus as an expiatory gift. Myron was an unhappy lover. Venus was angry with him, and he propitiated her by dedicating a gold bracelet to her. Bear in mind that *fecit* is very often used with the meaning of *consecravit*; the terms are synonymous. I could show you more than one example if I had Gruter or Orelli* to hand. It's only natural that a lover should dream of Venus, and that he should imagine her to be commanding him to give a gold bracelet to her statue. Myron dedicated a bracelet to her. Then the barbarians, or perhaps some sacrilegious thief . . . '

'Ah! How easy it is to see that you have written novels!' exclaimed my host, reaching out a hand to help me down. 'No, sir, it is a work of the school of Myron. Just look at the workmanship and you will agree.'

Having made it a rule never to persist in contradicting stubborn antiquarians, I lowered my head as if conceding defeat and said: 'It is an admirable piece.'

'Good Heavens!' cried Monsieur de Peyrehorade, 'another act of vandalism! Someone has been throwing stones at my statue!'

He had just noticed a white mark a little above the breast of the Venus. I noticed a similar trace of white on the fingers of the right hand. At the time I supposed that they had been grazed by the stone in its flight, or that a fragment had broken off on impact and ricocheted onto the hand. I recounted to my host the insult I had witnessed and the prompt punishment which had been its sequel. He laughed a good deal at this, comparing the apprentice to Diomedes and expressing the wish that, like the Greek hero, he might see all his companions changed into white birds*.

The bell for lunch interrupted this classical discussion, and, as on the evening before, I was obliged to eat enough for four. Then some of Monsieur de Peyrehorade's tenant farmers called by, and while he was attending to them his son took me out to see a carriage which he had bought in Toulouse for his fiancée, and for which, needless to say, I expressed admiration. Then I went with him to the stables, where he detained me for half an hour, boasting of his horses, giving me their pedigrees, and recounting to me the prizes they had won at races in the *département*. Finally, by way of a grey mare that he was reserving for her, he brought the conversation round to his bride-to-be.

'We shall see her today,' he said. 'I don't know whether you will find her pretty. You Parisians are hard to please, but everyone here and in Perpignan finds her charming. The best thing about her is that she's got lots of money. Her aunt in Prades left everything to her. Yes, I shall be very happy!'

I was deeply shocked to see a young man seemingly more moved by his bride's dowry than by her beautiful eyes.

'You know all about jewels,' Monsieur Alphonse continued. 'What do you think of this? It's the ring I shall be giving her tomorrow.'

As he spoke he drew from the first phalange of his little finger a large ring encrusted with diamonds, in the form of two interlocked hands—an allusion I found profoundly poetic. It was an ancient piece of workmanship, but I judged that the diamonds were a later addition. Inside the ring, in gothic lettering, were engraved the words *Sempr'ab ti*, that is, 'always with you'.

'It's a pretty ring,' I said. 'But these diamonds that have been added detract from its character somewhat.'

'Oh, it's much finer like that,' he replied with a smile. 'There's twelve hundred francs' worth of diamonds there. My mother gave it to me. It's a family ring, and very old—it dates from the age of chivalry. It used to be my grandmother's, and she had it from her own grandmother. Lord knows when it was made.'

'In Paris,' I said, 'it is customary to give quite a simple ring, usually composed of two different metals, such as gold and platinum. Look, that other ring, the one you've got on that finger, would be most appropriate. This one, with its diamonds and the hands in relief, is so large that you couldn't wear a glove over it.'

'Oh, Madame Alphonse will do as she sees fit. I'm sure she'll always be very pleased to own it—it's nice to have twelve hundred francs on one's finger. That little ring', he added, looking with an air of satisfaction at the perfectly plain ring he wore on one hand, 'was given to me by a woman in Paris one Mardi Gras. Ah, what a time I had when I was in Paris two years ago! That's the place to enjoy yourself . . .' And he sighed with regret.

We were to dine that day at Puygarrig, with the bride's relatives. We got into a carriage and drove to the château, which was about a league and a half from Ille. I was introduced and welcomed as a friend of the family. I shall not speak of the dinner, nor of the conversation that followed, in which I took little part. Monsieur Alphonse, seated next to his bride, spoke one word in her ear every quarter of an hour. As for the bride, she scarcely raised her eyes, and each time that her fiancé spoke to her she blushed modestly but replied without embarrassment.

Mademoiselle de Puygarrig was 18 years old; her supple and delicate figure contrasted with her robust fiancé's angular form. She was not only beautiful, but captivating. I admired the perfect spontaneity of all her responses; and her air of kindness, not without a tinge of mischief, put me involuntarily in mind of the Venus of my host. Comparing them mentally, I wondered whether the superiority in beauty that one had surely to concede to the statue was not very largely attributable to its tigress-like expression; for energy, even in evil passions, always awakens in us a feeling of astonishment and a kind of instinctive admiration.

'What a pity', I said to myself on leaving Puygarrig, 'that such a delightful person should be rich, and that her dowry should earn her the attentions of a man so unworthy of her!'

Returning to Ille, and unsure what to say to Madame de Peyrehorade, to whom I felt it proper to address a few words now and then, I exclaimed:

'You are certainly free-thinkers down here in Roussillon! Why, madam, you are celebrating a marriage on a Friday! In Paris we would be more superstitious. No one would dare to get married on that day.'

'Goodness, don't even speak of it!' she said. 'If it had been up to me, we would certainly have chosen another day. But it's what Peyrehorade wanted, and we had to let him have his way. But it distresses me all the same. Suppose there were some misfortune? And there must be a good reason for it, for why else should everyone be afraid of Fridays?'

'Friday', exclaimed her husband, 'is the day of Venus! A splendid day for a wedding! You see, my dear colleague, I think only of my Venus. Upon my word, it was on her account that I chose a Friday. If you like, tomorrow, before the wedding, we will make her a little sacrifice; we will sacrifice two wood-pigeons, and if I knew where to get hold of some incense . . .'

'Shame on you, Peyrehorade!' interrupted his wife, utterly scandalized. 'Burning incense before an idol? That would be an abomination! Whatever would they say about us in the district?'

'At least', said Monsieur de Peyrehorade, 'you will allow me to place a wreath of roses and lilies on her head:

*Manibus date lilia plenis.**

You see, sir, the constitution is mere empty words: we do not enjoy freedom of worship!'

The arrangements for the following day were as follows: everyone was to be ready and dressed for the occasion at ten o'clock prompt. Having drunk our chocolate, we would go by carriage to Puygarrig. The civil ceremony was to take place at the village *mairie*, and the religious service at the chapel in the château. Next would come lunch. After lunch we would amuse ourselves as best we could until seven o'clock. At seven o'clock we would return to Ille, to Monsieur de Peyrehorade's house, where the two families were to dine together. The rest would follow as a matter of course: as there would be no dancing, the intention was to eat as much as possible.

At eight o'clock I was already seated before the Venus, pencil in hand, beginning my twentieth attempt at drawing the statue's head, yet still not managing to capture its expression. Monsieur de Peyrehorade kept hovering around me, giving me advice, repeating to me his Phoenician etymologies; then arranging bengal roses on the pedestal of the statue and, in tragi-comic tones, addressing prayers to it for the couple who were soon to live under his roof. Around nine o'clock he went indoors to see about getting dressed, and at the same moment Monsieur Alphonse appeared, wearing a tight-fitting new dress coat, white gloves, patent leather shoes, chased buttons, and a rose in his buttonhole.

'Will you do a portrait of my wife?' he said to me, leaning over my drawing. 'She is pretty too.'

At that moment a game was beginning on the *pelota* court of which I have spoken; this at once attracted Monsieur Alphonse's attention. And, weary of drawing and despairing of ever rendering that diabolical face, I too soon went over to watch the players. Among them were some Spanish muleteers who had arrived the day before. They were from Aragon and Navarre, and almost all wonderfully skilled at the game. Consequently, though spurred on by the presence and advice of Monsieur Alphonse, the men from Ille were rapidly vanquished by these new champions. The local spectators were dismayed. Monsieur Alphonse looked at his watch; it was still only half-past nine. His mother had not yet finished having her hair dressed. He hesitated no longer: he took off his dress coat, asked for a jacket, and challenged the Spaniards. I watched him, smiling and a little surprised.

'The honour of the province must be upheld,' he said.

It was then that I found him truly handsome. He was in the grip of his enthusiasm. His clothes, about which he had been so concerned a moment before, had ceased to matter to him. A few minutes earlier he would have been afraid to turn his head for fear of disarranging his cravat. Now he had no thought for his curled hair or his carefully pleated jabot. And what of his fiancée? Upon my word, if it had been necessary, I believe he would have had the marriage postponed. I watched him hastily don a pair of sandals, roll up his sleeves, and place himself confidently at the head of the defeated side, like Caesar rallying his troops at Dyrrhachium.* I leaped over the hedge and placed myself comfortably in the shade of a nettle tree, so as to have a good view of the two camps.

Contrary to general expectation, Monsieur Alphonse missed the first ball; admittedly it came skimming low over the ground, driven with surprising force by an Aragonese who seemed to be the captain of the Spanish team.

He was a man of about 40, lean and sinewy, six feet tall, with an olive complexion that was almost as dark as the bronze of the Venus.

Monsieur Alphonse hurled his racquet to the ground in fury.

'That confounded ring!' he exclaimed. 'It stopped me bending my finger, and made me miss an easy ball.'

Not without difficulty, he removed the diamond ring. I stepped forward to take it, but he forestalled me, ran to the Venus, slipped the ring on to her third finger, and returned to his place at the head of the men from Ille.

He was pale, but calm and determined. From then on he didn't once miscalculate, and the Spaniards were soundly beaten. The spectators' enthusiasm was a fine sight to see: some cheered exuberantly and threw their caps in the air; others shook him by the hand, calling him a credit to the province. Had he repelled an invasion, I doubt that he would have received livelier and more sincere congratulations. The chagrin of the losers added still more to the lustre of his victory.

'We shall play you again, my good fellow,' he said to the Aragonese in a tone of condescension, 'but I shall give you points.'

I could have wished Monsieur Alphonse more modest, and I was quite upset at his rival's humiliation.

The Spanish giant keenly resented this insult. I saw him go pale under his tanned skin. He looked dejectedly at his racquet and clenched his teeth; then, in an undertone, he muttered the words: '*Me lo pagarás.*'*

The sound of Monsieur de Peyrehorade's voice cut short his son's triumph; my host was greatly astonished not to find him supervising the preparation of the new carriage, and even more so to see him standing drenched in sweat and with a racquet in his hand. Monsieur Alphonse ran to the house, washed his face and hands, again put on his new coat and patent leather shoes; and five minutes later we were trotting briskly along the road to Puygarrig. Every *pelota* player in the town and a large number of spectators followed us with cries of joy. The sturdy horses that drew us could barely keep ahead of the intrepid Catalans.

We were at Puygarrig, and the procession was about to set off for the *mairie*, when, striking his brow, Monsieur Alphonse whispered to me:

'What a blunder! I've forgotten the ring! It's still on the Venus's finger, devil take her. Whatever you do, don't mention it to my mother. Perhaps she won't notice.'

'You could always send for it,' I said.

'Not a chance. My servant stayed behind in Ille, and I don't trust any of the servants here. Twelve hundred francs' worth of diamonds might be too much of a temptation for some of them. And besides, what would people think of my absent-mindedness? I should seem too ridiculous. They would say I was married to the statue. . . . Just so long as nobody steals it! Fortunately that rabble are afraid of the idol, they daren't go within an arm's length of it. Oh well, no matter, I've got another ring.'

The two ceremonies, civil and religious, were performed with suitable pomp; and Mademoiselle de Puygarrig received the ring of a Paris milliner, never suspecting that her fiancé was sacrificing a love-token on her behalf. Then we sat down to table, where we drank, ate, and even sang, all at great length. I pitied the bride for the outbursts of vulgar mirth to which she was exposed; yet she put a better face on it than I would have expected, and her embarrassment was neither gauche nor affected.

Perhaps courage comes to us in difficult situations.

It was four o'clock when a merciful Heaven saw fit to put an end to lunch. The men went to stroll in the grounds, which were magnificent, or watched the peasant-girls of Puygarrig, decked out in their holiday best, dancing on the lawn of the château. In this way we filled a few hours. Meanwhile the women were fussing around the bride, who was showing off the wedding presents to them. Then she got changed, and I noticed how she covered her beautiful hair with a bonnet and a plumed hat; for women are in a great hurry to assume at the earliest opportunity the adornments that custom forbids them to wear whilst they are still unmarried.

It was almost eight o'clock when we prepared to leave for Ille. But first there occurred a pathetic scene. Mademoiselle de Puygarrig's aunt, a very old and very devout lady, who was like a mother to her, was not to accompany us to the town. On our departure, she gave her niece a touching lecture on her conjugal obligations, which led to a torrent of tears and interminable embraces. Monsieur de Peyrehorade compared this separation to the rape of the Sabine women. We finally managed to get away, and on the road home we all did our utmost to entertain the bride and bring a smile to her lips; but to no avail.

At Ille, supper was waiting for us—and what a supper! If the vulgar mirth of that morning had shocked me, I was far more shocked by the jokes and *double entendres* that were now directed particularly at the bride and groom. The groom, who had disappeared for a moment before sitting down to table, was pale and chillingly grave in his manner. He kept taking gulps of old Collioure wine that was almost as strong as brandy. I was seated next to him, and I felt obliged to warn him:

'Take care! They say that wine . . .' I do not remember what stupid remark I made so as to enter into the spirit of the festivities.

He nudged my knee and said to me in a very low voice:

'When we leave the table, . . . may I have a word with you?'

His solemn tone surprised me. I looked more closely at him, and I noticed how extraordinarily his features had changed.

'Are you feeling ill?' I asked him.

'No.'

And he resumed his drinking.

Meanwhile, amidst cheers and applause, an 11-year-old child, who had crawled under the table, was showing the company a pretty pink and white ribbon, commonly known as a garter, which he had just removed from the bride's ankle. It was immediately cut into bits and distributed to the young men, each of whom put a piece of it in his buttonhole, in accordance with an age-old custom that still survives in a few ancient families. This caused the bride to blush to the roots of her hair. But her confusion was crowned when, having called for silence, Monsieur de Peyrehorade sang her some verses in Catalan, made up on the spur of the moment, or so he claimed. This is how they went, if I understood them correctly:

'What then is this, my friends? Is the wine I have drunk making me see double, or are there two Venuses here?'

The groom turned his head sharply with a startled look, causing everybody to laugh.

'Yes,' continued Monsieur de Peyrehorade, 'there are two Venuses under my roof. One I found in the ground like a truffle; the other, descended from the skies, has just shared out her girdle among us.'

He meant her garter.

'My son, choose, between the Roman and the Catalan Venus, the one whom you prefer. The rogue has chosen the Catalan Venus, and he has the better of the bargain. The Roman Venus is black, the Catalan Venus is white. The Roman is cold, the Catalan enflames everything that approaches her.'

This ending provoked such acclaim, such clamorous applause, and such uproarious laughter that I thought the ceiling was going to fall about our heads. Around the table there were only three serious faces, those of the bride and groom, and my own. I had a fearful headache; and besides, I don't know why, but a wedding always depresses me. This one, furthermore, disgusted me rather.

When the last couplets had been sung by the deputy mayor—and pretty ribald they were, I must say—we moved into the drawing-room to celebrate the departure of the bride, who was soon to be escorted to her chamber, for it was nearly midnight.

Monsieur Alphonse drew me into the embrasure of a window and, averting his eyes, said to me:

'You're going to laugh at me . . . but I don't know what's the matter with me. I'm bewitched! The Devil's making off with me!'

The first thought that occurred to me was that he felt threatened by some misfortune of the sort alluded to by Montaigne and by Madame de Sévigné: '*All Love's empire is full of tragic histories*', et cetera.* 'I thought misfortunes of that sort only befell men of intelligence,' I said to myself.

'You've drunk too much of that Collioure wine, my dear Monsieur Alphonse,' I said to him. 'I warned you.'

'Yes, no doubt. But there's something far worse than that.'

His voice kept breaking. I thought he was completely drunk.

'You know that ring of mine?' he went on after a silence.

'Well? Has it been taken?'

'No.'

'In that case, have you got it?'

'No. I . . . I can't get it off the finger of that damned Venus.'

'So, you didn't pull hard enough!'

'Yes, I did. But the Venus . . . has bent her finger.'

He was staring at me wild-eyed, clutching the window-hasp to prevent himself from falling.

'A likely story!' I said. 'You pushed the ring on too far. Tomorrow you can get it off with some pliers. But be careful not to damage the statue.'

'No. I tell you the finger of the Venus is bent, curled in. Her fist is clenched, don't you understand? It seems she is my wife, since I've given her my ring. Now she won't give it back.'

I felt a sudden shudder, and for a moment I had gooseflesh. Then he heaved a great sigh that sent a blast of wine fumes in my direction, and all my emotions evaporated.

'The wretch is completely drunk,' I thought.

'You are an antiquarian, sir,' added the bridegroom plaintively. 'You are familiar with these statues. Perhaps there is some spring, some fiendish device I don't know about. Could you go and see?'

'Gladly,' I said. 'Come with me.'

'No, I'd rather you went alone.'

I went out of the drawing-room.

The weather had changed during supper, and rain was beginning to fall heavily. I was about to ask for an umbrella when a thought stopped me short. I would be a complete fool, I said to myself, to go out to confirm a drunken man's story. Besides, perhaps he means to play some practical joke on me, to raise a laugh among these good provincials; and the very least I can expect is to get soaked to the skin and catch my death of cold.

From the door I cast a glance at the statue, which was streaming with water, and I went up to my bedroom without returning to the drawing-room. I went to bed, but sleep was a long time coming. All the scenes of that day passed through my mind. I thought of that girl, so beautiful and chaste, abandoned to a brutal drunkard. What an odious thing a marriage of convenience is, I said to myself. A mayor dons a tricolour sash, a priest a stole, and lo and behold, the most charming girl in the world is delivered up to the Minotaur! What can two beings who are not in love find to say to one another at such a moment, which two lovers would purchase with their lives? Can a woman ever love a man when once she has seen him acting boorishly? First impressions are never obliterated, and I am certain that Alphonse will richly deserve to be hated.

During my monologue, which I have abridged a good deal, I had heard much to-ing and fro-ing in the house, the sound of doors opening and closing and of carriages leaving; then I thought I could hear on the stairs the light footsteps of several women heading for the other end of the corridor on which my bedroom was situated. No doubt it was the bride being escorted to bed by her entourage. Then I heard people returning downstairs. Madame de Peyrehorade's door closed. How distressed and ill at ease that poor girl must feel!, I said to myself. I was tossing and turning in my bed with ill-humour. A bachelor cuts a ridiculous figure in a house where a marriage is being celebrated.

Silence had reigned for some time when it was disturbed by heavy footfalls mounting the stairs. The wooden steps creaked loudly.

'What an oaf!' I exclaimed. 'I'll lay odds he's going to fall downstairs!'

Everything became quiet again. I picked up a book to turn my thoughts to other things. It was a volume of statistics on the *département*, graced with an article by Monsieur de Peyrehorade on the Druidic monuments of the Prades arrondissement. I nodded off on page three.

I slept badly and woke several times. It must have been five in the morning, and I had been awake for more than twenty minutes, when the cock crew. Day was breaking. At that moment I distinctly heard the same heavy footfalls, the same creaking of the stairs that I had heard before falling asleep. This struck me as strange. Yawning, I tried to fathom why Monsieur Alphonse should be getting up so early. I could think of no plausible explanation. I was on the point of closing my eyes again when my attention was once more aroused by strange scufflings, soon joined by the sound of bells being rung and of doors being noisily opened. Then I heard confused shouts.

'My drunken friend must have set fire to something!' I thought as I leaped from my bed.

I dressed hastily and went out into the corridor. From the other end came cries and lamentations, with one piercing voice dominating all the rest: 'My son, my son!' It was clear that some misfortune had befallen Monsieur Alphonse. I ran to the bridal chamber; it was full of people. The first sight that greeted me was the young man, half undressed and sprawled across the bed, the timber frame of which was broken. He was ashen-faced and motionless. His mother was weeping and lamenting by his side. Monsieur de Peyrehorade was bustling about, rubbing his son's temples with eau de cologne and holding smelling-salts to his nose. Alas! his son had been dead for some time. On a couch at the other end of the bedroom lay the bride, in the throes of dreadful convulsions. She was uttering inarticulate cries, and two strong maidservants were having the utmost difficulty in restraining her.

'What in Heaven's name has happened?' I exclaimed.

I approached the bed and lifted the body of the unfortunate young man; it was already stiff and cold. His clenched teeth and blackened features betokened the most dreadful anguish. It was quite apparent that his death had been violent and his last struggle a terrible one. Yet there was no trace of blood on his clothes. I lifted his shirt and saw on his chest a livid imprint that extended to his ribs and back. It was as if he had been squeezed in an iron hoop. I trod on something hard which was lying on the carpet; I bent down and saw the diamond ring.

I hauled Monsieur de Peyrehorade and his wife away to their room; then I had the bride taken there. 'You still have a daughter,' I said to them. 'You owe her your care.' Then I left them alone.

It seemed to me that Monsieur Alphonse had undoubtedly been the victim of murderers who had found a way into the bride's bedroom in the night. Those bruises on the chest, however, and their circular conformation, puzzled me greatly, for they could not have been caused by a stick or an iron bar. Suddenly I remembered having heard that, in Valencia, *bravos* use long leather bags filled with fine sand to strike down those they have been hired to kill. At once I remembered the Aragonese muleteer and his threat; however, I hardly dared think that he would have exacted so terrible a vengeance for a trivial jest.

I was going around the house searching for evidence that it had been broken into, but I found none anywhere. I went into the garden to see whether the murderers might have got in that way; but I found nothing definite. The previous day's rain had in any case made the ground so wet that it would not have retained any distinct traces. I did, however, observe some deep footprints in the ground; there were two sets, running in opposite directions but along the same path, from the corner of the hedge adjoining the *pelota* court to the front door of the house. They might have been the footprints left by Monsieur Alphonse when he went to fetch his ring from the statue's finger. On the other hand, since the hedge was less thick at this point than elsewhere, it might have been here that the murderers had penetrated it. Walking back and forth in front of the statue, I stopped for a moment to gaze at it. This time, I must confess, I could not contemplate without awe its expression of vicious irony; and, with my head still full of the horrible scenes I had just witnessed, I felt as if I were looking at an infernal deity applauding the misfortune which had overtaken this house.

I returned to my room and stayed there until midday. Then I emerged and enquired after my hosts. They were somewhat calmer. Mademoiselle de Puygarrig, or rather Monsieur Alphonse's widow, had regained consciousness. She had even talked to the public prosecutor from Perpignan, who happened to be in Ille on circuit at the time, and that judge had received her deposition. He asked me for mine. I told him all I knew, and did not conceal from him my suspicions regarding the Aragonese muleteer. He ordered the man to be arrested at once.

'Did you learn anything from Madame Alphonse?' I asked the public prosecutor when my deposition had been written and signed.

'The unfortunate lady has gone mad,' he told me with a sad smile. 'Mad! Totally mad! This is her story:

'She had been in bed, she says, for a few minutes, with the bed-curtains drawn, when her bedroom door opened and someone came in. At the time Madame Alphonse was lying at the very edge of the bed with her face turned towards the wall. She did not move, sure that it was her husband. After a moment the bed groaned as if under an enormous weight. She was very frightened, but did not dare turn her head. Five minutes, perhaps ten minutes—she cannot say how long— passed in this way. Then she made an involuntary movement, or else the person in the bed did, and she felt the contact of something as cold as ice—those were her words. She pressed herself closer to the side of the bed, trembling in every limb. A little later, the door opened a second time, and someone came in and said, "Good evening, my little wife". Soon afterwards the curtains were drawn back. She heard a stifled cry. The person who was in the bed beside her sat upright and seemed to reach out their arms. Thereupon she turned her head and saw, so she says, her husband kneeling by the bed

· with his head on a level with the pillow, in the arms of a sort of greenish giant that was crushing him in a tight embrace. She says—and she repeated it a score of times, poor woman—she says that she recognized—can you guess?—the bronze Venus, Monsieur de Peyrehorade's statue. Ever since it turned up, everyone has been dreaming about it. But to return to this poor crazed woman's story: at this sight she fainted, and she had probably taken leave of her senses several moments before. She is quite unable to say how long she remained in a faint. When she came to, she again saw the ghost, or the statue, as she persists in calling it, motionless, with its legs and the lower part of its body in the bed, its torso and arms extended forwards, and in its arms her husband, quite still. A cock crew. Thereupon the statue got out of bed, dropped the corpse, and went out. Madame Alphonse made a grab for the bell pull and the rest you know.'

They brought in the Spaniard. He was calm, and defended himself with great composure and presence of mind. In any case, he did not deny saying the words I had overheard; but he explained them by claiming he had meant nothing more than that, on the following day, when he was rested, he would have defeated his victorious opponent in another game of *pelota*. I remember him adding:

'When he is insulted, a man from Aragon does not wait till the next day to take his revenge. If I had thought that Monsieur Alphonse had meant to insult me, I would have run my knife into his belly there and then.'

They compared his shoes with the footprints in the garden; his shoes were much larger.

Finally the keeper of the inn at which he was staying assured us that the man had spent the whole night rubbing down and administering medicine to one of his mules that was sick.

Besides, the Aragonese was a man of good repute, well known in the region, which he visited every year on business. So he was released, with apologies.

I almost forgot to mention the statement of a servant who had been the last person to see Monsieur Alphonse alive. It was at the moment when he was about to go up to his wife, and he had called this man and asked him anxiously if he knew where I was. The servant replied that he had not seen me. Monsieur Alphonse heaved a sigh and stood in silence for more than a minute. Then he said: 'Oh well, the Devil must have made off with him too!'

I asked this man whether Monsieur Alphonse had had his diamond ring when he spoke to him. The servant hesitated before replying. Finally he said that he thought not, but that in any case he had not paid any attention to the matter. On second thoughts he added, 'If he'd been wearing the ring I'm sure I would have noticed it, since I supposed he had given it to Madame Alphonse.'

Questioning this man, I experienced something of the superstitious terror that Madame Alphonse's statement had spread throughout the household. The prosecutor looked at me, smiling, and I refrained from questioning him further.

A few hours after Monsieur Alphonse's funeral, I prepared to leave Ille. Monsieur de Peyrehorade's carriage was to take me to Perpignan. Despite his weak state, the poor old man wished to accompany me as far as his garden gate. We passed through the garden in silence; he could barely drag himself along, supporting himself on my arm. As we parted, I looked one last time at the Venus. I was confident that, although he did not share the fear and hatred it inspired among one section of his family, my host would wish to be rid of an object which would serve as a constant reminder of a dreadful misfortune. My intention was to urge him to place it in a museum. I was plucking up the courage to broach the subject when Monsieur de Peyrehorade turned his head mechanically in the direction in which he could see me staring. He saw the statue and at once burst into tears. I embraced him, and, not daring to say a single word to him, I got into the carriage.

Since my departure I have not heard that any new light has been shed on this mysterious catastrophe.

Monsieur de Peyrehorade died a few months after his son. In his will he left me his manuscripts, and perhaps I shall have them published one day. I found no trace among them of the monograph concerning the inscriptions on the Venus.

P.S. My friend Monsieur de P—— has just written from Perpignan, informing me that the statue no longer exists. After her husband's death Madame de Peyrehorade's first concern was to have it melted down and recast into a bell, and in this new shape it serves the church in Ille. But, adds Monsieur de P——, it seems that misfortune dogs those who possess this bronze. Since the bell has been ringing at Ille the vines have frozen twice.

Colomba

(1840)

Pè far la to vendetta,
Sta sigur', vasta anche ella.
VOCERU DI NIOLO*

I

EARLY in the October of 181–, Colonel Sir Thomas Nevil, an Irishman and a distinguished officer in the British army, alighted with his daughter at the Hôtel Beauvau in Marseilles on his way home from a tour of Italy. The unfailing enthusiasm of admiring travellers has led to a reaction, and nowadays, in order to stand out from the crowd, many tourists are taking Horace's *nil admirari** as their motto. It was to this category of dissatisfied travellers that Miss Lydia, the Colonel's only daughter, belonged. Raphael's *Transfiguration* she had found second-rate, and an eruption of Vesuvius scarcely more impressive than the factory-chimneys of Birmingham. Briefly, her main criticism of Italy was that the place lacked local colour and character. It is anyone's guess what these words mean, words which a few years ago I understood perfectly, but which nowadays mean nothing to me. At first Miss Lydia had flattered herself that she would find things beyond the Alps that she would be the first to have seen, things that she would be able to discuss 'with civilized people', as Monsieur Jourdain* puts it. But soon, finding that wherever she went her fellow-countrymen had beaten her to it, and despairing of ever making a discovery, she threw in her lot with the opposition. It certainly is most disagreeable when one cannot speak of the wonders of Italy without someone saying to you, 'Of course, you know the Raphael in the *** Palace, at ***? It's the finest thing in Italy!'—this, of course, being the very thing one has neglected to see. Since it would take too long to see everything, the simplest course is to condemn everything as a matter of principle.

At the Hôtel Beauvau Miss Lydia had a bitter disappointment. She had brought back with her a pretty sketch of the

Pelasgic or Cyclopean gate at Segni, which she believed the
artists had overlooked. However, on meeting her in
Marseilles, Lady Frances Fenwich showed Lydia her album,
in which, between a sonnet and a dried flower, the gate in
question was to be found, embellished with lavish applications
of burnt sienna. Miss Lydia gave the gate at Segni to her
chambermaid, and quite lost her esteem for Pelasgic edifices.

This regrettable attitude was shared by Colonel Nevil who,
since his wife's death, had seen things only through Miss
Lydia's eyes. For him, Italy had committed the heinous crime
of boring his daughter, and consequently it was the most
tedious country in the world. Admittedly, he did not have a
word to say against the paintings and statues; but he could
vouch for the fact that the sport there was wretched, and that
in the countryside around Rome you had to cover ten leagues
in the heat of the day in order to kill a few paltry red-legged
partridge.

The day after his arrival in Marseilles, he invited Captain Ellis,
his former adjutant, who had just spent six weeks in Corsica, to
dine with him. The Captain gave Miss Lydia a spirited account
of a tale of bandits, which had the virtue of being quite unlike the
stories of robbers with which she had so often been regaled on the
road from Rome to Naples. Over dessert, left alone with some
bottles of claret, the two men talked of hunting, and the Colonel
learned that nowhere is finer, more varied, and more abundant
shooting to be had than in Corsica.

'You see plenty of wild boar there,' said Captain Ellis, 'but
you have to learn to tell them from the domestic pigs, which
are astonishingly similar, because if you kill any pigs you get
into trouble with the men that tend them. They come out
from the thickets, *maquis* they call it, armed to the teeth, make
you pay for their animals, and hurl abuse at you. And then
there are the moufflon, wild mountain sheep, a most curious
animal found nowhere else; excellent game, but tricky to hunt.
Red deer, fallow deer, pheasant, partridge—it would take
all day to enumerate the various kinds of game with which
Corsica teems. If you like shooting, Colonel, go to Corsica,
where, as one of my hosts put it, you'll be able to shoot every
possible variety of game, from a thrush to a man.'

Over tea the Captain again delighted Miss Lydia with a story of *vendetta transversale*[1] even more bizarre than the first, and he set the seal on her enthusiasm for Corsica by describing to her the strange, wild appearance of the country, its inhabitants' idiosyncrasies, their hospitality, and their primitive customs. Finally, he laid at her feet a charming little stiletto, remarkable less for its shape and its brass handle than for its provenance. A notorious bandit had relinquished it to Captain Ellis, with an assurance that it had been thrust into four human bodies. Miss Lydia tucked it into her belt, placed it on her bedside table, and before falling asleep removed it twice from its sheath. Meanwhile, the Colonel dreamed that he was killing a moufflon and that the owner was making him pay for it, which he was glad to do, for it was a most curious animal, resembling a wild boar with a stag's antlers and a pheasant's tail.

'Ellis tells me the shooting in Corsica is first-rate,' said the Colonel, as he and his daughter breakfasted alone together. 'If it weren't so far away I'd like to spend a fortnight there.'

'Well, then,' replied Miss Lydia, 'why don't we go to Corsica? While you went shooting, I could sketch. I should be delighted to have a picture in my album of that cave Captain Ellis was talking about, where Bonaparte used to go and study when he was a child.'

This was perhaps the first time that any wish expressed by the Colonel had met with his daughter's approval. Delighted at this unexpected accord, he nevertheless had the good sense to raise a few objections in order to fuel Miss Lydia's happy impulse. In vain did he speak of the wildness of the country and of the hardships awaiting a woman travelling there: she was fearless; she liked nothing better than to travel on horseback; she relished the prospect of sleeping in the open; she threatened to go to Asia Minor. In short, she had an answer to everything, for no Englishwoman had ever been to Corsica, so she had to go there. And think of the pleasure, back in St James's Place, of showing people her album!

---

[1] The vengeance visited upon a more or less distant relative of the perpetrator of the offence.

'Now, my dear, why have you not shown us that charming drawing?'

'Oh, that's nothing. It's a sketch I made of a famous Corsican bandit who acted as our guide.'

'What! Have you been to Corsica?'

Since at that time there were no steamers between France and Corsica, they enquired whether any ship was about to sail for the island Miss Lydia was proposing to discover. That same day the Colonel wrote to countermand the apartment that was awaiting him in Paris, and struck a bargain with the skipper of a Corsican schooner that was about to sail for Ajaccio. There were two cabins of sorts. Provisions were taken aboard. The skipper swore that an old sailor in his crew was an excellent cook and that there was no one to touch him when it came to preparing a bouillabaisse. He promised that mademoiselle would be comfortable, and that there would be a fair wind and a calm sea for her.

At his daughter's wish, the Colonel also stipulated that the Captain would take no other passenger aboard, and that he would arrange to hug the shore of the island, so as to afford them a pleasant view of the mountains.

II

On the day fixed for the departure, everything was packed and on board by early morning. The schooner was due to set sail with the evening breeze. While waiting, the Colonel was strolling with his daughter on the Canebière when the skipper approached him with a request for permission to take on board one of his relatives, to wit, his elder son's godfather's second cousin, who was returning to his native Corsica on urgent business and could find no ship to take him across.

'He's a charming lad,' Captain Matei added. 'A soldier, an officer in the Foot Guards. He'd already be a colonel if *the Other* were still emperor.'

'As he's a soldier . . .' said the Colonel; he was about to continue, '. . . I am perfectly willing for him to accompany us.' But Miss Lydia exclaimed in English:

'An infantry officer!' (Her father had served in the cavalry, and she despised every other arm.) 'Perhaps a man of no education, who will be seasick, and ruin our crossing for us!'

The skipper did not understand a word of English, but he seemed to understand what Miss Lydia was saying from the way she pouted her pretty lips, and he launched into a three-part panegyric of his relative, which he concluded with an assurance that he was a most respectable man, that he was from a family of *caporali**, and that he would not put the Colonel to any inconvenience, since he, the skipper, would make himself responsible for accommodating him in some place where they would be unaware of his presence.

The Colonel and Miss Nevil thought it rather odd that in Corsica there were families in which the rank of corporal was handed down from father to son. But, as they genuinely supposed that the man in question was an infantry corporal, they concluded that it must be some poor wretch whom the skipper wanted to take on board out of charity. If he had been an officer, they would have been obliged to speak to him, to mix with him; but, with a corporal, one need not stand on ceremony, and he is a person of no consequence, unless his squad is there with bayonets fixed, waiting to escort you somewhere you do not wish to go.

'Does your relative get seasick?' asked Miss Nevil drily.

'Never, mademoiselle. A strong stomach, as steady at sea as on land.'

'Very well, you may take him with you,' she said.

'You may take him with you,' repeated the Colonel; and they resumed their walk.

Around five o'clock in the afternoon Captain Matei came to fetch them on board the schooner. On the quay, near the captain's gig, they found a tall young man wearing a blue frock coat buttoned to the chin, with a tanned complexion, dark, alert, almond-shaped eyes, and a candid and intelligent expression. From the way he drew back his shoulders, and from his small, curled moustache, it was not difficult to tell he was a soldier; for at that time moustaches were not two a penny, and the National Guard had not yet introduced barrack-room dress and manners into every home.*

On seeing the Colonel the young man removed his cap and

thanked him politely and unaffectedly for the service he was rendering him.

'Delighted to be of use to you, my boy,' said the Colonel, giving him a friendly nod. And he got into the gig.

'He doesn't stand on ceremony, this Englishman of yours,' the young man said quietly to the skipper in Italian.

The skipper placed his forefinger beneath his left eye and drew down the corners of his mouth. To anyone versed in sign language, this meant that the Englishman understood Italian, and that he was an eccentric. In reply to the sign from Matei, the young man gave a hint of a smile and touched his forehead, as if to say that the English were all slightly crazy; then he sat down next to the skipper and, attentively but with no trace of impertinence, contemplated his pretty travelling companion.

'These French soldiers are well turned out,' the Colonel said to his daughter in English. 'They make good officer material.'

Then, addressing the young man in French, he asked:

'Tell me, my good man, what regiment have you been serving in?'

Gently nudging the father of his second cousin's godson, and suppressing an ironic smile, he replied that he had been a chasseur in the Foot Guards, and that he had just left the 7th Light Infantry.

'Were you at Waterloo? You're rather young.'

'Excuse me, Colonel. It was my only campaign.'

'It's worth two others,' said the Colonel.

The young Corsican bit his lip.

'Papa,' said Miss Lydia in English, 'ask him whether the Corsicans are very fond of their Bonaparte.'

Before the Colonel had had time to translate the question into French, the young man replied in fairly good, though strongly accented English:

'You know, miss, that no man is a prophet in his own land. We fellow-countrymen of Napoleon perhaps love him less than do the French. Personally, although his family and my own used to be at daggers drawn, I love and admire him.'

'You speak English!' exclaimed the Colonel.

'Very badly, as you can tell.'

Although somewhat shocked by his off-hand tone, Miss Lydia could not prevent herself from laughing at the thought of a personal enmity between a corporal and an emperor. It seemed to her to be a foretaste of Corsica's peculiarities, and she promised herself she would record the detail in her diary.

'Were you by any chance a prisoner in England?' asked the Colonel.

'No, Colonel. I learned English in France, at an early age, from an English prisoner.'

Then, addressing Miss Nevil, he said:

'Matei tells me you are just back from Italy. I suppose you speak pure Tuscan, miss. I fear you would find it a little difficult to understand our dialect.'

'My daughter understands all the Italian dialects,' replied the Colonel. She has a gift for languages. I cannot say the same for myself.'

'Would the young lady understand these lines from one of our Corsican songs, for instance? A shepherd says to a shepherdess:

> *S'entrassi' ndru paradisu santu, santu,*
> *Et nun truvassi a tia, mi n'esciria.*[1]

Miss Lydia understood, and, finding the quotation impudent, and still more so the look that accompanied it, she replied with a blush, '*Capisco.*'

'And are you returning to your country on six months' furlough?' asked the Colonel.

'No, Colonel. They've put me on half-pay, probably because I was at Waterloo and because I am a compatriot of Napoleon. I'm returning home with little hope and light of purse, as the song goes.'

And he looked up at the sky and sighed.

The Colonel felt in his pocket; he was turning a gold coin over in his fingers, and searching for the right words with which to slip it politely into the hand of his unfortunate enemy.

---

[1] 'If I entered holy, holy paradise, and did not find you there, I would leave again' (*Serenata di Zicavo*).

'They've put me on half-pay too,' he said good-humouredly. 'But with your half-pay you don't have enough to buy tobacco. Take this, corporal.'

And he attempted to put the gold coin into the closed hand that the young man was resting against the gunwale of the gig.

The young Corsican flushed, drew himself up, bit his lip, and seemed on the point of making a heated reply; but suddenly his expression changed, and he burst out laughing. The Colonel stood with the coin in his hand, dumbfounded.

'Colonel,' said the young man, regaining his composure. 'Allow me to give you two pieces of advice. The first is, never to offer money to a Corsican, for there are some of my compatriots impolite enough to throw it in your face. The second is, not to give people titles to which they do not lay claim. You call me a corporal, and I am a lieutenant. No doubt, the difference is not great, but . . .'

'Lieutenant!' exclaimed Sir Thomas. 'Lieutenant! But the skipper told me you were a corporal, like your father and all the men in your family!'

At these words the young man leaned back and began to laugh more heartily than before, and so affably that the skipper and his two sailors joined in the laughter.

At last the young man said, 'Forgive me, Colonel, but there's been a most comical misunderstanding, and it's only just dawned on me. It's true that my family prides itself on numbering corporals among its ancestors. But Corsican corporals have never worn stripes on their sleeves. Around the year of grace 1100, a few municipalities rebelled against the tyranny of the mountain lords and chose chiefs for themselves whom they called *caporali*. In our island we count it an honour to be descended from these men, who were like tribunes among us.'

'Forgive me, sir!' exclaimed the Colonel. 'A thousand pardons. Now that you understand the cause of my mistake I hope you will be so good as to excuse it.'

And he offered him his hand.

'It is a fitting punishment for my petty pride, Colonel,' said the young man, still laughing, and shaking the Englishman's hand cordially. 'I do not bear you the slightest grudge. Since

my friend Matei made such a poor job of introducing me,
allow me to introduce myself. Orso della Rebbia is my name,
a lieutenant on half-pay, and if, as I presume, to judge from
those two fine dogs, you are coming to Corsica for the
shooting, I shall be very pleased to do you the honours of our
maquis and our mountains—that is, if I have not forgotten
them,' he added with a sigh.

At that moment the gig was drawing alongside the schooner.
The Lieutenant offered his hand to Miss Lydia, then helped
the Colonel on deck. There Sir Thomas, still most shame-
faced at his mistake, and not knowing how to make a man with
a pedigree stretching back to the year 1100 forget his impertinence, did not await his daughter's approbation before
inviting him to supper, amid renewed apologies and hand-
shakes. Miss Lydia certainly scowled rather, but when all was
said and done, she was not very sorry to have learned what a
caporal was. Her guest had made a favourable impression on
her, and she was even beginning to find something aristocratic
about him. The only trouble was that he seemed too frank and
too cheerful to pass for the hero of a novel.

'Lieutenant della Rebbia,' said the Colonel, greeting him
in the English fashion, with a glass of madeira in his hand.
'I came across a lot of your fellow-countrymen in Spain.
Splendid riflemen.'

'Yes. Many of them remained in Spain,' said the young lieutenant gravely.

'I shall never forget the conduct of a Corsican battalion at
the battle of Vitoria,' the Colonel went on. 'I have good cause
to remember it,' he added, rubbing his breast. 'All day they'd
been in extended order in the gardens, behind the hedges, and
had killed I don't know how many of our men and horses.
When the decision to retreat was taken, they rallied and began
to cut and run. On the plain we were hoping to get our
revenge, but the blighters . . . I beg your pardon, Lieutenant—
those stout fellows, I was saying, had formed a square, and
there was no way of breaking them. In the middle of the
square—I can still see him now—there was an officer on a
small black horse. He was right beside the standard, smoking
a cigar as if he were in some café. Sometimes, as if to taunt

us, a flourish of bugles would ring out. . . . I launched my first two squadrons on them. But instead of tackling the square head-on, my damned dragoons went and attacked them on the flanks, then wheeled about and returned in considerable disorder, with more than one horse minus its rider . . . and still those cursed bugles sounded! When the smoke surrounding the battalion cleared, I saw the officer, still standing next to the standard smoking his cigar. Incensed, I myself led a final charge. Their rifles had become fouled and were useless, but the soldiers had formed six ranks, with their bayonets turned on the horses. It was like a wall. There I was, shouting and exhorting my dragoons, gripping my horse close to urge it on, when the officer I was telling you about finally removed his cigar and pointed me out to one of his men. I heard him say something like, "*Al capello bianco!*"*—my helmet had a white plume on it. I heard no more, for a bullet pierced me through the chest.

'They were a fine battalion, Monsieur della Rebbia, the First Battalion of the 18th Light Infantry; all Corsicans, I was told later.'

'Yes,' said Orso, whose eyes had shone during this account. 'They covered the retreat and brought back their standard. But two-thirds of those fine men are now buried on the plain of Vitoria.'

'You don't by any chance know the name of the officer who commanded them?'

'It was my father. At that time he was a major in the 18th, and was promoted colonel for his conduct on that sad day.'

'Your father! Upon my word, he was a fine soldier! I should like to meet him again; and I'd recognize him, I'm sure of it. Is he still alive?'

'No, Colonel,' said the young man, paling slightly.

'Was he at Waterloo?'

'Yes, Colonel, but he didn't have the good fortune to fall on the field of battle. He died in Corsica . . . two years ago . . . Heavens, how beautiful the sea is! It's ten years since I saw the Mediterranean. The Mediterranean is more beautiful than the ocean, don't you think, miss?'

'I find it too blue. . . . And the waves lack grandeur.'

'Do you prefer wild beauty, miss? In that case I think you will like Corsica.'

'My daughter', said the Colonel, 'likes anything which is out of the ordinary. That's why she had so little time for Italy.'

'I don't know Italy at all,' said Orso, 'except Pisa, where I was at school for a time; but I can't think of the Campo-Santo, the Duomo, and the Leaning Tower without a feeling of admiration—especially the Campo-Santo. Do you remember Orcagna's *Triumph of Death**? I think I could draw it for you, it's so indelibly graven on my memory.'

Miss Lydia feared that the Lieutenant was about to launch into an enthusiastic tirade.

'Very pretty,' she said, yawning. 'Excuse me, father, I have a slight headache. I shall go down to my cabin.'

She kissed her father on the forehead, inclined her head majestically to Orso, and left.

The two men then talked of hunting and of war. They learned that they had been face to face at Waterloo, and must have exchanged many bullets. After establishing this they got on even better. In turn, they criticized Napoleon, Wellington and Blücher, then together they went in pursuit of fallow-deer, wild boar, and moufflon. At last, when the night was no longer young and the last bottle of claret had been finished, the Colonel again shook the Lieutenant by the hand and bid him goodnight, expressing the hope that they might cultivate an acquaintance that had begun on such a ridiculous note. They parted, and each betook himself to his bed.

III

The night was beautiful, the moon sported on the billows, the ship scudded smoothly at the bidding of a light breeze. Miss Lydia had no desire to sleep, and it was only the presence of a Philistine that had kept her from savouring those emotions any human being feels on a moonlit night at sea if he has an ounce of poetry in his soul. When she judged that the young Lieutenant was sound asleep, prosaic creature that he was, she got up, donned a pelisse, woke her maid, and went up on deck.

It was deserted except for a sailor at the helm, who was singing a sort of lament in the Corsican patois, to a wild monotonous strain. In the calm of the night this strange music had its charm. Unfortunately Miss Lydia could not understand everything the sailor sang. Amongst the commonplaces some forceful line would capture her attention; but soon, just at the climax, would come some words of patois she could not make out. Nevertheless, she realized it was about a murder. Imprecations against the murderers, threats of vengeance, praise of the dead man were all juxtaposed. She remembered a few lines; I shall try to translate them:

'Neither cannon nor bayonets—brought a pallor to his brow,—serene on a field of battle—as a summer sky. He was the falcon, a friend to the eagle,—honey of the sands to his friends,—to his enemies the raging sea.—Higher than the sun,—gentler than the moon.—He whom the enemies of France never expected,—murderers from his country—struck him from behind,—as Vittolo slew Sampiero Corso.[1]—Never would they have dared look him in the face.— . . . Place on the wall, before my bed,—my well-earned cross of honour.—Red is its ribbon.—Redder my shirt.—For my son, my son in a far-off land,— keep my cross and my bloodstained shirt.—He will see two holes in it.—For each hole, a hole in another shirt.—But will vengeance then be done?—I must have the hand that shot,—the eye that aimed,—the heart that contrived . . .'

The sailor suddenly stopped.

'Why don't you go on, my friend?' asked Miss Nevil.

With a nod of his head the sailor drew her attention to a figure emerging from the main hatch of the schooner; it was Orso, coming to enjoy the moonlight.

'Won't you finish your lament?' said Miss Lydia. 'I was so enjoying it.'

The sailor leaned towards her and said in a very low voice: 'I give the *rimbecco* to no one.'

'The *what*?'

Without replying, the sailor began to whistle.

[1] See Filippini, book XI.—Vittolo's name is still anathema to Corsicans. Today it is synonymous with treachery.

'I've caught you admiring our Mediterranean, Miss Nevil,' said Orso, advancing towards her. 'You must admit, you won't see a moon like that anywhere else.'

'I wasn't looking at it. I was engrossed in studying the Corsican language. This sailor was singing a most tragic lament, but he broke off just at the finest moment.'

The sailor stooped as if to read his compass better, and tugged Miss Nevil's pelisse sharply. Clearly, his lament was not one that could be sung in Lieutenant Orso's presence.

'What was it you were singing, Paolo Francè?' asked Orso. 'A *ballata*? A *vocero*?[1] The young lady can understand you, and would like to hear how it ends.'

'I've forgotten the rest, Ors' Anton,' said the sailor. And at once he began singing a hymn to the Virgin at the top of his voice.

Miss Lydia listened to the hymn with half an ear and did not press the singer further, but she vowed she would learn the answer to the riddle later. However, her maid, who came from Florence, and thus understood the Corsican dialect no better than her mistress, was also anxious to learn more; and, before Miss Lydia had a chance to give her a warning nudge, she turned to Orso and asked:

'What does "to give the *rimbecco*"[2] mean, Captain?'

'The *rimbecco*!' said Orso. 'Why, that's the most mortal

---

[1] When a man has died, particularly when he has been murdered, his body is placed on a table and the women of his family or, failing these, women friends, or even women from other parts known for their poetic talent, improvise verse laments in the local dialect before a large audience. These women are known as *voceratrici*, or, in the Corsican pronunciation, *buceratrici*, and the lament is called a *vocero*, *buceru*, or *buceratu* on the east coast, and a *ballata* on the opposite coast. The word *vocero*, along with its derivatives *vocerar*, *voceratrice*, comes from the Latin *vociferare*. Sometimes several women take turns to improvise, and often the dead man's wife or daughter herself sings the funeral lament.

[2] In Italian *rimbeccare* means 'to return, retort, throw back'. In the Corsican dialect the meaning is 'to reproach someone insultingly and publicly'. A murdered man's son is given the *rimbecco* by being told that his father has not been avenged. The *rimbecco* is a sort of summons to action addressed to the man who has not yet washed away an insult in blood. Under Genoese law, the author of a *rimbecco* was very severely punished.

insult you can offer a Corsican. It means to accuse him of not having taken his revenge. Who has been speaking to you of *rimbecco*?'

'Yesterday at Marseilles,' Miss Lydia replied hastily, 'the skipper of the schooner used the word.'

'Who was he talking about?' asked Orso sharply.

'Oh, he was telling us some old story . . . of the days of . . . why, I think it was about Vannina d'Ornano.'

'I daresay, miss, that Vannina's death did not inspire you with much love for our hero, the bold Sampiero?'*

'But do you really find what he did heroic?'

'The savage manners of the time excuse his crime. Besides, Sampiero was fighting a war to the death with the Genoese; how could his fellow-countrymen have had any confidence in him if he failed to punish the woman who was trying to negotiate with Genoa?'

'Vannina', the sailor said, 'had set off without her husband's permission. Sampiero was right to wring her neck.'

'But it was to save her husband, it was out of love for him, that she was going to intercede with the Genoese on his behalf!'

'To intercede for him was to dishonour him!' exclaimed Orso.

'And to have killed her himself!' Miss Nevil went on. 'What a monster he must have been!'

'You realize she asked it as a favour to die by his hand? What about Othello, mademoiselle, do you regard him as a monster too?'

'That's quite different! He was jealous; Sampiero was simply vain.'

'And isn't jealousy also a form of vanity? It's the vanity of love; and perhaps the motive will serve to excuse it.'

Miss Lydia gave him a look full of dignity and, addressing the sailor, asked him when the ship was due to reach port.

'The day after tomorrow,' he said, 'if the wind holds.'

'I wish we were already within sight of Ajaccio. I find this ship tiresome.'

She rose, took her maid's arm, and walked a few paces about the deck. Orso remained motionless by the helm, unsure whether he should walk with her or break off a conversation she seemed to find disagreeable.

'Blood of the Madonna, a fine girl!' said the sailor. 'If all the fleas in my bed were like her, I wouldn't mind being bitten by them!'

Perhaps Miss Lydia overheard this artless tribute to her beauty and was alarmed by it, for almost immediately she went down to her cabin. Shortly afterwards Orso too retired. As soon as he had quit the deck the maid returned to it and, after subjecting the sailor to a thorough interrogation, reported back to her mistress with the following information: the *ballata* interrupted by Orso's presence had been composed on the occasion of the death of Colonel della Rebbia, the aforesaid Orso's father, murdered two years previously. The sailor was in no doubt that Orso was returning to Corsica *to have his revenge*, as he put it, and affirmed that before long they would be seeing *fresh meat* in the village of Pietranera. Put into plain language, the long and the short of this national expression was that Signor Orso was proposing to murder two or three persons suspected of having murdered his father, persons who had in fact been prosecuted for this deed, but had emerged without a stain on their characters, in view of the fact that judges, lawyers, the Prefect, and the gendarmes could all be relied on to rally to their support.

'There's no justice in Corsica,' the sailor added. 'I set more store by a good gun than by a judge in the King's court. If you've got an enemy, you must choose one of the three S's.'[1]

This interesting information produced a significant change in Miss Lydia's behaviour and attitude towards Lieutenant della Rebbia. He suddenly acquired distinction in the mind of the romantic Englishwoman. The jaunty air and frank, good-humoured manner, which had at first prejudiced her against him, now lent him additional lustre in her eyes, for they concealed a forceful personality, that betrayed no hint of his innermost feelings.

She saw Orso as another Fieschi*, concealing grand designs

---

[1] A national expression: *Schiopetto, stiletto, strada*; that is, gun, dagger, or flight.

beneath a mask of levity; and although to kill a few ne'er-do-wells is not so fine a deed as to liberate one's country, a fine revenge is a fine thing for all that; and besides, women prefer their heroes not to be politicians. Only then did Miss Nevil notice that the young Lieutenant had very large eyes, white teeth, and an elegant figure, and that he was well educated and versed in the ways of society. In the course of the following day she spoke to him often, and found his conversation interesting. He was questioned at length about his country, and spoke eloquently of it. His recollections of Corsica, which he had left at a very early age in order to go, first to school, then to the military academy, were of a land suffused with poetry. He grew animated when speaking of its mountains and forests and of the strange customs of its inhabitants. As can be imagined, the word vengeance cropped up more than once in his tales, for it is impossible to speak of the Corsicans without either attacking or justifying their proverbial passion. Orso rather surprised Miss Nevil by his general condemnation of his fellow-countrymen's protracted feuds. However, he attempted to excuse them in the case of the peasantry, claiming that the vendetta is the poor man's duel.

'So much so', he said, 'that people never murder one another unless a challenge has been issued in proper form. "On your guard, I am on mine"; these are the ritual words exchanged by enemies before lying in ambush for one another. There are more murders in our country', he added, 'than anywhere else. But you will never find a base motive for these crimes. We have a lot of murderers, it's true, but not a single thief.'

When he uttered the words vengeance and murder, Miss Lydia watched him closely, but failed to detect the slightest trace of emotion on his features. As she had decided that he had the necessary strength of character to make himself impenetrable to all eyes (except, of course, her own), she continued firmly to believe that it would not be long before Colonel della Rebbia's ghost received the satisfaction it claimed.

The schooner was already within sight of Corsica. The skipper named the principal points along the coast, and, although they were all totally unknown to Miss Lydia, she derived a certain pleasure from learning what they were called. Nothing

is more tedious than a landscape without names. Sometimes
the Colonel's telescope would pick out some islander, clad in
brown cloth, armed with a rifle, mounted on a small horse,
and galloping down steep slopes. Miss Lydia supposed each
one to be a bandit, or else a son going to avenge his father's
death; but Orso assured her it was some peaceable resident of
the neighbouring market-town travelling on business; that he
carried a rifle less out of necessity than in order to *cut a dash*,
to follow the fashion, just as a dandy never goes out without
an elegant cane. Whilst a rifle is not such a noble and poetic
weapon as a stiletto, Miss Lydia considered that, for a man,
it was more elegant than a cane, and she remembered that all
Lord Byron's heroes die by a bullet, and not by the traditional
dagger.

After three days at sea they reached the Sanguinaire Islands,
and the magnificent panorama of the Gulf of Ajaccio unfurled
before our travellers' eyes. It has rightly been compared to the
Bay of Naples; and at the moment the schooner entered port, a
maquis that was ablaze, covering the Punta di Girato with
smoke, put one in mind of Vesuvius and added to the
resemblance. For it to be complete, one of Attila's armies would
have had to come and devastate the area around Naples: for
around Ajaccio everything is barren and desolate. Instead of the
elegant buildings that dot the landscape from Castellammare to
Cape Miseno, around the Gulf of Ajaccio one sees only sombre
maquis, and, behind it, bare mountains. Not a villa, not a dwelling is to be seen, save, here and there on the heights around the
town, a few white structures that stand out against a background
of greenery. These are mortuary chapels and family tombs.
Everything in this landscape has a grave, melancholy beauty.

The town's appearance, particularly at the time of these
events, further heightened the impression conveyed by
its solitary surroundings. Nothing stirs in the streets, in
which one meets no one but a few idlers, and always the
same ones. There are no women about, save for a few
peasants coming to sell their produce. There are no raised
voices, laughter, or singing, such as would be heard in
an Italian town. Sometimes, in the shade of a tree along the
promenade, a dozen armed peasants play a game of cards

or watch one in progress. They do not shout, never argue; if
the game grows animated one will hear pistol-shots, an invariable prelude to the threat. The Corsican is grave and silent
by nature. In the evening a few figures turn out to enjoy the
cool air, but these strollers on the Cours Napoléon are
almost always foreigners. The islanders remain at their door-
ways; each seems to be on the look-out, like a falcon in its
eyrie.

IV

Two days after landing in Corsica, and after visiting
Napoleon's birthplace and procuring, by more or less licit
means, a small piece of its wallpaper, Miss Lydia felt herself gripped by a profound melancholy, of the sort that
must assail every foreigner finding himself in a country
whose unsociable customs appear to condemn him to total
isolation. She regretted her sudden impulse, but to leave
at once would have meant jeopardizing her reputation for
being an intrepid traveller. Miss Lydia therefore resigned
herself to waiting patiently and killing time as best she
could. In the wake of this noble resolution she took pencils
and paints, sketched views of the Gulf, and painted a portrait of a sunburnt peasant who sold melons like any market-
gardener on the mainland, but had a white beard and looked
like the most ferocious rascal you ever set eyes on. As all this
failed to keep her amused she resolved to make the descendant
of the *caporali* fall head over heels in love with her; and this
was not difficult, for, far from being in a hurry to see his
village again, Orso seemed to be greatly enjoying life in
Ajaccio, despite the fact that he saw no one there. Besides,
Miss Lydia had set herself the noble mission of civilizing this
bear from the mountains, and of inducing him to renounce the
sinister designs that had brought him back to his island. Since
taking the trouble to study him, she had told herself that it
would be a shame to allow this young man to rush to his
doom, and that it would be a glorious exploit if she were to
convert a Corsican.

Our travellers' days passed in the following fashion: in the mornings the Colonel and Orso went shooting, and Miss Lydia sketched or wrote to her lady-friends, in order to be able to give Ajaccio as her address. Around six o'clock the men would return home laden with game; dinner was eaten, Miss Lydia sang, the Colonel dozed, and the young people stayed up very late chatting.

Some formality or other in connexion with his passport obliged Colonel Nevil to call on the Prefect. This man, who, like most of his colleagues, was mortally bored, had been delighted to learn of the arrival of a Britisher who was rich, a man of breeding, and the father of a pretty daughter. Consequently, he had extended him a lavish welcome and had overwhelmed him with offers of assistance. What is more, only a few days later, he returned his visit. The Colonel, who had just risen from table, was stretched out comfortably on the sofa, on the point of nodding off. His daughter was singing at a dilapidated piano. Orso was turning the pages of her music and looking at the lady virtuoso's shoulders and flaxen hair. The Prefect was announced; the piano fell silent, the Colonel rose, rubbed his eyes, and introduced the Prefect to his daughter.

'I won't introduce Monsieur della Rebbia to you,' he said. 'No doubt you already know him?'

'Are you Colonel della Rebbia's son, monsieur?' asked the Prefect, with an air of slight embarrassment.

'Yes, monsieur,' replied Orso.

'I had the honour of knowing your father.'

The commonplaces of conversation were soon exhausted. Despite himself, the Colonel yawned rather frequently. As a liberal, Orso had no wish to talk to a henchman of the regime; Miss Lydia was left to keep up the conversation. For his part, the Prefect did not allow it to languish, and it was obvious that he derived a keen pleasure from talking of Paris and the fashionable world with a woman who knew everyone of note in European society. From time to time, as he talked, he would observe Orso with intense curiosity.

'Was it on the mainland that you came to know Monsieur della Rebbia?' he asked Miss Lydia.

Miss Lydia replied with some embarrassment that she had

made his acquaintance on the boat that had brought them to Corsica.

'He's a very respectable young man,' said the Prefect in an undertone. 'Did he tell you', he continued, dropping his voice still more, 'what motive he has in returning to Corsica?'

Miss Lydia assumed her majestic air. 'I didn't enquire,' she said. 'You can ask him yourself.'

The Prefect held his peace. But a moment later, hearing Orso address a few words to the Colonel in English, he said:

'You seem to have travelled a good deal, monsieur. You must have forgotten Corsica, and its . . . customs.'

'It's true I was very young when I left.'

'Are you still in the army?'

'I'm on half-pay.'

'Having spent so long in the French army, you cannot have failed to become thoroughly French, I don't doubt, monsieur.'

He uttered the last words with marked emphasis.

It is scarcely flattering for Corsicans to be reminded that they belong to the Great Nation. They wish to be a nation apart, and they justify the claim sufficiently well for it to be conceded to them. Somewhat nettled, Orso replied: 'Do you think, Prefect, that a Corsican needs to have served in the French army in order to be a man of honour?'

'Indeed no,' said the Prefect. 'Far from it. I'm simply referring to certain customs of this country, some of which are not all an administrator could wish them to be.' He dwelt on the word 'customs', and assumed the most serious expression of which his face was capable. Soon afterwards he stood up and left, taking with him a promise that Miss Lydia would call on his wife at the *préfecture*.

When he had gone, Miss Lydia said: 'It has taken a visit to Corsica for me to find out what a Prefect is. I rather like this one.'

'Speaking for myself,' said Orso, 'I couldn't say as much, and I find him most odd, with his pompous, mysterious airs.'

The Colonel was dead to the world. Miss Lydia glanced in his direction and, lowering her voice, said: 'Well, I don't believe he's as mysterious as you claim, for I think I understood him.'

'You are indeed most perspicacious, Miss Nevil. If you can extract any sense from what he's just been saying, you must certainly have put it there yourself.'

'It was the Marquis de Mascarille* who said that, I think, Monsieur della Rebbia. But would you like me to give you proof of my perspicacity? I'm a bit of a witch, and it doesn't take me long to read a person's thoughts.'

'Heavens, you alarm me! If you could read my thoughts, I shouldn't know whether to be pleased or sorry . . .'

'Monsieur della Rebbia,' Miss Lydia went on, blushing, 'we have only known one another for a few days; but at sea, and in uncivilized countries—you will forgive me, I hope—in un-civilized countries one makes friends more quickly than in polite society. So don't be surprised if I speak to you as a friend about some rather personal matters, which perhaps are no business of a stranger.'

'Oh, don't use that word, Miss Nevil. I much preferred the other.'

'Well, I must tell you that, without having sought to learn your secrets, I find I have been partially apprised of them, and that there are some which distress me. I know what mis-fortune has befallen your family, I have heard much of the vindictive nature of your compatriots and of their way of avenging themselves. Was it not to this that the Prefect was alluding?'

'Miss Lydia, how could you think . . .!' And Orso grew deathly pale.

'No, Monsieur della Rebbia,' she said, interrupting him. 'I know you are a gentleman, and the soul of honour. You yourself told me that nowadays vendettas are unknown except among the common people; a kind of duel, you were pleased to call it.'

'Do you suppose I would ever be capable of committing a murder?'

'As I raised the matter with you, Monsieur Orso, you must clearly see that I have confidence in you. And if I spoke to you,' she went on, lowering her eyes, 'it's because I realized that, once back in your own country, perhaps surrounded by barbarous, old-fashioned beliefs, you would be glad to know there is someone who admires you for your courage in resisting them. Come,' she said, getting up, 'don't let's talk any more of such unpleasant matters. They give me a headache, and besides, it's very late. You're not cross with me, are you? Let's say goodnight, English fashion.' And she offered him her hand.

Orso clasped it gravely and earnestly.

'Do you know, Miss Nevil,' he said, 'there are moments when my native instinct awakens in me. Sometimes, when I think of my poor father, terrible ideas obsess me. Thanks to you, I am rid of them for ever. Thank you, thank you!'

He was about to continue. But Miss Lydia dropped a teaspoon, and the sound awoke the Colonel.

'Della Rebbia, tomorrow at five o'clock, with your gun! Be prompt.'

'Yes, Colonel.'

V

The next day, a little before the sportsmen's return, Miss Nevil was coming back from a walk along the seashore, and had just got as far as the inn with her maid when she noticed a young woman entering the town, dressed in black and riding a small but sturdy horse. She was followed by a man who looked like a peasant, also on horseback, wearing a brown cloth jacket in holes at the elbows, with a water-bottle slung over his shoulder, a pistol hanging from his belt, and in his hand a rifle whose butt rested in a leather pocket attached to the saddle-bow; in a word, dressed for all the world like a brigand of melodrama, or a Corsican citizen on his travels. It was the woman's remarkable beauty that first attracted Miss Nevil's attention. She looked about 20. She was tall, fair-skinned, with dark blue eyes, rosy lips, and teeth like enamel. Her expression was one of mingled pride, anxiety and sadness. On her head she wore a black silk veil called a *mezzaro*, which was introduced into Corsica by the Genoese and shows women off to great advantage. Long braids of brown hair formed a sort of turban around her head. Her attire was neat, but of the utmost simplicity.

Miss Nevil had plenty of time to contemplate her, for the lady in the *mezzaro* had halted in the street to question someone, with a good deal of interest, or so it seemed from the expression in her eyes. On receiving a reply, she gave her mount a flick of the riding-switch and, setting off at a fast trot, did not stop until she reached the door of the hotel where Sir Thomas Nevil and Orso were staying. There, after exchanging a few words with the innkeeper, the young woman leaped nimbly from her horse and sat down on a stone seat beside the front door, whilst her squire led the horses to the stable. The stranger did not raise her eyes as Miss Lydia walked past her in her Parisian attire. Opening her window a quarter of an hour later, Miss Lydia saw the lady in the *mezzaro* still seated in the same place and in the same attitude. Soon the Colonel and Orso appeared, returning from their shooting. Thereupon the innkeeper spoke a few words to the young woman in mourning, and pointed out young della Rebbia to her. She blushed, rose with alacrity, took a few steps forward, then stopped short as if in bewilderment. Orso stood before her, contemplating her with curiosity.

In a voice tinged with emotion she said, 'Are you Orso Antonio della Rebbia? I am Colomba.'

'Colomba!' exclaimed Orso.

And taking her in his arms he kissed her tenderly, rather to the surprise of the Colonel and his daughter; for in England people do not kiss in the street.

'Brother,' said Colomba, 'forgive me for coming without having been summoned. But I learned through our friends that you had arrived, and it was such a great comfort for me to see you.'

Orso kissed her again. Then, turning to the Colonel, he said: 'This is my sister. I should never have recognized her if she hadn't told me her name.—Colomba, Colonel Sir Thomas Nevil. I hope you will forgive me, Colonel, but I won't be able to have the honour of dining with you today. My sister . . .'

'Where the devil else are you going to dine, my boy?' exclaimed the Colonel. 'You know very well there's only one dinner in this confounded inn, and it's for the lot of us. The young lady will give my daughter great pleasure by joining us.'

Colomba looked at her brother, who did not need much persuading, and together they entered the largest room in the inn,
which served as a living-room and dining-room for the
Colonel. On being introduced to Miss Nevil, Mademoiselle
della Rebbia dropped her a low curtsy, but said not a word.
It was clear that she was very timid and that this was perhaps
the first time in her life she had found herself in the presence
of strangers and people of fashion. Yet there was nothing provincial in her manner. The impression she gave was one of
strangeness rather than awkwardness. It was precisely this
that endeared her to Miss Nevil; and as no room was available
in the hotel that the Colonel and his entourage had com-
mandeered, Miss Lydia went so far, whether through
graciousness or curiosity, as to offer to have a bed made up
for Mademoiselle della Rebbia in her own room.

Colomba faltered out a few words of thanks, and hastened
to follow Miss Nevil's maid, in order to make those minor
adjustments to her appearance rendered necessary by a
journey on horseback in the dust and sun.

On returning to the living-room she paused in front of the
Colonel's guns, which the sportsman had just placed in a
corner.

'Fine weapons!' she said. 'Are they yours, brother?'

'No, they're English guns belonging to the Colonel.
They're good as well as handsome.'

'I should like you to have one like that,' said Colomba.

'One of those three certainly belongs to della Rebbia,' exclaimed the Colonel. 'He uses them well enough. Why, today he
brought down fourteen head of game with fourteen shots!'

A contest of generosity at once ensued, in which Orso was
defeated, much to his sister's satisfaction, as was readily
apparent from the expression of childish joy that suddenly
shone on her face, so serious a moment before.

'Choose, my boy!' the Colonel urged. Orso refused.

'Well then, your sister shall choose for you.'

Colomba did not need asking twice. She took the least
ornate of the guns, an excellent heavy-calibre Manton.

'This one', she said, 'must have a good range.'

Her brother was groping for words with which to express

his thanks when, in the nick of time, dinner appeared and spared him further embarrassment. Miss Lydia was charmed to see that Colomba, who had shown some reluctance to sit down to table, and had only yielded at a look of behest from her brother, crossed herself like a good Catholic before eating. 'Now that's what I call primitive,' she said to herself. And she promised herself this would not be the last interesting observation she would make regarding this young representative of Corsica's ancient customs. As for Orso, he was evidently somewhat ill at ease, no doubt fearing his sister might say or do something that savoured too much of her village. But Colomba observed him constantly and modelled all her movements on those of her brother. Sometimes she would contemplate him fixedly with a strange expression of sadness; then, if Orso's eyes met hers, he was the first to look away, as if he wanted to evade a question his sister was addressing him mentally and which he understood only too well. They spoke French, for the Colonel had a poor command of Italian. Colomba understood French, and even pronounced reasonably well the few words she was obliged to exchange with her hosts.

After dinner the Colonel, who had noticed that there seemed to be some kind of restraint between the brother and sister, asked Orso with his customary frankness whether he would not like to speak with Mademoiselle Colomba alone, offering, should this be the case, to retire to the next room with his daughter. But Orso hastened to thank him, saying that they would have plenty of time to talk at Pietranera. This was the name of the village in which he was to take up residence.

So the Colonel took his accustomed place on the sofa; Miss Nevil, after essaying several topics of conversation, gave up hope of prevailing upon the beautiful Colomba to talk, and asked Orso to read her a canto from Dante, her favourite poet. Orso chose the canto from *Inferno* containing the episode of Francesca da Rimini*, and began to read, putting all the expression of which he was capable into those sublime tercets, that tell so well how perilous it is for two people to read a love story together. As he read, Colomba drew closer to the table and raised her head, that hitherto had been bowed; her dilated pupils shone with extraordinary fire; at one moment she blushed, the next she grew pale and shifted convulsively on her chair. What an admirable temperament the Italians have, that enables them to appreciate poetry without the need for a pedant to expound its beauties!

When the reading was over she exclaimed, 'How beautiful it is! Who made it up, brother?'

Orso was somewhat disconcerted, and Miss Lydia smilingly replied that it was the work of a Florentine poet who had been dead for several centuries.

'You shall read Dante when we're at Pietranera,' said Orso.

'Heavens, how beautiful it is!' Colomba repeated; and she recited three or four tercets she had remembered, first in an undertone, then, growing more excited, declaiming them aloud with more expression than her brother had put into his reading of them.

Miss Lydia was astonished. 'You seem to be very fond of poetry,' she said. 'How I envy you the pleasure you will get from reading Dante as if he were the latest author.'

Orso said, 'You can see the power of Dante's verse, Miss Nevil, that it can have such an effect on a little savage who can barely recite her Lord's Prayer.—But I'm mistaken. I remember now, Colomba is a poetess by profession. As a young child she used to slave away, composing verse, and my father wrote to me that she was the best *voceratrice* in Pietranera and for two leagues around.'

Colomba cast a look of entreaty at her brother. Miss Nevil had heard tell of the Corsican women who recite extempore poems, and was longing to hear one. She therefore lost no time in asking Colomba to give her a sample of her talent. At this Orso intervened, extremely vexed at having recollected so well his sister's gift for poetry. In vain did he swear that nothing was duller than a Corsican *ballata*, and protest that it was tantamount to a betrayal of his country to recite Corsican verse after Dante's; he only made Miss Nevil the more determined to have her own way, and was finally obliged to say to his sister, 'Very well then, improvise something, but make it short!'

Colomba heaved a sigh, scrutinized the tablecloth for a

minute, then the beams in the ceiling. Finally, covering her eyes with her hand, like a bird that takes comfort from the belief that it cannot be seen when it cannot itself see, she sang, or rather, declaimed in a quavering voice, the following *serenata*:

THE MAIDEN AND THE WOOD-PIGEON

'In the valley, far, far beyond the mountains,—the sun strikes it but once a day—in the valley there is a sombre house—grass grows about its threshold.—Doors and windows are forever closed.—No smoke rises from the roof.—But at noon, when the sun reaches it—then a window opens,—and the orphan-girl sits, spinning at her wheel.—She spins, and sings as she works—a melancholy song.—But no song comes in reply to hers.—One day, one spring day,—a wood-pigeon perched on a nearby tree,—and heard the maiden's song. "Maiden," she said, "thou dost not weep alone:—a cruel sparrowhawk has robbed me of my mate."—"Wood-pigeon, show me the predatory sparrowhawk. Were it as high as the clouds,—I shall soon have brought it to ground.— But as for me, a poor maiden, who will give me back my brother,—my brother who is now in a distant land?"—"Maiden, tell me where thy brother is,—and my pinion shall bear me close to him." '

'There's a well-bred wood-pigeon!' exclaimed Orso, kissing his sister with an emotion that contrasted with the bantering tone he affected.

'Your song is charming,' said Miss Lydia. 'I should like you to write it down for me in my album. I shall translate it into English and have it set to music.'

The gallant Colonel, who had understood not a word, added his compliments to those of his daughter. Then he added:

'I suppose, mademoiselle, that the pigeon you're referring to was the bird we had today boned and broiled?'

Miss Nevil fetched her album and was not a little surprised to find the poetess strangely niggardly in her use of paper when writing down her song. Instead of setting it out line by line, she wrote the verse continuously, across the full width of the page, so that it no longer answered to the well-known definition of a poem as 'short lines, of unequal length, with a margin on either side'. One could also have made a number of other observations regarding Mademoiselle Colomba's somewhat wayward spelling, which more than once brought a smile to Miss Nevil's lips, whilst Orso's fraternal pride underwent torments.

Bedtime having arrived, the two girls retired to their room. There, while taking off her necklace, ear-rings, and bracelets, Miss Lydia observed her companion removing from her dress something long, like a corset-stay, but of an altogether different shape. Colomba put it carefully and almost furtively under her *mezzaro*, which she had placed on a table; then she knelt down and devoutly said her prayers. Two minutes later she was in bed. Miss Lydia, who was very curious by nature and, like all Englishwomen, liked to take her time over undressing, went over to the table and, pretending to look for a pin, lifted the *mezzaro* and saw a longish stiletto, with an unusual mounting of mother-of-pearl and silver. It was an ancient weapon, of remarkable workmanship, and of great value to a collector.

'Is it the custom here for young ladies to carry one of these little instruments in their corsets?' Miss Nevil asked smilingly.

'We have to,' Colomba replied with a sigh. 'There are so many wicked people about.'

'And would you really have the courage to use it, like this?'

And holding the stiletto, Miss Nevil made a stabbing motion, downwards, like an actor in a play.

'Yes, if it were necessary,' said Colomba in her gentle, melodious voice. 'To defend myself, or to defend my friends. . . But you're not holding it right; you might injure yourself, if the person you wanted to stab stepped back.' And sitting up in bed, she said, 'Look, like this, you must strike upwards. If you do that it's fatal, they say. How fortunate are those who have no need of such weapons.'

She sighed, let her head fall on to the pillows, and closed her eyes. No head could have looked more beautiful, more noble, more virginal. Phidias, when carving his statue of Minerva, could not have wished for a better model.

VI

It is in order to comply with Horace's precept that I have plunged *in medias res**. Now that everything is asleep, the fair Colomba, the Colonel, and his daughter*, I shall avail myself of this moment to inform the reader of certain particulars with which he will need to be acquainted if he wishes to penetrate further into this veracious history. He knows already that Colonel della Rebbia, Orso's father, was murdered. Now in Corsica, unlike France, one is not murdered by the first escaped convict who comes along and can find no better way of making off with one's silverware. One is murdered by one's enemies; but the reason why one has enemies is often very hard to ascertain. Many families hate one another by long-established tradition, and the original cause of their hatred has been forgotten.

The family to which Colonel della Rebbia belonged hated a number of other families, but was particularly virulent in its loathing for the Barricini family. Some said that in the sixteenth century a della Rebbia had seduced a Barricini, and had afterwards been stabbed by a relative of the dishonoured damsel. Admittedly, others gave a different account of the affair, claiming that it was a della Rebbia who had been seduced, and a Barricini stabbed. The fact remains that, to use a time-honoured expression, there was a blood feud between the two houses. However, contrary to custom, this murder had not led to others. In the event, della Rebbias and Barricinis had both been hounded by the Genoese authorities, and, with their young men forced to flee the country, for several generations both families had been deprived of their most vigorous scions. At the end of the last century a della Rebbia who was an officer in the service of Naples found himself in a gambling-den where he had an altercation with some soldiers who, among other terms of abuse, called him a Corsican goatherd. He put his hand to his sword but, outnumbered by three to one, would have had a lean time of it if a stranger, who was gambling in the same place, had not exclaimed, 'I too am a Corsican!', and taken up his defence. This stranger was a Barricini, and did not know the identity of his fellow-countryman. When the truth emerged, elaborate compliments and oaths of eternal friendship were exchanged; for, on the mainland, Corsicans strike up friendships easily; quite the reverse is true on their island. This was a case in point: della Rebbia and Barricini were bosom friends for the duration of their stay in Italy; but once they were back in Corsica it became rare for them to see one another, although they lived in the same village; and when they died, people said it was a good five or six years since they had spoken to one another. Their sons, too, *kept their distance*, as the saying goes on the island. One, Ghilfuccio, the father of Orso, was a soldier; the other, Giudice Barricini, a lawyer. Having become heads of their families, and separated by their callings, they had almost no occasion to see one another or hear one another's name mentioned.

However, one day in Bastia in about 1809, Giudice read in a newspaper that Captain Ghilfuccio had just been decorated, and he said, in the presence of witnesses, that this did not surprise him, in view of the fact that his family were protégés of General ***. The remark came to the ears of Ghilfuccio in Vienna, and he observed to a compatriot that on his return to Corsica he would find Giudice a very wealthy man, since he made more money from the cases he lost than from those he won. It was never established whether he was insinuating that the lawyer cheated his clients, or merely voicing the trite truth that a lawyer does better out of a bad business than out of a good cause. Be that as it may, Barricini got wind of the epigram, and did not forget it. In 1812, when he was seeking to become mayor of his commune and had every reason to suppose he would be appointed, General *** wrote to the Prefect to put in a good word for a relative of Ghilfuccio's wife. The Prefect made haste to comply with the General's wishes, and Barricini never doubted that his setback was attributable to Ghilfuccio's machinations. After the fall of the Emperor in 1814, the General's protégé was denounced as a Bonapartist and replaced by Barricini. In turn, the latter was stripped of office during the Hundred Days*; but after that tempestuous period, amid much ceremony he again took possession of the mayor's seal of office and the register of births, marriages, and deaths.

From that moment his star shone more brightly than ever. Colonel della Rebbia, who had retired to Pietranera on half-pay, had to endure an unrelenting campaign of petty harassment. Once he was served a writ for damages caused by his horse on the mayor's land; on another occasion, on the pretext of restoring the paving in the church, the mayor ordered the removal of a broken flagstone which bore the della Rebbia coat of arms and marked the tomb of a member of the family. If the goats ate the Colonel's seedlings, the animals' owners were protected by the mayor. One after another, the grocer who ran the post office at Pietranera and the rural policeman, a disabled veteran, both clients of della Rebbia, were dismissed and replaced by creatures of Barricini.

At her death the Colonel's wife had expressed the wish to be buried in a small wood in which she had often enjoyed walking. The mayor at once made it known that she was to be interred in the cemetery of the commune, since he had received no authorization for the burial to take place elsewhere. The Colonel, incensed, declared that pending such authorization his wife would be buried in the place she had chosen, and he had a grave dug for her there. The mayor retaliated by having one dug in the cemetery, and called in the gendarmes, to ensure, as he said, that the law should prevail. On the day of the funeral the two parties came face to face, and for a moment there were fears that battle might be joined for possession of Madame della Rebbia's remains. Around forty well-armed peasants, who had been brought in by the dead woman's relatives, compelled the priest to take the path leading to the wood as they left the church. The mayor, with his two sons, his retainers and the gendarmes, arrived from another direction to offer opposition. When he appeared and called upon the procession to turn back, he was greeted with jeers and threats; his adversaries outnumbered him, and they seemed determined. Several of the party cocked their guns on seeing him. One shepherd is even said to have taken aim at him, but the Colonel pushed aside the gun-barrel, saying, 'No one is to fire unless I give the order!' The mayor was *naturally fearful of blows*, like Panurge*, and, refusing battle, beat a retreat with his escort. Thereupon the funeral procession set off, taking care to go the long way round, in order to pass in front of the town hall. As they marched past, a half-wit who had joined the procession took it into his head to call out, 'Long live the Emperor!' Two or three voices took up the call, and the della Rebbia faction, growing more and more excited, proposed killing an ox belonging to the mayor which happened to be blocking the way. Fortunately the Colonel put a stop to this outrage.

Needless to say, the particulars of the incident were recorded, and the mayor submitted a report to the Prefect, in his loftiest style, in which he depicted divine and human law as trampled underfoot—his dignity as mayor and that of the parish priest slighted and insulted—with Colonel della Rebbia at the head of a Bonapartist plot to change the order of succession to the throne and inciting the public to take up arms against one another, crimes under Articles 86 and 91 of the Penal Code.

The exaggerated tone of the indictment detracted from its effect. The Colonel wrote to the Prefect and to the public prosecutor. One of his wife's relatives was connected by marriage to one of the deputies for the island, another was the cousin of the President of the royal court. Thanks to their protection the conspiracy came to nothing, Madame della Rebbia's bones remained in the wood undisturbed, and only the half-wit was sentenced to two weeks' imprisonment.

Dissatisfied with the result of this affair, the lawyer Barricini commenced hostilities on another front. He unearthed an old title-deed, on the basis of which he embarked on a dispute with the Colonel as to the ownership of a certain stream that turned a mill. A lengthy court case began. After a year, the court was about to pronounce judgment, and showed every indication of finding in favour of the Colonel, when Monsieur Barricini placed in the hands of the public prosecutor a letter signed by one Agostini, a famous bandit, threatening him, the mayor, with arson and death unless he withdrew his action. It is a well-known fact that in Corsica the protection of bandits is much sought after, and that to oblige their friends they often intervene in private quarrels. The mayor was turning this letter to good account when another incident further complicated the affair. The bandit Agostini wrote to the public prosecutor to complain that someone had been forging his handwriting and casting aspersions on his character, making him seem like a man whose influence could be bought. 'If I discover the forger,' he wrote, concluding his letter, 'I shall make an example of him.'

It was clear that Agostini had not written the threatening letter to the mayor; the della Rebbias accused the Barricinis and vice versa. Each side assailed the other with threats, and the law did not know where to turn to find the culprits.

It was at this point that Colonel Ghilfuccio was murdered. These are the events as established in court: on 2 August 18—, when it was already dusk, a woman, one Madeleine Pietri, who was bringing some corn to Pietranera, heard two shots in rapid succession, coming, she thought, from a sunken lane leading to the village, about a hundred and fifty paces from where she stood. Almost immediately afterwards she saw a man crouched low and running along a path through the vines, heading towards the village. The man stopped and turned for a moment, but at that distance it was impossible for the witness to make out his features, and in any case he held a vine-leaf in his mouth, which hid his face almost entirely. He made a sign to a companion whom the witness did not see, then disappeared among the vines.

The witness dropped her burden, ran up the path, and found Colonel della Rebbia lying in a pool of blood, pierced by two bullets, but still breathing. Beside him was his gun, loaded and cocked, as if he had been struck from behind while preparing to defend himself against someone attacking him from the front. He was in his death throes, fighting for breath but unable to utter a word. The doctors later attributed this to the nature of his wounds, that had perforated the lung. He was choking on his own blood, which oozed from him slowly like a red foam. The witness raised him, and questioned him, but in vain. She could see that he was trying to speak but was unable to make himself understood. Noticing that he was attempting to reach into his pocket, she quickly took from it a small notebook which she opened and handed to him. The wounded man took the pencil from the notebook, and attempted to write. The witness saw him manage to form several letters with considerable difficulty; but, being illiterate, she could not understand their meaning. Exhausted by this effort, the Colonel gave the notebook to Signora Pietri, clasping her hand tightly and looking at her in a singular manner as if he wished to say to her (these were the witness's words), 'This is important, it's the name of my murderer!'

The witness was on her way up to the village when she met mayor Barricini and his son Vincentello. It was then almost dark. She recounted what she had seen. The mayor took the notebook and ran to the town hall to don his sash of office and summon his secretary and the gendarmes. Left alone with young Vincentello, Madeleine Pietri suggested that they go to the aid of the Colonel, always supposing he was still alive. But Vincentello replied that if he approached a man who had been his family's sworn enemy, he was bound to be accused of having killed him. Shortly afterwards the mayor returned, found the Colonel dead, had the body removed, and prepared his report.

Despite his agitation, which was natural in the circumstances, Monsieur Barricini had lost no time in placing official seals on the Colonel's notebook and in making every enquiry that lay within his power; but these turned up nothing of importance. When the investigating judge arrived the notebook was opened to reveal a bloodstained page on which a few letters had been traced in a faltering, but nevertheless clearly legible hand. They spelled *Agosti. . .*, and the judge was in no doubt that the Colonel had intended to name Agostini as his murderer. However, when Colomba della Rebbia was summoned by the judge, she asked to examine the notebook. After leafing through it for some time she pointed towards the mayor and exclaimed, 'There is the murderer!' Then, with an accuracy and lucidity that were surprising in one so distraught with grief, she told how a few days previously her father had received a letter from his son, who had just changed garrison, and how he had burned the letter, but had first recorded Orso's new address in pencil in his notebook. Now the address was no longer in the notebook, and Colomba concluded that the mayor had torn out the page on which it was written, which, she alleged, was the same page on which her father had scrawled the name of the murderer; a name for which, in Colomba's submission, the mayor had substituted Agostini's. The judge saw that sure enough a page was missing from the quire of paper in which the name was written; but he soon noticed that pages were also missing from other parts of the same notebook, and witnesses testified that the Colonel was in the habit of tearing pages out of his notebook whenever he wanted to light a cigar. It was thus more than probable that he had inadvertently burned the address he had copied down. Furthermore, it was established that by the time he received the notebook from Signora Pietri it would have been too dark for the mayor to read what it contained; that he had not once stopped before entering the town hall; and that the sergeant of gendarmes had gone in with him, and had seen him light a lamp, place the notebook in an envelope, and seal it in his presence.

When the sergeant had finished making his deposition, Colomba fell at his knees in a frenzy and implored him, by all that he held most sacred, to declare whether at any time he had left the mayor alone for a moment. After some hesitation the sergeant, visibly moved by the girl's intense emotion, admitted that he had gone to look for a large sheet of paper in an adjoining room, but that he had only been gone a minute, and that the mayor had been talking to him throughout the time he was rummaging in a drawer for the paper. In any case, he testified that on his return the blood-stained notebook was in the same place on the table where the mayor had thrown it on entering the room.

Monsieur Barricini gave his evidence with perfect composure. He forgave, he said, Mademoiselle della Rebbia's anger, and was quite prepared to go to the trouble of vindicating his character. He proved that he had spent the whole evening in the village; that his son Vincentello was with him outside the *mairie* at the time of the crime; and that his son Orlanduccio, who had been taken ill with a fever that same day, had not stirred from his bed. He produced all the guns in his house, none of which had been fired recently. He added that, on the matter of the notebook, he had immediately realized its importance, and had placed official seals on it and handed it over to his deputy, foreseeing that suspicion might attach to him on account of his enmity with the Colonel. Lastly, he reminded the judge that Agostini had threatened to kill whoever it was that had written the letter purporting to come from him, and insinuated that it was the wretched Agostini who, suspecting no doubt that the Colonel was the culprit, had murdered him. Such a revenge for a comparable motive is not without precedent in the bandit code of honour.

Five days after Colonel della Rebbia's death, Agostini was surprised by a detachment of *voltigeurs** and died fighting to the bitter end. On his body they found a letter from Colomba, in which she adjured him to say whether or not he was guilty of the murder imputed to him. Since the bandit had not replied to it, the view was fairly generally taken that he had not felt equal to the task of telling a daughter that he had killed her father. However, those who claimed to be conversant with Agostini's character gave it as their private opinion that if he had killed the Colonel he would have boasted of having done so. Another bandit, who was known as Brandolaccio, sent Colomba a declaration in which he vouched 'on his honour' for his comrade's innocence; but the only evidence he adduced for his assertion was that Agostini had never told him that he suspected the Colonel of the forgery.

The upshot was that the Barricini family were not put to any inconvenience. The investigating judge heaped praise on the mayor, who added lustre to his conduct by waiving all claim to the stream over whose ownership he had taken Colonel della Rebbia to court.

In accordance with the custom of the country Colomba improvised a *ballata* over her father's body, in the presence of his assembled friends. In it she gave vent to all her hatred of the Barricinis and formally accused them of the murder, also threatening them with her brother's vengeance. This *ballata*, which had become very popular, was the one that the sailor had sung in Miss Lydia's presence. On learning of his father's death, Orso, who was in the north of France at the time, applied for leave but was refused it. At first, on the basis of a letter from his sister, he had believed that the Barricinis were guilty, but soon he received copies of all the documents relating to the investigation; and a personal letter from the judge left him in virtually no doubt that the bandit Agostini was wholly to blame. Every three months Colomba wrote to him, repeating her suspicions, which she regarded as proofs. Despite himself, these accusations made his Corsican blood boil, and sometimes he was close to sharing his sister's prejudices. Nevertheless, whenever he wrote to her he repeated that there were no firm grounds for her allegations and that no credence should be given to them. He even forbade her to raise the subject with him again, though to no effect. Two years passed in this way, after which he was put on half-pay. At this juncture his thoughts turned to seeing his country again; not so as to take revenge on people he believed to be innocent, but to marry off his sister and sell his small properties, always supposing he could raise enough from them to enable him to live on the mainland.

VII

Whether because his sister's arrival had reminded him more forcibly of his ancestral home, or because Colomba's primitive costume and manners caused him some embarrassment in the presence of his civilized friends, the very next morning Orso announced his intention of leaving Ajaccio and returning to Pietranera. However, he made the Colonel promise to come and stay in his humble dwelling on his way to Bastia, and in return he undertook to provide deer, pheasant, wild boar, and the like, for him to hunt.

On the day before his departure, Orso suggested that, rather than going shooting, they should take a walk along the bay. Offering his arm to Miss Lydia, he was able to talk freely, for Colomba had stayed behind in the town to make some purchases, while the Colonel kept dashing off to take pot shots at gulls and boobies, much to the surprise of passers-by, who could not understand why anyone should want to waste gunpowder on such a quarry.

They were following the path that leads to the Greek chapel, which affords the best view of the bay; but they paid no attention to it.

'Miss Lydia,' said Orso, after a silence that had lasted long enough to become embarrassing. 'Tell me frankly, what do you make of my sister?'

'I find her most agreeable,' replied Miss Nevil. 'More so than you,' she added with a smile, 'for she's a true Corsican, whereas you're too civilized for a savage.'

'Too civilized! . . . The fact is, despite myself, ever since I set foot on this island, I've felt as if I were turning into a savage again. A thousand dreadful thoughts agitate and torment me—and I needed to talk with you a little before disappearing into the wilderness.'

'You must have courage, monsieur. See how resigned your sister is, and follow her example.'

'Don't be deceived! Don't suppose she really is resigned. She hasn't said a word to me about it yet, but I can tell from her every look what it is she expects of me.'

'So, what is it she wants you to do?'

'Oh, nothing. . . Just to see whether your father's gun will kill a man as well as it kills a partridge.'

'The very idea! How could you think such a thing! When you've just admitted that she hasn't said anything to you yet. Why, it's monstrous of you!'

'If she weren't thinking of revenge, she would have spoken to me about our father right away. But she has said nothing. She would have spoken of those she regards—wrongly, I know—as his murderers. But no, not a word. The fact is, you see, we Corsicans are a cunning race. My sister realizes that she does not yet have me completely in her power, and she doesn't want to frighten me off while I am still able to escape from her. Once she has led me to the edge of the precipice and my head is spinning, she will push me into the abyss.'

Orso went on to give Miss Nevil some details concerning his father's death, and enumerated the main facts which, taken together, led him to conclude that Agostini was the murderer.

'Nothing will make Colomba change her mind,' he added. 'I realized this when I read her last letter. She has sworn death to the Barricinis, and—Miss Nevil, I know I can trust you. . . Perhaps they would already be dead, but for the fact

that, thanks to one of those primitive ideas for which her
barbarous upbringing is to blame, she is convinced that it
is incumbent on me, as head of the family, to exact the
vengeance, and that my honour is at stake.'

'Really, Monsieur della Rebbia,' said Miss Nevil, 'you
slander your sister.'

'No. You said so yourself: she is a Corsican; she thinks as
they all do. Do you know why I was so sad yesterday?'

'No, but for some time now you've been prone to these fits
of depression. You were more pleasant when we first knew
one another.'

'On the contrary, yesterday I was more cheerful and happier
than usual. You'd been so kind, so indulgent towards my
sister! The Colonel and I were returning by boat. What do you
suppose one of the boatmen said to me in his infernal dialect?
"You've killed a lot of game, Ors' Anton', but you'll find that
Orlanduccio Barricini is a better hunter than you."'

'Well, what's so dreadful about that? Are you really so conceited about your skill as a hunter?'

'But can't you see, the wretch was saying I wouldn't have
the courage to kill Orlanduccio.'

'Do you know, Monsieur della Rebbia, you alarm me. It
seems that not only does the air of your island cause fever, but
it also drives people mad. Fortunately we are leaving soon.'

'Not before visiting Pietranera. You promised my sister that
you would.'

'And if we broke that promise, I suppose we should have to
be prepared for some kind of revenge?'

'Do you remember what your father was telling us the other
day about the Indians who threaten to starve themselves to
death if the East India Company Governors don't grant their
petitions?'

'You mean you would starve yourself to death? I doubt it.
You would go without food for one day, then Mademoiselle
Colomba would bring you such an appetizing *bruccio*[1] that
you would abandon your project.'

'You are cruel in your mockery, Miss Nevil. You should

---

[1] A sort of cooked cream cheese. It is a Corsican national dish.

treat me more leniently. After all, I am alone here. There was no one but you to prevent me from going mad, as you put it. You were my guardian angel; and now . . .'

'—Now,' said Miss Lydia seriously, 'to prop up your precarious reason you have your honour as an officer and a gentleman; that, and . . .', she added, turning aside to pick a flower, 'if it's of any help to you, the memory of your guardian angel.'

'Ah, Miss Nevil! If I could believe that you really took some interest . . .'

'Listen, Monsieur della Rebbia,' said Miss Nevil with some emotion, 'since you are a child I shall treat you like a child. When I was a little girl, I coveted a beautiful necklace; my mother let me have it, but she said to me: "Every time you wear this necklace, remember that you cannot speak French yet." The necklace somehow fell in my esteem; it was as if it were reproaching me. But I wore it, and I learned French. Do you see this ring? It's an Egyptian scarab, found, if you please, in a pyramid. That curious shape that you probably take for a bottle, denotes *human life*. There are people in my country who would find the hieroglyph most appropriate. This one, that follows it, is a shield, with an arm holding a spear. It means *combat, conflict*. So the two characters together form this motto, which I find rather admirable: *Life is a conflict*. Don't run away with the idea that I can read hieroglyphs fluently: it was some dry-as-dust antiquary who explained these to me. Here, I shall give you my scarab. When you have some wicked Corsican thought, look at my talisman and tell yourself that we must emerge victorious from the war our base passions wage against us.—I must say, I preach rather well.'

'I shall think of you, Miss Nevil, and I shall tell myself . . .'

'Tell yourself you have a friend who would be sorry . . . to learn you had been hanged. Besides, your ancestors the *caporali* would be most upset.'

At these words she relinquished Orso's arm with a laugh, and running towards her father, she said, 'Papa, leave those poor birds alone, and come and compose poetry with us in Napoleon's grotto.'

VIII

There is always something solemn about a departure, even when one is going away for only a short time. Orso was due to leave with his sister very early in the morning, and he had taken his leave of Miss Lydia the evening before, for he had no hope that she would belie her habitual laziness by rising early on his behalf. Their farewells had been cold and formal. Since their conversation by the seashore, Miss Lydia had been afraid she might perhaps have shown too keen an interest in Orso, whilst for his own part Orso still resented her mockery, and especially her tone of levity. For a moment he had thought he detected a feeling of incipient affection in the young Englishwoman's manner; now, put out by her jokes, he told himself that she regarded him as a mere acquaintance, who would soon be forgotten. Great, then, was his surprise when, as he was sitting taking coffee with the Colonel that morning, he saw Miss Lydia enter, followed by his sister. She had risen at five o'clock, and for an Englishwoman, particularly Miss Nevil, the effort this involved was sufficiently great for him to derive some self-satisfaction from it.

'I'm sorry you have been disturbed so early,' said Orso. 'I suppose my sister must have woken you despite my instructions. You must be cursing us. Perhaps you wish I was already *hanged*?'

'No,' said Miss Lydia, very quietly and in Italian, evidently so that her father should not hear her. 'But you sulked with me yesterday because of my innocent jokes, and I didn't want to let you leave with bad memories of your humble servant. What terrible people you are, you Corsicans! Farewell, then, I hope we will meet again soon.' And she held out her hand to him.

Orso could only sigh in reply. Colomba approached him, drew him into a window-bay, and, showing him something she held beneath her *mezzaro*, spoke to him in a low voice for a moment.

'My sister wishes to give you a strange present, mademoiselle,' said Orso to Miss Nevil. 'But we Corsicans have little to give . . . , except our affection, which time does not diminish. My sister tells me you showed an interest in this stiletto. It's a family heirloom. Probably it once hung from the belt of one of those *caporali* to whom I owe the honour of your acquaintance. Colomba considers it so precious that she has asked my permission to give it to you, and I'm not really sure whether I should allow her to, for I fear you may laugh at us.'

'The stiletto is delightful,' said Miss Lydia. 'But it's a family weapon. I cannot accept it.'

'It isn't my father's stiletto,' Colomba at once exclaimed. 'It was given to one of my mother's grandparents by King Theodore*. Mademoiselle will give us much pleasure by accepting it.'

'Come, Miss Lydia,' said Orso, 'do not scorn a king's stiletto.'

For a collector, relics of King Theodore are infinitely more precious than those of the mightiest monarch. The temptation was strong, and Miss Lydia was already thinking of the effect the weapon would produce when placed on a lacquered table in her rooms in St. James's Place. Taking the stiletto with the hesitation of someone who would like to accept it, and giving Colomba her most amiable smile, she said, 'Dear Mademoiselle Colomba, I cannot. I would not dare to let you leave like this, unarmed.'

'My brother is with me,' said Colomba proudly, 'and we have the fine gun your father gave us. Orso, have you loaded it?'

Miss Nevil kept the stiletto, and in order to avert the danger one courts by making a present of a cutting or stabbing weapon to one's friends, Colomba demanded a sou in payment.

At last the time came to leave. Orso again shook Miss Nevil's hand. Colomba kissed her, then went to proffer her rosy lips to the Colonel, who was enchanted by this mark of Corsican politeness. From the window of the living-room Miss Lydia saw the brother and sister mount their horses. Colomba's eyes shone with a vindictive joy she had never before noticed in them. This tall, powerful woman, with her fanatical ideas of primitive honour, pride written on her brow, her lips curled in a sardonic smile, leading away this young man armed as if for a sinister expedition, reminded her of Orso's forebodings, and she felt as if she were watching his evil genius leading him away to his doom. Orso, already astride his horse, looked up and noticed her. Whether because he had guessed her thoughts, or to bid her a last goodbye, he took the Egyptian ring, which he had hung from a cord, and raised it to his lips. Miss Lydia left the window, blushing; then, returning to it almost at once, she saw the two Corsicans galloping swiftly away on their little ponies, heading towards the mountains. Half an hour later, through his telescope, the Colonel picked them out for her as they skirted the end of the bay, and she could see Orso, turning frequently to look back towards the town. At last he vanished beyond the marshlands where today a fine plantation of young trees grows.

Looking at herself in her mirror, Miss Lydia thought she looked pale.

'What must this young man think of me?' she asked herself. 'And what do I think of *him*? And why do I think about him? A person encountered by chance on my travels! . . . Why did I come to Corsica? . . . Oh! I do not love him, indeed no. Anyway, it's out of the question. And Colomba. . . . Imagine me, the sister-in-law of a *voceratrice*, who carries a great stiletto!'

Then she noticed that in her hand she was holding King Theodore's stiletto. She threw it onto her dressing-table. 'Imagine Colomba in London, dancing at Allmack's!* Heavens, what a lion[1] for us to parade! Perhaps she would be all the rage. . . . He loves me, I'm sure of it. He's a story-book hero whose career of adventure I've interrupted. . . . But did he really want to avenge his father in Corsican fashion? There was something of the Conrad* about him, and something of the dandy. Now I've turned him into a dandy pure and simple, and one with a Corsican tailor!'

She threw herself onto her bed and tried to sleep, but this proved impossible; and I shall not undertake to continue her monologue, in which she told herself more than a hundred times that Monsieur della Rebbia had not been, was not, and never would be, anything to her.

---

[1] At that period in England, this was the name given to fashionable persons who made themselves conspicuous by some remarkable trait.

IX

Meanwhile Orso and his sister were proceeding on their way. At first the rapid motion of their horses prevented them from conversing; but when the ascents became too steep and forced them to slow to a walking pace, they exchanged a few words about the friends they had just left. Colomba spoke enthusiastically of Miss Nevil's beauty, of her fair hair, and of her gracious manners. Then she asked whether the Colonel was as rich as he appeared to be, and whether Mademoiselle Lydia was an only child. 'She must be a good match,' she said. 'It seems her father has taken a great liking to you . . .' And, as Orso made no reply, she continued: 'Our family was rich once, and is still one of the most highly regarded in the island. Those *signori*[1] are a bastard breed. They are no nobler than the *caporal* families, and you are aware, Orso, that you are descended from the foremost *caporali* in the island. You know our family originally came from beyond the mountains,[2] and that it was civil wars that forced us to cross to this side. In your place, Orso, I wouldn't hesitate, I would ask Miss Nevil's father for her hand.' (Orso shrugged his shoulders.) 'With her dowry I would buy the woods at La Falsetta and the vines below our home. I would build a fine house of quarried stone, and add an extra storey to the old tower in which Sambucuccio killed so many Moors in the time of Count Henry, the *bel Missere*.'[3]

'Colomba, you are mad,' replied Orso, breaking into a gallop.

---

[1] *Signori* is the name given to the descendants of the feudal lords of Corsica. The families of *signori* and *caporali* vie with one another, each group claiming nobler descent than the other.

[2] That is, from the east coast. *Di là dei monti* is a very frequently used expression, and one which changes its meaning according to the location of the person employing it, Corsica being divided by a chain of mountains running from north to south.

[3] See Filippini, book II. Count Arrigo bel Missere died around the year 1000. At his death, a voice is said to have been heard in the sky, singing these prophetic words:

> *E morte il conte Arrigo bel Missere:*
> *E Corsica sarà di male in peggio.*

> [(He is dead, Count Henry, the fine Messire:
> Corsica will go from bad to worse.)]

'You are a man, Ors' Anton', and no doubt you know better than a woman what you must do. But I should like to know what possible objection this Englishman could have to our becoming related. Do they have *caporali* in England?'

After covering quite some distance conversing in this vein, the brother and sister arrived at a small village not far from Bocognano, where they stopped to dine and spend the night with a friend of their family. There they were received with that Corsican hospitality which one has to have experienced to appreciate fully. The next morning their host, who had stood godfather to Madame della Rebbia, accompanied them for a league from his dwelling.

'You see those woods and that maquis,' he said to Orso as they took their leave of one another. 'A man who had *done away with* someone could live in peace in them for ten years without fear of pursuit by gendarmes or *voltigeurs*. The woods border on the forest of Vizzavona, and if you've got friends in Bocognano or thereabouts you won't go short of anything. That's a fine gun you've got there, it must have a good range. Blood of the Madonna, what a calibre! You could kill better game than wild boar with that!'

Orso replied impassively that the gun was of English manufacture, and carried *the lead* a great distance. They embraced, and went their separate ways.

Our travellers were already nearing Pietranera when, at the entrance to a gorge through which they had to pass, they came upon seven or eight men armed with guns, some seated on rocks, others lying on the grass, and others on their feet, apparently on the look-out. Their horses were grazing a short distance away. Colomba scrutinized them for a moment through a field-glass which she took from one of the big leather pouches that all Corsicans carry with them on a journey.

'They're our people!' she exclaimed joyfully. 'Pieruccio has done his work well.'

'What people?' asked Orso.

'Our shepherds,' she replied. 'The evening before last I sent Pieruccio off to collect these good people to accompany you home. It would not be proper for you to enter Pietranera without an escort, and furthermore, you must realize that the Barricinis are capable of anything.'

'Colomba!' said Orso severely. 'I've asked you a number of times not to speak to me again of the Barricinis, and of your groundless suspicions. I'm certainly not going to make myself ridiculous by returning home in the company of this band of ruffians, and I'm most displeased that you have assembled them without informing me.'

'Brother, you have forgotten your country. It is my business to guard you when your imprudence exposes you to danger. I did what I had to do.'

At that moment the shepherds noticed them and, running to their horses, galloped down to meet them.

'*Evviva Ors' Anton'!*' exclaimed a robust old man with a white beard, who, despite the heat, was swathed in a hooded cloak of Corsican cloth, thicker than the fleece on his goats. 'He's the spitting image of his father, only bigger and stronger. What a fine gun! We'll be hearing more about the gun, Ors' Anton'.'

'*Evviva Ors' Anton'!*' the shepherds repeated in chorus. 'We knew he'd come back in the end!'

'Ah, Ors' Anton'!' said a strapping fellow with a complexion the colour of brick, 'how happy your father would be if he were here to welcome you! Bless him! You would be seeing him now, if he had listened to me, if he'd allowed me to settle with Giudice. . . . Poor fellow, he didn't believe me. Now he knows how right I was.'

'Right,' the old man resumed. 'Giudice's turn will come.'

'*Evviva Ors' Anton'!*' And a volley of shots accompanied this acclamation.

Extremely annoyed to find himself surrounded by this group of men on horseback, all speaking at once and crowding round to shake his hand, Orso waited for some time without being able to make himself heard. Finally, adopting the manner he had used before his half-company when handing out reprimands and days in the guardroom, he said:

'My friends, thank you for the affection you have shown for me, and that you showed for my father; but I do not intend, and I shall not allow, anyone to give me advice. I know what it is I must do.'

'He's right, he's right!' exclaimed the shepherds. 'You know you can count on us.'

'Yes, I'm counting on you, but I need no one at present, and no danger threatens my house. Make a start by turning back, and returning to your goats. I know the way to Pietranera, and I need no guides.'

'Have no fear, Ors' Anton',' said the old man. '*They* would not dare show themselves today. The mouse retreats to its hole when the tom-cat returns.'

'Tom-cat yourself, old grey-beard!' said Orso. 'What is your name?'

'What! Don't you recognize me, Ors' Anton', who used to carry you so often behind me on my mule, the one that bit? Don't you recognize Polo Griffo? A worthy man, for sure, and devoted to the della Rebbias body and soul. Say the word, and when your big gun speaks, this old musket, that is as old as its master, will not remain silent. You can count on it, Ors' Anton'.'

'All right, all right. But, devil take it, clear off and allow us to continue on our way!'

At last the shepherds moved off, heading for the village at a brisk trot; but every so often they stopped, at every vantage point along the road, as if to make quite sure there was no ambush awaiting them, and all the while they kept fairly close to Orso and his sister so as to be available to come to their aid should the need arise. And old Polo Griffo said to his companions, 'I understand him, I understand him! He's not letting on what he wants to do, but he'll do it. He's the spitting image of his father. So be it! Say you wish harm to no one! You've made a vow to Saint Nega.[1] Good for you! If you ask me, I wouldn't give a fig for the mayor's hide. Before the month is out it won't be fit to use as a water-skin.'

Thus preceded by this troop of scouts, the scion of the della Rebbias entered his village and arrived at the ancient seat of his ancestors the *caporali*. The della Rebbia faction, long bereft of leaders, had turned out in force to meet him, and the

---

[1] This saint does not figure in the calendar. To make a vow to Saint Nega is to deny everything as a matter of course.

villagers themselves, who remained neutral, were all at their front doors to see him pass by. The Barricini faction remained in their houses, watching through the chinks in their shutters.

Like all Corsican villages, the small town of Pietranera is very irregular in its layout; in order to see a street you must go to Cargèse, which was built by M. de Marbeuf*. The houses, scattered at random with no regard for alignment, occupy the summit of a small plateau, or rather a shelf of the mountainside. Near the middle of the town stands a large holm oak, and close by can be seen a granite trough, into which a wooden pipe carries the water from a nearby spring. The cost of erecting this public edifice was borne jointly by the della Rebbias and the Barricinis, but one would be quite wrong to see this as an indication of the two families' erstwhile harmony; on the contrary, its existence is the result of their rivalry. Once, when Colonel della Rebbia had sent the municipality a small contribution towards the erection of a fountain, the lawyer Barricini lost no time in making a similar donation, and it is to this contest of generosity that Pietranera owes its water supply. Around the holm oak and the fountain there is an empty space which they call the square, where people gather in the evenings to while away the time. Sometimes they play games of cards, and once a year at carnival time there is dancing. At either end of the square stand tall, narrow buildings constructed of granite and schist. These are the *towers* of the warring della Rebbias and Barricinis. Their architecture is identical, they are of the same height, and it can be seen from them that rivalry has always existed between the two families and that fortune has not decided in favour of one or the other.

Perhaps this is the moment to explain what should be understood by the word tower. It is a square building about 40 feet high, which in any other country would go by the less grandiose name of a dovecot. The narrow door is eight feet above ground level, and is reached by a very steep flight of steps. Above the door is a window with a sort of machicolated balcony, which enables one to render an over-persistent visitor *hors de combat* without risk to one's own person. Between the window and the door can be seen two crudely carved shields. One of them formerly bore the cross of Genoa; but today it is so battered that only an antiquary could make anything of it. On the other are carved the arms of the family to whom the tower belongs. To complete the ornamentation, throw in a few bullet-marks on the shield and the casements, and you have a good idea of a medieval fortified dwelling in Corsica. I should not omit to mention that the living quarters adjoin the tower, and often communicate with it internally.

The della Rebbias' tower and house occupy the north side of the square of Pietranera, the Barricinis' tower and house the south side. From the northern tower to the fountain is the della Rebbias' stamping ground; the Barricinis' is on the further side. Since the Colonel's wife had been laid to rest, no member of either family had ever been seen to venture beyond the side of the square that had been assigned to him by a sort of tacit convention. To avoid making a detour, Orso was about to take the way that led past the mayor's house, when his sister alerted him, and urged him to turn down an alleyway which would bring them to their own house without their crossing the square.

'Why go out of our way?' said Orso. 'Doesn't the square belong to everyone?' And he urged his horse on.

'Valiant heart!' said Colomba under her breath. 'Father, you shall be avenged!'

Arriving in the square, Colomba took up position between the Barricinis' house and her brother, and kept a constant watch on her enemies' windows. She noticed that they had recently been barricaded, and that they had been equipped with *archere. Archere* is the name given to the narrow openings shaped like loopholes, left between the thick logs used to board up the lower part of a window. Persons fearing an attack barricade themselves in this way and, protected by the logs, can then fire on their assailants from behind cover.

'The cowards!' said Colomba. 'See, brother, they're beginning to protect themselves already; they're barricading themselves in. But they'll have to come out one day!'

Orso's presence on the south side of the square caused a sensation in Pietranera, and was considered evidence of daring verging on recklessness. For the neutrals gathered round the holm oak in the evening, it was the subject of ceaseless comment.

'It's a good thing', it was observed, 'that Barricini's sons haven't yet returned, for they're less tolerant than the lawyer, and they might not have allowed their enemy to set foot on their ground without making him pay for the bravado.'

'Mark my words, neighbour,' added an old man who was the town oracle. 'I observed Colomba's face today; she's got something in mind. I can smell gunpowder in the air. Before too long there'll be butcher's meat going cheap in Pietranera.'

X

Orso had been separated from his father at an early age, and had thus had little chance to get to know him. He had left Pietranera at the age of 15 to study at Pisa, and from there had gone on to the Military Academy while Ghilfuccio was bearing the imperial eagles around Europe. On the mainland Orso had seen him only occasionally, and it was not until 1815 that he found himself in the regiment commanded by his father. But the Colonel was inexorable in matters of discipline, and treated his son like all the other young lieutenants, that is, with considerable severity. Orso's memories of him were of two sorts. He remembered his father at Pietranera, entrusting his sabre to him, allowing him to unload his gun when he returned from his shooting, or seating him for the first time at the family table when he was a small child. Then he recalled Colonel della Rebbia sending him to the guardroom for some thoughtless action, and never addressing him otherwise than as Lieutenant della Rebbia. 'Lieutenant della Rebbia, you are not at your battle station. Three days' detention.—Your skirmishers are five metres too far from the reserve, five days' detention.—You are still in your forage cap at five past midday, a week's detention.' Once only, at Quatre-Bras*, he had said to him, 'Well done, Orso; but be prudent.' In any case, these were not the memories that Pietranera brought back to him. The sight of the familiar places of his childhood, and of the furniture used by his mother, whom he had loved devotedly, aroused in his soul a flood of tender and poignant emotions; then, the sombre future that lay in store for him, the vague feeling of unease his sister inspired in him, and, above all, the idea that Miss Nevil was going to visit his house, which now seemed to him so small, so poor, so ill-suited for a person accustomed to luxury, the contempt that it might perhaps inspire in her—all these thoughts mingled chaotically in his brain and left him profoundly discouraged.

He sat down to supper in a large armchair of darkened oak, from which his father had formerly presided over the family meals, and smiled on seeing Colomba hesitate before taking her place with him at table. He was nonetheless grateful to her for remaining silent during supper and for withdrawing promptly once the meal was over, for he felt too agitated to resist the assaults she was doubtless preparing for him. But Colomba spared him, wishing to allow him time to collect himself. With his head resting in his hand, he remained motionless for a long time, going over in his mind the scenes he had lived through over the last fortnight. He viewed with alarm the expectations everyone seemed to have of him regarding the Barricinis. He realized that he was already beginning to regard the opinion of Pietranera as if it were that of the world at large. He would be obliged to have his revenge, or else be taken for a coward. But on whom was he to take revenge? He could not believe that the Barricinis were guilty of murder. Certainly they were the enemies of his family, but it needed the crude prejudices of his compatriots to make one capable of attributing a murder to them. Sometimes he would contemplate Miss Nevil's talisman, and would softly repeat its motto: *'Life is a conflict!'* Finally he said to himself firmly, 'I shall win the day!' On this fine thought he rose and, taking the lamp, was about to go up to his bedroom when there came a sound of knocking at the front door. It was hardly the hour for social calls. Colomba instantly appeared, followed by the servant woman. 'It's all right,' she said, running to the door. Nevertheless, before opening it, she asked who was knocking. A gentle voice answered: 'It's me.' At once the wooden bar placed across the door was removed, and Colomba reappeared in the dining-room, followed by a small girl about 10 years old, barefoot and in rags, with her head covered by a dirty handkerchief from beneath which strayed long locks of hair, black as a raven's wing. The child was thin and pale, her skin burned by the sun; but her eyes shone with intelligence. Seeing Orso, she stopped timidly and dropped him a rustic curtsy; then she spoke softly to Colomba and handed her a freshly killed pheasant.

'Thank you, Chili,' said Colomba. 'Thank your uncle. Is he well?'

'Very well, miss. At your service, miss. I couldn't come sooner because he was very late. I was three hours in the maquis waiting for him.'

'So you've had no supper?'

'Why, no, miss, I had no time.'

'You shall be given some supper. Has your uncle still got enough bread?'

'Not much, miss, but it's gunpowder he's really short of. The chestnuts are ready now, so he only needs gunpowder.'

'I'll give you a loaf for him, and some gunpowder. Tell him to be sparing with it, it's expensive.'

'Colomba,' said Orso in French, 'who is that you're giving charity to?'

'A poor bandit from this village,' Colomba replied in the same language. 'This little girl is his niece.'

'It seems to me you could give to a worthier cause. Why provide a scoundrel with gunpowder, when he will use it to commit crimes? If it weren't for the deplorable partiality everyone here seems to have for bandits, Corsica would long since have been rid of them.'

'The wickedest people in our land are not those who have *taken to the country*.[1]'

'Give them bread if you wish, no one should be refused it. But I won't have you giving them ammunition.'

'Brother,' said Colomba gravely, 'you are the master here,

---

[1] To be *alla campagna* means to be a bandit. *Bandit* is not a term of disparagement; it is used in the sense of 'proscript', the 'outlaw' of the English ballads.

and everything in this house belongs to you. But, I give you due warning, if need be I will give this little girl my *mezzaro* to sell, sooner than refuse gunpowder to a bandit. Refuse him gunpowder! You might as well hand him over to the gendarmes. How is he to defend himself against them, except with his cartridges?'

Meanwhile the little girl was devouring a piece of bread voraciously, and looking attentively, first at Colomba, then at her brother, trying to read from their expressions the meaning of what they were saying.

'Anyway, what has he done, this bandit of yours? What crime has driven him to take refuge in the maquis?'

'Brandolaccio has committed no crime,' exclaimed Colomba. 'He killed Giovan' Opizzo, who had murdered his father while he was away in the army.'

Orso turned away, took the lamp, and without replying went up to his bedroom. Thereupon Colomba gave gunpowder and provisions to the child and accompanied her back to the door, repeating to her: 'Above all, make sure your uncle takes good care of Orso!'

XI

It took Orso a long time to get to sleep, and consequently he woke up very late, at least by Corsican standards. The first sight which greeted him as he rose from his bed was the house of his enemies with its newly installed *archere*. He went downstairs and asked for his sister.

'She's in the kitchen casting bullets,' replied the servant Saveria. It seemed he could not move an inch without being dogged by images of war.

He found Colomba seated on a wooden stool, surrounded by newly cast bullets, trimming the leaden sprues from them.

'What the devil are you up to?' her brother asked her.

'You had no bullets for the Colonel's gun,' she replied in her gentle voice. 'I've found a bullet mould of the right calibre, and today, brother, you will have twenty-four cartridges.'

'I won't be needing them, thank God!'

'It wouldn't do to be caught off your guard, Ors' Anton'.

You have forgotten what your country and the people around you are like.'

'If I had forgotten, you'd soon remind me. Tell me, did a large trunk arrive a few days ago?'

'Yes, brother. Do you want me to take it up to your room?'

'You take it up? Why, you'd never be strong enough to lift it. Is there no man here who can do it?'

'I'm not so weak as you suppose,' said Colomba, rolling up her sleeves and revealing a plump white arm, which was perfectly proportioned but which betokened exceptional strength. 'Come, Saveria,' she said to the servant, 'help me.' She was already lifting the heavy trunk unaided, when Orso hastened to help her.

'There's something for you in this trunk, dear Colomba,' he said. 'Forgive me for offering you such sorry presents, but the purse of a lieutenant on half-pay isn't very well lined.' As he spoke he opened the trunk and took out some dresses, a shawl, and other objects which a young person could put to good use.

'What beautiful things!' exclaimed Colomba. 'I'll put them away at once, in case they get spoiled. I shall keep them until my wedding,' she added, smiling sadly, 'for at present I'm in mourning.' And she kissed her brother's hand.

'It's an affectation to stay so long in mourning, sister.'

'I swore I would,' said Colomba firmly. 'I shan't go out of mourning . . .' And she looked out of the window, at the Barricini house.

'Until the day you marry?' said Orso, trying to prevent her from finishing her sentence.

'I shall only marry a man who has done three things,' said Colomba. And she continued to gaze at her enemies' house with a sinister expression.

'I'm amazed that a pretty girl like you isn't already married, Colomba. Come now, tell me who is courting you. In any case, I shall certainly hear their serenades. They'll have to be good, to please a great *voceratrice* like yourself.'

'Who would want a poor orphan-girl? . . . Besides, the man who gets me to leave off my mourning clothes will give the women over there cause to don them.'

'This is becoming an obsession,' Orso thought to himself. But he said nothing, so as to avoid discussion.

'Brother,' said Colomba, in a wheedling voice, 'I've got something to give you, too. Those clothes you're wearing are too good for this country. Your nice frock coat would be torn to pieces inside two days if you wore it in the maquis. You must keep it for when Miss Nevil comes.' Then, opening a cupboard, she took from it a suit of hunting clothes.

'I've made you a velvet jacket, and here's a cap, the kind well-dressed people here wear. I embroidered it for you some time ago. Will you try them on?'

And she helped him into an ample green velvet jacket with an enormous pocket in the back. She placed on his head a black velvet pointed cap embroidered in jet and silk of the same colour, with a sort of tassel on top.

'Here's our father's *carchera*[1],' she said. 'His stiletto is in your jacket pocket. I'll fetch the pistol for you.'

'I look like some stage brigand straight out of the *Ambigu-Comique**,' said Orso, looking at himself in a little mirror that Saveria offered him.

'How well they suit you, Ors' Anton',' said the old servant. 'The handsomest *pinsuto*[2] in Bocognano or Bastelica couldn't look more elegant.'

Orso dined wearing his new costume, and during the meal he told his sister that his trunk contained a number of books, and that he was intending to have more sent from France and Italy, and to make her study hard. 'For it's shameful, Colomba,' he went on, 'that a girl of your age still doesn't know things children on the mainland learn as soon as they are weaned.'

'You are right, brother,' said Colomba. 'I'm well aware of my shortcomings, and I would be only too happy to study, especially if you're willing to give me lessons.'

Some days passed without Colomba alluding to the Barricinis. She continued to be full of attentions for her brother, and often spoke to him of Miss Nevil. Orso got her to read French and Italian books, and was surprised both by the occasional acuity and good sense of her observations, and by her profound ignorance of the most everyday matters.

---

[1] A belt designed to hold cartridges. A pistol is attached to its left side.
[2] The name given to those who wear the pointed cap (*barreta pinsuta*).

One morning, after breakfast, Colomba went out for a moment and returned, not with a book and paper, but with her *mezzaro* on her head. Her manner was even more serious than usual. 'Brother,' she said, 'be so good as to come with me.'

'Where do you want to take me?' asked Orso, offering her his arm.

'I don't need your arm, brother. But bring your gun and your cartridge-box. A man should never go out without his weapons.'

'Very well then. One must comply with custom. Where are we going?'

Without replying Colomba secured the *mezzaro* round her head, summoned the watch-dog, and led her brother out. Walking briskly away from the village, she turned down a sunken lane which wound through the vineyards, sending the dog on ahead and giving him a sign with which he seemed to be familiar; for he at once began to zigzag through the vines, first to one side, then to the other, always keeping fifty paces ahead of his mistress, and sometimes stopping in the middle of the road to look back at her, wagging his tail. He appeared to acquit himself admirably of his duties as a scout.

'If Muschetto barks, cock your rifle, brother, and don't move,' said Colomba.

Half a mile from the village, after a good many detours, Colomba suddenly came to a halt at a point where the road turned sharply. There stood a small pyramid of branches, some green, others withered, piled up to a height of about three feet. The tip of a black-painted wooden cross could be seen protruding from the top of the pile. In several districts of Corsica, especially in the mountains, an extremely ancient custom, which may be connected with pagan superstition, requires passers-by to throw a stone or a branch onto the spot where a man has met a violent death. Over the years, for as long as men still remember his tragic end, this curious offering gradually mounts up from day to day. It is known as a person's 'cairn' or *mucchio*.

Colomba halted before this pile of foliage and, tearing a branch off an arbutus, added it to the pyramid.

'Orso,' she said. 'This is where our father died. Let us pray for his soul, brother.' And she fell to her knees. Orso at once followed suit. At that moment the village bell began to toll slowly, for a man had died during the night. Orso burst into tears.

After a few minutes Colomba got up; her eyes were dry, but her face was flushed. With her thumb, she hastily made the sign of the cross with which her compatriots normally accompany their solemn vows; then, leading her brother away, she set off on the road back to the village. They re-entered their house in silence. Orso went up to his room. A moment later Colomba followed him up, carrying a small casket which she placed on the table. She opened it and took from it a blood-stained shirt.

'Here is your father's shirt, Orso,' she said. And she threw it into his lap. 'Here is the lead that struck him down.' And she placed on the shirt two tarnished bullets. 'Orso, my brother!' she cried, throwing herself into his arms and embracing him violently. 'Orso, you shall avenge him!' She clasped him with a sort of frenzy, kissed the bullets and the shirt, then went out of the room, leaving her brother seated in his chair as if paralysed.

Orso remained motionless for some time, not daring to put the appalling relics out of his sight. At last, making an effort, he put them back in the casket and hastened to the other end of the room, where he threw himself onto his bed with his head turned towards the wall and buried in his pillow, as if trying to blot out the sight of some ghost. His sister's last words kept resounding in his ears, and he seemed to hear a fatal, inexorable oracle demanding blood of him, and innocent blood at that. I shall not attempt to convey the unfortunate young man's sensations, which were as confused as those that play havoc with a madman's reason. For a long time he remained in the same position, not daring to turn his head. At last he got up, closed the casket, rushed out of the house, and roamed the fields, walking blindly ahead with no clear conception where he was going.

Gradually the open air soothed him; he grew calmer, and considered dispassionately his situation and the ways in which he might extricate himself from it. He did not suspect the Barricinis of murder, as we already know. But he did suspect them of having forged the letter from the bandit Agostini; and that letter, in his opinion at any rate, had been the cause of his father's death. He felt sure that to prosecute them for forgery was out of the question. Sometimes, if the prejudices or instincts of his country returned to assail him with thoughts of an easy revenge at some bend in the road, he would repudiate them with horror, thinking of his comrades in the regiment, of the Paris *salons*, and above all of Miss Nevil. Then he would think of his sister's reproaches, and the vestiges of the Corsican in his make-up found these reproaches just, making them the more poignant. His one hope of resolving this conflict between his conscience and his prejudices was to find some pretext for starting a quarrel with one of the lawyer's sons and fighting a duel with him. To kill him with a bullet or a sword-thrust could be reconciled both with his French and with his Corsican ideas. Once the expedient had been accepted and he could ponder the means of implementing it, he at once felt relieved of a great burden; whereupon other, more tender thoughts came to contribute further towards calming his feverish agitation. Driven to despair by the death of his daughter Tullia, Cicero forgot his grief by rehearsing mentally all the fine things he might say on the subject. Discoursing in this strain on life and death, Tristram Shandy's father found consolation for the loss of a son*. Orso regained his composure by thinking how he would be able to reveal to Miss Nevil the state of his soul, a revelation in which that fair person could not fail to take a strong interest.

He was once again approaching the village, from which he had inadvertently strayed a considerable distance, when he heard the voice of a little girl who, no doubt supposing herself to be alone, was singing on a path that ran along the edge of the maquis. It was the slow, monotonous melody that is used for funeral laments, and the child was singing:

'*For my son, my son in a far-off land,—keep my cross and my bloodstained shirt.*'

'What's that you are singing, child?' said Orso angrily, suddenly appearing before her.

'Why, it's you, Ors' Anton'!' exclaimed the child, somewhat startled. 'It's one of Miss Colomba's songs.'

'I forbid you to sing it!' said Orso in a terrible voice.

The child, turning her head this way and that, seemed to be looking for the best way to run, and would doubtless have fled, had she not been held back by the need to look after a large parcel which could be seen lying on the grass at her feet.

Orso felt ashamed of his violence.

'What have you got there, child?' he asked her as gently as he could.

And as Chilina hesitated to reply, he lifted the cloth in which the parcel was wrapped, and saw that it contained a loaf of bread and various other supplies.

'Who is that bread for, my dear?' he asked her.

'My uncle, sir, as you well know.'

'But isn't your uncle a bandit?'

'At your service, Ors' Anton', sir.'

'If the gendarmes found you they'd ask you where you were going.'

Without hesitation the child replied: 'I'd tell them I was taking food to the Italians who've come over from Lucca to clear the maquis.'

'And supposing you came upon some famished hunter who wanted to dine at your expense and relieve you of your provisions?'

'He wouldn't dare. I'd say they were for my uncle.'

'I must say, he's not the sort of man to allow anyone to take his dinner. Is your uncle fond of you?'

'Oh, yes, Ors' Anton'! Ever since papa died he's looked after the family—mother, me, and my little sister. Before mother fell ill he used to put in a word for her with rich people so as they'd give her work. The mayor gives me a dress once a year, and the *Curé* has been teaching me to say my catechism and giving me reading lessons, since my uncle had a word with them. But your sister is the one who's kindest to us.'

At that moment a dog appeared on the path. The little girl placed two fingers in her mouth and gave a piercing whistle; the dog at once came and fawned on her, then plunged abruptly into the maquis. Soon two men, poorly clad but well armed, rose up from behind a stool of copse-wood a few feet from Orso. It was as if they had crawled forward like snakes through the tangle of cistus and myrtle that covered the ground.

'Oho! Ors' Anton', welcome!' said the elder of the two men. 'Well, don't you recognize me?'

'No,' said Orso, staring at him.

'It's funny how a beard and a pointed cap can alter a man's appearance. Come, Lieutenant, look carefully. Have you forgotten the veterans of Waterloo? Don't you remember Brando Savelli, who tore open so many cartridges* at your side on that ill-fated day?'

'What? Is it you, Brando? But you deserted in 1816!' said Orso.

'Quite right, Lieutenant. Let's face it, army routine is boring; and besides, I had a score to settle back here.—Ah! Chili, there's a good girl! Serve us quickly, we're hungry. You've no idea, Lieutenant, what an appetite one gets in the maquis. Who was it sent us this, Mademoiselle Colomba or the mayor?'

'No, uncle, it was the miller's wife who gave me this for you, and a blanket for mother.'

'What does she want of me?'

'She says that now the workers she hired from Lucca to clear the maquis are demanding thirty-five sous with the chestnuts thrown in, on account of the malaria down below Pietranera.'

'The bunch of idlers! I'll see about it. No ceremony, Lieutenant, will you share our dinner? We've made worse meals together, in the time of our poor compatriot that they've pensioned off.'

'No thanks. They've pensioned me off, too.'

'So I hear. But you weren't too upset about that, I'll be bound. You've got your own score to settle.—Come, *Curé*,' the bandit said to his companion. 'Dinner is served.—Monsieur Orso, allow me to introduce my reverend friend the *Curé*. Actually I'm not sure if he is a priest, but he has a priest's learning.'

'A poor theology student, monsieur,' said the second bandit, 'who has been prevented from pursuing his vocation. Who knows, Brandolaccio, I might have become Pope.'

'What was it that led to the Church being deprived of your wisdom?'

'A mere trifle; a score to settle, as my friend Brandolaccio puts it. A sister of mine had sown her wild oats while I was ploughing my way through the books at the University of Pisa. I had to come back here to marry her off. But the groom was in too much of a hurry, and went and died of malaria three days before I arrived. I then turned, as you would have done in my place, to the dead man's brother. I was told he was already married. What was I to do?'

'An awkward situation, and no mistake. And what did you do?'

'In cases such as these, there's nothing for it but the flintlock[1].'

'You mean . . . '

'I put a bullet through his head,' the bandit said nonchalantly.

Orso recoiled in horror. Yet curiosity, and perhaps also the desire to put off the moment when he would have to return home, made him remain where he was and continue his conversation with these two men, each of whom had at least one murder on his conscience.

While his comrade was speaking, Brandolaccio placed bread and meat before him; he served himself, then gave a share to his dog, telling Orso that the animal was called Brusco, and that he had the marvellous gift of being able to recognize a *voltigeur* instinctively, regardless of the disguise he assumed. Lastly, he cut a piece of bread and a slice of raw ham and gave them to his niece.

'It's a fine life being a bandit!' exclaimed the student of theology after a few mouthfuls. 'Perhaps you may be sampling it for yourself one day, Monsieur della Rebbia, and you'll see how delightful it is to know no master but one's own inclination.' Up until then the bandit had spoken in Italian; he continued in French.

'Corsica's no place for a young man. But for a bandit, it's a different matter. The women are crazy about us! Look at me, I've got three mistresses in three different parts of the island. Wherever I go I'm at home. And one of them's married to a gendarme.'

---

[1] *La scaglia*, a very commonly used expression.

'You speak a number of languages, monsieur,' said Orso gravely.

'If I speak French it's because, well, you know, *maxima debetur pueris reverentia**. Brandolaccio and me, we mean the child to turn out well and stay on the straight and narrow.'

'When she's 15,' said Chilina's uncle, 'I'll find her a good match. I've already got someone in mind.'

'Will you make the proposal yourself?' asked Orso.

'Assuredly. If I say to some rich man hereabouts, "I, Brando Savelli, would be pleased to see your son marry Michelina Savelli", do you suppose he will need his arm twisting?'

'I wouldn't recommend it,' said the other bandit. 'Our friend here doesn't know his own strength.'

'Now if I were a scoundrel,' Brandolaccio continued, 'a bad lot or a treacherous individual, I'd only have to open my satchel and the hundred-sou pieces would fall into it like rain.'

'Is there something in your satchel that attracts them?' asked Orso.

'No. But if I wrote to a rich man, as some have been doing, saying, "I need a hundred francs", he'd be quick enough to send me them. But I am a man of honour, Lieutenant.'

'Would you believe, Monsieur della Rebbia,' said the bandit whom his companion addressed as the *Curé*, 'that even in this land of simple customs, there are wretches who take advantage of the esteem our passports bring us' (he pointed to his gun) 'to forge our handwriting in order to draw bills of exchange?'

'I know,' said Orso abruptly. 'But what bills of exchange are you referring to?'

'Six months ago,' the bandit continued, 'I was walking over by Orezza when this fellow came up to me, doffed his hat while still some distance away, and said, "Ah, *Monsieur le Curé*," (they always call me that) "forgive me, allow me more time. I've only been able to find fifty-five francs. I swear that's all I've been able to grub together."

'Completely taken aback, I said to him, "Fifty-five francs? What are you talking about, you blackguard?" "I'm sorry, I mean sixty-five," he replied. "But as for the hundred you're asking for, that's out of the question." "What, you knave? Me ask you for a hundred francs? I've never seen you before in my life," I said. So then he handed me a letter, or rather, a filthy scrap of paper, in which he was called upon to leave a hundred francs at a specified place, failing which his house would be burnt down and his cows slaughtered by Giocanto Castriconi—that's my name. And they'd been despicable enough to forge my signature! The thing that hurt me most was that the letter had been written in dialect, and was full of spelling mistakes. Can you imagine, me, making spelling mistakes, when I'd won every prize at the university! I began by giving the fellow a thump that sent him spinning. "So, you take me for a robber, you swine!" I said to him, giving him a good kick you know where. I felt a bit better after that, and said to him, "When must you take the money to the appointed place?" "This very day," he said. "Right, off you go with it," I said.

'It was under a pine tree, the spot was clearly indicated. He took the money, buried it beneath the tree, and came back to join me. I had lain in wait close by. I remained there with the fellow for six solid hours. Monsieur della Rebbia, I'd have waited three days if necessary. After six hours a *Bastiaccio*[1] appeared, a vile usurer. He stooped to take the money, I fired, and my aim was so sure that his head struck the crowns he was unearthing as he fell. "Now, you rogue," I said to the peasant, "take your money, and never again take it into your head to suppose Giocanto Castriconi capable of any base action."

'Trembling all over, the poor devil picked up his sixty-five francs without bothering to wipe them. He thanked me, I fetched him a good kick to send him on his way, and he's still running now.'

'Ah, *Curé*,' said Brandolaccio, 'I envy you that shot. You must have laughed heartily.'

'I'd hit the *Bastiaccio* in the temple,' the bandit went on. 'It reminded me of those lines of Virgil:

> . . . . *Liquefacto tempora plumbo*
> *Diffidit, ac multa porrectum extendit arena.**

---

[1] Corsicans from the mountains detest the inhabitants of Bastia, refusing to acknowledge them as compatriots. They never refer to one as a *Bastiese*, but only as a *Bastiaccio*. The suffix *-accio* normally has a derogatory force*.

'*Liquefacto*! Do you suppose, Monsieur Orso, that a lead bullet can melt as a result of the speed with which it travels through the air? You've studied ballistics, you should be able to tell me whether or not it's possible.'

Orso was more inclined to discuss this problem of physics than to argue with the graduate about the morality of his action. Brandolaccio, who found this scientific dissertation little to his taste, interrupted him to remark that the sun was about to set.

'Since you didn't wish to dine with us, Ors' Anton',' he said, 'I advise you not to keep Mademoiselle Colomba waiting any longer. Besides, it's not always safe to be out of doors after sunset. And what are you doing out without a gun? There are some bad people about; look out for them. For today you have nothing to fear—the Barricinis are taking the Prefect home with them. They met him on the road, and he's going to spend the day at Pietranera before going on to Corte to lay a foundation stone, as they call it, or some such nonsense. He's sleeping at the Barricinis' place tonight, but tomorrow they'll be at large. There's Vincentello, who's a bad lot, and Orlanduccio, who's not much better. Try to deal with them separately, one at a time. But mind how you go, that's all I say to you.'

'Thank you for the advice,' said Orso. 'But there's no quarrel between us. Unless they come and seek me out, I have nothing to say to them.'

The bandit put his tongue in his cheek and clicked it to express irony, but did not reply. As Orso was getting up to leave, Brandolaccio said:

'By the way, I haven't thanked you for the gunpowder. It came in the nick of time. Now I've got everything I need;— though actually I could still do with some shoes. Still, one of these days I'll make myself a pair out of the skin of a moufflon.'

Orso slipped two five-franc coins into the bandit's hand. He said:

'It was Colomba who sent you the gunpowder. Here's something to buy yourself some shoes with.'

'Don't be a fool, Lieutenant,' exclaimed Brandolaccio,

giving him back the two coins. 'What do you take me for—a beggar? I'll accept the bread and the gunpowder, but I want nothing more.'

'I thought that, as old comrades-in-arms, we could help one another out. Oh well, farewell then!'

But, before leaving, he slipped the money into the bandit's satchel without his noticing.

'Farewell, Ors' Anton',' said the theologian. 'Perhaps we'll meet again in the maquis one of these days, and then we can continue our study of Virgil.'

It was a quarter of an hour after leaving his worthy companions that Orso heard a man running behind him as fast as his legs could carry him. It was Brandolaccio.

'This is going too far, Lieutenant,' he exclaimed breathlessly. 'A bit too far! Here, take your ten francs. If it had been anyone else, I would not forgive such a prank. My kind regards to Mademoiselle Colomba. Now I'm all out of breath! Goodnight.'

XII

Orso found Colomba somewhat alarmed at his long absence. But on seeing him she reassumed her habitual expression of sad serenity. During the evening meal they spoke only of unimportant topics, and Orso, emboldened by his sister's air of calm, told her of his encounter with the bandits and even ventured a few pleasantries about the moral and religious education little Chilina was receiving at the hands of her uncle and his honourable colleague, the worthy Castriconi.

'Brandolaccio is an honest man,' said Colomba. 'But, as for Castriconi, I've heard it said that he's unprincipled.'

'I don't think there's a great deal to choose between him and Brandolaccio,' said Orso. 'The pair of them are openly at war with society. One crime leads to another, and so it goes on, day after day. And yet, perhaps they're not as guilty as a good many people who haven't had to take to the maquis.'

For a second, his sister's brow lit up with joy.

'Yes,' continued Orso, 'these wretches have their own code of honour. It's a cruel convention, not base cupidity, that has plunged them into the life they lead.'

For a moment there was silence.

'Brother,' said Colomba, pouring out his coffee, 'perhaps you've heard, Charles-Baptiste Pietri died last night. Yes, he died of marsh fever.'

'Who was this Pietri?'

'A man of this town, the husband of Madeleine Pietri, who was given the notebook by our father as he lay dying. His widow has asked me to go to his wake and sing something there. It's only proper that you should come too. They're neighbours, and it's a social obligation one cannot ignore in a small place like ours.'

'Confound your wake, Colomba! I object to seeing my sister make a public exhibition of herself.'

'Orso,' replied Colomba, 'every man honours his dead after his own fashion. The *ballata* has been handed down to us from our ancestors, and we must respect it as an ancient custom. Madeleine does not have *the gift*, and old Fiordispina, who's the best *voceratrice* in the region, is ill. Someone must be there to perform the *ballata*.'

'Do you suppose Charles-Baptiste won't find his way to the next world unless someone declaims third-rate poetry over his bier? Go to the wake if you wish, Colomba. I will go with you, if you feel I ought to. But don't improvise a *ballata*. It's unseemly in one of your age, and . . . Sister, I implore you not to.'

'Brother, I have promised. It's the custom here, as you know, and, I repeat, there is no one but me to improvise.'

'It's a foolish custom!'

'It pains me greatly to have to sing. It reminds me of all our own misfortunes. Tomorrow I shall be ill as a result, but it has to be. Give me leave, brother. Remember how, at Ajaccio, you told me to improvise to entertain that English girl who makes fun of our ancient customs. Yet am I not to be allowed to improvise today for poor people who will be grateful to me for it, and whom it will help to bear their grief?'

'All right, do as you will. I suppose you've already

composed your *ballata* and you don't want it to go to waste.'

'No, I couldn't compose it beforehand, brother. I stand before the dead man and I think of those he leaves behind. Tears come to my eyes, and then I sing whatever comes into my head.'

All this was said so artlessly that it was impossible to suspect Mistress Colomba of the slightest trace of poetic vanity. Orso allowed himself to be prevailed upon, and went with his sister to Pietri's house. The dead man was laid out on a table, with his face uncovered, in the largest room in the house. The doors and windows were open, and candles burned around the table. At the dead man's head stood his widow, and behind her a large number of women occupied one whole side of the room; on the other stood the men, their heads bared, staring at the corpse in total silence. Each new visitor approached the table, kissed the dead man,[1] nodded to his widow and son, then took his place in the group without uttering a word. Nevertheless, from time to time one of those present would break the solemn silence to address a few words to the deceased. 'Why did you leave your good wife?' asked one of her cronies. 'Didn't she look after you properly? What did you lack? Couldn't you have waited another month? Your daughter-in-law would have given you a son.'

A tall young man, Pietri's son, clasped his father's cold hand and exclaimed, 'Oh, why did you not die the *malemort*[2]? We would have avenged you.'

These were the first words Orso heard on entering. Seeing him, the crowd parted, and a low murmur indicated the expectations of the assembled group, whose curiosity had been awakened by the arrival of the *voceratrice*. Colomba kissed the widow, took one of her hands, and remained for a few minutes with lowered eyes, collecting her thoughts. Then she pushed back her *mezzaro*, stared intently at the corpse, and, her face almost as white as the dead man's, leaned over him and began as follows:

'*Charles-Baptiste, Christ receive thy soul.—To live is to*

---

[1] This custom is still observed at Bocognano (1840).

[2] *La mala morte:* a violent death.

*suffer!—Thou goest to a place—wherein there is nor sun nor
chill.—No more dost thou need thy bill-hook,—or thy heavy
pick.—No more work for thee.—Henceforth all thy days shall be
Sundays.—Charles-Baptiste, may Christ receive thy soul!—Thy
son is now master of thine house.—I have seen the oak fall,—
withered by the wind from Libya.—I thought that it was dead.—I
passed this way again,—and from its root a shoot had sprung.—
The shoot has become an oak,—spreading its shade far and
wide.—Beneath its sturdy branches, Maddelè, take thy rest, and
think of the oak that is no more.'*

At this point Madeleine began to sob aloud, and two or
three men who, had the occasion arisen, would have shot a
Christian with as little compunction as they would a partridge, began to wipe great tears from their sunburnt cheeks.

Colomba continued in this strain for some time, addressing
now the deceased, now his family, and sometimes, using a
form of personification common in the *ballata*, making the
dead man himself speak, to console his friends or give them
advice. As she improvised, her face began to take on an exalted
expression, and her complexion was suffused with a rosy glow
that accentuated the brilliant white of her teeth and the fire
that flashed from her dilated pupils. She resembled the Pythia
on her tripod.* Except for a few sighs and stifled sobs, not the
slightest murmur came from the crowd pressing around her.
Although he was less susceptible than most to this wild
poetry, Orso soon felt himself affected by the general emotion.
Withdrawing into a dark corner of the room, he wept as
Pietri's son was doing.

Suddenly a slight stir ran through the assembly; the crowd
parted and several strangers entered. From the respect they
were shown and the haste with which room was made for
them, it was evident that these were people of importance who
were bestowing a signal honour on the house by their visit.
However, out of respect for the *ballata*, no one spoke to them.
The man who had been the first to enter looked about 40 years
old. From his black coat, the red rosette in his buttonhole, and
his expression of confidence and authority, one could immediately deduce that this was the Prefect. Behind him came an
old man, stooping, with a bilious complexion, wearing

green-tinted spectacles which failed to conceal the timidity
and anxiety in his eyes. He was wearing a black coat which
was too big for him and which, although it was still as good
as new, had obviously been made some years before. He was
constantly at the Prefect's side, as if he wanted to hide in his
shadow. Lastly, two tall young men followed him in, with
sunburnt complexions, their cheeks concealed by thick
whiskers, and with an expression of insolent curiosity in their
proud, arrogant eyes. Orso had had time to forget the faces of
the people from his village; but the sight of the old man in the
green-tinted glasses at once awakened old memories in his
mind. His presence in the Prefect's entourage was enough to
identify him: it was the lawyer Barricini, the mayor of
Pietranera, and his two sons, bringing the Prefect to hear a
performance of a *ballata*. It would be difficult to say precisely
what passed through Orso's soul at that moment; but the
presence of his father's enemy inspired him with a sort of
horror, and he felt more than ever prone to be swayed by the
suspicions against which he had struggled so long.

As for Colomba, at the sight of the man for whom she had
vowed mortal hatred her mobile features at once took on a
sinister expression. She turned pale; her voice grew harsh, the
phrase she was declaiming died on her lips. But soon, resuming her *ballata*, she continued with a new vehemence:

  '*When the sparrow-hawk laments—before its empty nest,—the
  starlings flutter around it,—mocking at its grief.*'

At this point a snigger was heard; it came from the two
young men who had recently arrived, and who apparently
found the image overstrained.

  '*The sparrow-hawk will awaken; it will unfurl its wings,—it
  will dip its beak in blood! And thou, Charles-Baptiste, let thy
  friends—bid thee their last farewell.—Their tears have flowed
  enough.—Only the poor orphan-girl will not weep for thee.—Why
  should she weep for thee?—Thou fellest asleep full of years—
  amidst thy family—prepared to meet the Almighty.—The orphan-
  girl weeps for her father,—surprised by craven murderers,—struck
  down from behind;—her father whose blood is red—beneath the
  heap of green leaves.—But she has gathered his blood,—that*

noble and innocent blood,—she has spread it over Pietranera,—
that it might become a deadly poison.—And Pietranera shall
remain stained—until some guilty blood—has wiped away the
traces of innocent blood.'

As she finished these words, Colomba slumped into a
chair, pulled her *mezzaro* down over her face, and could
be heard sobbing. The weeping women gathered around
the poetess; several men cast fierce glances at the mayor
and his sons; a few old people muttered protests at the
scandal the family had occasioned by their presence. The
dead man's son forced his way through the crowd, and was
preparing to ask the mayor to make himself scarce forth-
with. But the mayor had not waited to be asked. He had reached the door, and his two sons were already in the street. The
Prefect spoke a few words of condolence to young Pietri and
followed them almost at once. As for Orso, he went up to
his sister, took her by the arm, and led her out of the
room.

'Go with them,' said young Pietri to some of his friends.
'Make sure no harm befalls them!'

Two or three young men hastily slipped their stilettos
into the left sleeve of their jackets, and escorted Orso and his
sister as far as the door of their house.

XIII

Colomba, breathless and exhausted, was in no state to talk.
She rested her head on her brother's shoulder and held one of
his hands clasped between her own. Although inwardly he
rather resented her peroration, Orso was too alarmed to level
the slightest reproach at her. While he was waiting in silence
for her to recover from the hysteria which seemed to be gripping her, a knock was heard at the door and Saveria entered
in a fluster, announcing the Prefect. Hearing this name,
Colomba rose, as if ashamed of her weakness, and stood supporting herself against a chair, which shook visibly beneath
her hands.

The Prefect began by making a few routine apologies for
calling at such a late hour, offered his sympathy to

Mademoiselle Colomba, spoke of the danger of strong emotions, and deplored the custom of funeral laments, in which the talent of the *voceratrice* only served to increase the distress of those present. He skilfully slipped in a mild reproach regarding the tenor of the last improvisation. Then, in a different tone of voice, he said:

'Monsieur della Rebbia, I bring you many greetings from your English friends; Miss Nevil sends her kindest regards to your sister, Miss Colomba. I have a letter from her to give you.'

'A letter from Miss Nevil?' exclaimed Orso.

'Unfortunately I don't have it with me now, but you shall have it in five minutes. Her father has been unwell. For a moment we feared he might have caught one of our terrible fevers. Fortunately he has got over it, as you will be able to judge for yourself, for I imagine you will be seeing him soon.'

'Miss Nevil must have been most concerned for him?'

'Fortunately she didn't hear of the danger until it had already passed. Monsieur della Rebbia, Miss Nevil has spoken to me a good deal about you and your sister Mademoiselle Colomba.' Orso bowed. 'She is very fond of you both. Beneath her graceful exterior and her appearance of flippancy she conceals a wealth of sense.'

'She is a charming person,' said Orso.

'You could almost say she specifically asked me to come here, monsieur. No one is better acquainted than myself with a tragic story to which I would prefer not to have to allude. Since Monsieur Barricini is still mayor of Pietranera, and I am Prefect of this *département*, I need not tell you what store I set by certain suspicions which, if I am correctly informed, some imprudent persons have voiced to you, and which I know you have dismissed with the indignation one would expect of a man of your position and character.'

'Colomba,' said Orso, shifting on his chair, 'you're very tired. You should go to bed.'

Colomba shook her head. She had regained her customary composure and was gazing at the Prefect with flashing eyes.

'Monsieur Barricini', the Prefect continued, 'would be more than happy to see an end to what amounts to a state of enmity—that is, the uncertainty that characterizes your deal-

ings with one another. For my own part, I should be delighted
to see you establish relations of the sort that should exist
between men made to esteem one another.'

'Sir,' Orso interrupted in a voice full of emotion, 'I have
never accused the lawyer Barricini of murdering my father,
but he has committed an action which will make it impossible
for me ever to have any dealings with him. He forged a
threatening letter, purporting to come from a certain bandit;
or at least, he insinuated that it was from my father. You see,
sir, that letter was probably the indirect cause of his death.'

The Prefect collected his thoughts for a moment. 'That
your father, with his impetuous nature, should have thought
such a thing when he was engaged in litigation with Monsieur
Barricini, is pardonable. But, coming from yourself, such
blindness cannot be excused. Consider, Barricini had nothing
to gain from forging the letter. I shall not speak to you of his
character; you don't know him, you are biased against him;
but you cannot suppose that a man familiar with the law . . .'

'Sir,' said Orso, standing up. 'Kindly bear in mind that to
tell me the letter is not Monsieur Barricini's work, is tantamount to attributing it to my father. His honour, sir, is mine.'

'No one, monsieur,' continued the Prefect, 'is more convinced than myself of Colonel della Rebbia's honour. But the
fact is, we now know who wrote the letter.'

'Who?' exclaimed Colomba, advancing towards the Prefect.

'A wretch who is guilty of more than one crime—crimes of
the sort you Corsicans do not forgive. A thief, by the name of
Tomaso Bianchi, at present awaiting trial in prison in Bastia,
has confessed that he was the author of that fatal letter.'

'I don't know the man,' said Orso. 'What motive could he
have had?'

'He comes from this area,' said Colomba. 'He's the brother
of a former miller of ours. He's a rogue and a liar, a man
whose word is not to be trusted.'

The Prefect continued: 'You shall see what his motive was
in the affair. The miller to whom your sister Miss Colomba
is referring—his name was Théodore, I believe—rented a mill
from the Colonel, on the stream whose ownership Monsieur
Barricini was contesting with your father. The Colonel,

generous as ever, made almost no profit from his mill. Now Tomaso thought that if Monsieur Barricini acquired possession of the stream, he would have to pay him a substantial rent, for Monsieur Barricini is notoriously fond of money. In short, as a favour to his brother, Tomaso forged the letter from the bandit, and there's no more to it than that. You know that in Corsica family ties are so strong that they sometimes lead to crime. Be so good as to look at this letter written to me by the public prosecutor. It will confirm what I have just told you.'

Orso skimmed through the letter that set out Tomaso's confession in detail, and as he did so Colomba read it over her brother's shoulder.

When she had finished she exclaimed: 'Orlanduccio Barricini went to Bastia a month ago, when it was known that my brother was coming home. He must have seen Tomaso and paid him to tell this lie.'

'Mademoiselle,' said the Prefect impatiently, 'you explain everything by invidious suppositions; is that the way to discover the truth? You, monsieur, are a reasonable man: tell me, what do you think now? Do you think, like Mademoiselle, that a man who has only a comparatively light sentence ahead of him would cheerfully shoulder the responsibility for a forgery just to oblige someone he does not know?'

Orso reread the letter from the public prosecutor, weighing each word with the utmost attention; for, since setting eyes on the lawyer Barricini, he felt he had become harder to convince than he would have been a few days earlier. At length he found himself obliged to admit that the explanation seemed to him adequate. But Colomba exclaimed violently:

'Tomaso Bianchi is a scoundrel. He won't be sentenced, or else he'll escape from prison, I'm sure of that.'

The Prefect shrugged his shoulders.

'Monsieur,' he said, 'I have passed on to you the information I have received. I shall go now, and leave you to your reflexions. I shall wait for your reason to enlighten you, and I hope that it will carry more weight than your sister's . . . suppositions.'

After saying a few words of excuse for Colomba, Orso

repeated that he now believed that Tomaso was the sole guilty party.

The Prefect had stood up to leave.

'If it weren't so late,' he said, 'I would suggest that you come over with me to pick up Miss Nevil's letter. You could take the opportunity of repeating to Monsieur Barricini what you have just said to me, and there would be an end to the matter.'

'Orso della Rebbia shall never enter the home of a Barricini!' exclaimed Colomba impetuously.

'Mademoiselle is the *tintinajo*[1] of the family, it would seem,' said the Prefect with humorous mockery.

'Sir,' said Colomba firmly, 'you are deceived. You do not know the lawyer. He is the most scheming and villainous of men. I entreat you, do not make Orso commit an act which would cover him with shame.'

'Colomba!' exclaimed Orso. 'Your passion is driving you to delirium!'

'Orso! Orso! I implore you, by the casket I gave you, listen to me. There is blood between you and the Barricinis. You shall not go to their home!'

'Sister!'

'No, brother, you shall not go, or else I shall leave this house, and you will not see me again. Orso, have pity on me!'

And she fell to her knees.

'I am deeply sorry', said the Prefect, 'to see Miss Colomba so unreasonable. You will convince her, I am sure.' He opened the door a little and stopped, as if waiting for Orso to follow him.

'I cannot leave her now,' said Orso. 'Tomorrow, if . . .'

'I'm leaving early,' said the Prefect.

'Brother,' exclaimed Colomba with clasped hands, 'at least wait until tomorrow morning. Allow me to look again at my father's papers; you cannot refuse me that.'

'Very well, you shall see them this evening, but at least, don't torment me afterwards with this extravagant hatred of

---

[1] The bell-wether that leads the flock; figuratively, the name is applied to the member of a family who rules it in all important affairs.

yours. I beg your pardon, Prefect, I'm too much on edge myself tonight. It would be better if I left it till tomorrow.'

'Sleep on it,' said the Prefect, taking his leave. 'I hope that tomorrow all your doubts will be dispelled.'

'Saveria!' cried Colomba. 'Take the lantern and go with Monsieur. He will give you a letter for my brother.'

She added a few words that only Saveria heard.

'Colomba,' said Orso when the Prefect had left, 'you have caused me great distress. Will you always refuse to acknowledge the evidence?'

'You have given me until tomorrow,' she replied. 'I have very little time, but I am still hopeful.'

Then she took a bunch of keys and ran to an upstairs room. There she could be heard hurriedly opening drawers and rummaging in a writing-desk in which Colonel della Rebbia had been wont to lock up his important papers.

XIV

Saveria was away a long time, and Orso could no longer contain his impatience when at last she reappeared, carrying a letter and followed by little Chilina, who was rubbing her eyes, for she had been woken from her first sleep.

'What are you doing here at this hour, child?' asked Orso.

'Miss Colomba is asking for me,' replied Chilina.

'What the devil does she want with her?' thought Orso. But he made haste to unseal Miss Lydia's letter, and as he was reading it, Chilina went upstairs to his sister.

My father, sir, has been a trifle unwell (wrote Miss Nevil), and he is in any case so lazy when it comes to writing, that I am obliged to act as his secretary. The other day, as you know, he got his feet wet on the seashore instead of admiring the scenery with the rest of us, and that is quite sufficient to give you a fever in this charming island of yours. I can just imagine the face you are pulling; no doubt you are casting around for your stiletto, but I hope you no longer possess one. So, my father has had a slight fever, and I have had a great fright. The Prefect, whom I persist in finding most agreeable, provided us with a doctor, also a most agreeable man, who got us out of our predicament inside two days. The attack has not recurred, and my father wishes to return to his shooting; but I won't hear of it yet.

How was your castle in the mountains on your return? Is the North Tower still in the same place? Is it really haunted? I'm asking you all this because my father recalls that you promised him fallow deer, wild boar, and moufflon—is that what they call that strange animal? On our way to take ship in Bastia we are intending to turn to you for hospitality, and I hope that the Château della Rebbia, which you say is so old and so dilapidated, will not tumble down about our heads. By the bye, although the Prefect is so agreeable that one is never short of a topic for conversation, I flatter myself that I have made a conquest. We spoke of your noble self. The men of law in Bastia have sent him some revelations from a rogue they've got under lock and key, which are such as to dispel your last suspicions. Consequently your enmity, which sometimes gave me cause for concern, must cease. You can have no idea how pleased this has made me. When you left with the fair *voceratrice*, with a gun in your hand and a sombre expression on your face, you seemed more than usually Corsican—too Corsican, even. *Basta!* I am writing to you at such length because I'm bored. The Prefect, alas, is leaving. We shall send you a message when we set off for your mountains, and I shall take the liberty of writing to Miss Colomba to ask her for a *bruccio, ma solenne**. Meanwhile, my fondest regards. I have much recourse to her stiletto, for I'm using it to cut the pages of a novel I brought with me; but the terrible blade is indignant at such treatment, and tears my book piteously. Farewell, monsieur. My father sends you his best love. Listen to the Prefect, he is a sensible man, and is travelling out of his way, I think, on your behalf. He is going to Corte to lay a foundation stone. I imagine it must be a most imposing ceremony, and I greatly regret that I shall not be attending it. Imagine, a gentleman in an embroidered coat, silk stockings, and a white sash, holding a trowel! And a speech. . . . The ceremony will conclude with endlessly reiterated cries of '*Vive le roi!*' You are going to be most conceited at having made me fill these four pages; but, I am bored, monsieur, I repeat, and for that reason I shall permit you to write me a very long letter. By the way, I find it extraordinary that you have not yet sent word of your safe arrival at Pietranera-Castle.

LYDIA.

P.S. I would ask you to listen to the Prefect, and to do what he tells you. The two of us have decided that this is what you must do, and it will give me pleasure.

Orso read this letter three or four times, accompanying each reading with innumerable mental commentaries. Then he wrote a long reply, which he instructed Saveria to take to a man in the village who was leaving that same night for Ajaccio. He scarcely gave a thought now to discussing with his sister her real or imagined grounds for complaint against the Barricinis; Miss Lydia's letter made him see everything through rose-coloured spectacles; all his suspicions and hatred had left him. After waiting a while for his sister to come back downstairs, seeing that she still did not reappear, he went to bed, more light-hearted than he had felt for a long time. Having dismissed Chilina with secret instructions, Colomba spent the best part of the night reading through various old papers. A little before dawn some small pebbles were thrown against her window. At this signal she went down to the garden, opened a concealed door, and ushered into the house two men of highly unprepossessing appearance. Her first concern was to take them to the kitchen and give them something to eat. Who these men were, we shall shortly learn.

XV

That morning, at about six, one of the Prefect's servants knocked at the door of Orso's house. He was admitted by Colomba, and told her that the Prefect was about to leave, and that he was awaiting her brother. Without hesitation Colomba replied that her brother had just fallen downstairs and sprained his ankle; that, since he was incapable of walking, he begged the Prefect to excuse him, and would be most obliged if that gentleman would deign to go to the trouble of coming to his house. Shortly after this message had been dispatched, Orso came downstairs and asked his sister whether the Prefect had sent for him.

'He asks you to wait here for him,' she said with imperturbable self-assurance.

Half an hour went by without the slightest sign of life from the Barricini house. Meanwhile, Orso asked Colomba whether she had brought anything to light. She replied that she would announce her findings when the Prefect arrived. She affected great composure, but her complexion and her eyes betrayed her state of feverish agitation.

At last the door of the Barricini house was seen to open; the Prefect, dressed for his journey, emerged first, followed by the mayor and his two sons. Great was the astonishment of the inhabitants of Pietranera, who had been at their posts since dawn in order to witness the departure of the first official of the *département*, when they saw him, accompanied by the three Barricinis, head straight across the square and enter the della Rebbia house.

'They've made peace!' exclaimed the village politicos.

'I told you so,' added an old man. 'Orso Antonio has lived too long on the mainland to settle this business like a man of spirit.'

'But notice it's the Barricinis who are going to meet him,' replied one of the della Rebbia faction. 'They're asking for mercy.'

'The Prefect has got round the lot of them,' replied the old man. 'Courage is a thing of the past, and from the store young people nowadays set by their fathers' blood, you'd think they were bastards to a man.'

The Prefect was not a little surprised to find Orso on his feet and walking about without difficulty. In a few words, Colomba admitted her lie and asked him to forgive her for it. 'If you had been staying anywhere else, sir,' she said to the Prefect, 'my brother would have gone to pay you his respects yesterday.'

Orso was profuse in his apologies, protesting that he had had no part in this ridiculous ruse, which was a source of profound humiliation to him. The Prefect and the oldest Barricini seemed to accept the sincerity of his regrets, which, moreover, were confirmed by his embarrassment and by the reproaches he addressed to his sister. But the mayor's sons seemed resentful.

'We're being made fools of,' said Orlanduccio, loudly enough to be heard.

'If my sister played tricks like that on me,' said Vincentello, 'I'd pretty soon cure her of the taste for them.'

These words, and the tone in which they were spoken,

offended Orso and caused his goodwill to wane somewhat. He and the young Barricinis exchanged looks that were far from benevolent.

Meanwhile, everyone had sat down except Colomba, who remained standing near the kitchen door. The Prefect began to speak and, after making a few commonplace remarks about the primitive conventions of the country, pointed out that, by and large, the most inveterate feuds were attributable entirely to misunderstandings. Then, addressing the mayor, he told him that Monsieur della Rebbia had never believed that the Barricini family had been directly or indirectly implicated in the deplorable event that had deprived him of his father; that admittedly he had continued to have misgivings regarding one circumstance of the lawsuit in which the two families had been engaged; that this was excusable in view of Monsieur Orso's long absence and the nature of the information he had received; and that, in the light of certain recent revelations, he now felt fully satisfied on that score, and wished to establish friendly and neighbourly relations with Monsieur Barricini and his sons.

Orso gave a forced bow; Barricini mumbled a few words that nobody could make out; his sons contemplated the beams in the ceiling. Continuing his harangue, the Prefect was on the point of addressing Orso in terms similar to those in which he had just spoken to Monsieur Barricini, when Colomba took some papers from beneath her shawl, stepped forward gravely, and, placing herself between the contracting parties, said:

'It would indeed give me great pleasure to see an end to the war between our two families. But if the reconciliation is to be sincere, we must have it out, and nothing must be left in doubt.—I was right, Prefect, to be suspicious of Tomaso Bianchi's statement, coming as it did from a man of such ill repute. I said that your sons had perhaps seen this man in prison in Bastia . . .'

'That's a lie,' Orlanduccio interrupted. 'I never saw him.'

Colomba cast him a look of contempt, and continued with every appearance of composure.

'Am I right in thinking that, according to you, Tomaso's motive for using the name of a dangerous bandit to threaten Monsieur Barricini was that he wished his brother Théodore to keep the tenancy of the mill my father was letting him for a low rent?'

'It seems plain enough,' said the Prefect.

'With a wretch of the sort this Bianchi seems to be, it would explain everything,' said Orso, deceived by his sister's air of moderation.

'The forged letter,' continued Colomba, whose eyes were beginning to shine more brightly, 'is dated 11 July. At that time Tomaso was with his brother, at the mill.'

'Yes,' said the mayor, a little uneasily.

'So what motive could Tomaso Bianchi have had?' exclaimed Colomba triumphantly. 'His brother's lease had expired. My father had given him notice to quit on 1 July. Here is my father's account book, the record of the notice to quit, and the letter to us from an agent in Ajaccio proposing a new miller.'

As she spoke, she handed the Prefect the papers she held in her hand.

There was a moment of general astonishment. The mayor grew visibly pale; frowning, Orso stepped forward to examine the papers the Prefect was reading with close attention.

'We're being made fools of!' Orlanduccio exclaimed again, standing up angrily. 'Let's go, father, we should never have come here!'

In no time Monsieur Barricini had recovered his composure. He asked to examine the papers; the Prefect handed them to him without a word. Then, pushing his green-tinted spectacles up onto his forehead, he scanned the papers without much apparent interest, whilst Colomba observed him with the expression of a tigress that sees a deer approaching the lair of her young.

'I suppose', said Barricini, replacing his spectacles and returning the papers to the Prefect, 'that, knowing the late Colonel's kindness . . . Tomaso thought . . . he must have thought . . . that the Colonel would reconsider his resolve to give him notice. And, indeed, he did keep possession of the mill, so . . .'

'I was the one who allowed him to retain it,' said Colomba in a tone of contempt. 'My father was dead, and in my situation I was responsible for taking care of my family's clients.'

'Yet,' said the Prefect, 'this Tomaso admits that he wrote the letter. That much is clear.'

'What's clear to me,' Orso interrupted, 'is that there's some kind of dirty work here.'

'I have to contradict yet another of these gentlemen's assertions,' said Colomba. She opened the kitchen door, and at once there entered the room Brandolaccio, the graduate in theology, and the dog Brusco. The two bandits were not armed, or at least not visibly so. Each wore a cartridge-belt around his waist, but not the pistol which is its invariable accompaniment. On entering the room they respectfully removed their hats.

The effect of their sudden appearance can easily be imagined. The mayor nearly fell over backwards with surprise. His sons threw themselves boldly in front of him, reaching into the pockets of their coats for their stilettos. The Prefect made a move for the door, whilst Orso seized Brandolaccio by the scruff of the neck and shouted at him: 'What are you doing here, you scoundrel?'

'It's an ambush!' cried the mayor, attempting to open the door. But Saveria had double-locked it from the outside, on the bandits' instructions, as it later transpired.

'Good people!' said Brandolaccio. 'Don't be afraid of me; I'm not so black as I'm painted. Our intentions are not evil. At your service, Prefect.—Gently, Lieutenant, you're strangling me.— We have come here to give evidence. Go on, *Curé*, you speak, you have a way with words.'

'Prefect,' said the graduate, 'I have not the honour of being known to you. My name is Giocanto Castriconi, better known as the *Curé*. Ah, you recollect me now! Mademoiselle, whom I did not have the pleasure of knowing either, sent someone to ask me to give her some information about a man by the name of Tomaso Bianchi, with whom I was detained three weeks ago in the prisons of Bastia. This is what I have to tell you . . .'

'Spare yourself the trouble,' said the Prefect. 'I do not listen to men such as you.—Monsieur della Rebbia, I'm glad that you seem to have had no part in this detestable conspiracy. But are you master in your own house? Order them to open that door. Your sister may well have to account for these strange dealings she has with bandits.'

'Prefect,' exclaimed Colomba, 'be so good as to hear what this man has to say. You are here to dispense justice to all, and it is your duty to get to the truth. Speak, Giocanto Castriconi.'

'Don't listen to him!' cried the three Barricinis in chorus.

'If everyone speaks at once,' said the bandit with a smile, 'then no one will be heard.—Well, then, in prison I had for a companion—I cannot say a friend—the man in question, this Tomaso. He received frequent visits from Monsieur Orlanduccio . . . '

'It's not true!' exclaimed both brothers at once.

'Two negatives make an affirmative,' observed Castriconi coolly. 'Tomaso had money; he ate and drank of the best. I've always been fond of good living—that's the least of my failings*—and despite my reluctance to associate with the fellow, I several times allowed myself to join him for dinner. To show my gratitude, I suggested that he escape with me. A young girl . . . that I'd been good to . . . had provided me with the means to do so—I don't wish to compromise anyone. Tomaso refused, telling me his case was sure to turn out well, that the lawyer Barricini had put in a word for him with all the judges, that he would leave prison as pure as the driven snow and with money in his pocket. For my own part, I plumped for the outdoor life. *Dixi**.'

'Everything this man is saying is a pack of lies,' Orlanduccio repeated resolutely. 'If we were out in the open country, each with his gun, he wouldn't talk like that.'

'A foolish way to talk!' exclaimed Brandolaccio. 'Don't tangle with the *Curé*, Orlanduccio.'

'Will you kindly allow me to leave, Monsieur della Rebbia?' said the Prefect, stamping his foot with impatience.

'Saveria! Saveria!' Orso was shouting. 'Devil take it, woman, open the door!'

'Just one moment,' said Brandolaccio. 'First we have to make our getaway. Prefect, it is customary, when meeting at the home of mutual friends, to declare a half-hour's truce on separating.'

The Prefect glared at him contemptuously.

'Humble servant to you, one and all,' said Brandolaccio. Then, holding his arm out parallel to the ground, he said to his dog, 'Come on, jump, Brusco, jump for the Prefect!'

The dog jumped, the bandits hastily retrieved their weapons from the kitchen and fled into the garden, and at the sound of a piercing whistle the door of the room flew open as if by magic.

'Monsieur Barricini,' said Orso with concentrated fury, 'I regard you as a forger. This very day I shall lodge a complaint against you with the public prosecutor for forgery and complicity with Bianchi. Perhaps I shall have another, more serious charge to bring against you.'

'And I, Monsieur della Rebbia,' said the mayor, 'shall have you charged with ambush and complicity with bandits. In the meantime, the Prefect will be mentioning your name to the gendarmes.'

'The Prefect will do his duty!' said that gentleman sternly. 'He will ensure that there is no breach of the peace in Pietranera, and he will see to it that justice is done. I am speaking to you all, gentlemen!'

The mayor and Vincentello were already out of the room, and Orlanduccio was backing out after them, when Orso said to him in an undertone: 'Your father is an old man, a slap in the face would finish him off. It's you I shall strike, you and your brother.'

Orlanduccio's reply was to draw his stiletto and fling himself on Orso like a madman. But before he could use his weapon, Colomba seized his arm, twisting it hard whilst Orso struck him in the face with his fist, causing him to stagger back several paces and fall heavily against the door-frame. The stiletto slipped from Orlanduccio's grip, but Vincentello had his ready, and was already returning to the room when, seizing a gun, Colomba convinced him that the contest was an unequal one. At the same time the Prefect interposed himself between the combatants.

'Farewell for now, Ors' Anton'!' cried Orlanduccio; and, slamming the door violently, he locked it, to give himself time to get away.

Orso and the Prefect spent a quarter of an hour in silence, at different ends of the room. With an expression of triumphant pride on her brow, Colomba considered each of them in turn, leaning on the gun that had been the decisive factor in the victory.

'What a country! What a country!' the Prefect finally exclaimed, rising to his feet impetuously. 'Monsieur della Rebbia, you were wrong. I ask you to give your word of honour that you will refrain from violence and wait for the law to settle this accursed affair.'

'Yes, Prefect, I was wrong to strike the wretch. But strike him I did, and I cannot refuse him the satisfaction he has demanded of me.'

'What? Rest assured he doesn't want to fight a duel with you! But what if he murders you? You've given him reason enough to wish to do that.'

'We shall be on our guard,' said Colomba.

'Orlanduccio seems to be a courageous lad,' said Orso, 'and I hope for better things from him, Prefect. He was quick to draw his stiletto but, in his place, perhaps I would have acted as he did. And I'm glad my sister has more strength in her arm than a lady of fashion.'

'You shall not fight!' exclaimed the Prefect. 'I forbid you!'

'Allow me to say, sir, that in matters of honour I recognize no authority but that of my own conscience.'

'I tell you, you shall not fight!'

'You can have me arrested—if I let myself be taken, that is. But if you did so, you would only postpone a piece of business which is now inevitable. You are a man of honour, Prefect, and you know it cannot be otherwise.'

'If you had my brother arrested,' added Colomba, 'half the village would side with him, and we should see a fine shoot-out.'

'I warn you, sir,' said Orso, '—and I implore you not to suppose that it is an idle boast—I warn you that if Monsieur Barricini abuses his authority as mayor by having me arrested, I shall defend myself.'

'As from today,' said the Prefect, 'Monsieur Barricini is relieved of his duties. I trust he will clear his name. Come, monsieur, I have your interests at heart. All I am asking of you is that you should remain quietly at home until my return from Corte. I shall only be gone three days. I shall return with the public prosecutor, and then we can get to the bottom of this unfortunate affair. Do you promise to refrain from hostilities until then?'

'I cannot promise that, sir, if, as I think will happen, Orlanduccio challenges me to a duel.'

'What! Do you mean to say, Monsieur della Rebbia, that you, a French officer, want to fight a duel with a man you suspect of forgery?'

'I struck him, sir.'

'But supposing you had struck a convict and he had demanded satisfaction, would you fight him? Come, Monsieur Orso! Very well then, I shall ask still less of you. Do not seek Orlanduccio out. I permit you to fight a duel with him if he challenges you.'

'He will do so, I'm in no doubt about that. But I promise not to strike him again so as to oblige him to fight me.'

'What a country!' the Prefect repeated, striding this way and that. 'Will I ever get back to France?'

'Prefect,' said Colomba in her softest voice, 'it's getting late. Would you do us the honour of joining us for breakfast?'

The Prefect could not prevent himself from laughing. 'I've already stayed too long. It will look like partiality. And there's that wretched foundation stone to attend to. . . . I must go. Mademoiselle della Rebbia, what a host of misfortunes you may have caused by your actions today!'

'At least, Prefect, you will credit my sister with having good grounds for her convictions. And now I'm sure that you yourself believe them to be well founded.'

'Goodbye, monsieur,' said the Prefect, raising his hand in farewell. 'I must warn you that I shall be ordering the sergeant of gendarmes to follow your every movement.'

When the Prefect had left, Colomba said: 'Orso, this isn't the mainland. Orlanduccio cares nothing for your duels, and besides, the wretch isn't destined to die a brave man's death.'

'Colomba, my dear, you are a fine woman. I'm deeply obliged to you for saving me from a knife in the ribs. Give me your little hand to kiss. But you must let me deal with this. There are some things you don't understand. Bring me something to eat, and as soon as the Prefect has set off, send for little Chilina. She seems a most accomplished messenger, and I shall be needing her to deliver a letter.'

Whilst Colomba was supervising preparations for the meal, Orso went up to his room and wrote the following letter:

You must be impatient for an encounter. I am no less so. We can meet tomorrow morning, at six, in the valley of Acquaviva. I am an excellent shot with a pistol, so I shall not propose that weapon. They say you handle a gun well. I suggest that each of us comes armed with a double-barrelled gun. I shall bring a man from this village. If your brother wants to accompany you, appoint another second and notify me. Then, and only then, I shall have two seconds.

Orso Antonio della Rebbia.

After spending an hour with the deputy mayor, and after calling at the Barricini house for a few minutes, the Prefect left for Corte with just one gendarme for an escort. A quarter of an hour afterwards Chilina took Orso's letter and delivered it to Orlanduccio in person.

The reply was a long time coming, and did not arrive until the evening. It was signed by Barricini senior, and it informed Orso that he was handing over to the public prosecutor the threatening letter addressed to his son. 'I shall wait with a clear conscience', he added in conclusion, 'for the courts to pronounce on your calumnies.'

Meanwhile, five or six shepherds summoned by Colomba arrived to garrison the della Rebbia tower. Despite Orso's protests, the windows overlooking the square were fitted with *archere*, and all that evening he received offers of service from various townspeople. There was even a letter from the bandit-theologian, with a promise from himself and Brandolaccio to intervene if the mayor turned to the gendarmes for help. It ended with this postscript:

'Dare I ask you what the Prefect thinks of the excellent education my friend is giving the dog Brusco? Apart from Chilina, I have never encountered a more docile or a more gifted pupil.'

XVI

The following day passed without hostilities. Both sides were on the defensive. Orso did not leave the house, and the Barricinis' door remained permanently closed. The five gendarmes left to garrison Pietranera could be seen walking in the square or round and about the village, assisted by the rural policeman, the sole representative of the town militia. The deputy mayor did not leave off his sash; but, apart from the *archere* at the windows of the two hostile houses, there was nothing to indicate a state of war. No one but a Corsican would have noticed that in the square around the holm oak, only women were to be seen.

Over supper Colomba joyfully showed her brother the following letter, which she had just received from Miss Nevil:

Dear Miss Colomba,

I read with great pleasure, in a letter from your brother, that your hostilities are at an end. Accept my congratulations. My father cannot abide Ajaccio now that your brother is no longer here to talk of warfare and hunting with him. We are leaving today, and we shall spend the night with your relative, for whom we have a letter. The day after tomorrow, at about eleven, I shall come and ask you to let me sample the *bruccio* from the mountains which, you say, is so superior to the town product.

Adieu, dear Miss Colomba, from your friend,

LYDIA NEVIL.

'She can't have received my second letter!' cried Orso.

'You can see from the date that Miss Lydia must already have set off by the time your letter reached Ajaccio. Did you write telling her not to come?'

'I said we were in a state of siege. It seems to me this is hardly the moment to receive visitors.'

'Bah! those English are an odd lot. The last night I slept in her room, she was saying she would be sorry to leave Corsica without seeing a real vendetta. If you said the word, Orso, we could mount an assault on our enemies' house for her amusement.'

'You know, Colomba, nature made a mistake when she made you a woman,' said Orso. 'You would have made an excellent soldier.'

'Perhaps. In any case I must go and make my *bruccio*.'

'Spare yourself the trouble. Someone must be sent to warn them, and to stop them before they set off on their journey.'

'You mean you want to send a messenger out in this weather, to be swept away by a torrent, and your letter with him? How I pity the poor bandits, in this storm! Fortunately they've got good *piloni*.[1]—You know what you must do, Orso? If the storm abates, set off very early tomorrow, and get to our relative's house before your friends have left. You'll manage it easily, Miss Lydia always gets up late. You can tell them what's happened here, and if they still insist on coming, it will be a great pleasure for us to welcome them.'

Orso was quick to assent to this proposal, and, after a few moments' silence, Colomba resumed:

'Perhaps you think I was joking, Orso, when I spoke of an assault on the Barricini house? You realize we outnumber them by at least two to one? Since the Prefect suspended the mayor, all the men here are on our side. We could cut them to pieces. It would be easy to get things going. If you liked, I could go to the fountain and jeer at their womenfolk. That would fetch them out. Or perhaps—for they're such cowards!—they would shoot at me through their *archere*. They would miss. In that case no more need be said, they would be the ones who had started it. Too bad for those who come off worst—in a free-for-all, who is to know whose shots have found their mark? Take your sister's word for it, Orso: those lawyers in black robes will cover a lot of paper with ink and waste a lot of breath. Nothing will come of it. That old fox would find a way of making them see stars in broad daylight. Ah, if only the Prefect hadn't stood in the way of Vincentello, there'd be one less of them to deal with.'

All this was said with the same composure with which, a moment before, she had spoken of preparing the *bruccio*.

Astounded, Orso contemplated his sister with mingled admiration and awe.

'Colomba, my dearest,' he said, getting up from the table, 'I fear you are the devil incarnate. But rest assured—if I don't manage to have the Barricinis hanged, I'll find some other way of dealing with them. *Palla calda u farru freddu!*[2] You see, I've not forgotten my Corsican.'

'The sooner the better,' said Colomba with a sigh. 'What

---

[1] Coats of very thick cloth, with hoods.
[2] *Hot bullet or cold steel*. A very frequent expression.

horse will you be riding tomorrow, Ors' Anton'?'

'The black one. Why do you ask?'

'So it can be given some barley.'

When Orso had retired to his room Colomba sent Saveria and the shepherds to bed, and remained alone in the kitchen where the *bruccio* was cooking. From time to time she listened, and seemed to be waiting impatiently for her brother to go to bed. When at last she reckoned he was asleep she took a knife, ascertained that it was sharp, slipped her little feet into a pair of shoes too large for her and, without making the slightest noise, went out into the garden.

The garden, enclosed by walls, adjoined quite an extensive piece of ground surrounded by hedges, in which the horses were kept, for Corsican horses seldom see the inside of a stable. Generally they are turned loose in a field to fend for themselves, finding food and shelter against the cold and the rain as best they can.

Colomba opened the garden gate with the same extreme precaution, entered the paddock, and whistled softly to call the horses, to whom she often brought bread and salt. As soon as the black horse was within her reach, she seized it firmly by the mane and slashed its ear with her knife. The horse gave a terrific leap and fled, emitting the shrill cry that acute pain sometimes wrings from these creatures. Satisfied with her work, Colomba was making her way back to the garden when Orso opened his window and shouted, 'Who goes there?' At the same time she heard him cocking his gun. Fortunately for her, the garden gate was in total darkness and partially concealed by a large fig tree. Soon, from the glimmers she could see intermittently in her brother's room, she deduced that he was trying to relight his lamp. At this, she hurriedly closed the garden gate and, keeping close to the walls so that her black clothes blended in with the dark foliage of the espaliers, she managed to reach the kitchen a few moments before Orso appeared.

'What's the matter?' she asked him.

'I thought I heard someone opening the garden gate,' said Orso.

'Impossible; the dog would have barked. Still, let's go and see.'

Orso went once round the garden and, after establishing that the gate leading from it was properly shut, he prepared to return to his bedroom, feeling somewhat sheepish at this false alarm.

'I'm glad to see, brother, that you're becoming prudent, as befits someone in your situation,' said Colomba.

'You're educating me,' replied Orso. 'Goodnight.'

Next morning Orso was up at dawn, ready to leave. His attire bespoke both the aspiration to elegance of a man about to appear before a woman on whom he wishes to make a good impression, and also the prudence of a Corsican engaged in a vendetta. He wore a narrow-waisted blue frock coat, with a little tin box containing cartridges hanging from a green silk cord slung across one shoulder. In a side pocket he carried his stiletto, and in his hand he held the fine Manton rifle, ready loaded with its bullets. Whilst he hastily drank the cup of coffee Colomba had poured him, a shepherd had gone out to saddle and bridle the horse. Orso and his sister followed close behind him and went into the paddock. The shepherd took hold of the horse, then dropped the saddle and bridle and stood, seemingly horrified, whilst the horse, remembering the wound it had received the previous night and fearing for its other ear, reared and lashed out, whinnying and kicking up an infernal din.

'Come on, hurry up!' Orso shouted at him.

'Ah! Ors' Anton', Ors' Anton'!' exclaimed the shepherd. 'Blood of the Madonna! . . .' (Here followed an interminable string of oaths, most of them unsuitable for translation.)

'What's happened?' asked Colomba.

They all approached the horse, and when they saw it covered with blood and with its ear slashed, there was a general exclamation of astonishment and indignation. It must be appreciated that, for a Corsican, to mutilate an enemy's horse is at once a vengeance, a challenge, and a death threat. '*Only a gunshot can atone for this crime.*'* Although Orso, who had lived so long on the mainland, felt the enormity of the outrage less keenly than another man would have done, nevertheless, if at that moment some member of the Barricini family had appeared before him, it is probable that he would instantly have made the man atone for an insult for which he held his enemies responsible.

'The cowardly blackguards!' he exclaimed. 'To take it out on a poor animal, when they dare not meet me face to face!'

'What are we waiting for?' exclaimed Colomba impetuously. 'Are they to come and provoke us, and mutilate our horses, while we stand idly by? Do you call yourselves men?'

'Vengeance!' replied the shepherds. 'We must parade the horse round the village and storm their house!'

'There's a thatched barn next to their tower,' said old Polo Griffo. 'I'll set it ablaze in two shakes.' Another proposed going to fetch the ladders from the church tower; a third suggested battering down the doors of the Barricini house with a beam that had been left lying in the square to be used in some building that was being constructed. Above all these angry voices, Colomba could be heard announcing to her henchmen that before getting down to business, everyone was to receive a large glass of anisette.

Unfortunately, or rather, fortunately, the cruel treatment she had inflicted on the poor horse largely failed to achieve its intended effect on Orso. He did not doubt that the savage mutilation was the work of one of his enemies, and he particularly suspected Orlanduccio, but he did not consider that the young man whom he had provoked and struck had blotted out his shame by slashing a horse's ear. On the contrary, this ignoble and absurd revenge increased his contempt for his adversaries, and he now took the Prefect's view that such people were not worthy to face him man to man. As soon as he was able to make himself heard, he announced to his dumbfounded supporters that they must renounce their warlike intentions and that justice, which was on its way, would exact revenge enough for his horse's ear.

'I am master here,' he added sternly, 'and I mean to be obeyed. If I hear another word from anyone about killing or burning, I'll give him a taste of his own medicine. Come! Saddle the grey for me.'

'What, Orso?' said Colomba, drawing him to one side, 'Will you allow us to be insulted? The Barricinis would never have dared maim one of our beasts when our father was alive.'

'I promise you, they will have reason to regret it; but it's for the gendarmes and the gaolers to punish wretches who are only brave enough to attack animals. I've told you, the law will avenge me for their insult. And if it fails to do so, you won't need to remind me whose son I am.'

'Patience!' said Colomba with a sigh.

'Don't forget, sister,' Orso continued, 'that if on my return I discover that there has been some show of force against the Barricinis, I shall never forgive you.' Then, more gently, he added: 'It's quite possible, quite likely even, that I shall be returning with the Colonel and his daughter; see that their rooms are made ready, that the meal is a good one—in short, that our guests suffer as little discomfort as possible. It's all very well to be courageous, Colomba, but a woman must also be able to keep house. Come, kiss me, there's a good girl. Here's the grey, ready saddled.'

'Orso,' said Colomba, 'you're not to go alone.'

'I don't need company,' said Orso, 'and I can assure you I won't allow anyone to slash me across the ear.'

'I won't have you going off alone in time of war. Hey! Polo Griffo! Gian' Francè! Memmo! Fetch your guns, you're going with my brother.'

After a fairly heated discussion Orso had to resign himself to being accompanied by an escort. He chose from among his most spirited shepherds those who had been most vociferous in advocating war; then, after renewing his injunctions to his sister and the remaining shepherds, he set off, this time going by a roundabout route so as to avoid the Barricini house.

They were already some distance from Pietranera, and travelling at a great pace, when, as they forded a small stream which flowed into a marsh, old Polo Griffo noticed several pigs lying contentedly in the mud, basking in the sunshine and enjoying the coolness of the water. At once he aimed at the largest and shot it through the head, killing it on the spot. The dead pig's companions rose to their feet and fled with surprising agility; and although the other shepherd also fired, they reached a thicket in safety and vanished into it.

'Imbeciles!' exclaimed Orso. 'Can't you tell a pig from a wild boar?'

'Indeed we can, Ors' Anton',' replied Polo Griffo. 'That herd belongs to the lawyer. That'll teach him to mutilate our horses.'

'What, you scoundrels?' cried Orso, beside himself with fury. 'Do you mean to say you would emulate our enemies' ignoble acts? Leave me, you wretches, I've no need of your services. You're only fit for fighting pigs. So help me God, if you follow me, I'll crack your skulls open!'

The two shepherds looked at one another in bewilderment. Orso spurred his horse and disappeared at a gallop.

'Well!' said Polo Griffo. 'That's rich! You love people, and look what you get for it! The Colonel, his father, had it in for you once because you pointed your gun at the lawyer. You were a fool not to have fired! And the son—you saw what I did for him . . . and he talks of cracking my skull open, like a gourd when it won't hold wine any more. That's what they teach you on the mainland, Memmo!'

'Yes, and if they find out you killed the pig, they'll take you to court, and Ors' Anton' won't have a word with the judges or settle with the lawyer. Fortunately no one saw you, and Saint Nega is here to take care of you.'

After a brief deliberation, the two shepherds concluded that the wisest course would be to throw the pig into a swamp, a plan they proceeded to put into execution—though not, of course, until they had first helped themselves to a few pork chops, carved from this innocent victim of the hatred between della Rebbias and Barricinis.

XVII

Rid of his unruly escort, Orso continued on his way, more preoccupied with the pleasure of seeing Miss Nevil again than with the fear of encountering his enemies. 'I shall have to go to Bastia,' he was saying to himself, 'on account of the action I shall be bringing against these wretched Barricinis. Why shouldn't I accompany Miss Nevil there? Perhaps from Bastia we could go on together to the waters at Orezza*?' Suddenly, childhood memories of this picturesque spot came flooding back to him. It was as if he had been transported to a green lawn beneath the century-old chestnut trees. On a carpet of lustrous grass dotted with blue flowers that seemed like eyes smiling at him, he pictured Miss

Lydia seated beside him. She had taken off her hat, and her fair hair, finer and softer than silk, shone like gold in the sunlight that broke through the foliage. Her intensely blue eyes seemed to him bluer than the firmament. With her cheek resting on one hand, she was listening pensively to the words of love he was tremulously addressing to her. She was wearing the mousseline dress she had worn the last day he had seen her at Ajaccio. From beneath the folds of her dress peeped a small foot clad in a black satin slipper. Orso told himself he would be only too happy to kiss that foot. One of Miss Lydia's hands was ungloved, and she was holding a daisy. Orso took the daisy from her, and Lydia's hand clasped his; and he kissed the daisy, and then the hand, and she didn't remonstrate. And all these thoughts kept him from paying attention to the road ahead as he trotted along. He was imagining himself about to kiss Miss Nevil's white hand for the second time, when suddenly he found he was about to kiss the head of his horse, which had pulled up abruptly. Little Chilina was barring its way and seizing it by the bridle.

'Where do you think you're going like that, Ors' Anton'?' she said. 'Don't you know your enemy is close by?'

'My enemy?' cried Orso, livid at finding his reveries interrupted. 'Where is he?'

'Orlanduccio is close by. He's waiting for you. Turn back, turn back!'

'Oh, so he's waiting for me? Have you seen him?'

'Yes, Ors' Anton', I was lying in the ferns when he passed by. He was looking all about him with his telescope.'

'Which way was he going?'

'Down there, the way you're heading.'

'Thank you.'

'Ors' Anton', wouldn't it be best to wait for my uncle? He'll be along soon, and you'd be safe with him.'

'Have no fear, Chili, I can manage without your uncle.'

'If you like, I could go on ahead.'

'Thank you, but no.' And urging his horse on, Orso headed rapidly in the direction the little girl had pointed out to him.

His first impulse was one of blind fury, and he told himself that fortune had presented him with an excellent opportunity to punish this coward who mutilated a horse as a revenge for a slap in the face. Then, as he continued on his way, the thought of the half-promise he had made to the Prefect, and especially the fear of missing Lydia Nevil's visit, made him see things differently, and almost hope he would not encounter Orlanduccio. Soon, the memory of his father, the outrage inflicted on his horse, and the Barricinis' threats rekindled his anger, goading him to seek out his enemy, provoke him, and compel him to fight. Torn between these conflicting resolves, he pressed on, but more cautiously now, scrutinizing the bushes and hedgerows, and sometimes even stopping to listen to those vague noises one hears in the countryside. Ten minutes after leaving young Chilina (it was now nine o'clock in the morning), he found himself at the crest of an extremely steep hillside. The road, or rather the barely distinguishable track he was following, passed over an area of maquis that had recently been burned off. At this spot the earth was covered with a layer of whitish ash. Here and there, shrubs and a few big trees, blackened by the flames and totally stripped of their foliage, still stood, though lifeless now. At the sight of an area of burned-off maquis, one would be forgiven for thinking that one had been transported to some northern clime in midwinter, and the contrast between the aridity of the expanses that have been burned and the luxuriant vegetation all around only makes them seem still more sad and desolate. But at that moment Orso had eyes for only one thing, though an important thing, admittedly, for someone in his position; since it was devoid of vegetation, the ground could not conceal an ambush, and anyone who fears that at any moment he may see a gun-barrel pointed at his chest from out of a thicket looks upon a level expanse of ground affording an uninterrupted view as a kind of oasis.

The burned-out maquis gave place to several cultivated fields, enclosed by the breast-high dry stone walls typical of the region. The track passed between these enclosures, in which enormous chestnut trees, planted at random, looked from a distance like a thick wood.

Obliged to dismount on account of the steepness of the slope, Orso had placed the bridle on his horse's neck and was slithering rapidly downhill over the ashes. He was barely more than twenty-five paces from one of the stone walls to the right of the track when he noticed, directly in front of him, first the barrel of a gun, then a head sticking up over the top of the wall. The gun was levelled, and he recognized Orlanduccio, ready to fire. Orso hastily raised his rifle and, as they took aim, the two men looked at one another for a few seconds with that poignant emotion the bravest man must feel when about to kill or be killed.

'Contemptible coward!' exclaimed Orso. Even as he spoke he saw the flame from Orlanduccio's gun, and almost simultaneously a second shot was fired, to his left, from the other side of the track, by a man he had not noticed, and who was aiming at him from behind another wall. Both bullets struck him; one, Orlanduccio's, went clean through his left arm, which was exposed as he took aim; the other hit him in the chest and tore through his jacket, but fortunately it struck the blade of his stiletto, flattening itself against it, and causing only a slight bruise. Orso's left arm fell to his side, immobilized, and the barrel of his gun dipped for a moment, but at once he raised it again and, aiming his weapon with his right hand alone, he fired on Orlanduccio. His enemy's head, which was exposed only from the eyes up, disappeared behind the wall. Turning to his left, Orso fired his second shot at a man wreathed in smoke whom he could scarcely make out. This figure, too, disappeared. The four gunshots had followed one another with astonishing speed, and trained soldiers could not have exchanged rapid fire more briskly. After Orso's final shot, silence reigned again. The smoke from his gun rose slowly into the air; from behind the wall there came no movement, not the slightest noise. But for the pain in his arm, he could have dismissed the men at whom he had just fired as figments of his imagination.

Expecting a second volley, Orso stepped forward to position himself behind one of the charred trees that stood in the maquis. Protected by this cover, he placed his gun between his knees and hastily reloaded it. Meanwhile, his left arm was causing him excruciating pain and felt as if it were supporting an enormous weight. What had become of his adversaries? He couldn't make it out. If they had fled, if they had been wounded, he would surely have heard some noise, some movement among the foliage. So, were they dead, or was it not more likely that they were waiting behind their wall for the opportunity to fire at him again? In his uncertainty, and feeling his strength seeping away, he placed his right knee on the ground, supported his injured arm on the other knee, and rested his gun on a branch projecting from the trunk of the charred tree. With his finger on the trigger, his gaze fixed on the wall, and his ears pricked for the slightest sound, he remained motionless for a few minutes, which seemed to him like an eternity.

At last, a long way behind him, he heard a distant shout, and soon a dog ran down the hillside, as swift as an arrow, and stopped beside him, wagging his tail. It was Brusco, the bandits' disciple and companion, no doubt heralding his master's arrival; and never was an honest man awaited more impatiently. His muzzle in the air, pointed in the direction of the nearest enclosure, the dog was sniffing uneasily. Suddenly he gave a muffled growl, leaped over the wall, and almost at once reappeared on the top, from where he stared at Orso, his eyes expressing surprise as clearly as any dog's could. Then he sniffed the air again, this time in the direction of the other enclosure, and again leaped over the wall. A second later he reappeared on top, with the same expression of astonishment and anxiety. Then he jumped down into the maquis with his tail between his legs, keeping his eyes on Orso, and slowly sidling away from him until he was some distance away. Then, starting to run again, he went back up the hill as fast as he had descended it, running to meet a man who was advancing rapidly despite the steepness of the slope.

'I'm here, Brando,' shouted Orso as soon as he thought he was within earshot.

'Ho! Ors' Anton'! Are you wounded?' Brandolaccio asked him, running up out of breath. 'In the body or a limb?'

'In the arm.'

'The arm! That's nothing. What about the other man?'

'I think I got him.'

Following his dog, Brandolaccio ran to the nearest enclosure and leaned over to see what was on the other side of the wall. Then, removing his hat, he said: 'May God be with you, Signor Orlanduccio!' Next, turning towards Orso, he raised his hat gravely to him, too, and went on: 'Now, that's what I call giving it to a man good and proper.'

'Is he still alive?' asked Orso, fighting for breath.

'Oh, not he! He took it badly, that bullet you put through his eye. Blood of the Madonna, what a wound! A fine gun, I'll be bound! What a calibre! Just the job for blowing someone's brains out! You know, Ors' Anton', when first I heard "pop!, pop!", I thought to myself, "I'll be damned, they're murdering the Lieutenant!" Then I heard "boom!, boom!" "Aha!" I said, "that must be the English gun; he's retaliating."—All right, Brusco, what is it, boy?'

The dog led him to the other enclosure. 'Would you believe it?' exclaimed Brandolaccio, astounded. 'A right-and-left, no less! Devil take it, you can tell powder's expensive, you certainly don't waste it!'

'What is it, in God's name?' asked Orso.

'Come, don't play the joker, Lieutenant! You bring down the game, and you expect someone else to pick it up for you! I know someone who's going to get an unpleasant surprise before today's out—the lawyer Barricini. If it's butcher's meat you want, here we have it! Who the devil will inherit now?'

'What? Is Vincentello dead too?'

'Dead as a doornail. Health to the rest of us![1] The nice thing about you is, you spare them needless suffering. Just come and take a look at Vincentello; he's still kneeling, with his head resting against the wall. He looks as if he's asleep. You might say he's dead to the world, poor devil!'

Orso turned his head in horror. 'Are you sure he's dead?'

'You're like Sampiero Corso, who never needed more than one shot. See there—in the chest, on the left—just where they got Vincileone at Waterloo. I bet the bullet's not far from the heart. A right-and-left!—Oh, that's me through with shooting . . . two in two shots! And with bullets, too! Both brothers! If he'd had a third shot he'd have killed the papa. Better luck next time! What a shot, Ors' Anton'! And to think a fine lad like me will never be able to kill two gendarmes with a right-and-left!'

As he spoke, the bandit was examining Orso's arm and cutting open his sleeve with his stiletto.

[1] *Salute a noi!* An exclamation commonly accompanying the word *dead*, as a sort of antidote to it.

'It's nothing,' he said. 'Mademoiselle Colomba will have some sewing to do on this frock coat. Hey, what's this I see, the breast torn? Did something get you there? No, or you wouldn't be in such good spirits. Now then, try to move your fingers—can you feel it when I bite your little finger? Not much?—It doesn't matter, you'll be all right. Let me take your handkerchief and your cravat. Your frock coat's past praying for. Why the devil were you dressed up so smartly—were you off on a spree? Here, have a drop of wine. And why aren't you carrying a drinking gourd? What Corsican ever goes out without a gourd?' Then, in the middle of dressing the wound, he broke off to exclaim, 'A right-and-left! Stone dead, the pair of them! How the *Curé* will laugh! A right-and-left! Ah, here's that little sluggard Chilina at last!'

Orso did not reply. He was as pale as death and trembling in every limb.

'Chili,' cried Brandolaccio, 'go and look behind that wall, will you?' The child clambered up the wall, and as soon as she saw Orlanduccio's body she made the sign of the cross.

'That's nothing,' the bandit went on. 'Now go and take a look over there.'

The child made another sign of the cross.

'Was it you, uncle?' she asked timidly.

'Me? An old good-for-nothing, that's what I've become. It's Monsieur Orso's work, Chili. Congratulate him.'

'Mademoiselle Colomba will be overjoyed,' said Chilina. 'And she'll be very sorry to hear you've been wounded, Ors' Anton'.'

'Come, Ors' Anton',' said the bandit, when he had finished dressing the wound, 'Chilina has brought your horse back for you. Mount, and come with me to the maquis of La Stazzona. It would take a clever man to find you there. We'll look after you there as best we can. When we reach the cross of Santa Cristina we'll have to continue on foot. You'll give your horse to Chilina, who'll go off and inform Miss Colomba; you can give her your instructions as we go along. You can say anything to the girl, Ors' Anton'; she'd sooner be hacked to pieces than betray her friends.' Affectionately, he went on: 'Away with you, you wicked creature, may you be excommunicated. A curse on you, good-for-nothing.' Brandolaccio, who, like many bandits, was superstitious, was afraid he might cast a spell on children by blessing or praising them; for it is well known that the mysterious powers governing the *Annocchiatura*[1] have the bad habit of granting the opposite of our wishes.

'Where am I to go, Brando?' asked Orso faintly.

'Why, it's for you to choose: to prison or else to the maquis. But the road to prison is not for a della Rebbia. To the maquis, Ors' Anton'!'

'So, farewell all my hopes!' lamented the wounded man.

'Your hopes? Devil take it, could you have hoped to do better with a double-barrelled gun? Now, then, how the deuce did they get you? Those fellows must have had as many lives as a cat.'

'They fired first,' said Orso.

'So they did, I was forgetting. First "pop!, pop!", then "boom!, boom!". A right-and-left shot, one-handed.[2] I'll be hanged if anyone could do better. There, that's got you in the saddle; before setting off, take a look at your handiwork. It's bad manners to leave people without saying goodbye.'

Orso spurred his horse. Nothing in the world would have induced him to look at the unfortunates he had just killed.

'Listen, Ors' Anton',' said the bandit, seizing the horse's bridle, 'do you want me to speak frankly? Very well then; without wishing to offend you, I grieve for those two poor young men. Please excuse me—they were so handsome, so strong, so young! Orlanduccio, with whom I've hunted so often—four days ago he gave me a packet of cigars. Vincentello, he was always so cheerful. True, you did what you had to do, and anyway, it was too fine a *coup* to be regretted. But as for me, I had no part in your vengeance. I know you are right—when you have an enemy, you must do away with him. But the Barricinis were an old family. And now

---

[1] A spell cast unintentionally, either with the eyes or with words.
[2] If any incredulous sportsman should take issue with me over Monsieur della Rebbia's right-and-left shot, I would urge him to go to Sartène and ask to hear the story of how one of the most distinguished and amiable residents of that town extricated himself single-handed, and with a broken left arm, from a situation at least as perilous as Orso's.

there's one more gone and left us in the lurch, all through one right-and-left shot! It's rum.'

Delivering this funeral oration to the Barricinis as he went, Brandolaccio swiftly led Orso, Chilina, and the dog Brusco towards the maquis of La Stazzona.

XVIII

Meanwhile, shortly after Orso's departure, Colomba had learned through her spies that the Barricinis were out and about, and from that moment on she fell prey to acute anxiety. She could be seen walking to and fro about the house, moving from the kitchen to the rooms that had been prepared for her guests, never idle yet accomplishing nothing, constantly stopping to look and see whether anything unusual was taking place in the village. At about eleven o'clock quite a numerous cavalcade rode into Pietranera: it was the Colonel, his daughter, their servants, and their guide. Colomba's first words on welcoming them were: 'Have you seen my brother?' Then she asked the guide which road they had taken, and at what time they had left. From his replies, she could not understand how they had not met.

'Perhaps your brother went by the upper road,' said the guide. 'We came by the lower road.'

But Colomba shook her head and asked more questions. Despite her natural strength of character, increased still more by the pride she took in concealing any weakness from strangers, it was impossiible for her to hide her misgivings, and soon she confided them to the Colonel, and especially to Miss Nevil, having first told them of the attempt at a reconciliation which had had such an unfortunate outcome. Miss Nevil grew agitated, and wanted to have messengers sent out in all directions. Her father offered to mount his horse again and go with the guide to look for Orso. Her guests' fears reminded Colomba of her duties as a hostess. She endeavoured to smile, urged the Colonel to be seated at table, and found twenty plausible reasons to account for her brother's lateness, each of which she herself rejected a moment later. Feeling it was incumbent on him to try to reassure the ladies, the Colonel put forward his own explanation.

'I'll wager', he said, 'that della Rebbia came upon some game. He couldn't resist the temptation, and we shall soon see him returning home with a full bag. By Jove!' he added, 'on the way over, we did hear four shots. Two of them were louder than the others, and I said to my daughter: "I bet that's della Rebbia out shooting. It can only be my gun making such a loud noise." '

Colomba turned pale and Lydia, who was observing her attentively, had no difficulty in guessing what suspicions the Colonel's conjecture had just suggested to her. After a few minutes' silence, Colomba asked abruptly whether the two loud reports had preceded or followed the others. But neither the Colonel, his daughter, nor the guide had paid much attention to this all-important detail.

At about one o'clock, since none of the messengers sent by Colomba had yet returned, she summoned all her courage and insisted that her guests come to the dinner table; but, apart from the Colonel, no one could eat anything. At the slightest sound from the square, Colomba would run to the window, then return sadly to her seat, and, still more sadly, endeavour to continue with her friends some trivial conversation to which no one was paying the slightest attention and which was interrupted by long intervals of silence.

Suddenly they heard the sound of a horse arriving at a gallop. 'Ah, that must be my brother this time!' said Colomba, getting up. But at the sight of Chilina astride Orso's horse, she exclaimed in a heart-rending voice, 'My brother is dead!'

'The Colonel's glass fell from his hand; Miss Nevil gave a cry, and everyone ran to the front door. Before Chilina had had a chance to dismount, she was snatched up like a feather by Colomba, who smothered her in her embrace. The child read her terrible expression, and her first words were those of the chorus in *Otello*: 'He lives!'* Colomba loosened her grip, and Chilina dropped to the ground as nimbly as a kitten.

'And the others?' asked Colomba in a hoarse voice.

Chilina made the sign of the cross with her index and middle fingers. At once the mortal pallor of Colomba's face gave way to a warm flush. She cast a fervent glance at the Barricini house, then said smilingly to her guests, 'Let's go back in for coffee.'

This Iris* sent by the bandits had a long tale to tell. Her patois, translated by Colomba into Italian as they went along, then into English by Miss Nevil, wrung many a curse from the Colonel, and many a sigh from Miss Nevil; but Colomba listened impassively, except that she twisted her damask napkin as if trying to tear it to shreds. She interrupted the child half a dozen times to have her repeat that Brandolaccio said the wound was not serious and that he had seen many like it. Chilina concluded by reporting that Orso had urgently requested writing paper, and that he instructed his sister to entreat a lady who might perhaps be in his house not to leave it before receiving a letter from him.

'That's what was tormenting him most,' added the child, 'and I was already on my way when he called me back to give me the message again. It was the third time he had repeated it to me.'

Hearing of her brother's injunction, Colomba gave a flicker of a smile and squeezed the Englishwoman's hand; Miss Lydia burst into tears, and did not deem it necessary to interpret this part of the narration for her father.

'Yes, you shall stay with me, my dear,' exclaimed Colomba, kissing Miss Nevil. 'And you shall help us.'

Then, taking a quantity of old linen from a cupboard, she began to cut it up to make bandages and lint. From her sparkling eyes, her heightened colour, and her mood, alternately anxious and composed, it would have been difficult to tell whether she was more concerned at her brother's wound or delighted at the death of his enemies. One moment she was pouring coffee for the Colonel and boasting of her skill at preparing it; the next, she was handing out needlework to Miss Nevil and Chilina, and exhorting them to sew bandages and roll them up. For the twentieth time, she asked if Orso's wound was giving him much pain. She was constantly breaking off from her work to say to the Colonel, 'Such skilful, such redoubtable fighters, the two of them! Yet, alone and injured, with only one good arm, he killed them both! What courage,

Colonel! Isn't he a hero? Ah, Miss Nevil, how fortunate one
is to live in a peaceful country like your own! I'm sure you
didn't really know my brother before! Didn't I say, *the
sparrow-hawk will unfold its wings*? You were taken in by his
air of meekness. When he was with you, Miss Nevil. . . . Ah,
if he could see you working away for him now . . . poor Orso!'

Miss Lydia was working scarcely at all, and was at a loss for
words. Her father was asking why they did not at once refer
the matter to a magistrate. He spoke of 'coroner's inquests'
and a number of other things equally unheard of in Corsica.
Finally he wanted to know whether the country home of the
good Monsieur Brandolaccio, who had given his assistance to
the injured man, was very far from Pietranera, and whether
it was possible for him to go himself to see his friend.

And Colomba replied with her accustomed calm that Orso
was in the maquis; that he was being looked after by a bandit;
that he would be in great danger if he showed himself before
the intentions of the Prefect and the judges had been ascertained; and, lastly, that she would ensure that he was attended
secretly by a skilled surgeon.

'Above all, Colonel,' she said, 'don't forget that you heard
four shots, and that you told me that it was Orso who fired
second.' The Colonel couldn't make head or tail of it all, and
his daughter did nothing but sigh and wipe her eyes.

The day was already far advanced when a sad procession
entered the village. They were bringing back to the lawyer
Barricini the bodies of his sons, each slung across a mule led
by a peasant. A crowd of hangers-on and idlers followed the
mournful procession. With them could be seen the gendarmes, who always arrive too late, and the deputy mayor,
raising his arms to the heavens and repeating endlessly, 'What
will the Prefect say?' A few women, including one who had
been Orlanduccio's nurse, tore their hair and uttered wild
shrieks. But their noisy grief was less impressive than the
mute despair of one individual who attracted everyone's attention. This was the unhappy father, who went from one body
to the other, lifting their earth-stained heads, kissing their
purple lips, supporting their already stiffened limbs, as if to
spare them from being jolted on their journey. Sometimes he

was seen to open his mouth to speak, but he was unable to utter a word or a cry. With his eyes constantly fixed on the bodies, he stumbled against rocks, trees, and every obstacle he encountered.

The women's lamentations, the men's imprecations, redoubled as they came in sight of Orso's house. At the cheer of triumph a few shepherds of the della Rebbia faction dared utter, their adversaries' indignation could no longer be contained. 'Vengeance, vengeance!' cried several voices. Stones were thrown, and two shots, aimed at the windows of the room occupied by Colomba and her guests, pierced the outer shutters, showering splinters of wood over the table near which the two women were sitting. Miss Lydia emitted dreadful screams, the Colonel seized a gun, and, before he could restrain her, Colomba dashed towards the front door and impetuously opened it. There, standing on the raised threshold, with both hands extended to curse her enemies, she exclaimed:

'Cowards! Would you fire on women and strangers? Call yourselves Corsicans? Call yourselves men? You're only good for murdering a man when his back is turned. Advance, I dare you! I am alone, my brother is away. Kill me, kill my guests; it's what one would expect of you. You dare not, cowards that you are! You know we shall have our revenge. Be off with you, go and weep like women, and be thankful we have not demanded more blood of you!'

There was something imposing and terrible in Colomba's voice and attitude. At the sight of her the crowd fell back in terror, as if confronted by those evil spirits about whom so many frightening tales are told on long winter evenings in Corsica. The deputy mayor, the gendarmes, and a number of women took advantage of this retreat to interpose themselves between the two parties, for the della Rebbia shepherds were already preparing their weapons, and for a moment it looked as if there would be a free-for-all in the square. But the two factions were bereft of their leaders, and Corsicans, disciplined in their furies, rarely come to blows in the absence of the protagonists of their internecine wars. Furthermore, Colomba had been rendered cautious by success, and kept her small garrison in check.

'Let the poor creatures weep,' she said. 'Let the old man bear away his dead. What's the use of killing an old fox who has no teeth left to bite with? Giudice Barricini, remember the second of August! Remember the bloodstained notebook in which you wrote in your forger's hand. My father recorded your debt in it, and now your sons have paid it. I discharge you of that debt, old Barricini!'

With her arms folded and a smile of scorn on her lips, Colomba watched the corpses being carried into her enemies' house and the crowd slowly dispersing. She shut her door again and, returning to the dining-room, said to the Colonel:

'I must ask you to excuse my fellow-countrymen, Colonel. I would never have believed Corsicans capable of firing on a house where there are strangers, and I am ashamed for my country.'

That evening, when Miss Lydia had retired to her room, the Colonel followed her and asked her whether their best course might not be to begin the next day by leaving a village in which one was liable to receive a bullet in the head at any moment, and to take the earliest opportunity thereafter to leave a country where one encountered nothing but murders and perfidy.

It was some time before Miss Nevil answered, and it was obvious that she was hard put to it to reply to her father's proposal. At last she said:

'How could we leave this unfortunate young woman at a time when she has so much need of consolation? Don't you think that would be cruel of us, father?'

'It's you I'm thinking of,' said the Colonel to his daughter. 'If I knew you were safe in the hotel at Ajaccio, I assure you I would be sorry to leave this accursed island without shaking hands with that stout fellow della Rebbia.'

'Very well then, father, let's wait a bit, and before we leave, let's make quite sure we can be of no service to them.'

'You're a kind-hearted girl!' said the Colonel, kissing his daughter's brow. 'I like to see you sacrifice yourself to relieve others' misfortune. We shall stay; one never regrets a charitable act.'

Miss Lydia tossed and turned in her bed, unable to sleep.

Sometimes the indistinct noises she could hear sounded to her like the preparations for an attack on the house. At other times, reassured for her own safety, she thought of poor Orso, wounded, no doubt at that very moment lying on the cold ground, with no assistance other than what he could expect from a bandit's charity. She imagined him covered in blood, writhing in terrible agony; yet the strange thing was that, each time she pictured Orso, he always appeared to her as she had seen him at the moment of his departure, pressing to his lips the talisman she had given him. . . . Then she thought of his gallantry. She told herself that it was on account of her, in order to see her a little sooner, that he had exposed himself to the terrible danger from which he had just escaped. She came close to persuading herself that it was in her defence that Orso had come by his shattered arm. She blamed herself for his wound, but she admired him all the more for it; and, although the much acclaimed right-and-left did not have as much merit in her eyes as it did for Brandolaccio and Colomba, she nevertheless thought that few story-book heroes would have shown such intrepidity and self-possession when faced with such peril.

The room she was occupying was Colomba's bedroom. On the wall above a sort of oaken prie-dieu, next to a consecrated palm branch, hung a portrait in miniature of Orso, wearing the uniform of a second lieutenant. Miss Nevil took down the portrait, contemplated it at some length, and finally put it by her bed, instead of replacing it where it belonged. It was daybreak before she fell asleep, and the sun was already high above the horizon when she awoke. At the foot of her bed she saw Colomba, who had been standing there motionless, waiting for her to open her eyes.

'Well, mademoiselle, I hope you weren't too uncomfortable in our poor house?' Colomba said to her. 'I fear you've hardly slept.'

'Have you any news of him, dear friend?' asked Miss Nevil, sitting up in bed.

She noticed the portrait of Orso, and hastened to throw a handkerchief over it.

'Yes, I have news of him,' said Colomba with a smile. And, picking up the portrait, she said:

'Do you think it's a good likeness? It doesn't do him justice.'

'Heavens!' said Miss Nevil shamefacedly. 'The picture! I must have taken it down . . . in a fit of absent-mindedness. I'm always picking things up and not putting them back again. How is your brother?'

'Reasonably well. Giocanto was here before four o'clock this morning. He came with a letter—a letter for you, Miss Nevil. The letter wasn't for me. It does say "To Colomba" on the envelope, but underneath he wrote "for Miss N. . .". We sisters are not jealous. Giocanto says that writing it caused him great pain. Giocanto, who has a fine hand, offered to take down a letter to his dictation, but he refused. He wrote with a pencil, lying on his back. Brandolaccio held the paper. My brother kept wanting to get up, but the slightest movement caused him atrocious pain in the arm. Giocanto said it was pitiful to see him. Here is his letter.'

Miss Nevil read the letter, which had been written in English, no doubt as an additional precaution. Here is what it said:

Dear Miss Nevil,

An unkind fate drove me to this. I do not know what my enemies will say, what calumnies they will invent. Little do I care, if you, miss, lend no credence to them. Since first I saw you I have indulged in foolish dreams. It has taken this catastrophe to make me realize my folly; now I have come to my senses. I know what future awaits me, and it will find me resigned to it. You gave me a ring, which I thought was a talisman that would bring me good luck. I dare not keep it now. I am afraid, Miss Nevil, that you may regret not having bestowed it more wisely—or rather, I am afraid it may remind me of my former folly. Colomba will return it to you. Farewell, Miss Nevil, you will leave Corsica, and I shall never see you again. But tell my sister that I still enjoy your esteem, and I shall be able to say with confidence that I still deserve it.

O.D.R.

Miss Lydia had turned aside to read this letter, and Colomba, who was observing her attentively, handed her the Egyptian ring with an enquiring look. But Miss Lydia did not dare raise her head, and sadly contemplated the ring, which she kept placing on her finger and then removing again.

'Dear Miss Nevil,' said Colomba, 'may I not know what my brother says to you? Does he say anything about his health?'

'Why—,' said Miss Nevil, blushing, 'he doesn't mention it. . . . His letter is in English. . . . He asks me to tell my father . . . He hopes the Prefect will be able to arrange . . .'

Smiling archly, Colomba sat down on the bed, took both of Miss Nevil's hands in her own, and, looking at her with her piercing eyes, said to her: 'You will be kind and reply to my brother, won't you? It will do him so much good. For a moment I thought of waking you when his letter arrived, but I didn't dare.'

'You were wrong not to have done so,' said Miss Nevil. 'If a word from me could . . .'

'I cannot send him any more letters now. The Prefect has arrived, and Pietranera is full of his henchmen. Later, perhaps. Ah! if you knew my brother, Miss Nevil, you would love him as I do. He is so good, so brave! Just think what he did! Outnumbered two to one, and wounded into the bargain!'

The Prefect had returned. Notified by an urgent dispatch from the deputy mayor, he had come with a retinue of gendarmes and *voltigeurs*, bringing public prosecutor, clerk of the court and the like for good measure, to investigate this dreadful new catastrophe which had come to complicate, or rather terminate, the feud between the families of Pietranera. Shortly after his arrival he saw Colonel Nevil and his daughter, and did not conceal from them his fear that things looked bad for Orso.

'You realize', he said, 'that there are no witnesses to the combat. And those two unfortunate young men were so renowned for their skill at arms and their courage that no one is prepared to believe Monsieur della Rebbia could have killed them without help from the bandits with whom they say he has taken refuge.'

'Impossible!' exclaimed the Colonel. 'Orso della Rebbia is the soul of honour, I'll vouch for him personally.'

'I don't doubt it,' said the Prefect. 'But the public prosecutor—you know how suspicious those fellows always are—doesn't seem to me to be very favourably disposed towards him. He's got hold of a document that could cause trouble for your friend. It's a threatening letter addressed to Orlanduccio, challenging him to a duel. And it looks to him like an ambush.'

'This Orlanduccio fellow had refused to fight like a man of honour,' said the Colonel.

'It's not the custom hereabouts. Lying in ambush, killing from behind, is the way they do things here. However, there is one favourable deposition; it comes from a child who claims to have heard four shots, the last two of which were louder than the others and came from a weapon of heavier calibre, like Monsieur della Rebbia's gun. Unfortunately the child is the niece of one of the bandits suspected of complicity, and she's got her lesson off pat.'

'Sir!' Miss Lydia broke in, blushing to the whites of her eyes. 'We were on the road when the shots were fired, and we heard the same thing.'

'Really? This is important! And I suppose, Colonel, that you noticed it too?'

'Yes,' Miss Nevil went on hastily. 'My father, who is familiar with firearms, was the one who said: "That's Monsieur della Rebbia firing my gun." '

'And the shots you recognized were definitely the last?'

'The last two, wasn't that so, father?'

The Colonel had rather a poor memory; but he took good care never to contradict his daughter.

'We must speak to the public prosecutor about this at once, Colonel. Then this evening we are expecting a surgeon who will examine the corpses and ascertain whether the wounds were caused by the weapon in question.'

'I was the one who gave it to Orso,' said the Colonel. 'I wish it were at the bottom of the sea. Though I must say, I'm glad he had it with him, brave lad! for, without my Manton, I'm really not sure how he would have managed.'

XIX

The surgeon was a little late arriving, having had his own adventure on the way. Met by Giocanto Castriconi, he had been summoned with the utmost courtesy to come and attend a wounded man. He had been taken to Orso, and had administered first aid to his wound. The bandit had then conducted him some distance away, and had proved extremely edifying, speaking to him of the most famous professors of Pisa, who, he said, were his intimate friends.

'Doctor,' said the theologian on leaving him, 'I have come to regard you too highly to think it necessary to remind you that a doctor must be as discreet as a confessor.' And he rattled the battery of his rifle. 'If anyone asks exactly where it was that we met, you will have forgotten. Goodbye, delighted to have had the honour of meeting you.'

Colomba begged the Colonel to attend the post-mortem.

'You know my brother's gun better than anyone,' she said, 'and your presence will be invaluable. Besides, there are so many wicked people here that we would be running a great risk if we had no one to defend our interests.'

Finding herself alone with Miss Lydia, she complained of a bad headache, and suggested they take a walk a little way out of the village.

'The fresh air will do me good,' she said. 'It's so long since I breathed it!'

As they walked she spoke of her brother; and Miss Lydia, who found this subject of considerable interest, failed to notice that she was leaving Pietranera some distance behind. The sun was setting when she became aware of the fact and urged Colomba to return. Colomba knew a way across country which, she claimed, shortened the return journey considerably; and, leaving the path she was following, she took another which was evidently much less frequented. Soon she began to climb a hillside so steep that she had constantly to support herself by clinging to the branches of trees with one hand, whilst with the other she pulled her companion after her. After a good quarter of an hour of this arduous ascent they found themselves on a small plateau covered with myrtle and arbutus, surrounded by great masses of granite that protruded from the soil on every side. Miss Lydia was exhausted, the village was nowhere in sight, and it was almost dark.

'Do you know, Colomba, my dear,' she said, 'I fear we are lost.'

'Don't be afraid,' answered Colomba. 'Let's keep walking; follow me.'

'But I assure you, you're mistaken. The village cannot be that way. I'm certain we're walking away from it. Look, those lights we can see such a long way off, that must certainly be Pietranera.'

'My dear friend,' said Colomba agitatedly, 'you are right. But two hundred paces from here, in the maquis . . .'

'Well?'

'My brother is there. If you were willing, I could see him, and kiss him.'

Miss Nevil gave a start of surprise.

'I was able to leave Pietranera without attracting attention because I was with you,' Colomba continued. 'Otherwise I would have been followed. To be so close to him and unable to see him! Why don't you come with me to see my poor brother? You would give him so much pleasure!'

'But, Colomba, it would not be proper for me to do so.'

'I see. You city women are always worried about what's proper. We village women think only of what is right.'

'But it's so late! And whatever will your brother think of me?'

'He will think that he has not been abandoned by his friends, and that will give him courage to suffer.'

'And what about my father? He will be so worried.'

'He knows you are with me. Come, make up your mind. You were looking at his portrait the morning,' she added, with a malicious smile.

'Really, Colomba, I dare not. What about those bandits who are with him?'

'Well, they don't know you, what can it matter? You said you wanted to meet some!'

'Oh, heavens!'

'Come, mademoiselle, decide. I cannot leave you here alone, there's no knowing what might happen to you. Let's either go and see Orso, or else return together to the village. I shall see my brother again—God knows when. Perhaps never.'

'What are you saying, Colomba? Very well, then, we shall go! But only for a minute, and we shall return at once.'

Colomba clasped her by the hand and, without replying, began to walk so rapidly that Miss Lydia could scarcely keep up with her. Fortunately, Colomba soon stopped, and said to her companion:

'We'd better not go any further without warning them, or they might fire on us.' Thereupon she began to whistle through her fingers. Shortly afterwards a dog was heard barking, and the bandits' advance guard soon appeared. It was the dog Brusco, with whom the reader is already acquainted, and who at once recognized Colomba and undertook to act as her guide. After many detours along narrow paths through the maquis, they saw two men coming forward to meet them, armed to the teeth.

'Is that you, Brandolaccio?' asked Colomba. 'Where is my brother?'

'Over there,' replied the bandit. 'But don't make a noise; he's asleep, for the first time since his accident. By God, it's true enough that where the Devil has passed, a woman is sure to follow close behind.'

The two women approached cautiously, and, beside a fire whose glow the bandits had taken the precaution of concealing by building a low screen of dry stones around it, they saw Orso lying on a pile of ferns and covered with a *pilone*. He was very pale, and they could hear his laboured breathing. Colomba sat down beside him, and contemplated him without speaking, with her hands clasped, as if silently praying. Miss Lydia covered her face with her handkerchief and huddled against her; but from time to time she raised her head to look at the wounded man over Colomba's shoulder. A quarter of an hour passed without anyone speaking. At a sign from the theologian, Brandolaccio had vanished with him into the maquis, much to the relief of Miss Lydia, who, for the first time, found that the bandits' big beards and accoutrements had too much local colour for comfort.

At last Orso stirred. Immediately Colomba leaned over him and kissed him several times, overwhelming him with questions about his wound, his sufferings, and his needs. After replying that he was as well as could be expected, Orso in turn asked her whether Miss Nevil was still at Pietranera, and whether she had written to him. Bent over her brother, Colomba completely concealed her companion from him, and in any case the darkness would have made it difficult for him to recognize her. In one of her hands she held Miss Nevil's, and with the other she gently supported the wounded man's head.

'No, brother, she gave me no letter for you. But if you are still thinking of Miss Nevil, does this mean you are fond of her?'

'Fond of her, Colomba! But, perhaps she . . . scorns me now.'

At that moment Miss Nevil made an attempt to withdraw her hand. But, though small and shapely, Colomba's hand was powerful, as we have had occasion to note, and it was not easy to make her relinquish her grip.

'Scorn you?' exclaimed Colomba. 'After what you have done? On the contrary, she speaks well of you. Ah, Orso, if I told you some of the things she has said about you!'

The hand was still trying to break free, but Colomba continued to draw it closer to Orso.

'But why ever didn't she reply to me?' asked the wounded man. 'Just one line and I would have been content.'

By dint of tugging at Miss Nevil's hand, Colomba finally managed to engage it in Orso's. Thereupon, suddenly moving away and bursting out laughing, she exclaimed, 'Orso, take care not to speak ill of Miss Lydia, for she understands Corsican perfectly.'

Miss Lydia at once snatched back her hand, stammering out a few unintelligible words. Orso thought he must be dreaming.

'Can it be you, Miss Nevil? Have you really ventured to come here? Ah, how happy you have made me!' And, raising himself with some difficulty, he tried to draw closer to her.

Miss Lydia replied: 'I came with your sister so that no one would suspect where she was going. And then . . . I also wanted . . . to be sure. . . . Alas, how uncomfortable you are here!'

Colomba had sat down behind Orso. She raised him carefully so as to support his head on her knees. She put her arms around his neck, and motioned Miss Lydia to come closer.

'Nearer, nearer,' she said. 'A sick man must not talk too loud.'

And, as Miss Lydia still hesitated, she took her hand and forced her to sit so close to him that her dress was touching Orso, and her hand, which Colomba was still holding, rested on the wounded man's shoulder.

'He's comfortable just as he is,' said Colomba spiritedly. 'Isn't it true, Orso, that it's good to be sleeping rough, out in the maquis, on a fine night like this?'

'A fine night, indeed!' said Orso. 'I shall never forget it!'

'How you must be suffering!' said Miss Nevil.

'I'm not in pain any more, and I should be happy to die here,' said Orso. And his hand drew closer to Miss Lydia's, which Colomba still held captive.

'It is absolutely essential to have you moved somewhere where you can be looked after, Monsieur della Rebbia,' said Miss Nevil. 'I won't be able to sleep, now I've seen what an uncomfortable bed you have, out here in the open . . . '

'If I hadn't been afraid I might meet you, Miss Nevil, I would have tried to make my way back to Pietranera and give myself up.'

'Why ever were you afraid of meeting her, Orso?' asked Colomba.

'I had disobeyed you, Miss Nevil, and I would not have dared face you now.'

'Do you realize, Miss Lydia, you can make my brother do anything you want?' said Colomba with a laugh. 'I shall stop you seeing him.'

'I hope this whole unfortunate affair will soon be cleared up, and that you will have nothing to fear,' said Miss Nevil. 'I shall be so happy if we can leave Corsica knowing that you have been vindicated, and that your honour and your bravery have been acknowledged!'

'Leave, Miss Nevil? Don't say that word yet.'

'What would you have us do? My father cannot go on hunting here indefinitely. He wants to leave.'

Orso's hand, which had been touching Miss Lydia's, dropped, and there was a moment's silence.

'Don't think we'll allow you to leave just yet,' Colomba continued. 'We still have plenty of things to show you in Pietranera. Besides, you promised you would paint my portrait, and you haven't even started it yet. And I promised I would compose you a *serenata* in seventy-five couplets. And then—but why is Brusco growling? There goes Brandolaccio, running after him. I'll see what it is.'

At once she got up and, placing Orso's head unceremoniously in Miss Nevil's lap, she ran after the bandits.

Somewhat astonished at finding herself left supporting a handsome young man, alone with him in the middle of the maquis, Miss Nevil was unsure what to do, for she feared that by drawing back suddenly she would hurt the wounded man. But Orso himself relinquished the easeful support with which his sister had just provided him and, raising himself on his right arm, he said:

'So, you are leaving soon, Miss Lydia. I never supposed you would prolong your stay in this unhappy country. And yet, since you have been here, I have suffered a hundred times more at the thought that I must bid you farewell. I am a poor lieutenant, with no future, an outlaw now. What a time to tell you that I love you, Miss Lydia. . . . Yet it may be the only chance I have of telling you so, and I seem to feel less unhappy, now that I have unburdened my heart.'

Miss Lydia turned her head away, as if the darkness were not sufficient to hide her blushing. 'Monsieur della Rebbia,' she said in a trembling voice, 'would I have come to this place if . . .' And, as she spoke, she was placing the Egyptian talisman in Orso's hand. Then, making a valiant attempt to resume her habitual bantering tone, she continued:

'It's very wrong of you to talk like that, Monsieur Orso. Here in the middle of the maquis, surrounded by your bandits, you know very well I would never dare to be angry with you.'

Orso moved to kiss the hand that was returning him the talisman; and, as Miss Lydia withdrew it somewhat abruptly, he lost his balance and fell on his injured arm. He was unable to suppress a groan of pain.

'You have hurt yourself, my friend!' she exclaimed, helping him up. 'It was my fault, forgive me!' They went on talking together in low voices for some time, very close to one another now. When Colomba came dashing towards them, she found them exactly as she had left them.

'The *voltigeurs*!' she shouted. 'Orso, try to get up and walk, I'll help you.'

'Leave me,' said Orso. 'Tell the other two to escape. I hardly care if I am captured, but get Miss Lydia away. In God's name, don't let her be seen here!'

'I won't leave you,' said Brandolaccio, who was following after Colomba. 'The sergeant of the *voltigeurs* is a godson of the lawyer. Instead of arresting you, he'll kill you and then say it was an accident.'

Orso tried to get up, and even took a few steps, but soon stopped, saying, 'I can't walk. The rest of you, run for it. Goodbye, Miss Nevil. Give me your hand, and goodbye.'

'We won't leave you!' the two women exclaimed.

'If you can't walk,' said Brandolaccio, 'I shall have to carry you. Come, Lieutenant, take courage. We'll have time to make a getaway along that gully, there behind us. The *Curé* will keep them occupied.'

'No, leave me,' said Orso, lying down on the ground. 'For God's sake, Colomba, get Miss Nevil away!'

'You're strong, Mademoiselle Colomba,' said Brandolaccio. 'Take hold of him by the shoulders and I'll take his feet. That's right, off we go!'

They began to carry him rapidly, despite his protests. As Miss Lydia began to follow them, in an agony of fear, a shot rang out, at once answered by five or six others. Miss Lydia uttered a scream, Brandolaccio an oath, but he increased his pace and Colomba followed his example, running through the maquis without heeding the branches that lashed her face or tore her dress.

'Keep low, keep low, my dear,' she said to her companion, 'or you may be hit.' In this fashion they advanced, or rather ran, about five hundred paces, whereupon Brandolaccio declared that he could go no further and slumped to the ground, despite Colomba's exhortations and reproaches.

'Where is Miss Nevil?' asked Orso.

Miss Nevil, frightened by the gunshots, and brought to a halt at every step by the dense maquis, had soon lost track of the fugitives, and had been left behind, in a state of acute distress.

'She's somewhere behind us,' said Brandolaccio. 'But she's not lost, women always manage to find their way. Just listen, Ors' Anton'—what a racket the *Curé* is making with your gun! Unfortunately it's pitch black, and you can't do much harm shooting at people in the dark.'

'Listen!' exclaimed Colomba. 'I can hear a horse. We're saved!'

And sure enough a horse, that had been startled by the sound of shots whilst grazing in the maquis, was heading in their direction.

'We're saved!' repeated Brandolaccio. It was the work of a moment for the bandit and Colomba to run to the horse, seize it by the mane, and slip a knotted rope into its mouth as a makeshift bridle.

'Now we'll warn the *Curé*,' he said. He whistled twice. This signal was answered by another whistle in the distance, and the deep voice of the Manton fell silent. Thereupon Brandolaccio leaped onto the horse. Colomba arranged her brother in front of the bandit, who gripped him tightly with one hand, whilst with the other he guided his steed. Despite its twofold burden the horse, spurred on by a couple of good kicks in the belly, moved off briskly and galloped down a steep hillside on which any but a Corsican horse would have broken its neck a hundred times over.

Colomba now retraced her steps, calling for Miss Nevil at the top of her voice, but no voice came in answer to hers. After wandering about for some time, attempting to find her way back to the track she had been following, she came upon two *voltigeurs* on a path, who challenged her.

'My word, gentlemen,' said Colomba mockingly. 'What a din! How many dead?'

'You were with the bandits,' said one of the soldiers. 'You can come along with us.'

'Willingly,' she said. 'But I have a friend here, and first we must find her.'

'Your friend has already been captured, and the two of you will be spending the night in prison.'

'In prison? That remains to be seen. In the mean time take me to her.'

The *voltigeurs* took her to the bandits' encampment, where the trophies of their expedition, to wit, the *pilone* that had covered Orso, an old cooking-pot, and a pitcher full of water, were being assembled. Also present was Miss Nevil, who had been found by the soldiers half-dead with fright, and who responded by bursting into tears each time they questioned her about how many bandits there had been and which direction they had taken.

Colomba threw herself into her arms, and whispered in her ear, 'They've got away.' Then, turning to the sergeant of the *voltigeurs*, she said to him, 'Sergeant, you can see the young lady knows nothing about what you are asking her. Let us return to the village, where we are eagerly awaited.'

'You'll be taken there all right, and sooner than you wish, my girl,' said the sergeant. 'And you'll have to explain what you were doing in the maquis at this time of night with those brigands who've just got away. I don't know what spell those scoundrels use, but they certainly charm the ladies, for wherever there are bandits, you're sure to find pretty girls too.'

'You are gallant, Sergeant,' said Colomba, 'but it will pay you to watch what you're saying. This lady is a relative of the Prefect, and is not to be trifled with.'

'A relative of the Prefect!' murmured one *voltigeur* to his superior. 'Why yes, look, she's wearing a hat.'

'Hat or no hat,' said the sergeant, 'they were both with the *Curé*, who's the biggest philanderer on the island, and it's my duty to take them in. Besides, we've nothing further to do here. Damn that Corporal Taupin—the drunken French fool showed himself before I'd had a chance to have the maquis surrounded properly. If it hadn't been for him they wouldn't have slipped through the net.'

'Seven of you, are there?' asked Colomba. 'You know what, gentlemen? If by any chance the three Gambini brothers, Sarocchi, and Théodore Poli happened to be at the cross of Santa Cristina with Brandolaccio and the *Curé*, they could give you something to think about. If you're going to have it out with the *Commandante* of the Island,[1] I wouldn't care to be in the vicinity. Bullets don't mind who they hit in the dark.'

---

[1] This was the title assumed by Théodore Poli.

The possibility of encountering the redoubtable bandits Colomba had just named seemed to make an impression on the *voltigeurs*. Still cursing Corporal Taupin, that dog of a Frenchman, the sergeant gave the order to retreat, and his little troop set off on the road back to Pietranera, bearing the *pilone* and the cooking-pot with them. As for the pitcher, it was dispatched with one good kick. A *voltigeur* tried to take Miss Lydia by the arm, but Colomba at once pushed him back, saying:

'No one is to touch her! Do you suppose we want to run away? Come, Lydia, my dear, lean on me, and stop crying like a child. We've had quite an adventure, but it will all end happily; in half an hour we shall be having supper. Speaking for myself, I'm famished.'

'What will people think of me?' said Miss Nevil softly.

'They will think you got lost in the maquis, that's all.'

'What will the Prefect say? And, above all, what will my father say?'

'The Prefect? You can tell him to mind his own business. As for your father, from the way you and Orso were talking, I should have thought you had something to tell your father.'

Miss Nevil squeezed her arm without replying.

'Isn't it true', Colomba murmured in her ear, 'that my brother deserves to be loved? Don't you love him a little?'

'Ah, Colomba!' replied Miss Nevil, smiling despite her embarrassment. 'You betrayed me—and I trusted you so!'

Colomba put an arm around her waist and, kissing her on the forehead, said softly: 'My little sister! Do you forgive me?'

'My terrible sister, I must,' replied Lydia, returning her kiss.

The Prefect and the public prosecutor were staying with the deputy mayor of Pietranera; and the Colonel, who was most anxious on his daughter's account, had come for the twentieth time to ask them for news of her, when a *voltigeur*, dispatched as a messenger by the sergeant, related to them the terrible combat with the brigands, a combat in which, admittedly, there had been neither dead nor injured, but in which they had captured a cooking-pot, a *pilone*, and two women who were, he said, the bandits' mistresses, or else their spies. Thus

heralded, the two prisoners appeared before the judges surrounded by their armed escort. One can picture Colomba's
radiant expression, her companion's shame, the Prefect's surprise, and the Colonel's joy and astonishment. The public
prosecutor took a malicious delight in subjecting poor Lydia
to a sort of interrogation which did not cease until he had put
her quite out of countenance.

'It seems to me', said the Prefect, 'that we can allow
everyone to go free. These young ladies went for a walk—
nothing more natural in fine weather; they chanced to meet an
agreeable young man who had been wounded—nothing more
natural than that either.' Then, taking Colomba aside, he said,
'Mademoiselle, you can send word to your brother that his
case is going better than I expected. The examination of the
corpses and the Colonel's deposition reveal that he was merely
retaliating, and that he was alone at the time of the combat.
It can all be sorted out, but he must come out of the maquis
at once and give himself up.'

It was nearly eleven o'clock when the Colonel, his daughter,
and Colomba sat down to a supper that had gone cold.
Colomba ate with a hearty appetite, scoffing at the Prefect, the
public prosecutor, and the *voltigeurs*. The Colonel ate, but
said nothing, and kept looking at his daughter, who did not
raise her eyes from her plate. Finally, he spoke to her gently
but gravely in English.

'So, are you engaged to della Rebbia, Lydia?'

'Yes, father, as from today,' she replied, with a blush, but
firmly.

Then she raised her eyes, and, seeing no sign of wrath on
her father's face, she threw herself into his arms and kissed
him, as well-bred young ladies do on such occasions.

'Good for you!' said the Colonel. 'He's a fine lad. But, by
God, we'll not stay in this confounded country of his, or else
I refuse my consent!'

'I don't understand English,' said Colomba, who was
watching them with extreme interest. 'But I'm sure I can
guess what you are saying.'

'We were saying', the Colonel replied, 'that we are going to
take you on a trip to Ireland.'

'I shall be delighted. And I shall be *la surella Colomba*. Is it settled, then, Colonel? Shall we shake hands on it?'

'In circumstances such as this, people kiss,' said the Colonel.

XX

One afternoon, a few months after the right-and-left shot which (in the language of the newspapers) had plunged the commune of Pietranera into consternation, a young man with his left arm in a sling rode out of Bastia and headed towards the village of Cardo, renowned for its spring, which, in summer, supplies the more fastidious townspeople with delicious drinking water. A young woman, tall and of remarkable beauty, accompanied him, riding a small black horse whose strength and elegance a connoisseur would have admired, but which had unfortunately suffered a torn ear in a bizarre incident. In the village the young woman leaped nimbly to the ground and, after helping her companion to dismount, unslung a couple of fairly heavy bags that were attached to her saddlebow. The horses were entrusted to the care of a peasant and the young man and woman, she holding the bags concealed beneath her *mezzaro*, he carrying a double-barrelled gun, headed up the mountainside, following an extremely steep path which did not appear to lead to any habitation. On reaching one of the high ledges of Mount Querciolo they halted, and both sat down on the grass. They seemed to be waiting for someone, for they constantly turned to gaze towards the mountain, and the young woman frequently consulted a pretty gold watch, perhaps as much so as to contemplate a piece of jewellery which seemed to be a recent acquisition, as to see whether the time fixed for an appointment had yet arrived. They did not have long to wait. A dog emerged from the maquis and, hearing the name Brusco called by the young woman, hastened to come and fawn on them. Soon afterwards two bearded men appeared, with guns under their arms, cartridge-belts round their waists, and pistols at their sides. Their torn, patched clothes contrasted with their shining weapons, which were of a famous continental make. Despite the obvious disparity in their stations, the four actors in this tableau greeted one another familiarly, like old friends.

'Well, Ors' Anton',' said the elder of the bandits to the young man. 'So it's all over. Case dismissed! My congratulations. I'm only sorry the lawyer is no longer on the island, to see him fret and fume. How's your arm?'

'They say that in a fortnight it can come out of this sling,' replied the young man. 'Brando, my friend, I'm leaving for Italy tomorrow, and I wanted to say goodbye to you, and to the *Curé*. That's why I asked you to come here.'

'You're in quite a hurry,' said Brandolaccio. 'Acquitted yesterday and you're leaving tomorrow?'

'We have business to attend to,' said the young woman gaily. 'Gentlemen, I've brought you some supper. Fall to, and don't forget my friend Brusco.'

'You're spoiling Brusco, Mademoiselle Colomba, but he is grateful. You shall see.—Come, Brusco,' he said, holding out his gun parallel to the ground, 'jump for the Barricinis!' The dog remained motionless, licking his muzzle and watching his master. 'Jump for the della Rebbias!' And he cleared the gun by a good two feet.

'Listen, my friends,' said Orso. 'Yours is an ugly trade, and even if you manage to avoid ending your careers in the square we can see down there,[1] the best you can hope for is to die in the maquis from a gendarme's bullet.'

'Well?' said Castriconi. 'It's as good a death as any, and better than dying in one's bed of a fever, surrounded by heirs whose lamentations may or may not be sincere. When you're used to life in the open air, like us, there's nothing to beat dying in your boots, as our country people put it.'

Orso continued, 'I should like to see you leave this country, and lead a quieter life. For instance, why don't you go and settle in Sardinia, as several of your comrades have done? I could easily arrange it all for you.'

'Sardinia?' exclaimed Brandolaccio. '*Istos Sardos?** Devil take them and their patois. They're no fit company for us.'

'Sardinia has nothing to offer,' the theologian added. 'Personally, I despise the Sardinians. They have a mounted

---

[1] The square in Bastia where executions take place.

militia to pursue bandits, which is a poor reflection on the
bandits and on the country.[1] A fig for Sardinia! I'm astonished, Monsieur della Rebbia, that you, a man of taste and
learning, have not adopted the outdoor life, now that you've
had a taste of it.'

'But', said Orso with a smile, 'when I had the pleasure of
being your table companion, I wasn't really in any state to
appreciate the delights of your situation, and my ribs still ache
every time I think of the ride I had, one fine night, slung like
a sack over a horse ridden bareback by my friend Brandolaccio.'

'And what of the pleasure of evading pursuit?' Castriconi
went on. 'Does that mean nothing to you? How can you be
insensitive to the charm of untrammelled freedom in a fine
climate such as ours? With this safe conduct' (he pointed to
his gun), 'you can be monarch wherever its bullets carry. You
can issue orders and redress wrongs—a most edifying and
agreeable recreation, monsieur, and one we don't deny
ourselves. There's no finer life than that of a knight errant—
always provided one is better armed and more sensible than
Don Quixote. For instance, the other day, I learned that little
Lilla Luigi's uncle, old skinflint that he is, didn't want to give
her a dowry. I wrote him a letter, no threats—that's not my
style. Well! the man soon saw reason. He married her off. I've
made two people happy. Believe me, Monsieur Orso, there's
nothing to compare with the bandit's life. Why, perhaps you
really would throw in your lot with us, if it weren't for a
certain English girl whom I only caught a glimpse of for a
moment, but whom they all speak of with admiration down in
Bastia.'

'My future sister-in-law doesn't care for the maquis,' said
Colomba with a laugh. 'She had too much of a fright there.'

'Very well,' said Orso, 'if you prefer to remain here, so be
it. Tell me if there's anything I can do for you.'

---

[1] I am indebted to an ex-bandit friend of mine for this criticism of
Sardinia, and he must take full responsibility for it. He means that bandits
who allow themselves to be captured by horsemen are imbeciles, and that a
militia that pursues bandits on horseback has precious little chance of
encountering any.

'Nothing,' said Brandolaccio, 'except to remember us sometimes. You have been more than generous. Chilina now has a dowry, and to get her settled there won't be any need for my friend the *Curé* to write any of those letters that contain no threats. We know your tenant will give us bread and gunpowder whenever we need them. So—farewell. I hope to see you again in Corsica one of these days.'

'In an emergency,' said Orso, 'a few gold coins can come in very useful. Now that we're old acquaintances, surely you won't refuse to accept this cash, to enable you to replenish your ammunition?'

'No money between us, Lieutenant,' said Brandolaccio firmly.

'Money works wonders in society,' said Castriconi, 'but here in the maquis the only things of value are a stout heart and a gun that doesn't misfire.'

'I wouldn't like to go away without leaving you something to remember me by,' Orso resumed. 'Let's see, what can I leave you, Brando?'

The bandit scratched his head and, casting a sidelong glance at Orso's gun, said:

'Goodness, Lieutenant! If I only dared— But no, you're too fond of it.'

'What is it you want?'

'Nothing. The thing in itself is no good unless one knows how to use it. I keep thinking of that infernal one-armed right-and-left shot. That doesn't happen twice!'

'Is it the gun you want? I brought it for you. But use it as seldom as possible.'

'I don't promise to use it as you have, but rest assured, when it belongs to someone else, then you will be able to say that Brando Savelli has laid down his arms for good and all.'

'And what about you, Castriconi? What can I give you?'

'Since you are determined to leave me some tangible memento of yourself, I shall ask you without more ado to send me an edition of Horace, the smallest available. It will keep me entertained and stop me forgetting my Latin. There's a little girl who sells cigars in Bastia, on the quayside. Give it to her, and she will deliver it to me.'

'You shall have an Elzevir,* learned sir. It so happens I have one among the books I was intending to take with me.—Well, my friends, we must go our separate ways. Give me your hands to shake. If one day you have second thoughts about Sardinia, write to me. The lawyer N—— will give you my address on the mainland.'

'Lieutenant,' said Brando, 'tomorrow, when you have left port, look up at the mountains, at this spot. We will be here, and we will wave to you with our handkerchiefs.'

Thereupon they separated; Orso and his sister headed towards Cardo, the bandits towards the mountains.

XXI

On a fine morning in April, Colonel Sir Thomas Nevil, his daughter—Orso's bride of a few days—Orso, and Colomba drove out of Pisa in a barouche to visit a newly discovered Etruscan hypogeum that all the foreigners were flocking to see. Having made their way down into the interior of the monument, Orso and his wife took out their pencils and set about sketching the paintings it contained. But the Colonel and Colomba, neither of whom cared much for archaeology, left them to themselves, and took a stroll in the vicinity.

'Colomba, my dear,' said the Colonel, 'we will never be back in Pisa in time for our luncheon. Aren't you hungry? Orso and his wife are busy with their antiquities. Once they start sketching together, there's no stopping them.'

'I know,' said Colomba. 'Yet they never seem to have a single sketch to show for it.'

'If you want my opinion,' the Colonel continued, 'our best course would be to go to that little farmhouse over there. We'll find some bread there, perhaps some *aleatico* wine, and, who knows, maybe even some strawberries and cream, and we'll wait there patiently for our artists.'

'You are right, Colonel. You and I, who are the sensible members of the family, would indeed be wrong to make martyrs of ourselves on account of these lovers, who live by poetry alone. Give me your arm. Don't you find I'm coming on well? I take men by the arm, I wear fashionable hats and dresses; I have jewels, I'm learning goodness knows how many fine things; I'm not at all the little savage any longer. Just look how gracefully I wear this shawl. That fop of an officer in your regiment, the one who was at the wedding—Lord! I can't recall his name. A tall man, with curly hair, whom I could fell with one blow . . . '

'Chatworth?' the Colonel hazarded.

'That's the one! But I'll never manage to pronounce it. Would you believe, he's madly in love with me!'

'Ah! Colomba, you're becoming a true coquette! Before too long we'll be having another wedding.'

'Me, marry? And then who will bring up my nephew—when Orso gives me one? Who will teach him to speak Corsican? Oh yes, he shall speak Corsican, and I shall make him a pointed cap, just to annoy you.'

'First, let's wait until you have a nephew; then you can teach him to wield a stiletto, if you still think fit.'

'No more stilettos,' said Colomba gaily. 'I have a fan now, and I shall rap you over the knuckles with it whenever you speak ill of my country.'

Conversing in this vein, they reached the farm, where wine, strawberries and cream were all forthcoming. Colomba helped the farmer's wife pick the strawberries, whilst the Colonel drank *aleatico*. At a turning in the path Colomba caught sight of an old man sitting in the sunshine on a straw-bottomed chair. It seemed he was an invalid, for his cheeks were hollow and his eyes sunken; he was extremely thin, and his stillness, his pallor, and his glassy stare made him look more like a corpse than a living creature. For several minutes Colomba contemplated him with such intense interest that the farmer's wife noticed the fact.

'That poor old man is a compatriot of yours, miss,' she said, 'for I can tell from the way you speak that you come from Corsica. He suffered misfortune in his own country—his children died in terrible circumstances. They say, begging your pardon, miss, that your fellow-countrymen make bad enemies. Be that as it may, left alone in the world, the poor gentleman made his way to the home of a distant relative here in Pisa, the lady who owns this farm. The old fellow's a bit cracked, what with his misfortune and the grief—it's embarrassing for milady, who gets a lot of visitors, so she sent him here. He's a quiet old chap, no trouble—doesn't say three words all day. The fact is, he's off his head. The doctor comes once a week, and he says he's not long for this world.'

'You mean there's no hope for him?' asked Colomba. 'In his state, death comes as a merciful release.'

'Why don't you talk to him a bit in Corsican, miss? Perhaps it would cheer him up to hear someone speak his own language.'

'We shall see,' said Colomba with an ironic smile. And she walked towards the old man until her shadow blotted out his sunlight. At this the poor crazed old man raised his head and stared at Colomba, who, still smiling, returned his stare. After a moment the old man put his hand to his forehead and closed his eyes as if to escape Colomba's gaze. Then he opened them again, inordinately wide. His lips trembled. He tried to reach out with his hands, but, mesmerized by Colomba, he remained riveted to his chair, incapable of speaking or moving. At last, great tears welled from his eyes, and sobs broke forth from his breast.

'I've never seen him like this before,' said the farm woman. 'This is a young lady from your country,' she said to the old man. 'She's come to see you.'

'Mercy!' he croaked. 'Mercy! Aren't you satisfied? The page—the one I burned—how did you manage to read it?— And why both of them? Why Orlanduccio? You could find nothing to say against him. You should have left me one—just one . . . Orlanduccio! His name was not written.'

'I had to have them both,' Colomba said to him quietly in Corsican. 'The boughs have been lopped; if the stump had not been rotten, I would have uprooted it too. Come, stop complaining, you don't have long to suffer. I suffered for two years!'

The old man gave a cry, and his head slumped on to his breast. Colomba turned her back on him, and walked slowly back towards the house, singing a few barely distinguishable words from some *ballata*:

'*I must have the hand that shot,—the eye that aimed,—the heart that contrived . . .*'

Whilst the farm woman made haste to help the old man,

Colomba, her face flushed and with fire in her eyes, was sitting down to table opposite the Colonel.

'What's the matter?' he asked. 'You are like you were that time at Pietranera, when they fired at us while we were having dinner.'

'It was memories of Corsica coming back to me. But all that's over. I'm going to be a godmother, aren't I? My, what fine names I shall give him: Ghilfuccio-Tomaso-Orso-Leone!'

At that moment the farmer's wife returned.

'Well?' asked Colomba with the utmost nonchalance. 'Is he dead, or was it just a faint?'

'It was nothing, miss. But it's extraordinary the effect that seeing you had on him.'

'And the doctor says he won't last long?'

'Maybe not two months.'

'He'll be no great loss,' Colomba observed.

'Who on earth are you talking about?' asked the Colonel.

'Some half-witted countryman of mine, who is living here as a paying guest,' said Colomba nonchalantly. 'I shall send for news of him occasionally. Why, Colonel Nevil! Leave some strawberries for my brother and Lydia!'

When Colomba left the farmhouse to get back into the barouche, the farmer's wife gazed after her for some time.

'You see that pretty lady there?' she said to her daughter. 'Do you know, I could swear she has the evil eye.'

Lokis

(1869)

I

'THEODOR,' said Professor Wittembach, 'pass me that book of notes bound in parchment, there on the second shelf above the writing desk. No, not that one, the small octavo notebook. It contains all the notes from my diary for 1866—or at any rate, the ones that relate to Count Szémioth.'

The professor put on his spectacles and, amid a hushed silence, read us the following manuscript:

LOKIS

Miszka su Lokiu
Abu du tokiu.[1]

When the first translation of the Holy Scriptures into Lithuanian was published, in London,* I wrote an article in the Königsberg* *Scientific and Literary Gazette*, in which, while paying full tribute to the work of the learned translator and the pious intentions of the Bible Society, I felt it my duty to draw attention to a few minor errors. I also pointed out that this rendering could be of benefit to only one section of the Lithuanian population, since the dialect used is barely intelligible to the inhabitants of the palatinate of Samogitia, where Low Lithuanian, called *Żmudź* in common parlance—a language which perhaps resembles Sanscrit even more closely than does High Lithuanian—is spoken.* Despite the savage criticism it earned me from a certain well-known professor at the University of Dorpat*, this observation drew the matter to the attention of the General Committee of the Bible Society, whose worthy members showed no hesitation in approaching

---

[1] Two of a kind; both tarred with the same brush. Lithuanian proverb. Word for word, Michael and Lokis, both the same; *Michaelium cum Lokide, ambo [duo] ipsissimi.*

me with a flattering invitation to direct and supervise the preparation of an edition of St Matthew's Gospel in Low Lithuanian. (At the time I was too busy with my research on the trans-Uralian languages to undertake to translate all four Gospels.) So, postponing my marriage to Fräulein Gertrud Weber, I set off for Kovno (Kaunas) with the intention of collecting all the linguistic records of Low Lithuanian I could lay my hands on, whether printed or in manuscript—not, of course, overlooking the folk poetry (daïnos) and the tales or legends (pasakos)—which would serve as the basis for a Low Lithuanian vocabulary, without which the task of translation could not be undertaken.

I had been given a letter of introduction to young Count Michael Szémioth, whose father, I had been assured, had once owned a copy of the famous Catechismus Samogiticus by Father Lawicki, a work so rare that some scholars—conspicuous among them the professor from Dorpat to whom I have alluded—have even denied its existence. According to the information I had been given, his library contained an old collection of daïnos and some poetry in the Old Prussian tongue. Having written to Count Szémioth to inform him of the purpose of my visit, I received a most cordial invitation to stay at his castle at Medintiltas for as long as it took me to complete my research. He concluded his letter most disarmingly by telling me that he prided himself on speaking Low Lithuanian almost as well as his peasants, and that he would be happy to do what he could to assist me in what he described as a 'great and absorbing' undertaking. Like a number of the richest landowners in Lithuania, he professed the Evangelical faith, which it is my honour to serve as a minister. I had been forewarned that the count's character was not entirely exempt from eccentricity, but that he was nonetheless extremely hospitable, a lover of the sciences and the arts, and particularly well disposed towards those who cultivate them. I therefore set off for Medintiltas.

On the front steps of the castle I was met by the count's steward, who at once escorted me to the rooms that had been prepared for me.

'The Count regrets that he is unable to dine with you today,

Professor,' he said to me. 'He is suffering from a migraine, a malady to which he is unfortunately somewhat prone. Unless you wish to take dinner in your room, you will be dining with Doctor Froeber, the Countess's physician. Dinner will be served in one hour; formal dress is not required. If you need anything, the bell is here.' He made a low bow and withdrew.

The rooms were spacious, well furnished, and embellished with mirrors and gilding. On one side they overlooked a garden, or rather the castle grounds, and on the other the main courtyard. Despite the admonition not to dress for dinner, I felt it incumbent on me to take my black dress coat from my trunk. I was in my shirt-sleeves, busy unpacking my hand-luggage, when the sound of a carriage drew me to the window that overlooked the courtyard. A fine barouche had just driven in. Inside were a lady dressed in black, a gentleman, and a woman attired like a Lithuanian peasant, who was so tall and sturdy that at first I was inclined to take her for a man wearing a woman's clothes. She was the first to alight; two other women, of no less robust appearance, were already waiting on the flight of steps. The gentleman leaned over the lady in black, and, much to my surprise, unfastened a broad leather belt which secured her in her seat in the barouche. I noticed that the lady had long, extremely dishevelled white hair, and that her eyes were wide open and vacant in expression. Her face was as lifeless as a waxwork.

After releasing her, her companion addressed her, hat in hand, with a good deal of deference; but she seemed not to pay the slightest attention to him. He then turned to the servants with a slight nod. At once the three women seized the lady in black and, despite her efforts to cling to the barouche, they picked her up as though she had been a feather and carried her into the house. The scene was witnessed by several of the servants, who seemed to find nothing in the least unusual about it.

The man who had directed the operation took out his watch and asked whether dinner would soon be ready. 'In a quarter of an hour, Doctor,' was the reply. It was not difficult to guess that this must be Doctor Froeber, and that the lady in black was the Countess. From her age I deduced that she was Count

Szémioth's mother, and it was fairly clear from the precautions taken concerning her that her reason was impaired.

A few moments later the doctor himself came into my room. 'Since the Count is unwell,' he said to me, 'I shall have to introduce myself personally, Professor. Doctor Froeber, at your service. Delighted to make the acquaintance of a scholar whose merits are well known to all readers of the Königsberg *Scientific and Literary Gazette*. Would you care to begin dinner?'

I replied to his compliments as best I could, and told him that if the time had come to sit down to dinner, then I was ready to follow him in.

We entered the dining-room and at once, as is customary in the North, a butler proffered us a silver tray laden with drinks and salted, highly spiced hors d'œuvres intended to stimulate the appetite.

'As a physician, Professor,' the doctor said to me, 'may I be allowed to recommend a glass of this *starka*, a spirit as good as the best cognac, matured in the cask for forty years. It's the prince of vodkas. Try a Trondheim anchovy—there's no better way of stimulating the gastric juices and preparing the alimentary canal, that most important organ. And now, to table. Shall we speak German? You're from Königsberg, I'm from Memel,* but I studied in Jena. That way we can talk freely without being overheard by the servants, who only understand Polish and Russian.'

At first we ate in silence; then, after a first glass of madeira, I asked the doctor whether the count was frequently plagued by the indisposition that had deprived us of his presence that day.

'Yes and no,' replied the doctor. 'It depends where his travels take him.'

'What do you mean?'

'When he goes in the direction of Rosienie, for instance, he comes back with a migraine, and in a bad temper.'

'I went to Rosienie myself without suffering the same misfortune.'

'That, Professor, must be because you're not in love,' he replied with a laugh.

I thought of Fräulein Gertrud Weber, and sighed.

'Does the Count's fiancée live in Rosienie, then?' I asked.

'Yes, nearby. Though I'm not sure that they are engaged. A shameless coquette! She'll drive him mad, the same as happened with his mother.'

'Well, yes, the Countess certainly seems to be . . . unwell.'

'She's mad, my dear sir—stark, raving mad! And I'm madder than she is, for coming here in the first place.'

'Let us hope that your ministrations will restore her to health.'

The doctor shook his head, appraising the colour of the glass of Bordeaux he held in his hand. 'You wouldn't credit it, but I was once an army surgeon in the Kaluga Regiment. At Sebastopol we were at it from dawn to dusk, sawing off arms and legs; to say nothing of the shells that kept landing on us like flies on a flayed horse. Yet, ill-housed and ill-fed as I was then, at least I wasn't bored as I am here. I eat and drink of the best, I'm housed like a prince and paid like a court physician; but oh for freedom, my dear sir! Can you imagine, with that crazy female one doesn't have a moment to oneself!'

'Has she been in your care for long?'

'Less than two years. But she's been insane for at least twenty-seven, since before the Count was born. Didn't you hear about it in Rosienie or Kovno? Then let me tell you about it, for I intend one day to write an article on her case in the St Petersburg *Medical Journal*. She went mad with fright.'

'Fright? How can that be?'

'From a fright she had. She's descended from Kiejstut. No misalliances in this household, dear me no! *We* trace our descent from Giedymin.* So anyway, Professor, three days, maybe two days after his marriage, which took place in this house in which we're dining . . . (your health!) . . . the count, the father of the present count, went hunting. As you know, our Lithuanian ladies are amazons. The countess accompanied him. She fell behind, or got ahead of the huntsmen— I'm not sure which. Suddenly, the count saw the countess's little servant boy, a child of 12 or 14, come galloping up hell for leather. "Master!" he said. "A bear is making off with my mistress!" "Which way did they go?" asked the count. "That way!" says the little servant. The whole party rushed in the direction in which he was pointing. No countess! There was her horse, mauled, and her pelisse torn to shreds. They searched and combed the woods high and low. At last one huntsman shouted, "There goes the bear!" Sure enough, the bear was passing through a clearing, still dragging the countess with him, no doubt intending to devour her at his leisure in a thicket, for the creatures enjoy their food. They like to eat undisturbed, like monks. The count, who had been married only two days, was extremely gallant, and was all set to fling himself upon the bear, hunting-knife in hand. But a Lithuanian bear doesn't allow itself to be knifed like a stag, my dear sir. Fortunately, the count's rifle-bearer, a villainous piece of work who was so drunk that day he couldn't have told a rabbit from a roe-deer, let fly with his rifle from more than a hundred paces—couldn't have cared less whether the bullet hit the animal or the woman.'

'And he killed the bear?'

'Stone dead. It takes a drunk to pull off a shot like that. Then of course, there are magic bullets too, Professor. We have sorcerers here who sell them at a very reasonable price.

'The countess was badly clawed, unconscious, needless to say, and had one leg broken. They carried her away. When she recovered consciousness, she'd lost her reason. They took her to St Petersburg. A great consultation ensued, with four doctors bristling with every conceivable decoration. They said: "The countess is pregnant; it is probable that her delivery will precipitate a favourable termination of the crisis. She should have fresh country air, and plenty of whey and codeine." Each of them was paid a hundred rubles. Nine months later the countess gave birth to a healthy boy; but as for the favourable termination of the crisis, not a bit of it! Her ravings grew worse. The count showed her son to her: that never fails—in novels. "Kill him! Kill the beast!" she shrieked. She all but throttled him. Ever since then it's been abject depression one moment, frenzied elation the next. Strong suicidal tendencies. She has to be tied up when we take her out for a ride. It takes three sturdy servant-women to hold her down. However,

Professor, let me tell you something: when I've exhausted every possibility without being able to get her to obey me, I have one way of calming her. I threaten to cut off her hair. It must have been very beautiful once. Vanity—the only human feeling she still retains. Isn't that odd? Of course, if I were allowed to have my way with her, perhaps I could cure her.'

'How?'

'By giving her a sound flogging. That's how I once cured twenty peasant women in a village where there had been an outbreak of howling,[1] that curious Russian form of hysteria. One woman starts to howl, her crony joins in; three days later, the whole village is howling. By dint of flogging them, I finally put a stop to it.—Have a hazel-grouse, they're delicious.— The count would never allow me to try it.'

'What! You expected him to agree to your abominable treatment?'

'Oh, he never really knew his mother. Besides, it would be for her own good. But tell me, Professor, would you ever have supposed that fear could drive a person insane?'

'The countess was in a horrifying situation. Imagine finding oneself in the clutches of such a savage creature!'

'Well, you can't say the same for the count. Less than a year ago he found himself in exactly the same situation, and by keeping a cool head he made a miraculous escape.'

'From the clutches of a bear?'

'A she-bear actually, the largest that's been seen for some time. The count was going for her with his hunting-spear. With one swipe of her paw she sent the spear flying, then seized the count and knocked him to the ground, as easily as I could knock over that bottle. He had the sense to play dead. The she-bear sniffed at him a couple of times, then, instead of tearing him apart, she gave him a lick. He had the presence of mind not to stir, and she went on her way.'

'The bear took him for dead. I've heard it said the creatures don't eat corpses.'*

'I'd sooner take your word for it than try the experiment personally. But on the subject of fear, let me tell you a story about

---

[1] In Russian, a hysterical woman is called a 'howler', *klikusha*, from the root *klik*, 'cry, howl'.

Sebastopol. There were five or six of us standing round a pitcher of beer that had just been brought to us behind the ambulance at the famous 5th bastion.* The vedette shouted, "Shell!" We all threw ourselves flat on our faces, except for one fellow, called . . . but never mind his name—a young officer who'd just joined us, who remained standing, holding a glass full of beer, just at the moment the shell exploded. It blew off the head of my poor comrade Andrey Speransky, a fine lad, and it shattered the pitcher. Fortunately it was almost empty. When we picked ourselves up after the explosion, we saw our friend standing in a cloud of smoke, tipping back the last mouthful of his beer as if nothing had happened. We took him for a hero.

'The next day I met Captain Gedeonov, just out of hospital. He said to me: "I'll be dining with you chaps today, and, to celebrate my return, the champagne's on me." We sat down to table. The young officer who'd been involved in the episode with the beer was one of the company. He wasn't expecting the champagne. Someone uncorked a bottle near him, and pop! the cork flew out and hit him on the side of the head. He gave a cry and fainted. Would you believe it, our hero had been scared stiff on the first occasion, and the reason why he drank his beer instead of taking cover was that he was frightened out of his wits, and simply performed the action automatically, without realizing what he was doing. The fact is, Professor, the machine we call the human body . . .'

'Doctor,' said a servant, entering the room, 'Zhdanova says that the countess is refusing to eat.'

'Confound her!' muttered the doctor. 'I'll go and see. When I've persuaded that she-devil to eat something, perhaps, Professor, you would care for a hand of preference or *durachki*?'

I pleaded my ignorance of these card-games, and when he went to see his patient I took myself off to my room and wrote a letter to Fräulein Gertrud.

II

It was a warm night, and I had not closed the window overlooking the grounds. Having written my letter, and still feeling no inclination to sleep, I started to go over the Lithuanian irregular verbs, trying to find an explanation for their various irregularities in the structure of Sanscrit. While I was absorbed in this work, a tree quite close to my window was violently shaken. I heard the cracking of dead branches, and a sound as of some very heavy animal trying to climb it. With the doctor's stories of bears still fresh in my mind, I got up, not without some trepidation, and, amid the foliage of the tree a few feet from my window, I saw a human head, clearly visible in the light cast by my lamp. The apparition lasted only a split second, but the peculiar brilliance of the eyes that gazed into my own made an indescribably powerful impression on me. I recoiled involuntarily, then ran to the window and asked the intruder sternly what his business was. Meanwhile, he was hurriedly scrambling down the tree and, grasping a large branch, he hung from it, dropped to the ground, and at once vanished. I rang the bell and a servant entered the room. I told him what had just happened.

'You must be mistaken, sir,' he said.

'There is no mistake,' I replied. 'I fear there may be a robber at large in the grounds.'

'Impossible, sir.'

'Then was it one of the household?'

The servant opened his eyes wide without replying. Finally he asked me if I had any orders for him. I told him to close the window and I got into bed.

I slept soundly, untroubled by dreams of bears or robbers. The next morning, I had almost finished washing and dressing when there was a knock at my door. I opened it, and saw before me an extremely tall and handsome young man wearing a bokhara dressing-gown and holding a long Turkish pipe in his hand.

'I have come to ask you to forgive me, Professor,' he said, 'for extending such a poor welcome to a guest as eminent as yourself. I am Count Szémioth.'

I hastened to reply that, on the contrary, I had to thank him humbly for his magnificent hospitality; and I asked him whether he had recovered from his migraine.

'More or less,' he said. 'Until the next attack,' he added, pulling a wry face. 'Are you reasonably comfortable? You must remember that you are among barbarians. One can't afford to be over-particular here in Samogitia.'

I assured him that I was perfectly comfortable. As I spoke to him, I could not prevent myself from contemplating him with a curiosity that I was aware must seem impertinent. There was something about his expression which reminded me irresistibly of the man I had seen climbing the tree the night before. But was it really likely, I asked myself, that Count Szémioth devoted his nights to climbing trees?

His forehead was high and well developed, though rather narrow. His features were well proportioned, except that the eyes were too close together: I reckoned that the tear glands were not separated by the width of one eye, as prescribed by the aesthetic canon of the Greek sculptors. His gaze was piercing. Several times our eyes met, and we averted them in some embarrassment. Suddenly the count burst out laughing and exclaimed: 'You've recognized me!'

'Recognized you?'

'Yes. It was me you caught last night, acting like a naughty schoolboy!'

'Why, Count!'

'I'd been cooped up all day in my study, feeling very unwell. By evening I was somewhat better, and took a turn in the garden. I saw a light burning in your room and my curiosity got the better of me. I ought to have given my name and introduced myself, but it was such a ridiculous situation that I was ashamed and ran away. Will you forgive me for disturbing you at your work?'

He spoke in a tone that was intended to sound bantering; but he was blushing, and was evidently ill at ease. I did everything in my power to assure him that I had retained no bad impression of this first encounter, and in order to put an end to the topic I asked him whether it was true that he was the owner of Father Lawicki's Low Lithuanian Catechism.

'Very probably. To tell the truth, I'm not very well acquainted with my father's library. He used to love old books and rare editions. Personally I seldom read anything except modern works. But we shall look for it, Professor. So you would like us to read the Gospels in Low Lithuanian?'

'Don't you think, Count, that it is eminently desirable that there should be a translation of the Scriptures into the language of this country?'

'Certainly. But if you will permit me one small observation, may I point out that if you take all those people who speak nothing but Low Lithuanian, you'll find that not a single one of them can read.'

'Perhaps. But might I point out to Your Excellency[1] that the main obstacle to their learning to read is the dearth of books. When the peasants of Samogitia have a printed text they will want to read it, and then they will learn to read. This has already happened with a number of savage peoples—not that I would wish to imply that the inhabitants of this region are savages. Besides,' I added, 'isn't it a deplorable thing that a language should be allowed to vanish without trace? Prussian became extinct thirty years ago. The last speaker of Cornish died only recently.'

'Yes, it's sad,' interrupted the count. 'Alexander von Humboldt* once told my father about a parrot he had seen in America, that still knew a few words of a language spoken by a tribe that had been completely wiped out by smallpox. Shall we ring for tea?'

At tea the conversation turned on the Low Lithuanian language. The count found fault with the Germans—and rightly so—for the system of transliteration they have adopted for printing Lithuanian.

'Your alphabet is not suited to our language,' he said. 'You don't have our *j*, our *l*, our *y*, or our *ë*. I have a collection of *daïnos* that was published last year in Königsberg, and I have the greatest difficulty in puzzling out the words, they're so distorted.'

'No doubt Your Excellency is referring to Lessner's edition of the *daïnos*?'

'Yes. The poetry is pretty uninspired, isn't it?'

'He might perhaps have found better. I grant you that, as it stands, the collection is of purely philological interest. But I think that by dint of searching it would be possible to gather finer flowers of your folk poetry.'

'Alas, for all my patriotism I very much doubt it.'

'In Vilna* a few weeks ago I was given a really fine ballad,

---

[1] *Siyatyel'stvo*, literally, *radiancy*, the title given to a count.

on a historical subject, too. As poetry it's outstanding. Would you allow me to read it to you? I have it in my portfolio.'

'With great pleasure.'

He settled back in his armchair, after first asking my permission to smoke. 'I need to be smoking to appreciate poetry,' he said.

'It's called *The Three Sons of Boudrys*.'

'*The Three Sons of Boudrys?*' exclaimed the count, with a start.

'Yes. Boudrys is a historical figure, as I need hardly remind you.'

The count gazed at me with his extraordinary stare. It had some indefinable quality, at once timid and fierce, whose effect was almost painful to one not accustomed to it. So as to escape his gaze I hastened to begin my reading.

THE THREE SONS OF BOUDRYS

To his castle courtyard, old Boudrys summons his three sons, three true Lithuanians like himself. He says to them, 'My sons, feed your warhorses, prepare your saddles; sharpen your swords and your javelins.

'It is bruited abroad that in Vilnius war has been declared against the three corners of the world. Algirdas will march against the Russians; Skirgaila against our neighbours the Poles; Kęstutis will fall upon the Teutons.[1]

'You are young, sturdy, bold, go and fight; may the gods of Lithuania protect you! This year I myself shall not campaign, but I wish to give you counsel. There are three of you; three roads lie before you.

'Let one of you accompany Algirdas into Russia, to the shores of Lake Ilmen, beneath the walls of Novgorod. Ermine pelts and brocades abound there. Roubles are as plentiful among the merchants as ice is in the river.

'Let the second follow Kęstutis in his ride. Let him dash the cross-bearing rabble to pieces! There amber, not sand, lies along the sea-shore; their cloth is without peer for its lustre and its colours; rubies adorn the vestments of their priests.

[1] The Knights of the Teutonic Order.

'Let the third cross the Niemen with Skirgaila. On the far side he will find lowly implements for tilling the soil. Yet there he will be able to choose good lances and sturdy bucklers, and thence will he bring me back a daughter-in-law.

'The daughters of Poland, my sons, are the fairest of our captives. Skittish as kittens, white as cream! Beneath their black eyebrows, their eyes shine like twin stars!

'When I was young, half a century ago, I brought back from Poland a fair captive who became my wife. She is long since dead, but I cannot look to that side of the hearth without thinking of her!'

He gives his blessing to the young men, already armed and in the saddle. They set off. Autumn comes, then winter; they do not return. Already old Boudrys has given them up for dead.

A blizzard comes; a horseman approaches, covering some precious burden with his black burka.[1] 'It is a sack,' says Boudrys. 'Is it full of roubles from Novgorod?'—'No, father. I am bringing you back a daughter-in-law from Poland.'

In the thick of a blizzard, a horseman approaches, and his burka bulges, concealing some precious burden. 'What is that, my child? Yellow amber from Germany?'—'No, father. I bring you a daughter-in-law from Poland.'

The snow falls in flurries. A horseman draws near, concealing some precious burden beneath his burka. . . . But before he has revealed his booty, Boudrys has invited his friends to a third marriage feast.

'Bravo, professor!' exclaimed the count. 'Your Lithuanian accent is perfect! But who was it passed on that charming *daïna* to you?'

'A young lady I had the honour of meeting in Vilna, at the home of Princess Katarzyna Pac.'

'And what was her name?'

'Miss Iwinska.'

'*Panna* Julka![2] exclaimed the count. 'The little madcap! I might have guessed! My dear Professor, you may know Low Lithuanian and any number of obscure languages; and you may have read all the old books; but you've allowed yourself to be hoodwinked by a girl who's never read anything

---

[1] Felt cloak.
[2] Miss Julia.

but novels. What she's done is to give you a translation, into more or less correct Low Lithuanian, of one of the charming *Ballads* by Mickiewicz*—one that you've never read for the simple reason that it's no more ancient than I am. If you like I'll show it to you in the Polish original, or if you prefer an excellent Russian translation, I can give you Pushkin's.'

I confess I was totally taken aback. What a triumph it would have been for the professor at Dorpat if I had published the ballad about the sons of Boudrys as an original *daïna*!*

Instead of showing amusement at my discomfiture, the count, with exquisite politeness, hastened to change the topic of conversation.

'So,' he said, 'you have met Miss Julka.'

'I have had the honour to be introduced to her.'

'And what do you make of her? Be frank.'

'She is a most delightful young lady.'

'If it pleases you to say so.'

'She is very pretty.'

'Hmm!'

'What? Don't you think she has the most beautiful eyes?'

'Yes . . .'

'And the most remarkably white skin? I am reminded of a Persian *ghazel** in which a lover sings of the whiteness of his mistress's skin. *"When she drinks red wine,"* he says, *"you can see it flowing down her throat." Panna* Iwinska put me in mind of those lines from a Persian poem.'

'Miss Iwinska may very well exhibit such a phenomenon, but I'm not so sure she has blood in her veins. She has no heart. She's as white as snow, and as cold, too.'

He got up and walked about the room for a while in silence, in order, I suspected, to conceal his agitation. Then he suddenly stopped and said, 'I beg your pardon; I believe we were discussing folk poetry.'

'So we were, Count.'

'Mind you, I must say, she's translated Mickiewicz charmingly. *"Skittish as a kitten, white as cream . . . her eyes shine like twin stars."* It captures her to a T, don't you think?'

'Absolutely, Count.'

'And as for that prank she played on you—quite uncalled

for, of course—the poor child lives with an aged aunt, and she's bored out of her wits. It's like being shut up in a convent.'

'In Vilna she was managing to get out into society. I saw her at a ball given by the officers of some regiment, I think it was the . . .'

'Ah! Young officers, that's the company for her. Laughing with one, swapping slanderous talk with the next, flirting with all and sundry. . . . Would you like to see my father's library, Professor?'

I followed him to a large gallery which contained a great many books, finely bound but rarely opened, to judge from the dust that had accumulated on them. Imagine my joy when one of the first volumes I took from a bookcase proved to be the *Catechismus Samogiticus*! I could not suppress a cry of delight. Surely there must be some form of mysterious attraction that exerts its influence unbeknown to us.

The count took the volume, and, after leafing through it cursorily, wrote on the endpaper: '*To Professor Wittembach, from Michael Szémioth.*' No words can express the gratitude I felt, and I made a silent vow that after my death this precious book would adorn the library of the university at which I had taken my degree.

'Please regard this library as your study,' the count said to me. 'You will never be disturbed here.'

III

After lunch the next day the count suggested going out for a ride. We were to visit a *kapas* (this is the Lithuanian word for those burial mounds to which the Russians gave the name *kurgan*) which was famous throughout the district, because in olden times bards and sorcerers—who were one and the same—used to gather there on solemn occasions. 'I can offer you an extremely docile horse,' he said to me. 'I'm sorry I cannot take you there by barouche, but the fact is, the path we shall be taking is quite unsuitable for vehicles.'

I would sooner have stayed in the library taking notes, but I thought it incumbent on me not to oppose my generous host's wishes, and I accepted his proposal. The horses were ready for us at the front steps. In the courtyard a manservant was holding a dog on a leash. The count stopped for a moment and, turning towards me, said:

'Do you know much about dogs, Professor?'

'Very little, Your Excellency.'

'The *starosta** of Zorany, where I have some land, has sent me this spaniel, of which he speaks very highly. Do you mind if I take a look at it?' He called the manservant, who brought the dog over to him. It was an extremely fine beast. Already accustomed to this man, the dog frisked and seemed full of high spirits; but when it was a few steps from the count, it put its tail between its legs, backed off, and seemed smitten with sudden terror. The count fondled the animal, at which it howled pitifully. After appraising it for a while with an expert eye, he said: 'I think he'll be all right. See that he is taken good care of.' Then he mounted his horse.

'Professor,' the count said to me as soon as we were in the avenue leading away from the castle, 'you've just witnessed that dog's fright. I wanted you to see it for yourself. As a scholar you are called on to explain riddles. Why is it that animals are afraid of me?'

'Really, Count. You take me for an Oedipus. I am simply a humble professor of comparative linguistics. Perhaps . . .'

'Mark you,' he interrupted, 'I never ill-treat horses or dogs. I would scruple to whip a poor beast that doesn't know it has misbehaved. Yet you cannot imagine the aversion I inspire in them. It takes me twice as much time and effort to get them used to me as it would anyone else. That horse you're riding, for instance: it took me an age to break him in. Now he's as docile as a lamb.'

'I suspect, Count, that animals are good physiognomists, and that they can immediately tell whether or not a person they see for the first time is fond of animals. I suspect that you only like animals because of the things they can do for you. Some people, on the other hand, have a natural partiality for certain animals, and they can tell this immediately. I myself, for instance, have had an instinctive fondness for cats ever since childhood. They hardly ever run away when I go up to them to stroke them. I've never once been clawed by a cat.'

'It's quite possible,' said the count. 'The fact is, I'm not what they call an animal-lover. They're little better than humans.—I am taking you now, Professor,' he continued, 'into a forest where, at this very moment, the Kingdom of the Animals exists and prospers: into the *matecznik*, the great matrix, the great breeding-place of beings. Our national traditions tell how no one has penetrated its innermost recesses, no one has managed to reach the heart of those woods and swamps—except, of course, those worthy gentlemen the bards and the sorcerers, who turn up everywhere. There lives the Republic of the Animals—or maybe it's a constitutional monarchy, I'm not altogether sure. Lions, bears, elks, *zubr* (that's our name for the aurochs), all live in harmony together. The mammoth has survived there, and is held in the highest esteem—I believe he's Marshal of the Diet. They have a very strict police, and if any animal is vicious they make it stand trial and exile it. Then it's a case of out of the frying-pan and into the fire, for it has to venture out into the 'world of men. Few survive.'[1]

'A most intriguing legend!' I exclaimed. 'But tell me, Count: you mentioned the aurochs, that noble animal described by Caesar in his *Commentaries*,* that was once hunted by the Merovingian kings in the forest of Compiègne. Is it really still to be found in Lithuania, as I have been told?'

'Certainly. My father once killed a *zubr*—with a permit from the Government, of course; you may have seen its head in the great hall. I've never seen one myself—I understand they're extremely rare. But we have wolves and bears in great numbers. It's in case we should happen to run into one of those gentlemen that I brought this along.' (He pointed to a Circassian *chekhol*[2] slung across his shoulder.) 'And my groom is carrying a double-barrelled carbine on his saddle-bow.'

---

[1] See Mickiewicz, *Pan Tadeusz*; Charles-Edmond, *La Pologne captive* (*Poland Enslaved*).

[2] A Circassian gun-case.

We were beginning to enter the forest. Soon the very narrow path we were following vanished altogether. We had constantly to negotiate huge trees whose lower branches barred our way. Sometimes, one that had bowed to the years lay across our path like a sort of rampart crowned with an impenetrable line of *chevaux de frise*. At other times we encountered deep pools covered with water-lilies and duckweed. Further on we saw clearings carpeted with brilliant emerald-green grass; but woe betide anyone venturing into them, for that lush yet treacherous vegetation often conceals muddy bogs that would engulf a horse and its rider for ever.

The difficulties of the path had forced us to abandon our conversation. My attention was fully taken up with following the count, and I marvelled at the unfailing sagacity with which he made his way without a compass, invariably finding the best way ahead in order to bring us to the *kapas*. It was clear that he had frequently hunted in these primeval forests.

At last the burial mound came into view, standing in the middle of a large clearing. It was very high, and was surrounded by a defensive ditch that was still clearly visible, despite the undergrowth and the soil that had begun to fill it. It seemed already to have been excavated. At the summit I saw vestiges of a structure built of stones, some of which showed signs of exposure to flame. A substantial quantity of ash, mingled with coals and scattered fragments of crude pottery, bore witness to the fact that a fire had been kept lit on the summit for some considerable time. If popular tradition is to be believed, these burial mounds were once the scene of human sacrifices; but there is scarcely any vanished religion to which such abominable rites have not been attributed, and I doubt whether there is any historical evidence to support such a claim in the case of the ancient Lithuanians.

The count and I were descending the mound in order to return to our horses, which we had left beyond the ditch, when we saw an old woman coming towards us, leaning on a stick and holding a basket in her hand.

'Kind sirs,' she said, coming up to us, 'give me of your charity, for the love of God. Give me something to buy a glass of vodka to warm my poor frame.'

The count tossed her a silver coin and asked her what she was doing in the forest, so far from any human habitation. She replied by pointing to her basket, which was filled with fungi. Although my knowledge of botany is extremely limited, it seemed to me that several of the fungi were of poisonous species.

'My good woman,' I exclaimed, 'you're surely not intending to eat those?'

'Kind sir,' said the old woman, smiling sadly, 'the poor eat whatever the good Lord gives them.'

'You don't know Lithuanian stomachs,' the count added. 'They're tin-plated. Our peasants eat all the fungi they find, and thrive on them.'

'At least stop her from eating that *agaricus necator* I can see in her basket!' I exclaimed.

And I reached out my hand to take an extremely poisonous toadstool. But the old woman snatched away the basket abruptly. 'Take care!' she said in alarm. 'They are guarded. *Pirkuns, Pirkuns.*'

Pirkuns, it should be explained, is the name given in Samogitia to the divinity the Russians call *Perun*, the *Jupiter tonans* of the Slavic peoples. If I was surprised to hear the old woman invoke a pagan god, I was still more so when I saw the toadstools move, and the black head of a snake emerge from them and rise a good foot out of the basket. I stepped back smartly, and the count spat over his shoulder—a superstition widespread among the Slavs, who believe, like the ancient Romans, that this is a way of warding off evil spells.

The old woman placed her basket on the ground, squatted beside it, then, stretching out her hand towards the snake, uttered some unintelligible words that sounded like a magic spell. The snake remained motionless for a moment, then coiled itself round the old woman's scrawny arm and disappeared into the sleeve of her skeepskin coat, which, along with a squalid undergarment, represented, I think, the sum total of the Lithuanian Circe's apparel. The old woman looked at us with a short laugh of triumph, like a conjurer who has just pulled off a difficult trick. Her features wore that look of mingled cunning and stupidity which is not uncommon

among self-styled sorcerers, who are, for the most part, both
dupes and scoundrels.

'Here', the count said to me in German, 'is a sample of "local
colour": a witch charming a snake at the foot of a *kapas*, in the
presence of a learned professor and an ignorant member of the
Lithuanian gentry. It would make a fine subject for a genre
painting by your compatriot Knauss.* Do you want to have
your fortune told? This would be a splendid opportunity.'

I replied that I would be extremely loath to encourage such
practices. 'I should prefer to ask her whether she knows
anything about the curious tradition you spoke to me of,' I
added.—'My good woman,' I said, turning to her, 'have you
heard tell of an area of this forest where there lives a community of animals, that knows nothing of the tyranny of
mankind?'

The old woman nodded, and with her short laugh, half-
cunning and half-naïve, she said: 'I've just returned from it.
The animals have lost their king. Noble, the Lion,* is dead.
The animals are going to elect another king. Go to them—
perhaps you will become their king.'

'What are you talking about, woman?' laughed the count.
'Do you know who it is you're talking to? Don't you know that
this gentleman is—how the devil do you say *professor* in
Lithuanian?—the gentleman is a great scholar, a sage, a
wajdelota[1].'

The old woman looked at him intently. 'I was wrong,' she
said. 'You are the one who must go there. It is you who shall
be their king, not he. You are big and strong, and you have
teeth and claws.'

'What do you make of these epigrams she keeps coming out
with?' the count asked me.—'Do you know the way, my dear?'
he asked her.

She pointed to a part of the forest.

'Oh indeed?' replied the count. 'And what about the
swamp? How do you manage to cross that?—Let me explain,
Professor, that in the direction she indicates there is an im-
passable swamp, a lake of liquid mud covered with green

---

[1] Mistranslation of the word *professor*. A *wajdelota* was a Lithuanian bard.

vegetation. Last year a stag I had wounded plunged into that
confounded marsh. I watched it slowly sink. In two minutes
only its antlers were visible. Soon it had vanished altogether,
taking two of my dogs with it.'

'But I'm not heavy,' said the old woman, with an evil cackle.

'I think you can cross the swamp easily enough on your
broomstick.'

The old woman's eyes glinted with anger.

'Kind sir,' she said, resuming the drawling, snuffling tone
of voice used by beggars, 'can you spare an old woman a pipe
of tobacco?—You would do better', she added, lowering her
voice, 'to look for the way through the swamp than to go to
Dowgielly.'

'Dowgielly?' exclaimed the count, flushing. 'What do you
mean?'

I could not but notice the extraordinary effect this word had
on him. He was visibly embarrassed; he lowered his head and
concealed his confusion by fumbling with the strings of his
tobacco pouch, which hung from the handle of his
hunting-knife.

'No, don't go to Dowgielly,' the old woman continued. 'The
little white dove is not for you. Is she, Pirkuns?' Thereupon,
the snake's head emerged from the neck of the old coat and
craned towards its mistress's ear. The reptile, which had no
doubt been trained to perform this trick, moved its jaws as if
it were speaking.

'He says I am right,' the old woman added.

The count placed a handful of tobacco in her hand. 'Do you
know who I am?' he asked her.

'No, good sir.'

'I am the master of Medintiltas. Come and see me one of
these days. I'll give you some tobacco and some vodka.'

The old woman kissed his hand and strode off. In a moment
we had lost sight of her. The count stood there pensively,
absent-mindedly tying and untying the strings of his tobacco
pouch.

'Professor,' he said to me after a fairly long pause, 'you're
going to laugh at me. That villainous old crone must know me
better than she lets on, and the road she's just referred to . . . .

When all is said and done, there's nothing so very strange about it. Everyone knows me hereabouts. The old crone must have seen me more than once on the road to the castle at Dowgielly. There is a marriageable young lady there: she's jumped to the conclusion that I'm in love with the girl. Or else some handsome lad may have bribed her to warn me of misfortune. It's as plain as day—yet, I don't know why, her words make me uneasy. You could almost say they frighten me. You're right to laugh. The fact is, I had been intending to go to the castle at Dowgielly and ask to join them for dinner, and now I'm in two minds. Fool that I am!—come, Professor, you shall decide. Shall we go?'

'I shall take good care not to express an opinion,' I replied with a laugh. 'I never give advice on matters of marriage.'

We had rejoined our horses. The count leaped nimbly into the saddle, dropped the reins, and exclaimed: 'Let the horse decide for us!' The horse did not hesitate, but at once set off down a narrow path which, after a good many twists and turns, joined a made-up road that led to Dowgielly. Half an hour later we were on the steps of the castle.

At the sound of our horses a pretty, blonde head appeared at a window from between two curtains. I recognized the perfidious translator of Mickiewicz.

'Welcome,' she said. 'You couldn't have timed your arrival better, Count Szémioth. I've just this moment taken delivery of a dress from Paris. I'll look so beautiful in it you won't recognize me.'

The curtains closed again. As he climbed the steps the count muttered: 'I'll wager it wasn't for my benefit that she was showing off her new dress.'

He introduced me to Miss Iwinska's aunt, *Pani* Dowgiello, who welcomed me very civilly and spoke to me of my most recent articles in the Königsberg *Scientific and Literary Gazette*.

'The professor', said the count, 'has come to complain to you about Miss Julia, who played a very wicked trick on him.'

'She is a mere child, Professor. You must forgive her. She often drives me to despair with her follies. I had more sense at 16 than she has at 20. But she's a good girl at heart and she has sterling qualities. She is an excellent musician, paints flowers exquisitely, speaks French, German, and Italian equally well. She embroiders . . .'

'And composes poetry in Low Lithuanian!' added the count with a laugh.

'I wouldn't have credited it!' exclaimed her aunt, after we had told her of her niece's prank.

Pani Dowgiello was an educated woman, well versed in her country's antiquities. I found her conversation extraordinarily gratifying. She often read our German reviews, and had very sound ideas on philology. I must admit that I didn't notice the time it took Miss Iwinska to change into her new dress; but it seemed interminable to Count Szémioth, who kept getting up and sitting down again, looking out of the window and drumming on the window panes with his fingers like a man whose patience is wearing thin.

At last, after three quarters of an hour, Miss Julia appeared, followed by her French chaperon, proudly and gracefully wearing a dress which it would need an expertise far superior to my own to describe.

'Don't I look fine?' she asked the count, executing a slow pirouette to enable him to view her from all sides. She did not look at the count or myself, but only at her dress.

'Why, Julka!' said *Pani* Dowgiello. 'Aren't you going to say good afternoon to the professor, who has come with a complaint about you?'

'Ah, Professor!' she exclaimed with a charming little moue. 'What have I done? Are you going to punish me?'

'It would be a punishment for us, Miss Julia, to deprive ourselves of your company,' I replied. 'I have nothing with which to reproach you: on the contrary, I am delighted to have learned, thanks to you, that the Lithuanian muse has been born again, more glorious than before.'

She lowered her head, covering her face with her hands, but taking care not to disarrange her hair. 'Forgive me, I won't do it again!' she said, like a child caught stealing sweetmeats.

'I shall not forgive you, my dear young lady,' I said, 'until you have kept a promise you were so good as to make me in Vilna, at the home of Princess Katarzyna Pac.'

'What promise was that?' she asked, raising her head with a laugh.

'Have you forgotten already? You promised me that if we met in Samogitia you would show me one of your regional dances, about which you spoke very enthusiastically.'

'Oh, the *russalka**! I dance it ravishingly, and here's the very man I need!'

She ran to a table on which lay some volumes of printed music, hurriedly leafed through one, placed it on the music rest of a piano, and, turning to her chaperon, said: 'Like this, my dear friend, *allegro presto*.' And without sitting down she played the ritornello herself, to indicate the tempo. 'Come here, Count Michael,' she continued. 'A true Lithuanian like yourself must be good at dancing the *russalka*. But dance it as a peasant would. Do you understand?'

Pani Dowgiello tried to remonstrate, but to no avail. The count and I insisted. He had his reasons, for his role in this dance was a most agreeable one, as will shortly be seen. After trying it out a couple of times the chaperon said that she thought she would be able to play the piece, which, bizarre as it was, was not unlike a waltz; and, having cleared away a few chairs and a table that might have got in the way, Miss Iwinska took her partner by the coat collar and led him to the centre of the room.

'I should tell you, Professor, that I am a *russalka*, and at your service.' She dropped a low curtsy. 'A *russalka* is a water-nymph. There is one in each of the dark pools that adorn our forests. Don't go near! The *russalka* emerges, even more beautiful than myself if that were possible, and draws you down to the bottom where, apparently, she devours you.'

'A veritable siren!' I exclaimed.

'He', continued Miss Iwinska, pointing to Count Szémioth, 'is a young fisherman, innocence itself, who falls into my clutches, and so as to prolong the pleasure I'm going to fascinate him by dancing around him for a while. Oh! but to do it properly I should be wearing a *sarafan*[1]! What a shame! You will have to excuse this dress, it's not at all in character—no

---

[1] Peasant women's dress, without a bodice.

local colour. Oh, and I'm wearing shoes! How can anyone dance the *russalka* with shoes on? And shoes with heels, too!'

She raised her dress, and, gracefully shaking one charming little foot, at the risk of allowing us a glimpse of her leg, she sent one shoe flying to the far end of the room. The other soon followed it, and she stood on the parquet in her silk stockings. 'Now we're ready!' she said to the chaperon; and the dance commenced.

The *russalka* turns and weaves around her partner. He reaches out his arms to seize her; she passes beneath, eluding his grasp. It is all most graceful, and the music is lively and original. The figure ends when, just as her partner thinks he is going to seize the *russalka* and give her a kiss, she leaps into the air, strikes him on the shoulder, and he falls at her feet as if dead. The count, however, improvised a variant on this figure, and, clasping the mischievous young woman in his arms, did indeed kiss her. Miss Iwinska gave a little cry, blushed deeply, and flung herself sulkily onto a canapé, complaining that he had hugged her like the bear he was. I could see that the count was not pleased by this comparison, with its reminder of a family misfortune. His brow darkened. For my own part, I thanked Miss Iwinska warmly, and praised her dance, which seemed to me quite antique in character, and reminiscent of the sacred dances of the Ancient Greeks.

I was interrupted by a servant announcing General and Princess Veliaminov. Miss Iwinska leaped up from the sofa to retrieve her shoes, hastily thrust her little feet into them, and ran to meet the princess, to whom she dropped a low curtsy twice in rapid succession. I noticed how each time she curtsied she raised her heels adroitly. The general had brought two *aides de camp* with him and, like us, was taking pot luck. In any other part of the world I think the mistress of the house would have been hard put to it to cater simultaneously for six unexpected guests with hearty appetites. But such is the lavishness and hospitality of Lithuanian homes that I believe dinner was no more than half an hour late being served; though it must be said that there were rather too many hot and cold pies.

IV

Dinner was a most lively occasion. The general gave us some most interesting details about the languages of the Caucasus, some of which are Indo-European and some Turanian, despite the remarkable uniformity in the customs and way of life of the various peoples that speak them. I was myself obliged to speak of my travels, for, having been congratulated on my horsemanship by Count Szémioth, who told me he had never known a minister or a professor cope so skilfully with a ride such as the one we had just accomplished, I had to explain to him that I had once been commissioned by the Bible Society to make a study of the language of the Charrua Indians, and had spent three-and-a-half years in the Republic of Uruguay, almost constantly on horseback, living among the Indians of the pampas. While telling of this, I happened to mention that once, after spending three days lost on those endless plains, without food or water, I had been reduced to imitating my companions the gauchos by bleeding my horse and drinking its blood.

The ladies all shrieked in horror. The general remarked that the Kalmucks did the same in similar extremities. The count asked me what I had thought of the beverage.

'From the ethic standpoint,' I replied, 'I found it repugnant. But physically, I throve on it, and I have it to thank for the honour of dining here today. Many Europeans—by which I mean white men—who have lived for a long time among the Indians grow accustomed to it, and even acquire a taste for it. My worthy friend don Fructuoso Rivera, President of the Republic,* rarely lets slip an opportunity to satisfy it. I remember how one day, when he was on his way to Congress, wearing full-dress uniform, he rode past a *rancho* where they were bleeding a colt. He stopped and dismounted to ask for a *chupón*, a suck, after which he went on to deliver one of his most eloquent speeches.'

'Your President friend is a perfect monster!' exclaimed Miss Iwinska.

'Excuse me, *panno*,' I said. 'He is a man of great distinction and the highest intelligence. He has a wonderful command of several of the Indian languages, which are extremely difficult—especially Charrua, on account of the innumerable forms its verb may take, depending on the direct or indirect object, and even on the social relationship between the speakers.'

I was about to give some rather curious examples of the workings of the verb in Charrua when the count interrupted me to ask how one set about bleeding a horse if one wanted to drink its blood.

'Don't tell him, for heaven's sake, Professor!' exclaimed Miss Iwinska in mock horror. 'I wouldn't put it past him to slaughter his entire stable and then devour us when there are no horses left.'

With this sally, the ladies left the table amid much laughter, and went off to prepare the tea and coffee, leaving us to smoke. After a quarter of an hour the general was summoned to the drawing-room. We were all about to follow him, but were told that the ladies wanted only one man at a time. Soon we heard great gusts of laughter and the sound of applause coming from the drawing-room. 'Miss Julka is up to her tricks,' said the count. Then he himself was sent for. More laughter and applause ensued. After that it was my turn. When I entered the room every face had assumed a semblance of gravity that boded no good. I prepared myself for some practical joke.

'Professor,' said the general, in his most official manner. 'These ladies claim we have partaken too liberally of their champagne, and want us to submit to a test before being admitted to their presence. You will be asked to make your way blindfold from the middle of the room to that wall, and to touch it with your finger. As you can see, nothing could be simpler; all you have to do is walk in a straight line. Are you in a fit state to keep a straight course?'

'I think so, General.'

Thereupon Miss Iwinska slipped a handkerchief over my eyes and proceeded to bind it around my head as tightly as she could. 'You're in the middle of the room,' she said. 'Reach out your hand. That's right! Now, I bet you can't touch the wall.'

'Forward, march!' said the general.

The distance was only five or six paces. I walked forward

very slowly, convinced that I was about to encounter some cord or stool placed treacherously in my path to make me stumble. The stifled laughter I could hear increased my discomposure. At last, just as I thought my outstretched arm must be about to touch the wall, I felt one finger suddenly penetrate something cold and sticky. I grimaced and leaped back, at which everyone present burst out laughing. I snatched off my blindfold and saw Miss Iwinska standing close to me, holding the pot of honey into which, under the impression that I was about to touch the wall, I had thrust my finger. My only consolation was to see the two *aides de camp* undergo the same ordeal and emerge looking as sheepish as myself.

For the remainder of the evening Miss Iwinska continued to give free rein to her skittish humour. None of us was spared her relentless mockery and mischief. I noticed, however, that more often than not she singled out the count, who, I must confess, never took offence, and even seemed to take pleasure in her teasing. In fact, whenever she turned her attention to one of the *aides de camp*, he glowered, and I could see that smouldering gleam in his eye which was truly somehow frightening. *'Skittish as a kitten, white as cream.'* I thought that Mickiewicz must have had Miss Iwinska in mind when writing that line.

V

We retired to bed rather late. Many great Lithuanian houses boast magnificent silverware, fine furniture, and valuable Persian carpets, yet cannot offer a weary guest a good feather bed such as is to be found in our beloved Germany. Rich or poor, gentry or peasantry, the Slavic peoples are not in the least averse to sleeping on a plank. The castle of Dowgielly was no exception to this general rule. The room into which the count and I were ushered was empty, save for two couches upholstered in morocco leather. This scarcely deterred me, for during my travels I had often slept on the bare ground, and I was scornful of the count's protestations regarding his compatriots' uncivilized ways. A servant came to pull our boots

off, and gave us dressing-gowns and slippers. Having taken off
his coat, the count paced the room for some time in silence,
then, stopping in front of the couch on which I was already
stretched out, he asked me: 'What do you think of Julka?'

'I find her charming.'

'Yes, but she's such a coquette. Do you think she's really
taken a liking to that little fair-haired captain?'

'The *aide de camp*? How should I know?'

'He's a conceited idiot, so women are bound to like him.'

'I reject your conclusion, Count. If you want my honest
opinion, Miss Iwinska would far rather make a favourable
impression on Count Szémioth than on all the *aides de camp*
in the army.'

He flushed, and made no reply. But I had the impression
that he was decidedly pleased by my words. He continued to
pace for a while in silence, then, after looking at his watch,
said: 'Well, we'd better get some sleep. It's late.'

He took his gun and his hunting-knife, which had been
brought to our room, put them in a cupboard, and removed
the key. 'Would you look after this?' he said, handing it to me,
much to my surprise. 'I might leave it somewhere. Your
memory is certainly better than mine.'

'The best way to avoid forgetting your weapons would be
to put them on that table near your couch,' I said.

'No. Look, to tell the truth, I don't like sleeping with
weapons near me. The reason is this: when I was in the
Grodno Hussars I was once sleeping in a room with a comrade, with my pistols placed on a chair next to me. I was
woken in the night by a detonation. I had a pistol in my hand,
I'd fired it, and the bullet had missed my comrade's head by
two inches. To this day I don't remember what it was I'd been
dreaming about.'

This anecdote disturbed me somewhat. I could now be quite
sure of not receiving a bullet in the head; but when I considered my companion's great stature, his herculean build,
and his sinewy arms covered in black hair, I could not but
acknowledge that he was perfectly capable of strangling me
with his bare hands, if he were to have a nightmare. However,
I was careful not to show the slightest sign of uneasiness—

though I did place a light on a chair beside my couch, and
settled down to read Lawicki's Catechism, which I had
brought with me. The count bade me goodnight, stretched out
on his sofa, and tossed and turned on it half a dozen times. At
last he seemed to doze off, though he was curled up in a ball
like the lover in Horace who is shut up in a chest with his
knees tucked up against his head:

> . . . *Turpi clausus in arca,*
> *Contractum genibus tangas caput* . . .*

From time to time he sighed heavily, or emitted a sort of
nervous growl, which I attributed to the strange position in
which he had elected to sleep. About an hour passed in this
way. I was on the point of falling asleep myself. I closed my
book, and was arranging myself as comfortably as I could on
my couch when a strange, sinister laugh from my companion
made me come to with a start. I looked at the count. His eyes
were closed, his whole body was quivering, and he was
muttering indistinct words through half-open lips.

'Nice and fresh! Nice and white! The professor doesn't
know what he's talking about! Never mind the horse . . . what
a tasty morsel!' Then he began voraciously biting the cushion
beneath his head, and at the same time he gave a sort of roar,
so loud that it woke him up.

I did not stir on my couch, and pretended to be asleep. But
I was watching him. He sat up, rubbed his eyes, sighed unhap-
pily, and remained for almost an hour in the same position,
apparently immersed in thought. Meanwhile I was extremely
uneasy, and vowed in no circumstances to allow myself to fall
asleep in the count's company. At length, however, my fatigue
got the better of my anxiety, and when the servants came into
our room the next morning, we were both sound asleep.

VI

After lunch we returned to Medintiltas. There, finding myself
alone with Doctor Froeber, I told him that I thought the
count was unwell, that he was having nightmares and perhaps

walking in his sleep, and that in such a state he might be dangerous.

'I've noticed it too,' the doctor said to me. 'For all his athletic constitution, he's as highly strung as a pretty girl. Perhaps he gets it from his mother: she was a confounded nuisance this morning. I don't set much store by the tales of pregnant women, with their phobias and cravings. But one thing is sure: the countess is insane. And insanity can be inherited.'

'But the count is perfectly sane,' I protested. 'He's a man of sound judgement, he's well educated—much more so than I was expecting, I must confess. He loves reading . . .'

'Quite so, quite so, Professor. But he often acts strangely. Sometimes he shuts himself away for days on end. He often prowls about at night. You'd never believe the books he reads—German metaphysics, physiology, and what have you. Another great parcel of them arrived from Leipzig only yesterday. Do I have to spell it out?—Every Hercules needs a Hebe.* Some of the peasant girls around here are very pretty. On Saturday evenings, after their bath, they could pass for princesses. There's not one of them who wouldn't esteem it an honour to entertain His Excellency. Dammit, when I was his age. . . . Why, he doesn't have a mistress, he's unmarried—it's all wrong. What he needs is some wholesome distraction.'

I found the doctor's gross materialism utterly shocking, and abruptly terminated the conversation by expressing the devout hope that Count Szémioth would find a spouse worthy of him. It was not without surprise, I must confess, that I had learned from the doctor of the count's taste for philosophy. That this former officer in the Hussars and fanatical hunter should devote himself to reading German metaphysics and studying physiology seemed inconceivable. But the doctor was right, and what he told me was confirmed that same day.

'Professor,' the count said to me suddenly towards the end of dinner, 'how do you account for the duality or dichotomy of our nature?' And, seeing that I was not entirely clear what he meant, he went on: 'Have you never stood on top of a tower, or on the brink of a precipice, and felt simultaneously an impulse to plunge into the abyss and a totally conflicting feeling of terror?'

'It can be accounted for by purely physical causes,' said the doctor. 'To begin with, the fatigue one experiences after an ascent causes a rush of blood to the brain, which . . .'

'Never mind about the rush of blood, doctor,' exclaimed the count impatiently. 'Let's take another example. You are holding a loaded firearm. Your best friend is there with you. Suddenly it occurs to you to put a bullet through his head. You have the utmost abhorrence for murder, and yet you entertain the idea. I think, gentlemen, that if all the thoughts that pass through our heads in the course of an hour—I think that if all *your* thoughts, Professor, and I regard you as a wise man—could be written down, they would probably fill a folio volume on the basis of which any lawyer would call for you to be stripped of your civil rights, and any judge would have you locked up in prison or committed to a madhouse.'

'I'm sure, Count, that the judge wouldn't condemn me for having spent more than an hour this morning trying to discover the mysterious law whereby verbs in the Slavonic languages take on a future meaning when a preposition is prefixed to them. But if by some chance I had had some other thought, how could this be held against me? I am no more master of my thoughts than of the external accidents which suggest them to me. The fact that a thought enters my head does not imply that I have begun to put it into execution, or even a decision to do so. I have never once contemplated killing anyone, but if the thought did enter my head, is my reason not there to banish it?'

'It's all very well to talk of reason. But is it always there to direct us, as you claim? If reason is to speak and be heeded, we first need time and composure in which to reflect. Do we always have them? On the battlefield I see a piece of round shot ricochet and head straight towards me. I step aside, thereby exposing my friend, for whom I would have laid down my life, had I had time to reflect.'

I tried to speak to him of our duties as men and as Christians, of our need to emulate the warrior of the Scriptures, always prepared for combat; and finally I put it to him that by constantly struggling against our passions we acquire new strength with which to diminish and dominate them. I fear I only succeeded in reducing him to silence, and he did not seem convinced.

I stayed ten more days at the castle. I made one more visit to Dowgielly, but we did not spend the night there. As on the first occasion, Miss Iwinska acted like a mischievous, spoilt child. She exerted a sort of fascination on the count, and I did not doubt that he was deeply in love with her. Yet he was well aware of her faults, and had no illusions on that score. He knew her to be flirtatious, frivolous, and indifferent to everything but her own pleasure. I could often see him suffering inwardly from the knowledge that she was so unreasonable; but she had only to grant him some trifling favour and he would forget the past, his face would light up, and he would beam with joy.

He wanted to take me one last time to Dowgielly, on the day before my departure—perhaps because it was my habit to remain indoors conversing with the aunt, while he strolled in the garden with the niece. But I had a great deal of work to get through and had to decline his offer, though he was insistent. He was back for dinner, although he had told us not to wait for him. He sat down to table but ate nothing. Throughout the meal he was gloomy and ill-humoured. From time to time he scowled, and a sinister expression crept into his eyes. When the doctor left to pay his visit to the countess, the count followed me into my room and unburdened himself to me.

'I deeply regret having abandoned you', he exclaimed, 'to go and see that flighty creature who laughs at me and only cares for new faces. Fortunately it's all over between us. I'm heartily sick of her, and I shall never see her again.' He paced back and forth for a while, as was his custom, then continued:

'Perhaps you think I'm in love with her? That's what that fool of a doctor thinks. No, I never loved her. That laughing face of hers amused me, I enjoyed the sight of her white skin. Those are the only things she has to commend her . . . her skin, especially. A pretty head, but no brains.* I never considered her as anything other than a pretty doll, nice to look at when you're bored and you don't have a new book to read. I suppose she could be described as a beauty—her complexion is marvellous! The blood that flows beneath her skin must be better than a horse's blood, eh, Professor?'

And he burst out laughing. But his laugh was painful to hear.

The next day I took my leave of him, to continue my explorations in the north of the palatinate.

VII

These lasted about two months, and I can say that there is hardly a village in Samogitia that I did not visit, and in which I did not gather a few documents. May I be permitted to take this opportunity of thanking the inhabitants of the province, and in particular the local clergy, for the zeal with which they assisted me in my researches and the excellent contributions with which they enriched my dictionary.

After a week's stay in Siaulai, I was proposing to go and take ship at Klaipėda (the port we call Memel) in order to return home, when I received the following letter from Count Szémioth, brought to me by one of his lackeys:

'Dear Professor Wittembach,

Forgive me if I write to you in German. I would commit even more solecisms if I were to write in Lithuanian, and you would lose what little esteem you may at present have for me. In any case, the news I have to communicate to you will perhaps do nothing to increase it. Without more ado, I am getting married, and of course you can guess to whom. *Jupiter mocks at lovers' oaths.** So does Pirkunas, our Samogitian Jupiter. So, then, I shall be marrying Miss Julia Iwinska on the 8th of next month. You would do me the utmost kindness by attending the ceremony. All the peasantry of Medintiltas and the vicinity will come to my home to devour a few oxen and prodigious numbers of pigs, and when they are drunk they will dance in the meadow to the right of the avenue with which you are well acquainted. You will see costumes and customs worthy of your attention. I shall be delighted if you can attend, and so will Julia. I should add that your refusal would place us in a most embarrassing situation. You are aware that I belong to the Evangelical communion, as does my fiancée. Our minister, who lives about thirty leagues away, is laid up with gout, and I ventured to hope that you would be willing to officiate in his stead.

Your devoted servant,

MICHAEL SZÉMIOTH.'

At the foot of the letter, the following postscript had been added in Lithuanian, in an elegant feminine hand:

'I am the muse of Lithuania, so I shall write in Lithuanian. It is impertinent of Michael to doubt your approval. The fact is, it is I who am mad to want anything to do with a boy like him. On the 8th of next month, Professor, you will see quite a *chic* bride. The word is French, not Lithuanian. Whatever you do, don't allow yourself to be distracted during the ceremony!'

Neither the letter nor the postscript pleased me. I considered that the betrothed couple were displaying inexcusable levity in view of the solemn circumstances. But how was I to refuse? I must also confess that the prospect of the forthcoming festivities was in some respects a tempting one: there was every indication that, among the large number of gentlefolk who would be gathering at the castle of Medintiltas, I would be bound to encounter some educated persons whose knowledge might be of use to me. My Lithuanian glossary contained a wealth of material, but the meaning of a number of words I had learned from the lips of uncouth peasants was still far from clear to me. The combination of all these considerations was enough to sway me to agree to the count's request, and I wrote to say that I would be at Medintiltas on the morning of the 8th. Alas, I had cause to regret my decision.

VIII

On entering the avenue leading up to the castle I noticed a large number of ladies and gentlemen in morning dress standing together on the castle steps or sauntering along the paths in the park. The courtyard was full of peasants dressed in their Sunday best. The castle had a festive air about it: everywhere there were flowers and garlands, flags and festoons. The steward led me to the room that had been prepared for me on the ground floor, apologizing for being unable to offer me a better one: there were so many guests at the castle that it had proved impossible to let me keep the same rooms I had occupied during my first visit, since these were being reserved for the wife of the Marshal of the Nobility. Nevertheless, my new room was very adequate, with a view of the grounds, and was directly beneath the count's rooms. I hastily dressed for the ceremony; I donned my vestments; but there was no sign of the count or his fiancée. The count had gone to fetch her at Dowgielly. They should have been back some time before, but a bride's *toilette* is no small matter, and the doctor warned the guests that, since lunch would not be served until after the religious ceremony was over, those who could not contain their appetites would do well to take appropriate precautions at a refreshment table that had been set with cakes and drinks of every description. During this time I observed how waiting makes people prone to malicious gossip: the mothers of two pretty girls who had been invited to the festivities kept up a constant torrent of malicious epigrams at the bride's expense.

It was past noon when a salvo of firearms and mortars heralded her arrival; and soon afterwards a ceremonial barouche drawn by four magnificent horses pulled into the avenue. From the foam that covered their breasts it was evident that the horses were not responsible for the delay. The barouche contained only the bride, *Pani* Dowgiello, and the count. He alighted and offered *Pani* Dowgiello his hand. With a graceful gesture of childlike coquetry, Miss Iwinska made as if to hide behind her shawl so as to shield herself from the curious stares directed at her from all sides. However, she stood up in the barouche, and was on the point of taking the count's hand when the shaft-horses, perhaps frightened by the hail of flowers with which the peasants were pelting the bride, or perhaps also experiencing that strange terror the count inspired in animals, suddenly reared and snorted. One wheel struck the marker-stone at the foot of the steps, and for a moment it looked as if there was about to be an accident. Miss Iwinska gave a little cry. Our minds were soon set at rest. Seizing her in his arms, the count carried her up the flight of steps as effortlessly as if she had been a dove. We all applauded his nimbleness and chivalrous gallantry. The peasants uttered resounding cheers, while the bride, blushing deeply, laughed and trembled all at once. The count, who was in no hurry to relinquish his charming burden, seemed jubilant as he displayed her to the crowd surrounding him.

Suddenly a tall, pale, thin woman appeared at the top of the flight of steps, her clothes in disarray, her hair dishevelled, and her features distorted by terror. No one seemed to know where she had appeared from.

'The bear!' she cried in a piercing voice. 'The bear! Fetch your guns! He's making off with a woman! Kill him! Shoot, shoot!'

It was the countess. The bride's arrival had brought everyone to the front steps, out into the courtyard, or to the castle windows. Even the servants who were supposed to be guarding the poor madwoman had forgotten their instructions. She had escaped and had slipped in among us unnoticed. A most distressing scene ensued. She had to be carried away shouting and struggling. Many of the guests did not know about her illness. They now had to be given an explanation. There was a good deal of whispering in low voices. Faces had grown solemn. 'A bad omen!' said the superstitious—and there is no shortage of such folk in Lithuania.

Meanwhile, Miss Iwinska asked for five minutes in which to tidy herself and don her bridal veil, an operation which took a good hour. This was more than enough time for those still ignorant of the countess's malady to be apprised of its cause and the form it took.

At last the bride reappeared, magnificently attired and glittering with diamonds. Her aunt introduced her to all the guests; then, when the time came to go into the chapel, to my astonishment *Pani* Dowgiello slapped her niece on the cheek in front of the entire company, hard enough for everyone, including those whose attention had been directed elsewhere, to notice. The slap was received with perfect resignation, and nobody seemed in the least surprised by it. However, a man dressed in black wrote something down on a piece of paper he had with him, and some of those present put their signatures to it as if this were the most natural thing in the world. It was not until after the ceremony was over that I learned the explanation for this mystery. Had I guessed it before, I should have made a point of protesting, with all the authority bestowed on me by my sacred ministry, at this abominable practice, the purpose of which is to establish grounds for divorce by pretending that the marriage has taken place only because one of the parties was under duress.

After the religious ceremony I thought it my duty to address a few words to the young couple, in which I tried to stress to them the solemnity and sanctity of the commitment that had just united them; and as Miss Iwinska's tactless postscript still rankled with me, I reminded her that she was leaving behind her life of adolescent joys and amusements, to embark on a new life of serious duties and severe trials. I sensed that this part of my address made a profound impression on the bride, and on everyone present who understood German.

Salvos of firearms and cries of joy welcomed the procession as it left the chapel. Then we moved into the dining-room. The meal was magnificent, appetites had been well and truly whetted, and at first no sound was heard other than that of knives and forks being wielded. But soon, with the help of the wines of Champagne and Hungary, people began to chat, laugh, and even shout. The bride's health was toasted enthusiastically. Scarcely had we sat down again when an old gentleman with a white moustache rose to his feet and, in a formidable voice, said: 'I am distressed to see that our old customs are dying out. Our fathers would never have drunk this toast from crystal glasses. We used to drink from the bride's shoe, or even from her boot—for in my day ladies wore red morocco leather boots. My friends, let us show that we are still true Lithuanians.—And you, madam, be so good as to give me your shoe.'

Blushing, and with a little half-suppressed laugh, the bride replied: 'Come and take it, sir. But I shall not return the compliment by drinking from your boot.'

The gentleman did not wait to be asked twice, but knelt down gallantly, removed one small, white, red-heeled satin shoe, filled it with champagne, and tipped it back so quickly and deftly that not more than half of it spilled over his clothes. The shoe was passed round and all the men drank from it, not without difficulty. The old gentleman claimed back the shoe as though it were some precious relic, and *Pani* Dowgiello sent for a chambermaid to come and repair the damage to her niece's attire.

The toast was followed by a number of others, and soon the guests became so noisy that I thought it would not be proper to remain any longer among them. I made my escape from the table unnoticed, and stepped outside to take a breath of fresh air; but there too I came upon a spectacle that was scarcely edifying: most of the servants and villagers, who had had beer and vodka *ad libitum*, were already drunk. There had been quarrels, and fights had broken out. Here and there on the grass men lay sprawled in a drunken stupor, and the general appearance of the festivities was strongly reminiscent of a battlefield. I would have been curious to take a closer look at the folk dances, but most of them were led by brazen Gypsy women, and I did not think it would be seemly to venture into this mêlée. So I returned to my room, where I read for a while, then undressed, and soon fell asleep.

When I woke up the castle clock was striking three. It was a bright night, although the moon was partially obscured by a slight mist. I tried to get back to sleep but was unable to do so. As is my wont on such occasions, I decided to take up a book and study, and I reached for the matches but could not find them. I got up, and was groping around my room, when a very large, opaque body fell past my window and landed with a thud in the garden. My first impression was that it was a man, and I thought that one of our drunken brethren must have fallen out of the window. I opened my own window and looked out; I saw nothing. At last I managed to light a candle and, returning to bed, looked over my glossary until my tea was brought to me.

At about eleven o'clock I went into the drawing-room, where I found a good many dark-ringed eyes and haggard faces, and learned that, sure enough, the party had broken up very late. Neither the count nor the young countess had yet put in an appearance.

At half-past-eleven, after a good deal of malicious joking, voices began to be heard protesting, first in an undertone, then quite audibly. Doctor Froeber took it upon himself to send the count's valet to knock on his master's door. After a quarter of an hour the man came back downstairs and informed Doctor Froeber somewhat uneasily that he had knocked more than a dozen times but had obtained no response. *Pani* Dowgiello, the doctor, and myself conferred. The valet's anxiety had infected me. The three of us went back upstairs with him. At the door we found the young countess's maid in a fluster, insisting that some misfortune must have occurred, since her mistress's window was wide open. I remembered with alarm the heavy body that had dropped past my window. We knocked loudly. There was no response. Finally the valet brought an iron bar and we broke down the door.

I cannot bring myself to describe the spectacle which met our eyes. The young countess was stretched out dead on her bed, her face hideously lacerated, her throat torn open, and drenched in blood. The count had vanished, and nothing has ever been heard of him since.

The doctor contemplated the young woman's dreadful wound.

'No steel blade ever inflicted a wound like that!' he exclaimed. 'That's a bite!'

The professor closed his book and gazed pensively at the fire.

'And is that the end of the story?' asked Adelaide.

'Yes,' replied the professor dolefully.

'But why did you give it the title *Lokis*?' she went on. 'None of the characters has that name.'

'It's not the name of a person,' said the professor. 'Well, Theodor, do you understand the significance of the name *Lokis*?'

'I haven't a clue.'

'If you had thoroughly mastered the law of transformation from Sanscrit to Lithuanian, you would have recognized the word *lokis* as the Sanscrit *arkcha* or *rikscha*. *Lokis* is the Lithuanian word for the animal the Greeks called 'άρκτος, the Romans *ursus*, and the Germans *Bär*. Now you will understand the epigraph:

> *Miszka su Lokiu*
> *Abu du tokiu.*

As you know, the bear in the *Roman de Renart* is called *Damp Brun*. Among the Slavs he is called Mishka (Michael), and in Lithuania, Miszka, a sobriquet which almost always replaces the generic word *lokis*. In the same way, the French have forgotten their Latin-derived word for a fox, *goupil* or *gorpil*, which has been supplanted by the word *renard*. Let me give you some other examples . . .'

But Adelaide remarked that it was late, and we parted company.

APPENDIX

The final chapter of *Carmen* added
edition

IV

Spain is one of the countries where large numbers of those
nomads who are scattered throughout Europe, and are known
by such names as *Gypsies*, *Bohémiens*, *Gitanos*, and *Zigeuner*,
may still be found today. Most of them inhabit, or rather
roam, the provinces of the south and east—Andalusia,
Extremadura, and the kingdom of Murcia. A fair number of
them live in Catalonia, often crossing over into France, where
they can be seen at any of our southern fairs. Usually the men
make a living as horse dealers, horse doctors, or mule clippers;
they supplement this work by occupations such as repairing
saucepans and copper utensils, to say nothing of smuggling
and other illicit activities. The women tell fortunes, beg, and
deal in all sorts of drugs, innocuous and otherwise.

The physical characteristics of the race are easier to recognize
than to describe, yet once you have seen one, you could spot
a Gypsy in a crowd of a thousand faces. It is above all in the
cast and expression of their features that they differ from the
indigenous peoples of the same country. Their complexion is
very swarthy, always darker than that of the people among
whom they live: hence the name *Calé*, blacks, by which they
often refer to themselves.[1] Their eyes have a pronounced slant
and are almond-shaped, very dark, and fringed with long thick
eyelashes. Their expression can best be compared to that of a
wild beast. It expresses both boldness and timidity, and in this
respect their eyes faithfully reflect the character of the people,
wily, daring, but, like Panurge, 'naturally fearful of blows.'*

---

[1] I got the impression that, although they understand the term *Calé* well
enough, the Gypsies of Germany dislike being referred to in this way. Their
own term is *Romané tchavé*.

ost part the men are muscular, slim, and lithe; I can-
call ever having seen one who was running to fat. In
ermany the Gypsy girls are often very pretty, but beauty is
a truly rare attribute among the *gitanas* of Spain. While they
are still very young, their ugliness may be not unattractive;
but once they have borne children they become positively
repulsive. The filthiness of both sexes has to be seen to be
believed. Picture to yourself the most unkempt, the greasiest,
and the dustiest mane imaginable, and you will still find it
hard to conceive of the state of a Gypsy matron's hair unless
you have seen the reality. In some of the large towns in
Andalusia a few of the girls are rather more attractive than the
rest, and take greater care of their personal appearance. Girls
of this kind earn money by performing dances very similar to
those it is forbidden to perform in public at our Shrovetide
carnivals.

Mr Borrow*, an English missionary and the author of two
extremely interesting works on the Spanish Gypsies, whom he
was sent by the Bible Society to convert, assures us that it is
unheard of for a Gypsy woman to show any partiality towards
a man not of her race. It seems to me that his praise for their
chastity is somewhat exaggerated. In the first place, what Ovid
wrote of the ugly girl can also be said of most Gypsy women:
Casta quam nemo rogavit*. As for the pretty ones, they are like
all Spanish women—difficult to please when it comes to choos-
ing a lover. Not only must he be attractive to them; he must
also be worthy of them. Mr Borrow cites one trait as evidence
of their virtue, which does credit to his own virtue, though it
is also a measure of his naïveté: he tells how a rake of his
acquaintance tried unsuccessfully to seduce a pretty Gypsy
girl by offering her some gold *onzas*. An Andalusian to whom
I told this anecdote claimed that the rake would have stood a
better chance of success if he had shown her two or three
piastres, and that to offer gold *onzas* to a Gypsy girl was as
poor a way of going about persuading her as promising a
couple of million piastres to a barmaid. Be that as it may, it
is certain that Gypsy women are extraordinarily loyal to their
husbands. There is no danger or privation they will not
undergo to help them in their hour of need. One of the names

by which Gypsies refer to themselves, *Romé* or 'married folk', seems to me to testify to the respect their race feels for the institution of marriage. As a generalization it may be said that their chief virtue is their patriotism—if one can so characterize the solidarity that is a feature of their relations with people of the same origin as themselves, their readiness to help one another, and the scrupulousness with which they observe secrecy in their illicit dealings. And indeed, much the same is true of every mysterious association that lies beyond the pale of the law.

A few months ago I visited a band of Gypsies at their camp in the Vosges. In the hut of an old woman, the oldest of her tribe, lay a Gypsy who did not belong to her family, and who was suffering from a fatal illness. This man had left a hospital, where he had been well looked after, in order to come and die among people of his own race. For thirteen weeks he had been confined to bed in the home of his hosts, and was receiving much better treatment than the sons and sons-in-law living in the same home. He had a good bed of straw and moss, with fairly clean sheets; whereas the rest of the family, eleven people in all, were sleeping on boards three feet long. This is a measure of their hospitality. The same woman, who treated her guest so humanely, used to say to me within earshot of the sick man, '*Singo, singo, homte hi mulo*' ('Very soon, very soon, he is going to die'). The fact is, the life these people lead is so wretched that the imminence of death holds no terrors for them.

One remarkable feature of the Gypsy character is their indifference to religion. Not that they are unbelievers or sceptics: they have never professed atheism. On the contrary, they adopt the religion of the country in which they happen to find themselves; but they change it whenever they change their homeland. The superstitions which, among primitive peoples, replace religious feelings are equally alien to them. How, indeed, could superstition exist among a people used to living by the credulity of others? However, I noticed that Spanish Gypsies have a marked aversion to the company of corpses. Few of them would consent to bear a dead man to his grave, even for money.

I have said that most Gypsy women engage in fortune-telling. They make an excellent job of it. But their major source of income is the sale of charms and love philtres. Not only do they sell toads' feet to secure inconstant hearts, and powdered lodestone that will make even the most obdurate fall in love; but, if need be, they will utter powerful spells to oblige the Devil to come to their aid.

Last year a Spanish woman told me the following story. She was walking one day along the Calle de Alcalá, plunged in melancholy thoughts. A Gypsy woman squatting on the pavement called out to her, 'My pretty lady, your lover has betrayed you.' (This was in fact the case.) 'Do you want me to get him back for you?'

You can imagine the joy with which this proposal was greeted, and the confidence inspired by a person who could, at a glance, penetrate the inmost secrets of the heart. As it would have been impractical to perform the magic ceremonies there in the busiest street in Madrid, they arranged to meet the following day.

'Nothing could be simpler than to make your faithless lover fall at your feet again,' said the Gypsy woman. 'Do you happen to have a handkerchief, a scarf, or a mantilla given to you by him?' She was handed a silk shawl.

'Now, with crimson silk, sew a piastre into one corner of the shawl. Into another, sew half a piastre; into the next, a peseta, and in the last a two-*real* piece. Then you must sew a gold coin into the middle—a doubloon would be best.'

The doubloon and other coins were duly sewn into the shawl.

'Now give me the shawl. I shall take it to the cemetery on the stroke of midnight. If you want to see a fine piece of witchcraft, come with me then. I can promise that tomorrow you will see your beloved again.'

The Gypsy set off for the cemetery alone, for the lady was too afraid of black magic to accompany her. I leave you to guess whether the poor lovelorn creature ever saw her shawl or her faithless lover again.

Despite their poverty and the feeling of antipathy they inspire, Gypsies are held in some regard by uneducated folk, a fact of which they are extremely proud. They regard themselves as a race endowed with superior intelligence, and cordially despise the nation that gives them hospitality. 'The Gentiles are so stupid', a Gypsy woman in the Vosges said to me, 'that there is no merit in cheating them. The other day a peasant woman called to me in the street, and I went into her house. Her stove was smoking, and she asked me to cast a spell to put it right. First of all I got her to give me a largish piece of bacon. Then I began to mutter a few words in Romany. "You're a fool," I said. "You were born a fool, and a fool you'll die." When I was near the door I said to her in good German, "The surest way of stopping your stove from smoking is not to light it." At that I took to my heels.'

The history of the Gypsies is still a matter for conjecture. It is known that the first few isolated bands appeared in eastern Europe towards the beginning of the fifteenth century. But no one can say where they came from or why they came to Europe; and, strangest of all, no one knows how it came about that their numbers soon increased so prodigiously in several countries so far apart. The Gypsies themselves have preserved no tradition as to their origin, and although most of them talk of Egypt as their original homeland, they are merely repeating an old tale that others have told about them since time immemorial.

Most of the orientalists who have studied the language of the Gypsies believe that they originally came from India. It does indeed seem that a number of roots and many of the grammatical forms of Romany can also be found in the languages derived from Sanscrit. Understandably, the Gypsies have adopted many foreign words in the course of their long wanderings. A number of Greek words can be found in all dialects of Romany: for example, *cocal*, bone, from κόκκαλον; *petali*, horseshoe, from πέταλον; *cafi*, nail, from καρφί, and so forth. Today there are almost as many different Romany dialects as there are separate bands of their race. Everywhere they speak the language of their adopted country in preference to their own, which they seldom use except in order to communicate freely in front of strangers. If one compares the dialect of the German Gypsies with that of their Spanish kinsmen, who for centuries have been cut off from contact with those in Germany, one can identify a very large number of words common to both. But everywhere, though to varying extents, the original language has undergone significant changes through contact with the more developed languages these nomads have been obliged to use. German in the one case, and Spanish in the other, have so modified the basic Romany that it would be impossible for a Gypsy from the Black Forest to have a conversation with one of his brothers from Andalusia, although they would only need to exchange a few sentences to recognize that they were both speaking a dialect of the same language. A few very frequently used words are, I believe, common to all dialects. Thus, in every vocabulary I have been able to see, *pani* means 'water', *manro*, 'bread', *mâs*, 'meat', and *lon* 'salt'.

The numerals are more or less the same everywhere. The German dialect seems to me much purer than that spoken in Spain, for it has preserved a number of primitive grammatical forms, whereas the *Gitanos* have adopted those of Castilian Spanish. However, a few words are exceptions, providing evidence that the two languages were once one and the same. In the German dialect the preterites are formed by adding -*ium* to the imperative, which is always the root of the verb. In the Romany of Spain all verbs conjugate on the model of first-conjugation verbs in Castilian. From the infinitive *jamar*, to eat, the regular form would be *jamé*, I ate, from *lillar*, to take, *lillé*, I took. However, some of the old Gypsies prefer the form *jayon, lillon*. I have found no other verbs that have conserved this ancient form.

Whilst I am airing my scanty knowledge of the Romany language, I must draw attention to a few slang words borrowed from the Gypsies by our thieves here in France. Polite society has learned from *The Mysteries of Paris** that *chourin* means 'a knife'. This is pure Romany, *tchouri* being one of the words common to all dialects. Monsieur Vidocq* calls a horse *grès*, which again is the Gypsy word *gras, gre, graste, gris*. To this can be added the word *romamichel*, used to refer to Gypsies in Parisian slang. It is a corruption of *rommané tchave* (Gypsy lads). But one etymology of which I am proud is that of *frimousse* (face, expression), a word used by all schoolchildren, at least in my day. Note, firstly, that in his curious dictionary of 1640, Oudin records the word *firlimouse*. Now *firla* or *fila* in Romany means 'face', and *mui* has the same meaning, being the precise equivalent of *os* in Latin. A speaker of pure Romany instantly understood the combination *firlamui*, which, furthermore, is consistent with the spirit of the language.

This should be more than sufficient to give readers of *Carmen* an idea of my studies in the field of Romany. I shall finish with an appropriate proverb: *En retudi panda nasti abela macha*. A closed mouth, no fly can enter.

CARMEN

1 *Epigraph*: 'Every woman is as bitter as g.... good moments: one in bed, the other at her death.' This epig.... is a pun on the Greek words *thalamos* (bedroom, bridal chamber) and *thanatos* (death). Palladas lived in Alexandria in the fifth century AD. His writings are contained in the *Greek Anthology*.

Montilla: on 17 Mar. 45 BC, Julius Caesar defeated Cnaeus and Sextus Pompeius, the sons of Pompey, thereby ending the Civil Wars and definitively establishing his supremacy over all Roman dominions. The site of the battle is still disputed. The location close to Montilla favoured by the narrator of *Carmen* is about 40 km south of Córdoba, and thus more than 100 km north-north-east of the rival site to which he refers, at Monda, inland from Marbella in Málaga province.

Caesar's Commentaries: the *Commentarii* is the name usually given to the seven books by Caesar covering the first seven years of the Gallic Wars (*De bello gallico*) and to the three books covering the Civil Wars down to the beginning of the Alexandrine War (48–7 BC) (*De bello civili*). *De bello hispaniensi* is an anonymous continuation of Caesar's record of the earlier Civil Wars.

2 *Elzevir*: the Elzevirs were a Leiden-based family of Dutch booksellers, publishers, and printers of learned books in the period 1581–1712. They specialized in high-quality editions of literary classics, often in small format.

3 *the bad soldiers of Gideon*: cf. Judges 7: 5–7: 'So he brought down the people unto the water: and the Lord said unto Gideon, Every one that lappeth of the water with his tongue, as a dog lappeth, him shalt thou set by himself; likewise every one that boweth down upon his knees to drink. And the number of them that lapped, putting their hand to their mouth, were three hundred men: but all the rest of the people bowed down upon their knees to drink water. And the Lord said unto Gideon, By the three hundred men that lapped will I save you, and deliver the Midianites into thine hand: and let all the other people go every man unto his place.'

5 *the Venta del Cuervo*: the Raven Inn. A *venta* is a rural hostelry or wayside inn.

6 *gazpacho, a sort of salad consisting of peppers*: gazpacho is not in

ct a salad, but a soup served throughout the hotter regions of Spain. The ingredients vary widely from province to province, but almost invariably include olive oil, garlic, cucumber, and red or green peppers, usually with onion, tomato, breadcrumbs, and vinegar. The soup is served cold or iced.

7 *Milton's Satan*: cf. *Paradise Lost*, I. 589–604. Milton's lines had become well known in France in a translation by Chateaubriand contained in his *Génie du christianisme* (1802).

12 *Actaeon*: according to one version of the story, while hunting, Actaeon witnessed Diana bathing naked on Mount Cithaeron. To prevent him from recounting the incident she metamorphosed him into a stag, whereupon he was devoured by his own hounds.

by the dark light that shines down from the stars: an allusion to an earlier work of French literature with an Andalusian setting, Corneille's *Le Cid*, IV. 3, ll. 1273–4: '*Cette obscure clarté qui tombe des étoiles / Enfin avec le flux nous fait voir trente voiles*'. The line Mérimée quotes is well known, and is often cited as an example of an oxymoron.

13 *Francisco Sevilla*: (*c.* 1809–41), a figure renowned in the annals of tauromachy. His exploits are recounted in Gautier's *Voyage en Espagne* and in Mérimée's own first *Lettre d'Espagne* (1831), which contains an 1842 postscript announcing Sevilla's recent death. Despite the claim advanced here, Mérimée and Sevilla were not personal friends, though they did once dine together. However, it should be borne in mind that the narrator of the first two chapters of *Carmen* is himself a fictional creation who is not to be identified with Mérimée in every respect—a consideration Mérimée himself appears to have overlooked when he came to add a fourth chapter to *Carmen* in 1846. (See Appendix.)

14 *see Brantôme*: Pierre Brantôme, *c.* 1540–1614, soldier and chronicler. The passage in question appears in Book 2 of *Les Vies des dames galantes* (Lives of Gallant Ladies), where the following enumeration is to be found, in Spanish and in French: 'Three white things: her skin, her teeth, and her hands. Three dark: her eyes, her eyebrows, and her eyelashes. Three red: her lips, her cheeks, and her nails. Three long: her body, her hair, and her hands. Three short: her teeth, her ears, and her feet. Three wide: her bosom, her forehead, and the space between her eyebrows. Three narrow: her mouth (both of them), her waist, and her ankles. Three plump: her arm, her thigh, and her calf. Three delicate: her fingers, her hair, and her lips. Three small: her breasts, her nose, and her head.'

17 *corregidor*: at this period, the chief magistrate in some Spanish towns, with civil, administrative, and criminal jurisdiction.

18 *the prison chapel*: it was once the custom in Spain for prisoners condemned to death to spend the three days before their execution confined to the prison chapel, in the company of their confessors. Mérimée's second *Lettre d'Espagne* (1831) also contains an account of this practice.

'*verry preety leetle hanging*': a quotation from Molière's *Monsieur de Pourceaugnac*, III. 3. Molière's phrase imitates a Swiss, not a Spanish accent. Mérimée's intention is to stress the manifest relish with which the friar contemplates the impending execution.

19 *Old Christian*: in Spain the term *cristiano viejo* was formerly used to denote anyone of purely Christian ancestry, that is, with no known admixture of Moorish, Jewish, or 'pagan' blood.

that big building: this vast and imposing eighteenth-century Baroque edifice near the centre of Seville now houses the University.

22 *Triana*: a working-class district of Seville, south-west of the city centre across the Guadalquivir, much frequented by Gypsies.

to keep the flies off her: a reference to the *azotes*, a punishment prescribed for witches and habitual adulteresses. The guilty party was mounted on a donkey, paraded through the streets of the town, and flogged across the bare shoulders at every crossroads.

Street of the Serpent . . . twists and turns: the French text has *rue du Serpent*. Despite its narrowness, the *Calle de las Sierpes* (Street of the Serpents) is one of the main commercial thoroughfares of old Seville; however, it does not 'twist and turn', and is in fact quite straight. The name is thought to allude to the snakes depicted on a tavern sign that once hung there. This is not an oversight on Mérimée's part, or simply another example of the French tendency to Gallicize place-names: don José succumbs to Carmen the temptress in a street whose name evokes the serpent that tempted Adam and Eve in the Garden of Eden.

25 *Longa . . . Mina . . . Chapalangarra*: prominent figures in the guerrilla campaigns against the French during and after the Peninsular War (War of Independence), 1808–14. Francisco Tomás de Longa (b. Francisco Anchía, in Longa (Vizcaya), 1783; d. 1831) commanded the Iberia Division in the Peninsular War, in which he defeated the French in a number of guerrilla actions. Francisco Espoz y Mina (b. Indocín, Navarre, 1781; d. 1836) rose from partisan to general, but was forced to flee to France on the restoration of Fernando VII in 1814, on account of his liberal political views.

He returned to Spain in 1820 and fought against the conservative Absolutists and the French troops backing them, but again fled Spain from 1823 to 1833. Joaquín de Pablo y Antón, known as Chapalangarra, Governor of Alicante in 1823, resisted the French troops that had invaded Spain in an attempt to restore the absolute monarchy. He took refuge in England, returned to Spain in 1830 intending to organize a revolution, but was captured by Royalist forces and shot.

29 *manzanilla*: a very dry, fortified white wine, sometimes classed as a sherry. Sanlúcar de Barrameda is the centre for the trade in this wine. It has a slightly salty taste, supposedly attributable to the proximity of the vines to the sea.

Caliph Haroûn-al-Raschid: the historical Harun ar-Rashīd (b. 766 or 763, d. 809) was fifth caliph of the 'Abbāsid dynasty. From his capital, Baghdad, he ruled an empire that extended from the western Mediterranean to India, excluding only Byzantium. The opulence and luxury of his court were romanticized in the fabulous descriptions of the *Thousand and One Nights*, which contains many tales recounting his nocturnal wanderings in disguise through the streets of Baghdad.

39 *Saint Nicholas*: Mérimée appears to have overlooked the fact that in Spain Christmastide gifts are traditionally brought to children not by Saint Nicholas (Santa Claus), but by the Three Wise Men (*Los Reyes Magos*), on 6 Jan. (Epiphany).

40 *their shirts, of which we had urgent need*: this remark throws new light on the first narrator's reflexion in the third paragraph of the story (page 2): '. . . what would he want with my shirts and my Elzevir *Commentaries*?' Is it simply coincidence that five years earlier, in *Colomba* (chapter XX), Mérimée had made another bandit, Castriconi, request Orso della Rebbia to provide him with an edition of Horace, whereupon Orso had offered the bandit an Elzevir edition?

MATEO FALCONE

54 *When I was in Corsica in 18——*: the narrator's visit is presumed to have taken place some time prior to 1829, the date printed beneath the title of the story. Mérimée himself did not visit Corsica until 1839. On his return he made only minor changes to the 1829 text.

62 *the very wads*: Mateo's guns were muzzle-loaders; the powder and bullets were kept in place by a wad of cardboard or some similar material. When the gun was fired, the wad carried only a short distance. The thought uppermost in Gamba's mind is

that, were he to fire from such close range, Mateo could hardly fail to hit his two targets.

THE STORMING OF THE REDOUBT

67 *the Cheverino redoubt*: Cheverino is a garbled form of the name Shvardinó. The Shvardinó redoubt, west of Moscow, was taken on 5 Sept. 1812, two days before the battle of Borodinó. Mérimée is describing events that had taken place a mere 17 years earlier. While the device of using a 'military friend' as narrator is of course simply a literary convention, he did no doubt have the benefit of eye-witness accounts of the action. However, artistic and imaginative considerations here take precedence over historical accuracy, and Mérimée's account strays from the facts in a number of particulars. A very different version of these events, recounted by General Compans (the General C**** of the story's closing lines), was made public in 1912.

69 *non bis in idem*: this adage states the principle that a man may not be tried twice for the same offence. Here, it is used loosely to convey the idea that 'lightning does not strike twice in the same place'.

TAMANGO

72 *Ledoux*: the choice of name is intended as ironic (*doux* means 'gentle'). Similarly, Mérimée names the slave-ship *Espérance* ('Hope').

prize money: the spoils from captured enemy vessels were shared out among the officers and crew of ships that were in the vicinity at the time of the capture.

The Peace Treaty: this was the Treaty of Paris (30 May 1814), concluded between defeated France and the Allies and ratified at the Congress of Vienna on 9 June 1815, after Napoleon's brief return from Elba and prior to his final defeat at Waterloo.

When the slave trade was abolished: a declaration abolishing slavery had been signed at the Congress of Vienna on 8 February 1815. However, many years passed before an end was finally put to the trade.

barres de justice: according to the proceedings of the abolitionist *Société de la Morale chrétienne*, these were irons six feet long equipped with four pairs of rings with which to secure the legs of four slaves. They were manufactured in Nantes 'in thousands'.

76 *The Sicilian Vespers*: a tragedy by Casimir Delavigne first performed in 1819 (not Verdi's better-known opera of the same title, which dates from 1855).

80 *Mumbo Jumbo*: Mérimée's source here is Mungo Park's *Travels in the Interior Districts of Africa* (1797). In chapter 3 of that work, Park describes Mumbo Jumbo as 'a strange bugbear, common to all Mandingo towns, and much employed by the Pagan natives in keeping their wives in subjection'. He goes on to give a full description of Mumbo Jumbo, many details of which recur in the interpreter's account contained in this passage.

81 *balafos*: the *balafo*, the precursor of the modern marimba, is a pitched percussion instrument with wooden bars like a xylophone, to which are attached gourds that act as resonators.

82 *Martin-Bâton*: a *martin-bâton* is a stick used to beat recalcitrant animals, and, by extension, denotes the man who wields it. Sometimes, as in La Fontaine's *L'Âne et le petit chien* (*Fables*, IV. 5) and also in this passage, Martin-Bâton is the stick personified.

89 *Coriolanus*: Gnaeus Marcius Coriolanus, the legendary Roman general of the fifth century BC, the subject of Shakespeare's tragedy of that title. Driven from Rome as a result of his ultra-conservative policies, he sought refuge among his former enemies, the Volsci, and led a Volscian army against Rome. Although he was eventually prevailed upon by his mother to relent and withdraw the hostile Volscian forces, his name nonetheless became a byword for inflexibility and resolution.

THE ETRUSCAN VASE

93 *Mademoiselle Sontag's singing*: Henriette Sontag (1805–54), a German operatic soprano. She made her Paris début in 1826, as Rosina in Rossini's *The Barber of Seville*. The Théâtre-Italien is now the Opéra-Comique.

96 *That Russian Lovelace who served under Diebitsch*: Lovelace, the villain in Richardson's *Clarissa* (1747–8), typifies the unscrupulous rake. Hans Friedrich Anton, Count Diebitsch (1785–1831), a Russian general of German parentage, commanded the Russian forces in Europe during the Russo-Turkish War of 1828–9. He was promoted to the rank of Field Marshal for his role in the Turkish defeat.

98 *Judith Pasta*: *née* Giuditta Negri (1797–1865), prima donna who sang at the Théâtre-Italien in the 1820s and was renowned for the dramatic force she brought to her performances. This may account for Saint-Clair's description of her as a tragic actress.

99 *the fox that had had its tail cut off*: cf. La Fontaine, *Fables*, V. 5 (*Le renard ayant la queue coupée*). After losing his tail while

escaping from a trap, the fox tries unsuccessfully to persuade the other foxes to cut off their own tails.

Staub: a fashionable tailor, also patronized by characters in the novels of Balzac and Stendhal.

101 *Frailty, thy name is woman!*: *Hamlet*, I. 2.

102 *the Pasha? When will he declare independence?*: Muhammad Ali Pasha (1769–1849), the founder of the dynasty that ruled Egypt from the early nineteenth to the mid-twentieth century. Apparently of Albanian origin, he left Kavala (now in Greece) in 1795, in an Ottoman expeditionary force sent to oppose Napoleon's occupation of Egypt (at that time a semi-autonomous province of the Ottoman Empire). By 1805 he had risen to be the Sultan's viceroy in Egypt. He supported the Turkish attempt to suppress the Greek movement for independence, but in 1831 himself rebelled against the Sultan and invaded Syria. His successes led to intervention by the European Powers in 1840. However, in 1841, he and his descendants were granted the hereditary right to rule Egypt and the Sudan under the suzerainty of the Sultan.

102 *almehs*: Egyptian dancing-girls with a training in dance, music, and poetry. The form *alma(h)* is also found.

The statue of Memnon? And Ibrahim Pasha?: the so-called statue of Memnon was in fact one of the colossal statues of Amenhotep III, near Thebes. After being partially destroyed in an earthquake in 27 BC it began to emit musical sounds, resembling those of a plucked harp-string, when warmed by the rays of the rising sun—a phenomenon attributed to the circulation of air through the porous stone. In AD 170 the statue was restored and the sounds ceased. Ibrahim Pasha (*c.* 1792–1848) was one of Muhammad Ali's ninety-five children and, briefly, viceroy in succession to him in 1848. In the 1820s he had reorganized the Egyptian army along European lines.

103 *Bedouin, Copts, fellahin, moghrabbin*: Bedouin: the generic name for Arabs of the desert. Copts: native Egyptian Christians whose branch of the Eastern Church has its origins in St Mark's ministry in Alexandria in AD 61. Fellahin: Egyptian villagers. Moghrabbin: men of the west; whether this refers to inhabitants of Western Egypt, or of the lands to the west of Egypt, including the *Maghreb* (present-day Morocco, Algeria, and Tunisia), is unclear. At one time, units of Turkish infantry recruited from among the Moors went by this name.

a djerid that belonged to the famous Mourad Bey: a *djerid* is a weapon fashioned from a dry palm branch. It may be thrown like a javelin or used like a lance. Mourad Bey (d. 1801) was a Mameluke chief defeated by Napoleon at the battle of the Pyramids in 1798, and subsequently an ally of the French.

yataghan . . . khandjar . . . mashlah . . . burnous . . . haik: Yataghan: 'Sword without guard and often with double-curved blade, used in Muslim countries' (*Concise Oxford Dictionary*). Khandjar: a large knife or dagger, generally curved and double-edged. Mashlah: the French has *metchlâ*, a word that has caused widespread mystification among commentators. *Mashlah*, a Syrian word for a headscarf, may be what Mérimée intended, though it is not inconceivable that he had in mind *meç*, a Turkish word for a sword or rapier. Burnous: a hooded cloak. Haik: 'an Arab's outer wrapper for head and body' (*Concise Oxford Dictionary*).

Giourdina, c'est-à-dire Jourdain: the quotation is from Molière's *Le Bourgeois Gentilhomme*, v. 1, in which the gullible *parvenu* Monsieur Jourdain, bamboozled into believing that he has been elevated to the Turkish nobility, tries to convince his wife that his name is now Giourdina.

104 *Charlet's collection of illustrations*: Nicolas Charlet (1792–1845), painter and lithographer. He specialized in military subjects, and his work helped propagate the Napoleonic legend in the period after Waterloo.

which make Lamartine's seem like classical prose: in their style and themes Lamartine's *Méditations poétiques* (1820) epitomize the concerns of the French Romantic Movement in poetry. The Egyptian poet would appear to be a figment of Mérimée's imagination.

from the cedar tree even unto the hyssop: cf. 1 Kings 4: 33. This tag was a favourite with Mérimée (it recurs in *The Venus of Ille*). It is probable that he took it, not from the Old Testament, but from Molière's *L'Impromptu de Versailles*, scene v: '. . . les comédiens et les auteurs, depuis le cèdre jusqu'à l'hysope, sont diablement animés contre lui.'

106 *a fine English engraving . . . her hair dressed in this way*: the French text reads 'une belle gravure anglaise, la duchesse de Portland d'après Lesly (elle est coiffée de cette manière)'. In their note on this passage (Pléiade edition, p. 1372) Mallion and Salomon refer to an engraving by Charles Leslie (1794–1859) depicting the Duchess of Portsmouth, and surmise that *Portland* is an error for *Portsmouth*. No indication is given of the whereabouts of this engraving. Assuming their information to

be accurate (Leslie was a painter, and specialized in portraits and literary themes), to amend *Lesly* to *Leslie* nonetheless entails disregarding the word *d'après* in the French. It seems altogether more likely that the artist in question is Sir Peter Lely, whose paintings of aristocratic women of the court of Charles II include a number of portraits of the Duchess of Portsmouth, several of which were reproduced, with variations, in contemporary English engravings. If Mérimée did have some specific engraving in mind, it seems, on the evidence of the engravings, most likely that the sitter is the Duchess of Portsmouth. However, further amendment is unnecessary, since Lely also painted a portrait of Lady Portland.

107 *the École Polytechnique*: one of the *Grandes Écoles*, the prestigious French university schools. Founded in 1794 as an engineering school, it became a military establishment in 1804 and is still under the direction of the Ministry of Defence. Nowadays most of its students go on to posts in government service or business.

108 *The lark, the herald of the morn*: *Romeo and Juliet*, III. 5.

113 *Schroth's*: Schroth was an art dealer with premises at 353 rue Saint-Honoré.

THE GAME OF BACKGAMMON

116 *the famous bridge of boats at Essling*: on 21 and 22 May 1809, having crossed the Danube by means of two bridges of boats, Napoleon's army attacked the Austrians at Aspern and Essling, near Vienna. After two days' fighting, during which his troops sustained heavy losses, Napoleon withdrew to the island of Lobau. The engagement was his first major personal defeat.

Le Constitutionnel: a newspaper of liberal leanings that flourished during the Restoration period following Waterloo.

the prison ship at Cádiz: ten to twelve thousand French soldiers were imprisoned in hulks off Cádiz after the surrender at Bailén in 1808. Stories of attempted escapes were legion.

119 *napoleons*: the gold napoleon coin was worth twenty francs.

122 *prize money*: booty from captured enemy merchant vessels. See note to *Tamango*, p. 345.

123 *blocked his points as if he had been trying to lose*: each of the two compartments of the backgammon table is marked with two rows of six wedge-shaped triangles, known as points. If a player places two or more of his men on a point, that point is said to be blocked.

127 *Jean Bart*: (1650–1702), privateer and naval officer, famous for his exploits in Louis XIV's wars. On one occasion he was captured

by the British but escaped by rowing for fifty-two hours from Plymouth to the French coast. He went on to command a ship at the battle of Beachy Head (1690), and later a division. He was ennobled by Louis XIV for his services to France.

129 *the hulks at Portsmouth*: French prisoners of war were housed in these vessels during the Napoleonic wars.

THE VENUS OF ILLE

132 *Epigraph*: 'And I said: "May the statue be gracious and kindly, since it is so lifelike" ', Lucian, *The Lover of Lies*, section XIX. Lucian was a Greek rhetorician, pamphleteer, and satirist of the second century AD.

the little town of Ille: this is Ille-sur-la-Têt, 24 km west of Perpignan, in the *département* of Pyrénées-Orientales, formerly the province of Roussillon.

133 *the saints at Serrabona*: the monastery of Serrabona is 12 km from Ille. Mérimée had visited it during a tour of duty as Inspector-General of Historic Monuments in 1834.

134 *pelota*: to judge from the somewhat scanty details Mérimée goes on to give, this would seem to be an early form of the modern *pelota vasca* or *jai alai*, a very fast ball game associated particularly with the Basque country, but also popular elsewhere in northern Spain, in Southern France, and in Florida. Nowadays the game is played on a three-walled outdoor court, the ball being caught and thrown in a basket-like device strapped to the arm, known as a *cesta*. Earlier versions of the game were played with a flat wooden bat. The oldest *pelota* courts are to be found in the Basque country, and date from the late eighteenth century.

Don José Lizarrabengoa was also an enthusiastic *pelota* player (see *Carmen*, p. 19).

135 *a Roman Terminus*: a divinity presiding over boundaries and frontiers, whose statue consisted merely of a stone or post marking a boundary (such markers having originally been consecrated to Jupiter). This somewhat obscure simile echoes the lines '*Foi de peuple d'honneur, ils lui promirent tous / De ne bouger non plus qu'un terme*' ('They all gave their word of honour not to stir from the spot') from La Fontaine's *Fables*, IX. 19, *Le Berger et son troupeau*. Later developments in the story will lend the comparison ironic significance.

136 *everything from the cedar tree to the hyssop*: see note to *The Etruscan Vase*, p. 348.

137 *Coustou's lifeless figures*: Nicolas Coustou (1658–1733) and his brother Guillaume (1677–1746) were eminent sculptors whose work may be seen in Notre-Dame, the Louvre, and elsewhere in and around Paris and Versailles. Several sculptures by Nicolas, including *Venus with her dove* and a marble group representing the Seine and the Marne, stand in the Tuileries gardens.

With what irreverence / My wife doth speak of the Gods!: a parody of two lines from Molière's *Amphitryon*, I. 2: '*Comme avec irrévérence/ Parle des dieux ce maraud*' ('With what irreverence this rascal speaks of the gods').

Myron: a Greek sculptor of the fifth century BC, famous for his representations of athletes. The originals of his bronze statues are lost, but Roman marble copies survive, notably that of the 'Discobolus' in the Museo Nazionale delle Terme, Rome.

138 *Veneris nec praemia noris*: 'And shall you not know the gifts of Venus?', Virgil, *Aeneid*, IV. 33.

140 *mora*: a game of Italian origin in which the hand is briefly raised, the opponent then having to guess how many fingers of the hand were extended. The statue referred to is exhibited in the Louvre. It is no longer thought to portray Germanicus; however, the explanation for the statue's attitude put forward here is pure speculation.

141 *C'est Vénus tout entière à sa proie attachée!*: 'It is Venus intent on her prey!', Racine, *Phèdre*, I, 3, l. 306. This is arguably Racine's most frequently quoted line.

142 *Quid dicis, doctissime?*: 'What do you say, o most learned one?', Molière, *Le Malade imaginaire*, II. 6; an expression formerly used during *viva voce* examinations at universities.

143 *with much recourse to spectacles*: cf. Rabelais, *Gargantua*, chapter 1: 'I (though unworthy) was sent for thither, and with much help of those spectacles, whereby the art of reading dim writings, and letters that do not clearly appear to the sight, is practised, as Aristotle teacheth it, did translate the book . . .' (Urquhart and Motteux translation).

Eutychus Myron: a private joke for the benefit of the author's inner circle of acquaintants. Eutychus is a latinization (found in Acts, 20) of the Greek name ʼΕυτυχής, meaning 'fortunate'. The French equivalent is Prosper. 'Eutychus Myron' thus loosely renders the name Prosper Mérimée.

145 *Gruter or Orelli*: Jan van Gruytere (1560–1627), Dutch humanist and archaeologist, compiler of *Inscriptiones antiquae totius orbis Romani* (1603); Johann Kaspar von Orelli (1787–1849), Swiss philologist,

compiler of *Inscriptionum latinarum selectarum amplissima collectio* (1828–56); two classic works of epigraphy.

146 *changed into white birds*: Diomedes, king of Argos and companion of Odysseus, wounded Aphrodite (Venus) at the Siege of Troy (cf. Homer, *Iliad*, Book 5). In revenge she changed his companions into white birds (cf. Ovid, *Metamorphoses*, XIV. 496 *et seq*., and Pliny the Elder, *Historia naturalis*, X. 44, 126).

148 *Manibus date lilia plenis*: 'Give lilies in handfuls', Virgil, *Aeneid*, VI. 883.

150 *Dyrrhachium*: present-day Durrës, in Albania, the scene of Julius Caesar's defeat by Pompey in 48 BC. Caesar rallied his troops and retreated towards Thessaly, where he decisively defeated Pompey at the battle of Pharsalia later in the same year, thereby becoming master of the Roman world.

151 *Me lo pagarás*: 'You'll pay for this.'

154 *'All love's empire is full of tragic histories,' et cetera*: cf. Montaigne, *Essais*, Book I, chapter XXI, *De la Force de l'imagination*; Madame de Sévigné's letter to Madame de Grignan dated 8 Apr. 1671; and also the chapter *Des Fiasco* in Stendhal's *De l'Amour* (1822). The allusion is to states of temporary sexual impotence. The sentence that follows may be a recollection of Mérimée's own abortive liaison with Amandine-Aurore-Lucile Dudevant (the novelist George Sand).

COLOMBA

162 *Epigraph*: 'But, rest assured, she will be enough to avenge you', the closing lines of the folk ballad *Funeral Lament of Niolo* (Niolo is a region of central Corsica). The lines immediately preceding these in the ballad bring out the full significance of the quotation: 'From so great a family / you leave only one sister, / without first cousins, / poor, an orphan, without a husband . . .'

nil admirari: 'Marvel at nothing', Horace, *Epistles*, I. 6.

Monsieur Jourdain: the 'would-be gentleman' of Molière's *Le Bourgeois Gentilhomme*. (See also note to *The Etruscan Vase*, p. 348). The 'civilized people' referred to are those in whose company Monsieur Jourdain wishes to shine (III. 3).

166 *caporali*: see Mérimée's own footnote in *Mateo Falcone*, p. 56.

barrack-room dress and manners into every home: the National Guard was a civilian militia established in 1789, and subsequently several times disbanded and reformed. Mérimée is here alluding to the reforms introduced by Louis-Philippe in 1831.

171 *al capello bianco*: presumably, 'the one with the white hat'. Mérimée (or his first printer) seems to have confused *capello* (hair) and *cappello* (hat).

172 *Orcagna's Triumph of Death*: a fresco in the Campo Santo at Pisa, formerly attributed to Andrea Orcagna (1308–69), now thought to be the work of an unknown artist referred to as 'The Master of the Triumph of Death'. It provided the inspiration for Liszt's *Totentanz*. It was badly damaged by fire after a bombardment in July 1944, but has since been restored.

175 *Vannina d'Ornano . . . Sampiero*: Sampiero Corso (*c*. 1496–1567) attempted to liberate Corsica from Genoese domination. After the failure of the uprising his wife, Vannina d'Ornano, pleaded Sampiero's cause before the Genoese Senate. Regarding this as a betrayal, Sampiero strangled her. As the sailor's *ballata* recounts, he was later killed by Vittolo, a former associate, in an ambush organized by Vannina's brothers to avenge her death.

176 *Fieschi*: Gian Luigi Fieschi, a Genoese nobleman (1522–47) who plotted to overthrow Andrea Doria, the *de facto* ruler of Genoa. The conspiracy was the subject of Schiller's drama *Fiesco; or, the Genoese Conspiracy* (1782), with which Lydia Nevil, with her devotion to Romantic literature, would no doubt have been familiar.

182 *the Marquis de Mascarille*: in Molière's *Les Précieuses ridicules*, scene ix. In fact, Mascarille is the target of the remark, not its author.

186 *the canto from Inferno containing the episode of Francesca da Rimini*: Francesca da Polenta, a contemporary of Dante, married the deformed Gianciotto Malatesta of Rimini, but fell in love with his married younger brother Paolo. Gianciotto surprised the lovers *in flagrante delicto* and stabbed them. Dante retells the story in canto V of *Inferno*. Among subsequent treatments of the episode, the plays by Pellico (1814) and d'Annunzio (1901), an orchestral work by Tchaikovsky, and an opera by Rachmaninov are especially noteworthy.

190 *in medias res*: cf. Horace, *Ars poetica*, ll. 148–9: *semper ad eventum festinat et in medias res / non secus ac notas auditorem rapit . . .* ('The poet always hastens to the issue, and plunges the listener right into the midst of the plot, just as if it were well known').

everything is asleep, the fair Colomba, the Colonel, and his daughter: Mérimée here echoes, or parodies, Racine's famous line (from *Iphigénie*, I. 1): *Mais tout dort, et l'armée, et les vents, et Neptune* ('But everything is asleep, the army, the winds, and Neptune').

191 *the Hundred Days*: the period from Napoleon's return to Paris from exile on Elba (20 Mar. 1815) to the second restoration of Louis XVIII (28 June 1815).

192 *naturally fearful of blows, like Panurge*: Rabelais, *Pantagruel*, XXI: 'and with this he ran away as fast as he could, for fear of blows, whereof he was naturally fearful' (Urquhart and Motteux translation).

197 *voltigeurs*: see Mérimée's own footnote in *Mateo Falcone*, p. 56.

203 *King Theodore*: Theodor, Baron Neuhof (1694–1756), a German adventurer whose exploits included inciting a group of Corsican prisoners in Genoa to revolt against Genoese rule. He landed in Corsica in March 1736, and the following month was proclaimed king, but was forced to flee the country after a rule of only eight months. He twice returned to Corsica, but was eventually reduced to mortgaging his kingdom in order to secure his release from a London debtors' prison.

204 *Allmack's*: a prestigious assembly room in King Street, established by William MacCall in the 1760s and frequented by fashionable society.

Conrad: the hero of Byron's narrative poem 'The Corsair' (1813).

209 *M. de Marbeuf*: Louis, comte de Marbeuf, the first French administrator of Corsica after the island was ceded to France by Genoa in 1768.

211 *Quatre-Bras*: an engagement fought on 16 June 1815, two days before Waterloo.

216 *the Ambigu-Comique*: a Paris theatre that specialized in melodrama.

219 *Tristram Shandy's father found consolation for the loss of a son*: cf. Laurence Sterne, *The Life and Opinions of Tristram Shandy* (1760), vol. v, ch. 3: 'Now let us go back to my brother's death. Philosophy has a fine saying for every thing. For *Death* it has an entire set; the misery was, they all at once rushed into my father's head, that 'twas difficult to string them together, so as to make any thing of a consistent show out of them.—He took them as they came.'

221 *tore open so many cartridges*: the cartridge for a flintlock rifle was torn open with the teeth before loading, allowing a spark to ignite the gunpowder.

223 *maxima debetur pueris reverentia*: 'The greatest respect is due to children', Juvenal, *Satires*, XIV. 47.

224 *The suffix -accio normally has a derogatory force*: This observation is true of the Italian spoken on the mainland; in Corsica, however, the suffix is usually a simple diminutive.

Liquefacto . . . arena: 'With the now molten lead he split apart his skull, and stretched him out full-length upon the sand,' Virgil, *Aeneid*, IX. 587–8.

229   *the Pythia on her tripod*: the priestess of the Delphic oracle, who mounted a sacred tripod before making her oracular pronouncements.

237   *bruccio, ma solenne*: 'a *bruccio*, but an exceptional one'. For *bruccio*, see Mérimée's own footnote, p. 200.

243   *that's the least of my failings*: cf. La Fontaine, *Fables*, I. 1, *La cigale et la fourmi*: '*La fourmi n'est pas prêteuse; / C'est là son moindre défaut*' ('The ant is not given to lending; that is the least of her failings').

      Dixi: the word was often used at the conclusion of a speech made in Latin, with the meaning 'I have done (with my speech)', 'I have had my say'.

251   '*Only a gunshot can atone for this crime*': this parodies the lines '*Rien que la mort n'était capable / D'expier son forfait*' ('Only death could atone for his crime') from La Fontaine, *Fables*, VII. 1, *Les Animaux malades de la peste*.

254   *Orezza*: a village north-east of Corte, reputed for its curative mineral springs.

263   *Otello*: '*He lives!*': this is Rossini's opera drawn from Shakespeare's *Othello*, first performed in 1816, not, of course, Verdi's more famous opera of 1887. The words come from the finale of Act II.

264   *Iris*: the goddess Iris carried the messages of the gods. *Iris* is the Greek word for the rainbow, thought to connect heaven and earth. She was thus an appropriate bearer of such messages.

284   *Istos Sardos?*: 'Those Sardinians?' One would expect Castriconi, rather than Brandolaccio, to speak in Latin. This may be an authorial oversight.

286   *an Elzevir*: see notes to *Carmen*, pp. 341 and 344.

LOKIS

291   *the first translation . . . in London*: in fact, a translation of the Liturgical Epistles and Gospels into Lithuanian had appeared in Königsberg as early as 1579. A project to translate the whole Bible was begun in London around 1660, and the books from Genesis to Psalms were printed in 1662, though apparently never issued. A translation of the entire Bible into Lithuanian was published in Königsberg in 1735, and revisions of this version were financed or published by the British and Foreign Bible Society from 1816 on, first in Königsberg, later in Berlin, but never in London.

      Notwithstanding the professor's assertion later in the paragraph, versions of the Scriptures in the Samogitian dialect of Lithuanian had already been published in Vilna in 1816 and in Mitau (modern Jelgava, Latvian SSR) in 1844 (reprinted Berlin, 1866).

The British and Foreign Bible Society was founded in 1804, and still plays a key role in the preparation and distribution of Scriptures in English, though its former activities as a sponsor of translations are now undertaken by the United Bible Societies.

291 *Königsberg*: modern Kaliningrad, Russian SFSR; formerly the capital of German East Prussia and coronation city of the kings of Prussia. E. T. A. Hoffmann and Immanuel Kant were natives of the city, and Kant was a professor at the university. Largely destroyed in the last days of the Second World War, Königsberg and the surrounding area were annexed by the Soviet Union in 1945.

291 *the palatinate of Samogitia . . . where Low Lithuanian . . . is spoken*: Samogitia, in Lithuanian *Žemaitija* (*Low Country*), a region co-extensive with most of the modern Lithuanian SSR, bounded by East Prussia, Courland, and Lithuania proper (the region around Vilnius). Long disputed between the Teutonic Knights and Lithuania, it was permanently attached to the latter in 1422. The term *palatinate* is frequently used in historical literature to refer to administrative divisions of Lithuania. Curiously, however, Samogitia itself was never a palatinate.

Lithuanian, together with Latvian and a number of extinct languages including Old Prussian (to which reference is made later in the story), is one of the Baltic sub-family of the Indo-European language family. It is divided into a High (Eastern) and a Low (Western) dialect, the latter being also referred to as Samogit, Samogitian, or Zhmudian (in Polish, *Żmudź*). The Lithuanian dialects 'resemble' Sanscrit, the oldest Indo-European language that has come down to us, only in the sense that they are structurally the most archaic of surviving Indo-European languages, and thus the closest to the hypothetical Proto-Indo-European from which Sanscrit is also descended. In grammar and vocabulary the Baltic tongues show far greater resemblances to the Slavonic languages, with which they are still sometimes grouped.

291 *Dorpat*: Estonian, Tartu; Russian, Yurev. From 1704 until the end of the First World War it was part of Russia, in the *guberniya* of Livonia. In 1920 it passed to independent Estonia (now the Estonian SSR). Its university, opened in 1802, replaced one founded by Gustavus Adolphus of Sweden in 1632 but closed in 1710.

294 *Memel*: Lithuanian, Klaipėda. A Prussian town from the sixteenth century, the port remained German until taken by Russia in the First World War. After the war Memel and its hinterland were administered briefly by France under the League of Nations, before becoming an autonomous region within independent Lithuania in 1924. Klaipėda is now part of the Lithuanian SSR.

295 *Kiejstut . . . Giedymin*: Giedymin (Lithuanian, Gediminas), Grand Duke of Lithuania, the strongest contemporary ruler in eastern Europe and true founder of the Lithuanian state, reigned 1316–41. He made Vilnius his capital, and opened up Lithuania to European commercial and intellectual influences. Through diplomacy and marriage alliances he extended his domains far into Byelorussia and the Ukraine, as well as neutralizing the Teutonic and Livonian Knights on his western and northern frontiers. A pagan, he also achieved a precarious balance between his pagan subjects (the Lithuanians were the last pagan people in Europe), his Orthodox subjects in Russia, and occasional Catholic allies in Poland and elsewhere, even, for a time, contriving to make an ally of the Pope.

Kiejstut (Lithuanian, Kęstutis), a younger son of Gediminas, ruled 1381–2. In 1341 Jaunutis had succeeded Gediminas, but in 1345 Kęstutis overthrew him, made his brother Algirdas (Olgierd) official Grand Duke of Lithuania, but himself became *de facto* ruler of the western and southern domains.

In using the first person plural pronoun, Doctor Froeber appears to be ironically identifying himself with the patient in his charge.

297 *the creatures don't eat corpses*: cf. La Fontaine, *Fables*, v. 20, *L'Ours et les deux compagnons*.

298 *the famous 5th bastion*: the Siege of Sebastopol (October 1854 to September 1855) was the major operation of the Crimean War, in which French, British, and, from 1855, Piedmontese troops stormed and finally captured the main base of the Russian Black Sea fleet. The 5th bastion was the western fortification of the Sebastopol defence line. It is frequently referred to in Tolstoy's *Tales of Sebastopol* (1855–6), a work with which Mérimée was familiar.

301 *Alexander von Humboldt*: Prussian scientist, naturalist, and explorer, 1769–1859, one of the major scientific figures of the first half of the nineteenth century, a founder of ecology, and influential in encouraging the study of the earth sciences generally. Between 1799 and 1804 he undertook a scientific expedition to the Spanish possessions of Central and South America. On returning to Europe he lived until 1827 in Paris, preparing and publishing

his findings. His last years were spent in Berlin, where he was tutor to the Prussian crown prince. Mérimée is said to have met Humboldt during his Paris years.

Vilna: Russian name for the town called Vilnius in Lithuanian and Wilno in Polish. Gediminas made it his capital in 1323. At the period in which the story is set the town was Russian, having passed to Russia in the Third Partition of Poland (1795). Mickiewicz (see next note) was a student at the university. When Lithuania gained independence in 1920 Kaunas became the capital and Vilnius passed to Poland. It is now capital of the Lithuanian SSR.

304 *Ballads by Mickiewicz*: Adam Mickiewicz (1798–1855), the greatest poet of Poland and, in exile, a champion of Polish nationalism and liberty at a time when the nation had vanished from the political map of Europe. Chopin sought to evoke the atmosphere of Mickiewicz's ballads in his four *Ballades* for piano. The ballad of the three sons of Boudrys was composed by Mickiewicz in 1829 and translated into Russian by Pushkin in 1833. Boudrys is not in fact a historical character. Of the three warlords mentioned in the ballad, Algirdas (Olgierd) and Kęstutis (Kiejstut) were sons of Gediminas, while Skirgaila (Skirgiello) was a younger son of Algirdas (see note to p. 295).

an original daïna!: this whole passage is a reminiscence of an episode which earned Mérimée belated retribution for a hoax he had perpetrated in his youth. In 1827 he had composed and anonymously published *La Guzla*, a series of thirty-two ballads masquerading as translations of poems by one Hyacinthe Maglanovich, a Dalmatian bard and bandit wholly of Mérimée's imagining. Not only did this hoax deceive prominent scholars, but within a few years Mérimée had the satisfaction of seeing some of these ballads translated into Polish and Russian, by Mickiewicz and Pushkin respectively, both of whom took them for authentic examples of Serbian folk poetry. In 1838, however, Pushkin's translation of the ballad by Mickiewicz referred to in the previous note was reprinted in a collected edition of Pushkin's works, this time with no mention of its source. Here it was later discovered by Mérimée, who went on to translate it and quote it in his *Les Faux Démétrius* (1853), under the impression that it was an original work by Pushkin.

ghazel: a short lyric poem, Arabic in origin, and much imitated in Persian and Turkish poetry. Generally it is erotic in theme and consists of between five and twelve couplets with a recurrent rhyme.

306 *starosta*: literally *elder*, the village headman or mayor.

307 *aurochs . . . described by Caesar in his Commentaries*: 'Aurochs: Historically and properly, the name of an extinct species of Wild Ox . . . described by Caesar as *Urus*, which formerly inhabited Europe, including the British Isles, and survived until comparatively recent times in Prussia, Poland, and Lithuania. Since this became extinct, the name has often been erroneously applied to another species, the European Bison (*Bos Bison* Gesn., *B. bonasus* Linn.), still extant in the forests of Lithuania, in which sense it is used by some English naturalists.' Thus the *Oxford English Dictionary*. By going on to misinform the professor, Count Szémioth perpetuates this confusion: the *zubr* is the European bison, sometimes improperly called *aurochs*, not the *urus* referred to by Caesar in *De bello gallico*, VI. 28, which became extinct in the seventeenth century. The bison, too, was becoming extremely rare, and had been protected by a government ukase of 1812.

310 *Knauss*: Ludwig Knauss (1829–1910), a German genre painter, noted for his gifts of observation. He lived in Paris from 1852 to 1860 and was decorated by the French in 1867.

Noble, the Lion: Noble is the name of the Lion in the *Roman de Renart*, a group of anonymous French verse tales of the twelfth and thirteenth centuries, drawn from a number of sources and depicting contemporary society through the adventures of various animals. Other prominent characters are Brun the Bear and Renart the Fox, both of whom are referred to in the closing paragraphs of *Lokis*.

The reader may be forgiven for wondering why a Lithuanian peasant woman should be so well versed in medieval French literature. This is one of several unsatisfactory aspects of this chapter. Mérimée wrote to Turgenev that, when revising *Lokis* for inclusion in a volume of stories, he intended to replace this episode by an encounter with Gypsies, who were to be accompanied by a tame bear. However, he did not live to carry out his intention.

314 *russalka*: in Russian folklore, a water-nymph. The *russalka* is not found in Lithuanian or Polish folklore; nor is there a dance of that name.

316 *don Fructuoso Rivera, President of the Republic*: having distinguished himself in the War of Independence, José Fructuoso Rivera

(1778–1854) became the first President of independent Uruguay in 1830. In 1834 he relinquished power to Oribe, his elected successor, but later organized a revolt against him. He was again president from 1839 to 1843. In 1853 he was appointed to a governing triumvirate, but died shortly afterwards.

320 *Turpi . . . caput . . .*: Horace, *Satires*, II. 7, ll. 60–2: '*an turpi clausus in arca, / Quo te dimisit peccati conscia erilis / Contractum, genibus tangas caput?*' ('Or will you rather crouch, locked ignobly in some chest where a maidservant party to her mistress's wrongdoing hid you, with your head between your knees?').

321 *Hercules . . . Hebe*: Hebe (Latin, Juventas), daughter of Zeus and Hera, the personification of Youth. When, on his death, Heracles (Hercules) acquired divine status and was admitted to Olympus, he was given Hebe as his celestial bride.

323 *A pretty head, but no brains*: yet another echo of La Fontaine; this time, *Fables*, IV. 14, *Le Renard et le buste*.

324 *Jupiter mocks at lovers' oaths*: the allusion could be either to Ovid, *Ars amatoria*, I. 633 (*Jupiter ex alto perjuria ridet amantum*); or to Tibullus, III, Elegy VII, 17 (*Perjuria ridet amantum Jupiter*); or to Shakespeare, *Romeo and Juliet*, II. 2, 92–3 (*At lovers' perjuries, / They say, Jove laughs*).

CHAPTER IV OF CARMEN

333 *like Panurge, 'naturally fearful of blows'*: see note to *Colomba*, p. 192).

334 *Mr Borrow*: George Borrow (1803–81), English traveller, writer, and linguist. The works to which Mérimée refers are *The Zincali: An Account of the Gypsies in Spain* (1841) and *The Bible in Spain* (1842), an account of Borrow's travels in Spain between 1833 and 1840. As Foreign Agent of the British and Foreign Bible Society, Borrow was responsible, not for converting the Gypsies, but for organizing the printing and distribution of a Spanish New Testament in Madrid. His other writings include *Lavengro* (1851), usually regarded as his best work, and *The Romany Rye* (1857). Borrow was supposedly proficient in some twenty languages, and his linguistic accomplishments include a translation of St Luke's Gospel into Romany, undertaken on his own initiative and subsequently published by the Bible Society. For the Bible Society, see note to *Lokis*, pp. 355–6.

Casta quam nemo rogavit: 'Any girl is chaste if she's never been asked', Ovid, *Amores*. I, viii, 43.

338 *The Mysteries of Paris: Les Mystères de Paris* by Eugène Sue, a master of the nineteenth-century French popular novel, serialized between June 1842 and October 1843 to enormous popular acclaim. One of the characters has the sobriquet *Le Chourineur*.

338 *Monsieur Vidocq*: François-Eugène Vidocq (1775–1857), a former criminal who, after several spells in prison, approached the Government with a proposal to set up and head a new police department, the *Brigade de la Sûreté*. This he did, but in 1827 he resigned in order to form an industrial enterprise employing ex-convicts. When this failed he again headed the detective department, but in 1832 was dismissed for allegedly instigating a theft. He subsequently set up the first private detective agency. Vidocq was the inspiration for the character Vautrin in *Le Père Goriot* and other novels by Balzac. His *Memoirs* (4 vols, 1828–9) and *Les Voleurs* (1836), published under his name, were apparently the work of other writers. *Les Voleurs* contains a glossary of thieves' jargon.

THE WORLD'S CLASSICS

A Select List